WILLIAM CLAI

C000110098

A SEA QUEEN

A NOVEL

Elibron Classics
www.elibron.com

Elibron Classics series.

© 2005 Adamant Media Corporation.

ISBN 1-4021-6305-3 (paperback)
ISBN 1-4212-8046-9 (hardcover)

This Elibron Classics Replica Edition is an unabridged facsimile
of the edition published in 1883 by Harper & Brothers,
New York.

A SEA QUEEN

A Novel

BY

W. CLARK RUSSELL

AUTHOR OF

"THE WRECK OF THE 'GROSVENOR'" "THE 'LADY MAUD'"
"A SAILOR'S SWEETHEART" ETC.

NEW YORK

HARPER & BROTHERS, FRANKLIN SQUARE

1883

A SEA QUEEN.

CHAPTER I.

I AM BORN AT NEWCASTLE-ON-TYNE.

I AM not only a sailor's daughter, but I may say that I was born among sailors, as much so as if my birth had taken place on board ship ; for on the evening on which I came into the world my father was entertaining a company of captains and mates in the parlor of his house, and my mother would say the doctor told her that when he went down-stairs, to give my father the news of my arrival, the room was so full of tobacco-smoke that the guests loomed through it like colliers in the mist of a Tyne fog, so that after peering about, and hitting, as he supposed, upon my father, and saying, "Captain, there's a bundle of troubles for you up-stairs, but she's a fine baby, and as far as I can make out promises to be like you," he found that he had addressed the wrong man.

The doctor, I say, told my mother that story, and what followed. My father, on hearing the news, flourished a long clay pipe, and pointing to a steaming bowl on the table, exclaimed, "Lads, here's punch enough to christen the lassie with. Sit down, doctor—sit down, man ; there's a pipe and yonder's a tumbler. What shall her name be, lads? I'll speak last."

This produced a dead silence, for not only did the presence of the doctor make the sailors shy, but one of them, a Blyth skipper, who was in Newcastle on business, said that "inventing was not in his line, and that Snowdon" (meaning my father) "had put him, for one, on a tack that there was no creeping with to windward at all."

My father, however, would not let them off. Singling out the youngest man present—a mate—and pointing his pipe at him, he told him to turn to and speak up and give the little 'un a name.

"Well," said the mate, "if I'm to have the naming of her, I'm for calling her Polly. It's a useful name, for if it comes too long when you're in a hurry, there's nothing to do but to take a sheepshank in it and make it Poll."

After musing awhile and looking around at his friends to see how this suggestion took, my father levelled his pipe at another man—likewise a mate—who, gulping down a mouthful of punch to clear his throat, said that he didn't deny Poll was a useful name, and that for his part he'd be sorry to say anything against it, as his mother had been called Poll; but if the bairn up-stairs was his, he'd not stick to the old charts in the matter of names, but take soundings for himself, and try and bring up something original—something that would make people stare when they heard it. What would Captain Snowdon say to Eurydice, now?

He pronounced it U-ree-dice—the *dice* long as in English.

Here the doctor declared he could hold his face no longer, and burst into a fit of laughter.

"U-ree what?" cried my father.

"Dice," answered an old skipper, in a hoarse, deep-sea voice. "There was a ship called by that name belonging to Hull. She was at Callao last year. It's a pagan word, my lad—the doctor there'll tell you that. You'd get no parson to relish giving such a term to a Christian infant, Snowdon."

"U-ree-dice!" grumbled my father, hanging upon the word, and looking somewhat severely upon the mate who had proposed it. "Pagan! Would you make her a gambler, William, that you're putting dice in her way before she's fairly settled down to draw the breath of life?"

This was accounted a good joke, and there was much laughter, in which my father, after several struggles to look serious, joined at the top of his voice. The general merriment, said the doctor, put the mates and captains at their ease, and many names were suggested, at all which my father shook his head.

At last a North Shields skipper, growing tired, and struggling with the irritability that is a rather common failing among elderly seamen, said :

"Look here, Snowdon ; we've all of us thought and thought until there is no thinking any deeper. We've come to the dunnage in our minds, master, and there's no use going below it. Shall I tell you why ? Because you've got a name for her yourself. He's had hold of the signal-halliards all the time," he continued, addressing the others, "and is only waiting for us to exhaust our flag-lockers to hoist away his own colors."

"Well, I don't mind owning it," said my father, with a beaming face. "I'll name her Jessie. It was my sister's name, and I like it because there's something about it that smells flowery and summer-like. Fill your glasses, lads, while I go and see my lass, and bid the little 'un welcome to this tempestuous ocean of life."

This little introduction shows that I was not only born in Newcastle-on-Tyne, but, as I have said, as much among sailors as if my first cry had been uttered in a ship's cabin. When my father returned to the parlor, his guests begged him to go back and fetch me, that they might have a look ; and I was told he would have enjoyed the errand, brought me into that tobacco-smoke, and sent me to go the rounds of the company, had not the doctor, putting on a stern face, declared that I must instantly expire if introduced into that atmosphere.

It has often amused me to think over the picture that would have been made had my father been allowed to have his way : no real experience could dwell more fixedly in my mind than the fancy of my wee body in my father's arms, and the dark, storm-swept faces of his friends looking down on my tiny face with the childlike tenderness that makes the honest sailor-man's character one of the few lovable things of this world.

In those days Newcastle-on-Tyne abounded in ancient houses, many of which survive to this hour in some of the streets, so that there is scarcely a town of the same size

in England fuller of architectural contrasts. One of these
streets, called the Side, begins in a steep lane that broadens
somewhat as you descend.   The road at the top is so narrow that the opposite neighbors can almost shake hands
with one another from their windows.   How ancient this
street is I do not know ; some of the houses are bowed
and warped, and lean wearily, like aged men who have
stood too long.   The gable roofs and overhanging stories
and large quaint windows, probably once crowded with
small squares or lozenges of glass, transport the observer
back two or three hundred years ; and when a child I
never passed down this steep and most romantically ven-
erable thoroughfare without imagining that I perceived
dim and dusty figures, queerly apparelled in faded colors,
stirring amid the shadows behind the windows.   As you
stand in this street the hum of the busy life surging and
swelling through the broader roads beyond, nay, the
shriek of the locomotive, and the roar of twoscore coal-
wagons, speeding swiftly along the railway metals upon
the lofty viaduct, sound unreal, as though they were the
echoes of a world whose realities have yet to be explored.
Nothing seems true but the dreams which are begotten
by the old structures around you, and the visions of unfamiliar shapes strangely attired, which flit in troops before the mind's eye, along the worn pavements of this
worm-eaten vestige of the dead centuries.   I believe it is
such relics as this, their power of enriching the mind with
gentle fancies and of perpetuating stirring traditions, their
influence as domestic dials, which indicate by tender contrast the growth and progress of the noble and renowned
old borough, which make all Tyneside lads and lasses love
Newcastle with the reverent and cordial heartiness that
distinguishes their loyalty to their town.   It is " canny
Newcastle " with us all, and our Runic dialect could invent or borrow no truer expression of the Tynesider's
affection for the place.

My father's house was much such a structure as sur-
vives in the Side, or gives beautiful quaintness to other
approaches to the river.   No matter the street in which
it stood—people who do not know the town would not
much value exactness in such matters; and to point out

its site I should have to enter a spacious building that has been erected, at this time of writing, about eight years. It was an extremely old-fashioned house, more than two centuries old when it was pulled down. The parlor is the room I best remember, a large, square, rather gloomy room, with a low ceiling; and that, and a massive beam overhead, and the furniture in it, made it more like a ship's cabin than a chamber in a dwelling-house. The greater portion of the "fittings"—that was my father's term for the chairs and tables—had crossed many leagues of ocean. The chairs had come out of an East Indiaman; the handsome brass oil-lamp that hung from the centre of the ceiling had drifted ashore in a wreck, and was bought by my father at an auction at South Shields; there was a remarkable sideboard, exquisitely carved, said to have been made in Arabia, which my father had purchased in a Mediterranean port a few months before he was married. The walls also were curiously decorated. First, the pictures and engravings were, without exception, representations of marine scenery, of well-known north-country ships—a view of the mouth of the Tyne in a storm, a collier dismasted off Whitby, and so forth. Scattered among these pictures hung a few charts, well "pricked," as the seamen's phrase goes—that is, covered with tracings denoting the progress of a vessel from one port to another, or across a certain space of ocean. The charts were fixed to rollers, and my father was constantly adding to them.

Other features of that room I vividly recall—and, indeed, I dwell upon the whole because it was a kind of education to me—particularly a small oval concave looking-glass, that made every figure it reflected a curved dwarf with a great head and huge feet—it would have served a giant so—around which were clustered numerous South Sea trophies, some of which had been brought from the Pacific by seamen who had served under Cook and Vancouver—long, sharp spears, a shield like the shell of a tortoise, a grass mat or cloak that resembled an ancient faded banner over a knight's stall, tomahawks, barbarous, ill-looking hatchets, and I know not what else besides. The mantel-shelf and side-tables were decorated with models of ships, canoes, lifeboats, and a great variety of

Chinese ivory work, such as card-cases, brooches, figures of animals, puzzles, and the like. In short, our parlor might well have been called a museum. My father always brought home from every voyage some fresh curiosity to swell our collection; the captains and mates who visited us rarely came empty-handed; and in course of time the parlor became so full of singular and interesting objects that, as our neighbors would tell us, we might have paid our rent over and over again by charging people sixpence a head for admission to view the wonders. Ay, and there were plenty of persons who would have thought sixpence cheap for the pleasure of seeing so many strange things.

I do not suppose that, had I not been born with a love for the sea and sailors, my being reared in an atmosphere so full of marine life would have colored my thoughts, and given my tastes the direction they took. The reverse is much nearer the rule, many children taking a disgust to their father's calling merely because they are continually associated with it, in a sense, and are always hearing of it until they grow up and leave home for good. But in my case, having been born with a love for the sea, all my surroundings educated and confirmed that disposition. Even when I was only just old enough to put words together, and when my mother would say, before friends (for the pleasure of calling me out, as the term is), "There is little Jessie; ask her what husband she will choose when she becomes a great girl?" my answer always was, "I will marry nobody but a sailor-lad, and we'll live in a fine ship."

Believe me, I earnestly meant what I said, even when I was a bairn; and that you may know all women are not the capricious creatures men call them, I was saying and meaning the same thing—but to myself—when I was twenty years old; only *then*, instead of a sailor-boy, I wanted a captain as a sweetheart.

CHAPTER II.

CHILDHOOD.

THE charm our old parlor had for me in my childhood
I have no words to convey.   I was strictly forbidden to
touch, yet I was never weary of looking at the "curios,"
as my father called them, which shows the fascination
they possessed for me.   For what child who may not
touch will look long?   Thoughts, full of childlike beauty,
visited me from those objects.   My father's talk, when
he was at home; my mother's stories to me about his voyages, and the wonders of the great sea, helped my fancies,
or rather, I suppose, I built them up on those founda-
tions; and the very earliest recollection I have is that of
associating the spears and shield over the oval glass with
leagues of still blue ocean, and green and shining islands
in the midst of it, as though fitted into a bed of glass,
and dusky figures sporting amid the creamy surf or racing
along the golden sands, and, all about, an atmosphere
filled with the sweetness of orange and lime trees, and
the fragrance of groves of spice.   The Chinese carvings
in ivory set me dreaming of elephants, and palm-trees
like great green umbrellas, and strangely-shaped temples,
sparkling inside with precious stones.   In truth, I was a
wanderer in my little heart almost before I was old enough
to sup porridge, and my love was with sailors and ships,
and flying, dove-like, abroad upon the face of the deep,
even when my tongue was barely formed to pronounce
words correctly.

I was the only surviving child of my parents, and, therefore, though I knew many children, and never wanted for
playmates out of doors, at home there was nobody but my
mother and the servant, or the friends who called, for me
to talk to.   For this reason, no doubt, I was considered
somewhat old-fashioned in my manners and behavior, and
intelligent above my years.

One noticeable peculiarity in me was that, beyond a certain inflection in my speech, there was nothing to distinguish my pronunciation from the English that is spoken in London and the south of England. I always thought, and do still think, this strange, for I scarcely know a *patois* more contagious than the Northumbrian. So far as I am concerned, I would sooner have the *burr* than not. In the mouths of the lower orders, Newcastle English is, I freely admit, a very rugged and grotesque tongue, as unintelligible to the ears of a stranger as Dutch; an extraordinary compound, plentifully flavored with raw lowland Scotch, in which most of the etymologies are hopelessly lost through sheer perversity of utterance. But, on the other hand, there is nothing sweeter than the pronunciation of an educated Tynesider. There is something fascinating to listen to in the silken rippling of a Newcastle lady's speech, and the *burr* and an unconscious sprinkling of expressive local words will make the veriest commonplaces attractive in a cultivated male speaker.

I probably owe my freedom from the colloquial oddities of my native town to my mother, who was a Sussex woman, belonging to a family that had lived for generations on the skirts of a village not far from Brighton. How my father and she became acquainted is a little romance that would make an interesting chapter; but I must be brief, for my story does not concern her nor Newcastle, but myself and what befell me when I became a wife and a mother, and fulfilled the early dream of my life by marrying a sailor and living in a ship with him.

Yet there is room for a narrow outline, and it is this. In such and such a year, my father was second mate of a ship homeward-bound from the East Indies. When in the latitude of the Cape of Good Hope they encountered a gale of wind which forced them to heave to—that is, to point their ship's head a little away from the direction of the wind, and lie in that posture, which is the safest a vessel in a strong sea can be put into, until the weather moderates.

While they lay, heavily rising and falling upon the roaring seas, the horizon cleared in the southeast, and my father, who had charge of the deck, spied a large ship in that quarter, with two of her masts gone, and the English ensign, union down, flying in the mizzen rigging. She was about four miles off. On examining her through the telescope, he perceived that she was very low in the water, and evidently in a sinking condition. He reported her to the captain, who, being a humane man, determined to make an effort to succor the people, and accordingly, heedless of all risks, put his vessel before the seas, and ran down to the wreck. On approaching the ship, ten men could be counted on her poop; and, to rescue them, my father volunteered to make one of a boat's crew. Others immediately offered themselves; and, though there never was a more dangerous errand undertaken at sea, yet my father twice made the journey between the vessels, amid waves as wild as ever ran in those stormy parallels, and succeeded in bringing off the whole of the people without the loss of a single life.

They proved to be a portion of the crew and passengers who had been left behind on the ship in consequence of the boats, in which the others had gone away early that morning, being loaded above their capacity.

One of the rescued men was a young gentleman, named Wills. On learning that he owed his life mainly to my father, he made him promise that he would pay him a visit at his home in Sussex on their arrival in England. My father was a shy man, as most sailors are, and would have backed out of that promise on his return home; but Mr. Wills, finding he did not come, wrote to say that he must fetch him, as his parents, who were old people, could not rest until they had shaken the hand of the man who had saved their son's life. Seeing he could not escape, and little dreaming, as you may suppose, how momentous this visit would prove, my father took the coach from Newcastle to London, and from London he went on to Brighton, and so got to the village where the Willses lived, where, among the inmates of the hospitable house, he found the girl—young Mr. Wills's sister, a pretty, tender little woman of nineteen, named Annie—who afterwards became his wife. They were engaged three years before they married, and even that term, I dare say, would have been prolonged had not old Mr. and Mrs. Wills died, one within a month

of the other, leaving my father's sweetheart alone, for her
brother had returned to India and settled there. She
brought my father a little money, but not much. But
something more precious than gold she brought him—the
most gentle, loving heart that ever beat in a woman's
breast.

I may fairly say that my father was one of a class of
English seamen who, now that steam has completely
changed the character and conditions of the seafaring
life, must soon be as extinct as that ancient 'long-shore
bird called by the Portuguese the dodo.

He was forty years of age when I was born, and at forty
a sailor is as old as a landsman at fifty. He had followed
the sea ever since he was thirteen, and, famous as our
northeastern coast is for the race of mariners who have
sailed from its ports, no better seaman ever helped to man
or sail a ship belonging to these English shores than
Thomas Snowdon. The men of his family had been sailors, and the women sailors' wives, for generations, and
salt water ran in his veins as blue blood runs in the veins
of lords and squires whose ancestry streams like a wake
through the sea of history.

It was impossible for the merest stranger to glance at
his face without being drawn by the attraction of the ster-
ling, generous, loyal, and hearty nature that was expressed
there. Whenever I think of him, I recall the words of
Dibdin's song, which no seaman ever sang more sweetly
than he :

> " His form was of the manliest beauty,
>   His heart was kind and soft;
> Faithful below he did his duty,
>   And now he's gone aloft."

You never met his fine gray eyes but that there was an
affectionate smile sparkling in them, and giving them such
a magic as defies every effort to define it. There was a
rich tone in his laugh that made every peal of merriment
as gay and melodious as a cheerful, tuneful song. Everything in his bearing and appearance denoted the ocean
sailor. Yet all nautical airs he denounced as lubberish;
and his argument was, that as the profession of the sea
was the noblest calling in the world—as I truly believe it

to be, and as every Englishman who values his country
and knows what sailors have done for it will own—so all
right-minded men who followed it would never let its dig-
nity suffer in the eyes of landsmen by leaving them to
suppose that the oaths, swagger, and drink which novelists and dramatists have used as pigments for the painting
of that deplorable caricature, nicknamed Jack Tar, were
truthful components of the English seaman's character.

No man who has "knocked about" from his boyhood
in all sorts of ships, and among all sorts of crews, is likely
to preserve, if, indeed, he ever possessed, the airs and polish of the drawing-room gentleman. But, though I do
not despise that sort of veneer—in truth, the want of it is
one of those things I consider inexcusable in a man who
has not the sailor's apology for being without it—yet certainly its absence is something more than compensated
in a seaman who reveres God, who faithfully discharges
every duty that comes in his way, who values the nobility
and greatness of his calling, who is gentle and honorable
in his home-life, and whose hand is always ready to receive the grasp of a shipmate who lags in the race.

This was my father's character, as it was the character
of many mariners in his day, and is of a large number in
ours—men who will never let their profession suffer in
the eyes of the world while they have charge of vessels
and are known as sailors ashore. Yet, as I have said, my
father belonged to a race of seamen who must shortly
be extinct. He could quit the command of a collier, with
her grimy decks, and the rough companionship of the men
who officered and manned that sort of craft, to take charge
of a passenger-ship, with a cuddy full of ladies and gentlemen, and bear himself among them with as much grace
as any living sea-captain carries who has been brought up
in an ocean steam-palace, and who has found his experiences among passengers. I know no collier-man that
could do that now.

If I can write as a sailor, I have to thank my father for
it. My husband taught me a little, but only a little. I
knew all about ships—the names of the masts, yards, and
gear—when I married; and truly believe that, even at the
age of fifteen, I could have passed an examination in that

part of practical seamanship which relates to rigging.
This I say here to account for the familiarity with nautical terms you will possibly find me exhibiting when we
get upon the sea.

It will seem strange, I have no doubt, that a woman
should have a knowledge of such things. A girl might
own to knowing all about soldiering—about barracks-rou-
tine, the goose-step, eyes right, shouldering arms, and such
stuff—with much less confusion of modesty than to knowing about the sea. This is true, but why? Because, no
doubt, even the most bucolic conception of the sea can
discover nothing feminine in the calling. Do you say the
same thing of the army? Ah! contrast soldiers and sailors, their talk, their dress, their manners, their airs, and
then consider which is the more masculine of the two vo-
cations. Nay, I have met some military officers who were
very manly fellows. But did you ever hear of a sailor
wearing stays? Would Jack, do you believe, borrow a
nursemaid's last half-crown to buy beer and tobacco with?
The soldier may not be able to help his pipe-clay and the
dandyism of his uniform; but there is nothing to stop him
minding his behavior, nor hinder him from acting as though
his jacket had been made out of more manly stuff than a
colored petticoat.

But to come back to what I was saying about a woman's
knowing the sea. Let me declare that I am not the only
sailor's daughter with what in the north we call a "nice"
knowledge of ships. I once saw a model of a full-rigged
ship, built and rigged by a sea-captain's lass, most perfect
in all respects; no shipwright could have put the hull together better, and no rigger fitted the toy aloft with prettier accuracy. Why should not my sex know all about
ships? A little nautical knowledge on the part of women
has saved more than one vessel full of valuable cargo, as
there are marine records to prove. It is true a woman
does not need to know the law to help her husband who
is an attorney. A musician can earn a living, though his
wife is unable to distinguish between "Yankee Doodle"
and "God save the Queen." But a sailor's wife who is a
sailor too may be more useful than a chief mate to a captain who carries her on a voyage with him. Not very

long ago, the wife of a captain whose crew were prostrated with fever steered the ship while her husband worked in the engine-room.* Had she not had a sailor's heart and a sailor's knowledge, how could her husband have saved his ship and their lives? My own story, too, ought to confirm my ideas on this subject. Moreover, the ignorance of landsmen on all that belongs to the sea should make women, in this age of pushing females, ambitious to prove their superiority on one platform.

I will not speak of my education, nor unnecessarily lengthen this preface. When I was nine years old, my father carried my mother and me with him on a voyage. He had then command of a bark. Our voyage was to the West Indies, and lasted six months. He took us two more trips after that, one to the Mediterranean, and one to the Baltic; and I believe he would have had us with him every voyage if my mother had consented. But she was a bad sailor; she suffered much from sea-sickness, and was easily alarmed by bad weather. Though these voyages did her health a great deal of good, yet, after our return from the Baltic, she said she would go to sea no more; and she kept her word, in spite of my father's entreaties. He then would have taken me, but my mother said no; she wanted me at home; I was her only child; she could not spare me and her husband too.

Her refusal vexed me much, and I cried heartily when she said she would not let me go. Indeed, in my little life I had never known such happiness as the being at sea in a ship gave me. The sailors would stop in their work and stand looking and laughing at me as I clapped my hands when the vessel buried her bows in the green and rushing surges, and flung up a veil of spray that shone in the sunshine like a sheet of white silk in the air. My

* The vessel was a steamer called the *Edgar*, homeward bound from Senegal. The newspaper accounts said: "On its way from Senegal the whole of the crew of the English steamer *Edgar*, with the exception of the captain and his wife and the mate, were stricken with sickness in such a manner that they could take no part in the navigation of the vessel. The captain suggested to his wife to take the post of the 'man at the wheel,' while he himself and the mate acted as engineer and fireman. The three brought the vessel safe from the West Coast of Africa to Europe." The name of the lady was Mrs. Lucy Dyson.

2

mother could scarcely keep me out of the forecastle. The men coaxed me one way and my mother's commands held me the other way, so that I was sometimes at my wits' end. Yet, in spite of my mother, I was much among the seamen, and when I think over that time now, the true spirit of the sailor's character comes to me in the tender respect those rough fellows showed the little girl who skipped and prattled among them, the hearty pleasure it gave them to watch and hear me, the loyalty of their hearts, that would have made them risk any peril sooner than that a hair of my head should come to harm on the great deep, whose cold and troubled bosom was their home, and with whose manifold perils they wrestled day and night for bare life for themselves, and for gold for their employers.

I learned a great deal about the sea during these voyages. I was shown how to steer, and have held the wheel for half an hour at a time, the man whose duty it was to steer standing by and explaining the various steering terms, such as "full and bye," "luff," "lee-helm," and so on. I studied the points of the compass until I was able to "box" it as glibly as my father, and whenever he asked me to run to the binnacle and see how the vessel headed, I could give him the course instantly to a quarter of a point. I also understood all about what is called at sea "dead-reckoning"—that is, the finding out of a place the vessel is in by counting the number of knots she has run during a given time, and tracing her progress upon a chart by a reference to the courses she has steered. This necessarily involved a knowledge of the use of the log-line, and a sailor will suppose I soon mastered that contrivance when I tell him that my father always allowed me to hold the sand-glass when I was on deck and the log was hove.

These and many other sea-matters which I had at my fingers' ends may look outlandish and puzzling to a landsman, yet few things are easier to learn. A ship seems an endless complication of ropes and spars, and certainly some of the nautical terms are very barbarous and bothersome. Yet the divisions of the complicated mechanism that towers above the hull greatly diminish the tax upon the memory. When you know the names of the rigging and yards upon one mast you pretty well know all. Sheets, braces, backstays, sails, and the like, have the same names on all three masts; they are merely distinguished by the prefix of the name of the mast to which they belong, as *mizzen*-topmast-backstay, *main*-brace, *fore*-topsail-sheet.

Hence, no great genius is required to understand sea-terms, and a girl like me, fond of ships, and much thrown with sailors, would find as little difficulty in mastering nautical names and understanding the use of the things so called, as in working a sewing-machine or knitting a pair of stockings.

Sometimes the seamen helped me up the rigging, and handed me over the maintop. I shall never forget the first impression I had of the sea surveyed from the height of the lower masthead. It was a bright, warm day; the sky was a rich blue, and the sea a radiant emerald green. There was a steady breeze that kept the vessel leaning. Below and high above me were the white and swelling cloths, in the hollows of which the wind hummed with a note that resembled the wailing of bagpipes heard at a distance. The waters flashed in the sunshine, and the brilliant white of the breaking heads of the little seas contrasted with lovely effect upon the glorious green of the deep, in the midst of which, a long way beneath me, were the sand-colored sloping decks of the vessel, outlined into perfect symmetry by the black rail of the bulwarks, while on either side ran a rushing stream of froth that united under the square counter, and went dancing away astern in a whirl of snow, until I thought I could perceive the faint glimmer of its pallid surface upon the delicate green, sun-touched, trembling beauty of the horizon. What pen could express the joyous sensations, the triumphant delight, the passionate feeling of liberty that possessed me as I looked from my high and windy seat, amid the cloud-like volumes of the steady sails, upon the leagues of shining ocean? No spirit soaring from its clay tenement on wings of light into the azure heavens could taste more perfect happiness than filled my young heart as I stood on the platform of the leaning mast and swept the amphitheatre of the deep with kindling eyes.

But, as I have said, when we returned from that voyage to the Baltic, my mother and I settled down in our home in Newcastle, and a good many years were to elapse before I found myself afloat again.

As time wore on my father was more at home than formerly, owing to his engaging in short voyages. He had been a saving man all his life, and put all his money into ships, which paid him very well in those days, and he would often talk of giving up the sea, saying that he had done his share, that he was getting old, that it was time he made way for younger men, until every voyage promised to be his last. Yet when it came to the point he would not give up.

"What am I to do," he would say, "if I leave the sea? How am I to amuse myself? There was William Thompson. William's friends advised him to give up when he was forty. He gave up, got married, and furnished himself a house down Byker way. But he couldn't stop at home. His wife put him to gardening, thinking if she could interest him in cabbages he'd be punctual at meal-times. But it was no good. He'd drop his spade for the river, and arrive home, when dinner was cold, as grimy as a pitman. 'I can do nothing with him, Captain Snowdon,' his wife said to me. 'William belongs to the water, and you might as well hope to make a duck happy in a hen-coop as keep William pleased by putting a rake into his hands and showing him where the weeds are. He goes away among the shipping, and whenever he spies a friend, he jumps on board, pulls off his coat, and begs, for mercy's sake, to be put to some job. The tar and grease I find on his clothes would ruin the temper of an angel. I now let him have his way. He is only happy when his hand is in the tar-bucket, and I've got something else to do than turpentine his trousers and waistcoats morning, noon, and night.' Now," my father would continue, "don't you think I had better take warning from the melancholy condition to which Bill Thompson reduced himself? Michael Hanson the other day recommended me to drop the sea, and set up ashore as a weather-prophet. But it's poor work telling others to look out for squalls you're never sure of yourself. I'd as lief take to out-door preaching. No, I'll go another voyage, and that'll give

me time to turn my mind over and come to some resolution."

CHAPTER III.

THE MOUTH OF THE TYNE IN A GALE.

HOWEVER, my father met with an experience at last
that finally determined him, though, had it not found him
strongly disposed to quit the sea, it would not in the least
degree have influenced him.

He had taken the command of a brig in which he was
part owner, for a voyage to Calais with a cargo of coals.
My mother received a letter from him, dated at that port,
in which he told us to look out for him on a Wednesday,
naming the date. Of course, we knew that his punctuality
would depend on the weather, but, as a rule, he was very
accurate in his forecasts, and seldom disappointed us by
more than a day or two—that is, I mean, when he performed short coasting voyages.

Well, Tuesday night came, and I was sitting talking to
my mother, who was busily knitting stockings—her favorite occupation, and never was Newcastle knitting better
than hers—when a moan of wind in the wide old chimney
made me go to the window and look out. The sky was
black and the air hazy with the smoke from the factories
along the Tyneside, and a faint drizzle, in which the street
lamps shone dimly, every one with a ring around it, such
as you may have seen the moon look out of when hanging bleared and dull in a thick sky. It was the middle
of November, the air bitterly cold. I said nothing to my
mother, for bad weather always made her wretched when
father was away ; but, letting fall the curtain, I stepped
into the passage and took a peep at a marine barometer
that hung there, and noticed that the mercury had sunk
by the length of my thumb-nail.

I came back to my place, and went on quietly with my
work. I see the picture of that old parlor now as plainly
as I saw it then. The bright flames of the coal fire vanquished the steady glare of the brass lamp, and set the

curiosities dancing and shaking in the quivering radiance.
Near the fire was my mother, in an arm - chair, peering
steadfastly down upon her hands through a pair of old-
fashioned spectacles, and nimbly plying her needles, her
dear face, tenderly touched with the fire-play, standing
out upon the high, dark wainscoting, in which the radiance rolled in many a soft ripple, so that from where I
sat her profile looked like a cameo.

But the moaning of the wind quickly grew into muffled
bellowings, and these my mother noticed, for, letting fall
her knitting, she bade me draw the curtain and see how
the night looked.

I told her it was so dark I could see nothing. She
came herself, and while she was peering a furious shower
of sleet and hail came, along with a violent blast of wind,
and rattled upon the window-panes, as though bucketsful
of gravel were being flung at the house.

This was the first of the storm. In less than half an hour
it had swept up into a furious gale from the southeast.
I never remember the like of that night. The thunder
of the tempest as it roared across the black sky was a distinct note, clearly audible above the fierce groaning and
shaking and shrill crying of the old house. Imagining I
heard a ring at the house-bell, and the servant not coming
quickly, I went to see who it might be ; but the instant
I raised the latch the door was swept open with the
speed of a shot from a cannon, and the house was filled
with the storm in a breath. The white sleet rushed in
like loads of feathers on the blast, and I had to call to
my mother and the servant to help me shut the door,
which I could no more have accomplished alone than I
could have pushed a wall down. The ringing of the bell
was a false alarm, but a real one came while we were bolt-
ing the door ; for there happened such a mighty crash
upon the pavement in front of the house that we stood
stock-still with amazement and dread, persuaded that the
roof was coming in, and that presently we should be
buried alive. On going to the window, all three of us
trembling, and our faces very white, to see what had happened, we perceived by the light of the street lamp that
an immense stack of chimneys from the house fronting

ours had been blown over and hurled by the wind right
across the road, that was wide enough to make such an
illustration of the fury of the tempest terrible indeed.

There was no sleep for my mother and me that night.
She asked me to come to her bed, and we lay talking of
father, and listening to the raging of the hurricane, until
the dawn glimmered upon the window - blinds. It was
Wednesday, the day on which my father had told us to
expect him; and wherever his brig might be, we knew
that, if she had outlived the fearful night, she would not
be far off.

"I must go down to Shields, Jessie," said my mother;
"I cannot rest here. I shall go crazy if I stay at home
listening and fearing."

It blew so fiercely that it was scarcely safe to venture
abroad. Our street was full of slates and tiles and chim-
ney-pots; and while we were at breakfast the servant ran
in to say the butcher had told her that dreadful mischief
was done, great trees blown down, windows forced in,
many houses at Gateshead and Newcastle unroofed, and
some scores of people killed in various parts while passing
through the streets; and that even now it was as much
as a person's life was worth to leave shelter.

But my mother was resolved; and I was as anxious as
she. I well knew that this southeast gale would sweep
my father's vessel northwards, and that, if he had not
sought shelter in some roadstead or port farther south,
he would, if his ship were afloat, be in the neighborhood
of the Tyne.

Very clearly I remember that morning—the howling
of the gale through the streets, the flying darkness overhead, and the frequent rush of horizontal sleet that seemed
to pierce the face like a shower of needles. We muffled
ourselves up to our noses, my mother grasped my arm,
and, at one time leaning against the wind until we took
the very posture of hobbling, doubled-up old women, at
another time helplessly swept around a corner, often
forced to turn our backs and pause to recover our breath,
which the gale in sudden bursts dashed from our bodies,
stepping fearfully over the fragments of masonry which
encumbered the pavements, and every moment expecting

to be struck down by some flying chimney-pot or tile, we finally succeeded in reaching the railway station, more exhausted than had we toiled up the side of a high mountain.

There were many people going to Shields ; some, like ourselves, wild with anxiety as to the safety of relatives at sea ; others concerned only in a commercial sense, and whose thoughts were with the cargoes rather than the human lives upon the deep ; and others, again, who were making the journey merely to behold the great sight which they very well knew the sea would present. It was moving to see the people, the look of consternation on the faces even of those whom the storm could not defraud of either relatives or property ; to observe women, strangers to one another, speaking eagerly together in groups, made akin by the fears bred by the terrible storm ; to hear them as they poured forth their hopes and their dread in the rugged Newcastle dialect, often gesticulating with something even of frenzy in their motions, while their voices sometimes rose into a sound of wailing and lamentation.

It took us an hour to reach South Shields, for not only did the train stop at every station down the line, but the gale seemed to be right in our teeth, as it howled along the metals, and at some of the curves it was as much as the locomotive could do to drag the carriages at the rate of five miles an hour. It is a bit of a walk from the railway station at South Shields to the Lawe, as it is called, a point of cliff directly looking on to the mouth of the Tyne. We went along in a crowd, fighting with the wind, that appeared to have the fury of a cyclone now that we were near the sea. Few people were to be seen in the street, but this had been explained at the railway station, where we were told that there were four or five vessels ashore, and that the whole population was down at the water's side.

I looked at my mother when I heard about those vessels being ashore ; she turned her face up to God, but said nothing, and we hurried along with the crowd in silence. To understand our feelings you must have a brother, a husband, a father, some one dearly loved, at sea; you must be waiting for his return and be near the sea in the midst of a tempest, and then be told that there are many vessels ashore. Inland, the news of shipwreck, the dread that the dear one's ship may be one of the wrecks, cannot break into your heart as it will when you behold the vessels with your own eyes, when your ears are filled with the roaring of the hurricane that may have bereaved you, when the dreadful reality of the ocean is there before you, white, blind, and raving.

We saw it on a sudden. The bend of the path opened the mouth of the Tyne, and laid bare the North Sea to the near horizon of iron-gray mist. It was a sight to give such a memory to the mind as the longest lifetime could not weaken. I had often viewed this sea in stormy weather from the Tynemouth cliffs; but here now was a scene of boiling, deafening commotion that awed, ay, and almost stunned me, as a revelation of the unspeakable might and remorseless ferocity of the deep. The harbor bar had not then been dredged to the depth it now stands at, and as the steady, cliff-like heights of dark, olive-colored water—their summits melting, as they ran, into miles of flashing foam — came to this shoaling ground, they broke up into an amazing whirling and sparkling of boiling waters, filling the air with driving clouds of spray, like masses of blowing steam, and whitening the pouring and roaring waves in the mouth of the Tyne beyond the bend at Shields, and as high, maybe, as Whitehill point. The horizon was barely two miles off, owing to the darkness that stood up like a gray wall from the sea to the heavens; and this near demarcation, therefore, exaggerated the aspect of the surges, as they came towering in the shape of ranges of hills out of the fog-curtain.

The tumult, the uproar of the trampling seas, no image could express. The huge breakers coiled in mighty, glass-smooth combers, and burst in thunder and in smoke upon the yellow sands, and the air was blinding with the flying of the salt rain from these crashing liquid bodies.

Across the river the Tynemouth cliffs were black with crowds gazing upon the wonderful, terrible sight, and I cannot describe the solemnity given to this scene of strife betwixt the powers of the earth and the air by that immense concourse of human beings, thronging the summits of the chocolate-colored rocks up which the breakers, as they fell against the base in ponderous hills, darted long, flickering tongues of milk-white spume, which streamed downwards again like mountain torrents among the dark-green, withe - like herbage which covers those cliffs in places.

There were three vessels ashore on our side, between the Trow rocks and where the long south pier now forks out. Others were stranded out of our sight, around the point on which Tynemouth lighthouse stands. Whether their crews were saved or drowned, whether any sort of assistance was being rendered them, I did not know; I could scarcely see. My senses were dulled by the violent thundering of the gale in my ears, by the uproar of the rushing seas, mingled with the voices of the people round me, and, above all, by the terror that sickened my heart as I thought of my father.

Yet, one thing we knew; that his vessel was not among the wrecks. They were all of them schooners and brigantines. This my mother was told by a seaman who stood near her, who had sailed with my father, and also in the brig my father was now at sea in, called the *Countess of Durham;* and, remarking my sinking aspect, she cried the news out in my ear to comfort and rally me.

I had asked this sailor, a man named Taylor, a question, and was trying to catch his answer, when his voice was drowned by a general shout, and, looking quickly, I spied a hundred arms pointing into the southeast. The moment my eyes were upon that quarter of the sea I saw the outline of a vessel heaving and staggering out of the thickness. She was, when I first beheld her, merely a smudge upon the mist, but in a short time she grew into a clearly defined object upon the hard green of the pelting seas. Taylor, who kept close at my mother's side, pointed a little pocket-glass at the vessel. I waited to hear him speak, but he was so long silent that in an agony of impatience I cried out to him to tell me if the vessel was my father's brig.

"Noa, miss," he answered; "aw thowt she was it forst. She's awlmyest heed on. She's a little bark. Thor's the

Danish ensign i' thi mizzen rigging. Her fore-topmist is gyen," he continued, keeping his eye at the glass, "her mainyard's i' two. God hev mercy on her foak! She's a doomed ship!"

The voices of the crowd had risen into a kind of roar as the people exclaimed together, when the vessel first hove in sight; but no sooner was it seen that she was not under control, and that she was drifting with the send of the seas and with the force of the gale dead on to the beach, which, it was thought, she would take a little to the right of where we stood, than a deep, impressive silence fell; every eye seemed transfixed; every face grew as hard and pale as stone, under the influence of the pity and horror the spectacle filled the soul with. A few men could be seen in her main rigging. Her furious tossing was sickening and distracting to watch. Now she was thrown up on the crest of a sea, and there hung an instant, poised on the dark pinnacle, suspended in the gray, cold, apparently motionless heaven of sullen cloud, half her keel out of water, the outline of her small, black hull showing clearly, and her wrecked spars aloft, and the confused tracery of her rigging limned in sharp lines as though drawn in India-ink; then, swooping down as the sea that supported her ran hissing past in a storm of snow, her hull and masts as high as the maintop disappeared, and nothing was visible but her topgallant-mast, that stood up no thicker than a hair out of the roaring hollow in which the vessel lay. It was a wonder to see her rise from those abysms; indeed, every sweeping heave of hers to the summit of the surges was like the coinage of a ship from the raging heart of the deep; yet, regularly as the swing of a pendulum did she draw nearer and nearer, watched with scarcely a stir—as though some blighting curse had gone forth and turned all life into marble—by the immense multitude that crowded the rocks and the shores.

She took the ground on a sudden. Her striking was known by the fierce smother of spray that burst up all round her, in the midst of which her masts reeled and fell; a second dreadful sea roared over her, and when it was spent she lay clean over on her port bilge, her decks up and down like the side of a house; a third breaker struck her—I believed I could hear the dull boom of the concussion rise above the hooting and the crashing of the tempest; and now the wreck was in halves—one black fragment fixed, the other a dozen fathoms nearer the beach.

Heart had been taken from me by fears for and thoughts of my father, and the sight of this wreck was more than I could bear. The sudden extinction of those poor seamen, who a few minutes before were holding on for life in the rigging, and looking with yearning, dying eyes upon the land, filled me with a soul-moving consternation.

"Oh, mother!" I cried, "let us go. We can wait for news of father in the town."

She looked at me, and seeing how bitterly distressed and shocked I was, she asked Taylor to come to us at once when a brig should heave in sight, and told him where he would find us; and then, taking my arm, she walked with me into the town, though she was constantly pausing to take a backward look at the sea, until a turning shut out the raging picture.

The widow of a Wesleyan minister, a kind and grave old body of seventy, named Mistress Robson—we say mistress in the north—who had known my father all his life, and who never failed to visit us when she was in Newcastle, which happened about once a year, lived just out of King Street, and to her house we went, that being the address my mother had given Taylor.

She put her aged face to the window when my mother knocked, and, catching sight of us, came to the door and hurried us into her little parlor, where a noble fire roared in the chimney.

"I expected ye would be coming to Shields, Mistress Snowdon," said she. "Ye've had no bad news, I hope, hinny?"

"No," answered my mother, "but my husband is at sea, and his vessel is due in the Tyne this very day. My trust is in God's mercy," she added, looking up; "but, oh, Mrs. Robson, have you been as far as the Lawe? Have you seen the sea? Only just now another vessel has come ashore with men in the rigging, and gone to pieces!"

Mrs. Robson clasped her old hands on her lap and shook her head. Her eldest son had been a sailor, and was drowned in a shipwreck on the Goodwin Sands, and no one better than she could understand the aching in the heart of a sailor's wife and child while listening to the storming of such a gale as was now blowing.

But she had a very cheerful, tender character, and knew what to say to keep our spirits hopeful. I never recall that horrible day without thinking of that ancient north-country dame bidding us come close to the fire and warm ourselves, removing my mother's cloak with her trembling hands, calling me " hinny," and stroking my cheek, and listening eagerly to what we said, being somewhat hard of hearing. Her room was very cosey; the bright fire blazed in the deep grate; there was a large Bible in a recess, and over it hung a portrait of the late Mr. Robson. I remember a couple of tapestry pictures—one representing the Last Supper; also the high-backed arm-chair in which the old lady sat; a large silver jug or tankard under a glass shade, a presentation to the late pastor; and, above all, do I remember the oppressive, leaden gloom of the sky over the house-tops opposite, as I saw it through the window, with masses of sulphur-colored scud sweeping along it, and the voices of the tempest, which shrieked like tortured children at the hall-door and the window-casements, and roared like the discharge of heavy ordnance in the chimneys.

I had come to that cheerful room nearly frozen, for we had lingered hard upon three hours on the Lawe. The warmth, I believe, helped to support our minds. Worry is chilling enough of itself, and though it may not be softened by a good fire, may be better borne near one than in a freezing wind. "Him too cold for brave to-day," says the negro sergeant in "Tom Cringle," meaning that he had no courage unless the sun shone warm. Old Mrs. Robson, hearing that we had eaten nothing since breakfast, bustled about to get some dinner for us, and, with the help of her servant, had us presently seated at her table with a good meal before us. We took her hospitality as a matter of course: we should have treated her in the same way, and been treated so by any other friends on whom we had called. Indeed, it was not until I visited other towns away from Newcastle and its neighborhood that I discovered that hospitality was reckoned a virtue. In the north we give and take. When people drop in they take a bite of whatever is going, and no fuss is made, and no name, that ever I heard of, given to the custom.

So we sat down to Mrs. Robson's little dinner as though we had been in our own house; but we could scarcely taste the food put before us. I knew what mother's thoughts were, and as for myself, I was fitter to cry than to eat when I glanced through the window at the scowling sky, and hearkened to the booming and shrieking of the wind.

The time wore on. We were listening to our aged friend, who was telling us of such another gale as this, that had burst over the northeastern coast some thirty years before, when we were startled by a loud knocking on the hall-door. My impatience was too great to suffer me to wait for the servant to answer the summons. I ran out, and on opening the door found Taylor outside. He was out of breath, yet managed to make me understand that a brig had hove in sight, and that she was running for the Tyne, and he believed by the look of her that she was the *Countess of Durham*. He also said, without any pause in his speech, that the gale had broken; delivering the whole, indeed, as a boy whips out with a message made up of several sentences which he has got by rote.

I called out the news to my mother, but begged her not to face the wind again, saying that I would go to the cliff alone with the sailor. Her answer was merely a look of wonder that I should ask her to stay behind. So, putting on our cloaks and wraps, we kissed old Mrs. Robson, and hurried along the street with Taylor at our side.

The man had told me truly enough that the gale had broken. I looked up at the sky and was struck by the reddish tinge that covered the great curtain of cloud; but, on glancing behind me, I perceived that the heavens had opened in the west, and that there was an amazing glory of bright gold clouds there, floating swiftly over several streaks of pure sky of an exquisite faint green color; and though the sun was lower down than this open space, and hidden behind a long line of dark vapor, out of which the golden clouds were sailing like bursts of living fire from some concealed mighty volcano, yet the brightness cast down by the shining break was as sweet to our senses as though the sun himself was visible, and sent us along with beating hearts, which grew lighter with hope as the beautiful sunset tinge broadened into the stormy darkness which lay like the night upon the face of the east.

Whether the crowds had gone and come again I do not know; but Tynemouth cliffs, and our own side of the river's mouth, were thronged with a concourse as dense as I had seen in the morning. A little schooner under a shred of canvas, her main boom gone, and her decks littered with wreckage, had just safely crossed the bar as we came in sight of the sea, and we could hear the people on the opposite shore cheering her as she swarmed through the white smother of foam, and went staggering over the seas in the mouth of the river towards the smooth reaches beyond, like a breathless, broken, terrified, hunted creature.

But we had no eyes for her. When we had the sea before us, Taylor pointed into the southeast, into the very eye and wake of the gale, and we stopped, staring with all our might and main.

The aspect of the ocean had been terrific in the morning, and it was terrific still; but the wonderful light that lay upon it and upon the sky gave it a grandeur that was not to be found in it before. The wind yet blew hard enough to maintain the impulse of the rushing seas, though they were no longer the towering ranges of hills which had chased one another in endless succession out of the wild and dismal obscurity of the water-line. The horizon lay clear to its normal verge, and the surges there were distinctly visible in broken, tumultuous, wintry - sharp shapes against the faint orange of the heavens.

The vessel that had sent the sailor in a hurry to fetch us was the only object in sight upon that foaming, roaring, desolate expanse of ocean. She was not above three miles off, and was heading dead for the mouth of the Tyne, with nothing on her but a reefed foresail. I could see that she was brig-rigged, also that she had sustained some injury aloft; but I could not be equally sure that she was my father's ship, though Taylor, after looking again, said that if she was not the *Countess of Durham* he'd pay any man five good shillings down.

We had been watching some few minutes when the skies, opening wider yet in the west, let down a long and slanting beam of sunlight which illuminated, as if by magic, the farthest confines of the sea in the east. The glorious radiance flashed upon the heaving and rushing waters in the mouth of the river, and upon the whirling snow of the surges, leaping in fury upon the Black Middens under the Tynemouth heights, and upon the stately pouring of the grass-green seas beyond the bar. In that wondrous beam of light which appeared to divide the heavens, the ocean and the coasts, and the little toiling brig that was rapidly approaching the river's mouth, made a picture incomparably noble and majestic. Against the reddish slate of the northeast sky—as it bore from where we stood—Tynemouth lighthouse reared its substantial white shape, and in that sudden gush of afternoon glory it resembled a height of solid marble, on whose summit the lantern glasses sparkled with innumerable fiery stars. The brightness gave sharpness to the colors of the apparel of the crowds upon the top of the cliffs, and a deeper hue to the brown of the great blocks of rock, from whose base the breakers were recoiling in clouds of smoke. But best of all was the vivid clearness it lent to the hull and rigging of the lonely little vessel, that was still far enough distant to resemble a toy upon the broken, headlong waters.

We were no longer in doubt about her: others as well as Taylor had recognized her, and I heard her name called out over and over again by the people we were standing among. My mother grasped my hand, and in that posture we stood watching the approach of the brig.

Much of the spite had gone out of the wind, yet it still blew a gale, and the raging of the surges upon the bar made the mouth of the Tyne resemble a whirlpool. It was a terrible sea for a small vessel to run before. The foresail helped the brig greatly by lifting her head as she swept into the hollows; yet, after I knew the vessel to be my father's, I could sometimes scarcely draw my breath when I saw her thrown up, her bowsprit pointed to the heavens, her stern out of sight on the slope of the wild sea behind her, her bows and some feet of her keel forward out of water; and then rush down into the fearful chasm —ay, just as a man might fall over the edge of a sheer cliff—and so vanish as though she had gone to the bottom.

But she struggled onwards stoutly and surely, and no one who saw her but must have known that the courage, coolness, and determination of an old and experienced seaman were watching over her, and conducting her through those sickening, giddy, thunderous acclivities. As she scaled the liquid heights it was a sight to stir the most languid blood to see her spurning the green seas from her bows, sending them recoiling a whole ship's length in advance of her, in a great surface and torrent of foam, and to follow the leaping and tossing path she had scored, by running the eye along the narrow stream of wake which marked her whereabouts, even when she was hidden, by the flashing of its snow-like, sinuous line upon the hinder surges, and tracing it until it was lost amid the warring of the foaming seas under the horizon.

"The maistor brings her weel throo'd," exclaimed Taylor, who kept close to us all this while. "He's it thi wheel ilang wiv inuther, an' thor's han's it thi releevin' ta'kils. Aw lay they divvent fynd them i' thi road. They've myed bettor weather iv it up iloft then aw forst thowt. Hees fore-topgallent-mist's gyen, and so's hes jibboom, an' awl sweer war ye ti cast thi gaskets adrift, ye wid fynd nowt but rags on thi main-topsil yards. Luik, mistress! ye'll see thi captain plain enuff ti wind'ard o' thi wheel, if ye kin only bring thi glass ti bear steadily."

But she was too agitated, her hands shook too much to enable her to keep the tube covering the bounding and ever-vanishing hull. She gave the little telescope to me, and just once I managed to catch a glimpse of my father's face; but it was like seeing it in a flash of lightning—it swept out of the field of the lens, and I could not catch it again. And yet, had I been able to look steadily for five minutes, I believe I should not have received a deeper im-

pression than that flying glance at his dear face gave me.
It was an instantaneous photograph, but I caught the
whole—the fixed and resolute stare of the eyes, the compressed lips, the iron-like steadiness of the head upon the
neck, the scrap of gray hair tossing like a wreath of smoke
upon his forehead under his sou'wester.

He and his brig seemed well known to the people about
me. I heard them mention his name and praise the manner in which he was bringing her along.

"He'll hit thi bar reet eneuff!" said one, speaking to
another close beside me. "Nivor feer! He knaws thor
wettors as he knaws hes fingers. Gannin' throo thi race
'ill be thi job. It's not thi Middens he'll faal fool on.
Thi bar's the thing. If thi trow o' thi sea drops him upon't,
it 'ill be ta-ta tiv him."

I very well knew what the speaker meant, and so did
my mother. At this time the depth of water at the entrance of the Tyne was at flood-tide not above twenty-two
feet, and at low water *scarcely seven feet.*

One would hardly believe this could be true—so late
even as the year 1860—of a river where now you may see
sailing-ships and steamers as large and stately as any that
pass up and down the Thames. Yet I am telling the
truth, as any old Tyneside sailor will assure you, and
though at this distance of time I cannot recall the state of
the tide at the hour when my father's brig was making for
the mouth of the river through that fearful sea, I very
well knew that even when the bar was best covered it was
still all too shallow for safe navigation; and that in such
a gale and in such a sea as were now raging—the furious
surges as they rushed one after another in frightful procession upon that shoaling ground shattering themselves,
for want of depth to maintain their elevation, in sickening
whirlpools and eddies and tramplings of white water—the
crossing of that bar by a brig of the tonnage of the *Countess of Durham* must be a passage full of deadly peril.

By this time the brig was close; too near to be lost
sight of even when she swept into the dark chasms and
veiled her forward decks in spray. My mother and I, our
hands tightly locked, our hearts hammering in our very
finger-tips, stood watching. The people about us were

silent, leaning forward, intently gazing; I saw them on the Tynemouth cliffs crowding into compact masses to get a view.

Suddenly there was a rush of men along the drenched and shining decks of the brig, and a fragment of sail was hoisted.

"That's weel dune!" said a hoarse voice behind me. "She'd nivvor 'a cum up withoot it!"

I looked hurriedly at the speaker, then swiftly again at the brig. Her stem was in contact with the raging milk-white water; a sea lifted her stern, and I saw the figures at the helm revolve the wheel; her bowsprit swept around, and the weight of the gale catching her laterally bent her over until her starboard bulwarks were hidden in the foam. The fierce, convulsed seas resembled a hundred thousand wolves snapping at her, trying to board her, jumping right over her; she seemed to sink in the foam like a piece of wood among soapsuds. Right and left she was struck—forward in blows which sent the water flying as high as her foretop in solid white pillars, which gleamed like salt, and blew away in radiant powder; aft by the maddened surges which thundered against her counter and burst in clouds of spume, which the gale caught up and swept towards the heavens in shapes of feathers.

I looked at my mother; she had her eyes shut.

"He is safe, mother!" I cried. "See! he will be abreast of us in a minute!"

As I said this, a deep-noted cheer, a continuous roaring noise, dulled by the storming wind, came across from the Tynemouth cliffs, and instantly it was taken up on our side, and such a shout was given as might have been heard a mile off. Hats and handkerchiefs were flourished to welcome the little storm-borne craft; and as she swirled over the short seas which rolled into the mouth of the river all white with the smother on the bar, and ran, with streaming decks and sluicing scuppers and trailing gear, past the point on which we stood, I saw my father wave his hand towards us as though he veritably spied his wife and child, and was saluting us, while the crew in their shining oilskins stood motionless in a group a little forward of the mainmast, like men newly rescued from the jaws of death, and awed by their great deliverance.

We stood watching the brig until she vanished round the bend of the river, when my mother, waking up as from a trance, and letting fall my hand, cried out hysterically:

"Oh, Jessie, let us make haste home and get all ready for father. Quick, dear child! He must not arrive and find no welcome prepared;" and though my heart was yearning to go and meet him as he came ashore from the brig, I knew he would be better pleased to find us, and the welcome of a cheerful fire and a hearty meal, awaiting him at home in Newcastle. So forthwith we walked to the railway station.

CHAPTER IV.

MY FATHER GIVES UP THE SEA.

It was a little before six o'clock when we reached Newcastle, and quite dark. We knew that father would be with us that night, no matter how late it should be when he came; so we built up a great fire in the parlor, and got ready the table for supper, and made the room very fit indeed for a man newly arrived from a voyage, and fresh from a dreadful hurricane, to light upon.

All the wind had gone. Going to the window to look at the night, I found the heavens clear, and the stars sparkling with a wintry vividness; but the air was icily keen, and the cold and the weariness would make such a room as this we had got ready—the capacious grate as bright as sunlight with a noble, roaring fire, the table laid for supper, the snow-white cloth ashine with glass and plate—a welcome sight to my father.

It was striking ten when I heard the house-door open, and running out to meet the only person beside ourselves who would enter without ringing the bell, I was clasped in my father's arms. It was a rare meeting, and mother could scarcely be made to let go his hand.

"We saw you arrive, father," said I. "We were down at Shields, and spied your brig when she was no bigger than a fly."

"What, ye were both at Shields!" said he, looking from me to mother, and smiling and well pleased. "I don't doubt you held your breath, Jessie, as we crossed the bar. Eh, my word, what a sea! Annie, d'ye know there are fifteen wrecks betwixt Blyth and Marsden Bay; and a matter of over tenscore sailors drowned, by rough reckoning! God help the widows and fatherless! The gale was all along the coast, as far as the Channel. There'll be heart-breaking news coming day after day for the next fortnight, or I'm sadly out."

He fell into deep thought, toasting his hands at the fire, and speaking to himself.

But supper was ready, and when at table he told us about the hurricane—how he was somewhat to the southward of Sunderland when the whole fury of the gale struck him, and forced him to heave to. But for the gale he would have made the Tyne last night, as he had got away from Calais earlier than he had reckoned upon doing, and had carried a fresh southwesterly wind to within a couple of hours of the change of weather.

I listened while he described the storm, too much excited to go on with my supper. All sailors—who can talk at all—are graphic as relaters: their language is picturesque and simple, the best in the world for putting their stories before you in; they notice points connected with the sea which a landsman would miss; and they are fertile in illustrations, making use of comparisons which are often extraordinarily well-contrived to convey their meaning. Indeed, one has only to notice the number of sailors' terms introduced into our every-day language to appreciate the wealth, color, and vividness of the marine phraseology.

All the qualities I have indicated my father had in a high degree; no seaman ever spun a yarn better. And when he spoke of the gale, described the slow gathering of livid clouds in the southeast, and the effect of the first outfly of the hurricane upon them—the whirling masses of black vapor, the wool-white sea under them, the infernal hooting and yelling of the tempest as it came along—I could not take my eyes from his face. I seemed to be in the little vessel, to see the fearful scene of storm he

described, to hear the crash and splintering of wood in
the revolving gloom overhead as the brig heeled under
the shattering blow, and buried her lee deck as high as
the main hatch upon the plain of foam that was levelled
by the fury of the wind as flat as a floor.

When supper was over we brought our chairs to the
fire. I filled my father's pipe, and put some spirits and
hot water upon the table; but in the midst of this, the
servant looked in and said that Captain Salmon had called
to ask if father's brig had fetched the Tyne.

"Is Salmon there?" sung out my father.

"Ay, Tom Snowdon, here he is!" echoed an old, rasp-
ing, shaky voice. "Hearty glad to find ye all alive O, and
snug in harbor, skipper."

"Come in, Salmon, come in," cried my father; and there
entered as strange and ancient a marine product as was at
that time to be found in Newcastle or anywhere else; an
aged, dried-up, retired sea-captain, two years over eighty.
His left eye was withered up and no sight left in it; but
the other eye, as if annoyed at having to do all the work,
stood out angrily, and shone like a brown glass ball with
a light behind it. A quantity of silver hair fell as low as
his coat-collar from either side of his head, leaving the top
as bald as a piece of marble; the loss of his teeth brought
his under-lip pretty nearly up to his nose; and what with
weather, years, and grog, the skin of his face was like an
old drum-skin—the part of it, I mean, where the drum-
sticks strike. He was dressed in a long pilot-cloth coat,
with an endless blue kerchief, embellished with white spots,
coiled round his neck, and a tall chimney-pot hat brushed
the wrong way, and of the color of bronze at the rims.

He nodded to mother and me, and looking slowly about
him, selected a chair, under which he put his hat, and then
painfully seated himself.

My father had known him pretty nearly all his life—I
mean my father's life—had sailed with him often, and was
his second mate in the last voyage the old man ever took.
Salmon had been a keelman, then a foremast hand, and
had saved up a trifle of money out of investments in coasters after he had got command; and, having buried all his
relatives, lived alone, cooking his own food and dusting

his own furniture, people said, in a little bit of a house out of Northumberland Street.

"I've been smoking a pipe with Ben Stephenson," said he, in a voice it was difficult to listen to without smiling; "but I wouldn't go home without first asking if aught had been heard of ye. Snowdon, ye'll have had a sneezer, my lad. What was the ship? I heard it was a brig."

"The *Countess of Durham*," answered my father, nodding at me to mix the old man a glass of spirits.

"I know her nicely," quavered the old fellow, bringing his solitary burning eye to bear upon my movements. "What weather did ye make?"

"So-so," exclaimed my father, puffing out a cloud of smoke. "We were in ballast, ye must know, crank as a top that's done spinning, and she jumped her fore-top-gall'nt-mast out of her, which dragged the jibboom along with it. Salmon, you were never out in more wind. It was like a wall, man."

The old fellow took a steady pull at the steaming tumbler I had placed before him, and then ran his eye round the room with a rather sour expression in his face, as if this challenge to his own experiences were not to his taste. His gaze coming to my mother, he looked at her attentively, and said, "Mistress, ye'll be making Tom Snowdon give up the sea now. He's filled his purse. He has no call to keep ye fretting your heart over every gale of wind that blows."

"If he knew what Jessie and I went through last night and this morning," she replied, glancing fondly at her husband, "he would never look at a ship again."

"Annie, my lass," said my father, solemnly, "you shall have your way. This day I give up the sea for good. The old ocean 'll play me no more tricks. The end of my tow-rope's coiled down. Henceforth Tom Snowdon's a landsman."

His pipe shook in his hand, as he turned his eyes first on mother, then on me; his weather-beaten face twitched with emotion, and he spoke in a broken voice. My mother jumped up and threw her arms round his neck, and when she had hugged him enough, I stepped forward. In spite of his having threatened to give up the sea time after time, and always going to it again, it was impossible to question his earnestness now.

"Oh, Tom," said my mother, as she returned to her chair, "this is glad news for me, dear!"

"But mind ye stick to your promise," exclaimed Captain Salmon, raising his glass with one hand and forking up a long, hornlike fore-finger over it. "I know what sailors are. I know what *I* was. More fathoms of cable go to holding Jack at his shore-anchor than he's got room to stow away aboard of himself. He rides with the ocean under his lee, and he'll find an excuse to slip, mistress," said he, turning to my mother, "if ye don't keep him well aft and under a taut hand."

"No fear of that, Salmon; no fear of that, Annie," answered my father, still speaking with much emotion. "When I looked to wind'ard last night, into the pitch-black roaring smother out there, and thought of how they'd be feeling in this old house when they heard the wind thundering, and sent their hearts out to me, I said to myself, 'Thomas, let Almighty Providence carry ye this time safe home and set you ashore, and you'll swab down, coil up, and *stop there*. Mind, Thomas,' I said, 'you'll do it. There must be no hankerings, no wanderings of fancy. You'll do your duty to those who love you, save them from the trouble you're causing them to pass through now, turn your attention to land-going diversions, and go down on your knees and give thanks that, after forty-seven years of seafaring life, you're able to knock off a whole man, all your limbs sound, appetite good, spirits middling hearty, and with enough shot in the locker to keep the bailiffs below th' horizon.' Those were my thoughts; and here I sit now, safe and whole, thanks be to God for the same! a resolved man, with a heart filled with gratitude. No," he exclaimed, with great energy and a violent shake of the head, "you'll not find me changing. Here you see me, and here I stop. I deserve rest, and I'll take it."

And so saying, he put his pipe to his lips, and smoked rapidly and with an air of great defiance, keeping his eyes fixed on Captain Salmon, as if, being sure that *we* believed in his sincerity, he was resolved that the old man should believe in it too.

"No man who is a husband and a father ought to keep at sea when he has money enough to excuse him leaving the calling," said my mother. "What life is more perilous? And it is as thankless as it is perilous. What honor does a man get for being a sailor? Last night and to-day, Tom, you went through dangers more dreadful than any a soldier meets with on a battle-field. But what reward do you receive? If you lose your ship, the chances are your captain's certificate is taken from you; and, if you are a poor man, you must get your living by begging. If you are drowned, your wife breaks her heart, and your daughter becomes a friendless orphan. If you come through it safely, not a word is said; nobody takes any notice, nobody praises your courage and skill."

"It's true enough," replied my father, shaking his head thoughtfully, and stealing a look at old Salmon. "There's no life more thankless than the sailor's. Shore-going people, including the parsons, take no interest in him, don't understand him, never trouble to make friends with him. His pay's poor, and he works with his life in one hand and his employer's interests in the other. When he dies they give him the last toss, nobody heaves a sigh, and the bubbles which rise as the hammock he's stitched up in goes down are the only version of his life and death that hits the truth."

Captain Salmon listened stolidly, with his under-lip moving.

"There are many who love sailors, father," said I, timidly. "At all hours of the night and day there are scores of prayerful hearts away out with sailors upon the sea."

"Well, I'm not so sure of that, my lass," exclaimed old Salmon, suddenly. "There's a deal of sentiment talked about sailors, and more songs written about 'em than I'd care to hear sung, if I was allowed to the year nineteen hundred and fifty-nine to listen to 'em in. All this here soft-soap about Jack has come up since I was at sea. A sailor was a sailor then. Ne'er a blue jacket but covered a man. But steam's corrupted the seaman. Being kept always warm in the engine-room has made his poor health delicate, and that's set the females writing poetry about him, and talking, as Miss Jessie here does, of fond hearts following of him."

"I wonder you can speak like that, with such a sailor as my husband listening to you, Captain Salmon," said my mother, taking him up rather quickly, and glancing at my father, whose face was full of ill-concealed amusement.

"Look here, Mistress Snowdon," answered the old man, with a good deal of asperity, and convulsively clutching his glass; "if there were fifty sailors present, and all of them the equals of Tom Snowdon, I'd repeat my observations, and fear no contradictions. I knew Tom Snowdon afore you did, ma'am, begging your pardon for a liberty that happened by accident. Tom Snowdon and me have sailed together in vessels of which, were ye to offer ten thousand pound for a sight of, ay, even a copper bolt belonging to 'em, your curiosity couldn't be satisfied, so dead and gone they be. There was never a better sailor in my time, nor in any time that went afore, nor that'll follow after me, than Tom Snowdon. There he sits, and he hears me. But his listening isn't going to make me say things I don't mean. I tell ye, mistress, that sailors aren't the men they used to be when I was at sea. Look at the ships they're building! Take your stand on the Lawe, and observe the iron tanks passing; see 'em with their ugly bows cocked up, as if they were ashamed of the derricks, called masts, which they carry forrards, and wanted to toss 'em over their starns. Watch 'em, with their midship beam so narrow that any man with long legs might span their decks with a foot on either bulwark rail; inspect their internal organization, and remark Jack, with a black face, earning his wages in the bunkers; and then ask yourself whether it's possible for men bred in such metal cisterns to answer to the name of sailors as folks in my day understood the word?"

"The whiskey's within reach of your arm, Salmon," said my father, soothingly. "All that you say is true enough;" and he gave my mother a wink, to let her know that he agreed with the old man merely to pacify him.

"If sailors are no longer sailors," said my mother, smiling, "they have no excuse for keeping to the sea for love of it when they can afford to quit it."

"They don't keep to it," rejoined my father. "It's only old shell-backs, like Salmon and me, who go on looking behind us after we're ashore."

"Nothing but infirmity drove me from it," said Captain Salmon. "If Time 'ud make a starnboard, ye'd find me afloat again, Thomas."

A gloomy look came into my father's face, and he squeezed a pinch of tobacco into his pipe with a very downcast air.

"What I'm going to say will mean nothing," said he, addressing Captain Salmon, but talking to mother, "for, as you know, I'm resolved. I'm ashore, and here I stop. But there's no woman in this wide world, and there's no landsman either, as can understand the struggle in the heart of a sailor who quits the sea loving it. Fresh from a hurricane as I am, and thankful to Almighty God for my preservation, I can skip that spell of storm, and slip back into the sunny days, and recall the joy the sea gave me, and my triumphs in the old buckets I've commanded. Nay, Annie, ye needn't fear. Here I sit, I tell ye, a resolved man; but, nevertheless, no matter how long I may yet be spared, I shall go to my grave remembering that for forty-seven years the sea served me well and used me kindly, and that from the days I first went apprentice, when it was my pride to ship the first handspike, to haul out the weather-earing, to be the first to run on deck in my watch below at the cry of all hands, down to the hour when, under Providence, I outlived last night's gale and brought the *Countess* safe over the bar, the lightest-hearted hours mortal man ever enjoyed were passed by me under the ocean sky, and in the midst of the blue circle that's been the grummet round my world ever since I was a boy."

"Ay," exclaimed old Salmon, who had listened with close attention and much satisfaction to this speech, "and let me tell ye, Mistress Snowdon, that in saying what he does, Thomas means no disrespect to you, but just leaves your share in the making of his happiness untouched."

"She knows that—she knows that," cried my father, in a broken voice.

"It's natural and it's beautiful," continued the old man, "that when a sailor leaves the sea he should give it his blessing. When Jack says good-bye to salt water, he's parting with an old friend. What's the occupation a man can quit — the calling that found him young and that leaves him old—without a wistful heart? Only last week I met Mr. Jackson standing opposite a little shop, looking at it. 'Why,' says I, 'yon was your old place of business, Mr. Jackson. Ye don't mean to begin afresh, do ye, that ye're eying it so steadily?' 'No, Salmon, no,' he answers, 'I don't mean to begin afresh. But I passed five-and-thirty year of my life yon, and when I look at it, I see myself, a young man, full of hope and strength, gazing through those windows, and I never can pass by without giving the old place a hand-shake, as it might be.' That's human nature, Mistress Snowdon; and if it's true of a retired linen-draper, which Mr. Jackson is, as I don't doubt ye know, how much truer is it of a sailor-man who leaves the sea that's tossed him for half a century on its breast, treating him as a mother treats her bairn, sometimes caressing him, often fretting him, often cuffing him, and then taking him to her heart again, and then giving him over to those who love him, with nothing to remember but what should make a good man proud to recall?"

"Say no more, Salmon," called out my father, almost tearfully. "You've put my case. A course of such arguments would end in making me feel I'm an ungrateful son of a swab."

"I am sure my husband doesn't need any excuses for giving up the sea, Captain Salmon," said my mother, a little crossly.

"Very well, ma'am, very well," answered the old fellow, laboriously securing his hat and rising. "I just called to hear about ye, Snowdon, and find I've stopped longer than I meant."

And so speaking, and shaking hands with us, and stopping to look at me as I opened the hall-door for him, and to mumble, "Eh, my word! ye're a great woman indeed; and it seems but yesterday that I could have stowed ye away in this old hat," he tottered out of the house.

We sat up talking for nearly an hour after he was gone.

None of us cared to leave the fire and the warm room. I thought that mother looked tired and pale, but when I advised her to go to bed, she said no, she was not sleepy. It did her good, after last night's anxiety, to sit talking.

"What a change, Jessie," said she, "in a few hours! This time last night, Tom, we could not hear ourselves speak for the dreadful crying of the wind and the shaking of the house; and now, hark! you can hear the kitchen clock ticking."

My father went to the window, and stood there awhile in silence with his face upturned, looking at the stars, which shone most gloriously in the frosty calm; then, breaking away from his thoughts, he came back to his chair, and said:

"Jessie, my lass, to-morrow maybe I'll introduce you to as handsome a young fellow as ever you read of in story-books. Annie, d'ye remember once going with me to Tynemouth, to call on a Mrs. Fowler — a quiet, pretty-faced woman in black, the widow of a Church of England clergyman?"

She did not remember.

"Why, surely you can't have forgotten. You thought her manners so fine—she had grand black eyes; you feared she was consumptive."

"Yes, I recollect now; but it must be ten years ago."

"It will be about ten years," said he. "Well, I mind she told us she had a son—a lad named Dick—an apprentice aboard a ship belonging to some London firm. Who should my mate be in this last trip in the *Countess* but that lad. His mother's been dead a year. He's six-and-twenty years old, and a better seaman I never want to meet. He was like my right hand in yesterday's gale, active as a cat, and as quiet. I've promised him my interest to help him to a ship, and I'll keep my word. He'll be here to see us to-morrow, and look to your heart, Jessie. If you have your father's eyes you'll admire him; and your mother'll tell you what admiration of a man means in a girl."

"Since he is a sailor, I shall like him," said I, laughing.

"What's Jessie's age, mother?" said he, running his

eyes over me with an expression half of pride, half of quizzing.

"She'll be twenty next month," answered mother, looking at me fondly.

"Ay, so she will. Jessie, you'll have to be seeking for a husband soon," said he, "if you don't want to end your days as one of those sheer hulks called old maids."

"Seeking!" cried my mother. "I hope not. The men who are got by seeking are but poor findings, as a rule. And why do you talk of Jessie marrying? You are only just returned home, after a dreadful storm, and while we're sitting here with our hearts full of gratitude for being united again, you're arranging, as it were, for scattering us for good."

"I was only joking, my lass," he answered, rising and tenderly kissing her. "No, no; Jessie must bide a wee with us yet. But, preserve us!" he exclaimed, pulling out a great old-fashioned gold watch, and comparing its time with the clock on the mantel-shelf, "what hour d'ye think it is? A quarter to twelve, as I'm a man!"

I was rising.

"Stay, Jessie," said he, sinking his voice, "there's a duty to be performed before we turn in. God has preserved me, and brought me home in safety, and we owe him thanks for his goodness."

There is an ancient proverb that says if you want to learn how to pray, you must go to sea. Anybody would have understood the meaning of that old saying who had heard my father giving thanks to God for preserving his life. There is no sacred memory that moves me as the recollection of that night does. I did not see the darkness then, but when I look back I behold the shadow of death in that old parlor, and my mother kneeling in the gloom of it. Solemn and mysterious, indeed, is the coloring that after-events give to circumstances which seemed but trifling matters when they happened.

When my father had concluded, mother rose from her knees, her face wet with tears, and stood looking at him. There was something in her expression that made her countenance unfamiliar; it startled me, and I glanced at my father to see if he noticed it; but he was smiling and about to speak, and when I looked at her again the strangeness was gone, and she was listening to some cheery words her husband addressed to her. I supposed my sight had deceived me, and that the swift change was some trick of the combined lamplight and firelight. But when I recalled it next day, I was sure then, and have never doubted since, that it was the presage in her soul that had wrought in her face, that it was the recognition by her instincts of the change that was coming—a recognition operating without the least reference to her reason—that had caused the subtle, passing alteration that had alarmed me.

However, after she had kissed me and said good-night, I thought no more of it, which affects me to think of to a degree I should be thought childish to confess.

CHAPTER V.

MY MOTHER'S DEATH.

LATE as it was when I got to bed, I lay awake a long while. One reason, no doubt, was, the day had been full of excitement, and my mind had not recovered from the effect of the fears and cruel expectations of the morning. But I will be honest, and own that there was another reason; and that was the thoughts which had been put into my head by my father's brief reference to the handsome sailor that was to visit us on the morrow—or, let me say, that day, for I heard the clock of St. Nicholas strike one as I lay thinking.

I had never yet had a sweetheart, nor can I remember that my fancies had ever run that way. It is true that, when a child, I would say that I would marry no one but a sailor, and that was still my resolution; but the want of a lover, or the wish to get married, had never troubled me. But, whether because I was ripe to listen to talk about such matters, or because my father's joking suggestion to me to seek a husband was the first expression of the kind that had ever escaped him—that is, since I had grown old enough to understand the meaning of such jokes—or because, not being sleepy, I was willing to let my imagination run upon that hint of the handsome sailor who was to visit us, I will confess that half my wakefulness, at least, was caused by thinking of my father's good-looking mate, wondering whether he would fall in love with me, and whether I should fall in love with him, with other fancies of a like kind, equally silly, if you please to think them so, though certainly not peculiar.

My notion is that a good many girls, who lead quiet lives, who grow up from infancy to womanhood in a regular routine of home duties, have the perception that they are women at last, and no longer young girls, flashed upon them as a revelation. Very often the discovery comes through falling in love. With me it came partly through those lightly spoken words of my father, and partly through the possibility of meeting some one who might fall in love with me. I am pretty sure that, up to that night, I had never fully realized that I was a woman, and no longer a little girl. Lying in my dark bedroom, not a sound upon the starlit night air without to distract my thoughts, and considering what being twenty years old meant, I found the number extraordinarily significant; and as a person who, falling asleep in a boat and waking up discovers that the current has carried him some distance out to sea, and that the shore is a long way off, so I, rousing up with a new intelligence from the quiet dream of my life, perceived that, all unconsciously, I had drifted far from my purely girlish boundary, and was indeed fairly afloat upon the great ocean of time.

These thoughts put me into good spirits, though, had they found me older, they would hardly have elated me. After inventing all sorts of faces and figures for Mr. Fowler, my father's mate, I came to myself, and wondered whether he would think me pretty. I believed I was, though a girl can never be sure on that head until the men leave her no room for doubting one way or the other. As for describing myself—which certainly no fear of being thought conceited would hinder me from doing if I possessed the art of putting a portrait before you in words; for, as I am the principal personage of this story, it is perfectly reasonable that I should wish to give you

the clearest possible notion of the woman who is addressing you—I say, as to describing myself, the mere cata-
loguing of my features would no more help you to know
me than—and I will borrow a fragrant simile—a list of
the flowers in a bouquet would give you a sense of their
perfume and an idea of the effect produced by the combination of their colors.

To say that I was fair, that my hair was a reddish
brown, my eyes gray, my stature slightly above the middle height of women, my figure tolerably well-shaped—
a little too stout, perhaps—and my carriage, to use the
expressive old word, so erect as to give strangers the
notion that I had a very good opinion of myself—I say
strangers, for those who knew me would never call me
conceited, whatever other ambiguous qualities the eye of
friendship might discern—to say all this, and ten times
more, if there were ten times more to say, would be saying nothing. A single physical characteristic—an oddly
shaped nose, a squint, a vague profile, a point that can be
expressed in a line—will often help the imagination when
twenty pages of microscopic description would still leave
the mind blank.

Such, however, as I was, there in my bed did I lie
wide awake for nearly two hours, in strangely good spirits, turning over all sorts of new fancies which I formed
in my mind, until I heard the church clock chime a quarter to two, when, feeling alarmed to discover myself awake
at so unreasonable an hour, I settled my head resolutely
on the pillow and fell asleep.

I was aroused by a hand laid upon me ; I opened my
eyes and saw father, dressed in his shirt and trousers,
standing at the bedside. It was broad morning, and the
sun shone brightly on the window. The moment I had
my senses thoroughly I perceived a most dreadful expression of grief in his face.

"Get up quickly, Jessie," said he. "A shocking thing
has happened. When you are dressed come to our bedroom ;" and speaking in a voice so hollow that I should
not have known it had I not seen his lips move, he left me.

I could not for the life of me imagine what shocking
thing to stir and break him down so deplorably could

4

have happened. I hurried on my clothes, my heart beating so fast that it made me feel ill and faint, and hurried across the passage to my mother's bedroom. My father stood at the window; he turned his head to look at me, and pointing to the bed, said, "She has left us, Jessie!"

I ran to the bed and saw mother lying as if asleep, with her face to the wall. Her features could not have been so composed—so happy and tranquil an expression as lay softly upon her countenance, and gave a surprising sweetness to it, could not have been there, had she indeed been asleep, and not dead. Nor had hers, instead of being the first, been but one of many corpses I had seen, could I have more instantly recognized the presence of death. I hung over the bed, stunned and petrified; I was as motionless as the beloved form I surveyed; my very breathing seemed to have ceased, so heart-crushing was this most terrible and unexpected shock; but my father creeping up to me took me in his arms, on which I turned and hid my face on his breast, and cried as I never had cried before.

My father, before he aroused me, had sent the servant for the doctor who lived close by. He arrived in a few minutes. He looked at my mother attentively, examined her, and then told us she had been dead some hours, and that her death was no doubt due to an affection of the heart. In this last he afterwards proved to be right, but I wished he had not said how long she had been dead, for my father broke down utterly on hearing the doctor, as though he found something unbearable in the thought of his lying quietly sleeping with his wife dead at his side. His deep and rending sobs, the terrible convulsions of his body, the picture of his strong, sunburned face partially concealed in his hands, the weather-beaten hue of which gave a peculiar smoke-like whiteness to his iron-gray hair, so terrified and affected me as to altogether draw my thoughts from mother to him; and I fell upon my knees at his side, and endeavored to calm him by caresses, and by entreaties that he should remember I had no friend now but him, and that his grief should not let him forget me.

The doctor, a kind-hearted man, though commonly his

manners were rough almost to coarseness, reasoned with
him too, and after a while we came away from the room
and went down-stairs. The sight of the old parlor brought
home our loss to me with cruel keenness ; every object
that my eye rested upon recalled her ; I dared not look
at the chair in which she would sit knitting. Little wonder that we pray against sudden death. An interval of
illness prepares the way ; you grow used to the absence
of the familiar figure amid the scenes associated with her
presence ; the withdrawal is slow ; her chair has stood
empty, her place at table has been vacant, when she was
still with you. But sudden death gives habit no time.
Whenever the door is opened you think the lost one is
coming in ; you hear her voice twenty times a day ; you
find yourself waiting for her, and as every trick of custom is exposed it becomes, so to speak, a fresh perception
of your loss.

There was a little sitting-room adjoining the parlor,
and my father, unable to bear the sight of the furniture
of the parlor, that was inseparably associated with my
mother, withdrew to it ; and there, with the window-
blind down, and in a mournful twilight, we sat, talking
of the dead.

It was about noon when I heard a gentle ring at the
house-bell. The servant answered the door, but I paid no
attention, my thoughts being with my mother. In a few
moments the servant put her head in to say that Mr. Fowler
had called. My father asked if he had left any message.

"Why, sir," said the servant, who was a raw kind of
girl belonging to Whitley, "he's in the parlor."

"Oh," exclaimed my father, rising suddenly, "I cannot
see him. I could not look any man in the face. I could
not talk to him. Did ye not tell him that the mistress
was—was—" the words stuck in his throat.

The poor fool of a girl stared and looked as if she had
a mind to whimper, but made no answer.

"He is here," said my father, addressing me ; "could
ye trust yourself to meet him, Jessie ? Mary," meaning
the servant, "would blunder over any message, and I
should be sorry to have his feelings hurt."

I had no heart to go, either. If I remembered the

curiosity and the fancies which had kept me waking till nearly two in the morning it was only with shame and grief that such idle thoughts should have possessed me on the eve of this blighting sorrow. But seeing my father's trouble, and knowing as well as he that any message the servant delivered would be blundered, so as to become almost as bad as turning the poor man into the street, I said, "Very well, father, I'll go. I'll tell him you cannot see him to-day."

"Nor to-morrow—no, nor till after the funeral," he exclaimed, with a grievous outburst of sorrow.

I left the room and entered the parlor, where I found Mr. Fowler standing near the fire, with his cap in his hand, looking puzzled, and yet not seeming to know that there was grief in the house. The window-blinds were down, but he would not think that that signified anything, as the sun shone full upon the front of the house. In spite of the drawn blinds the room was not dark. I could see him very plainly, and though the eyes I lifted to him were heavy and clouded enough, I was not so blinded by grief as not to perceive that my father had spoken the truth when he called his mate good-looking.

He bowed and asked to see Captain Snowdon.

"He cannot be seen," I answered; "a dreadful grief has befallen us. My mother was found dead in her bed this morning."

I thought I should have been able to say this without crying, but in spite of a hard struggle I gave way and sobbed bitterly, weeping the more, perhaps, because I strove to keep my tears back.

"Had I known this I should not have followed the servant into this room," said he, in a voice full of apology and sympathy, and looking shocked, too. "Are you Miss Snowdon?"

I answered that I was.

"Please tell your father, and believe yourself, that I am heartily grieved to have intruded upon you at such a time," said he.

"If you will call again—a little later—next week," said I, crying and stammering, "he will be glad to see you."

"Yes; and I hope, meantime, that neither of you will let this sorrow sink too deep," he exclaimed, so gently and kindly that I could not help looking at him. "There is no cure but time for wounds of this kind;" and giving me another bow, he stepped softly from the room and left the house.

Sad and overcome as I was, I could not help admiring the manner in which he had managed his behavior and going. To be met by a girl who could not speak without sobbing, to step unawares into a house of death, as he had, were such confrontments as might harass the tact of a man pretending to manners very different from what a plain merchant-mate is likely to have. What can you say to a person fresh from a death-bed, and weeping? The gentlest condolences are a mere impertinence at such a time. To quietly depart is the utmost you can do; but to manage that leave-taking capably, to be quick and yet not seem hurried, and yet to contrive that the mourner shall feel that your sympathy is honest, shows real judgment as well as a kind heart.

"Is Mr. Fowler gone?" said my father, when I returned.

I answered yes, and that I had told him we should be glad if he called next week. So there the matter ended. Nothing more was said about Mr. Fowler, and though now and again the remembrance of his handsome face would steal into my grief, I gave him very little thought, my mourning for my mother growing greater hour by hour, and wholly engrossing my mind, as old memories trooped up and deepened to my innermost senses the reality of my irreparable loss.

Before the day of the funeral, however, my father rallied considerably. He was a man of strong religious feelings, though he never aired them, and they would have been of little worth had they failed him at such a time as this. I heard that he broke down at the grave when the coffin was lowered, and that when the service was over his friends had much trouble to coax him away from the church-yard; but he recovered his composure on his way home, and calmly kissed me when he arrived, as though to convince me he had mastered his grief and that he was humbly content that God should have his own.

In writing of my mother's funeral, I cannot but recall that they were all sailors who attended it. Old Captain Salmon was one ; there was also Captain Tarbit, who had sailed several voyages with my father in one capacity or another ; altogether there were seven seamen, one of them being a mate, and they filled two mourning coaches. I thought Mr. Fowler would have been among them, but either my father had forgotten to invite him, or else he could not get away from his duties at South Shields.

I was in the parlor when they assembled and waited for the coffin to be conveyed to the hearse, and was struck by the hearty simplicity of their sympathy with father. They made no fuss; they stood here and there talking, endeavoring to subdue their voices, though some of the gruff sea-notes were not easily modulated to softness. I heard Salmon arguing with Captain Tarbit.

"No, no," said he, "ye can't liken it to your tow-line parting and sending ye adrift. Death's a haven, man; life's the ocean where ye get the tossing. Death's smooth water and good holding-ground, where there's nothing to do but let go the anchor and turn in;" and I watched him roll his single eye round the room in search of approval for his illustration.

"When young Joe Patten died," said one of the captains, whom I had not met before, a short, square, brown-faced man with bright, intelligent eyes—"that Joe Patten, I mean, whose father owned the old *Venus*—William Morris, who was a bit of a poet in his way, says to me, ' Well, poor young Joe's gone. He took five days dying, and he said to me the day afore his death, " William," says he, " when a man draws near the other world—when the coast's hove up and's as plain in sight as a spiritual shadow can be, my belief is that God A'mighty sends an angel aboard him to pilot him in. That's just the fancy I have," he says. " There's a strong hand steering me, William, and although I know no more than that I'm bound to a new life, yet I feel to be so well handled, all's so calm and steady with me, mate, that, so far from being afraid, I wouldn't take twenty years more of life in exchange for the happiness that's now in me."' William Morris," continued the skipper, "may have invented this, or it may be young Joe Patten's very words. *I* think it's true, and I'll tell 'ee why. The hardest part of death is being alone. Friends may be crying round ye, and holding your hands, but still ye're alone. But my notion is, th' A'mighty's too good to let a man drift out of this world like a derelict, no one aboard. And so, as we can't ship human friends for the last voyage, what more natural than that th' A'mighty should put an angel aboard us, as young Joe Patten said—a sort of pilot to keep us company and cheer us up, and navigate us truly? If nothing of that kind takes place, how do ye account for men dying smiling, as if they'd been having a pleasant talk with a shipmate up to the last moment?"

These and other fragments of the low-pitched conversation among our friends on that solemn day survive in my memory, with the bearing of the men, their tender-hearted efforts to say such things as they believed would cheer up father and me, though we were seldom or never addressed, but, on the contrary, treated with that kind of awe which the sanctity of deep sorrow never fails to excite in childlike minds.

CHAPTER VI.

MR. FOWLER'S SECOND VISIT.

THOUGH my father felt the loss of his wife at the time with a singular violence and passion of grief, he recovered himself quickly. Ever afterwards there was a change in him; indeed, anybody could have seen that something that had 'made a precious part of his life had gone out of it; but there was no pining, no sentimental bemoaning. He took his discipline as a simple-hearted sailor should, often quoting a favorite expression of his father, "That when the Captain of the universe gave orders we were never to doubt their wisdom, but to turn to and execute them with cheerful hearts, assured that we should never be put to a job that wasn't for our good."

Though Mr. Fowler called after the funeral, I did not see him. He came one day when I was up-stairs, had a long talk with my father, then went away, and was gone half an hour when I heard that he had called.

"Will he be here again?" said I.

"Not for another three months," answered my father. "He sails next week as chief mate of the *African Chief*."

I was a trifle put out by this, for my vanity wanted an earlier opportunity to improve on the wretched, moping figure I had made in that meeting on the day of my mother's death. But the annoyance was small enough. I had hardly thought of him, and his going away for three months promised to slip him clean out of my memory.

After my mother's death the passage of the days was terribly tedious, sorrow freighting them heavily; but time brought me the medicine I wanted, and every week after the first month found me thinking of her with less pain, and feeling her absence with less sharpness. I got used to her empty seat in the pew at St. Nicholas's Church, where we regularly worshipped, to her absence from the kitchen, where every morning we would settle the household business of the day, to her vacant place near the parlor fire, where her arm-chair stood, as though at any moment she might come in and seat herself with her work-basket and knitting.

Yet Christmas-day followed too fast upon her departure not to make it an empty and dismal festival for us. The cheerful ringing of the church bells, the holiday attire of the people, the thought of the family gatherings, recalled happy memories which only made this Christmastide the darker to me.

However, in the evening, Captain Tarbit, his wife, and a marine engineer—a hearty Scotchman, named Finlay, who had known my father some years, and who was a man fuller of extraordinary experiences than any person that ever I knew, having encountered when at sea pretty nearly every kind of marine disaster that can be named— I say these three persons came over from Shields to spend the evening with us and cheer us up, rightly enough suspecting that we should be dull and depressed; and though, no doubt, had we been asked the question, we should have said we would rather have been alone, secretly we were by no means displeased to be broken in on and forced out of the gloom of our thoughts into the daylight of living interests.

Mrs. Tarbit was a Cullercoats woman, with the richest rattle of an accent that can be imagined of a north-country born and bred person. When Tarbit courted her she was a widow, and kept a sailor's boarding-house in North Shields. I suppose the skipper liked her for her warm heart, and took her, as you would an oyster-shell, for the sake of the pearl inside it. Externally she was certainly no divinity. Not to speak of a small beard, about the eighth of an inch long, which she would lay hold of and twist about when listening, her complexion was yellow, her nose like a small cork strongly defined by a redness at the point; she had short legs and a long body, and in her large bonnet trimmed with yellow, a green silk dress, a loose cloth jacket, decorated down the front and upon the arms with rows of flaunting bows, she looked, with her beard, like a pitman masquerading in petticoats. But if all that was reported of her was true, a more tender, humane, and loving heart than hers never beat in a woman's breast. No sailor came under her care but would have risked his life to do her a service. No shipwrecked crew, bruised and dying from the sea, were brought ashore but that she was the first to be busy among them, finding money for them, sending them clothes, and at her own expense decently and reverently interring those who died among them.

When she spoke to father and me about my dead mother, there was such a cordial note of generous compassion, such a depth of moving sympathy in her plain, true words, that I felt a peculiar magic in her kindness, and, with the tears in my eyes, could have kissed her rough, masculine face for the encouragement she gave me, and for the Christian womanliness of her condolence. Such people are God's commentaries upon human nature. They are designed to show us the little value that is set by heaven on the beauty of the flesh; otherwise, what is the purpose of such reve-

lations of high and lovely characters encased in shapes
which seem to repel all sympathies but those which owe
nothing to the eyesight?

Our guests did us a deal of good. Mr. Finlay was as full
of wonders as the "Arabian Nights," and I see him now,
with a plentiful crop of hair tossed wildly upon his forehead and curling on his shoulders, a somewhat ragged beard
and mustache deepening the character of rough daring in
his face, a great brown hand sawing the air as he told his
stories in pure Aberdeen, and his eyes glowing like live
embers in their hollows, which nature had made extrava-
gantly deep by the projection of the bushy brows—I say
I see him now, telling his extraordinary adventures of
shipwreck, imprisonment, long days of lonely agony and
starvation in an open boat, and the like, while we all sat
listening, father with his arms folded and the red firelight
flickering on one side of his face, honest Mrs. Tarbit pluck-
ing at her beard and hearkening with open mouth, and
her husband as restless as a smack's dog-vane, turning
about in his chair, swinging his legs, and eagerly watching for an opportunity to slip in with some story of his
own, while outside the street was white with snow, the
velvet-black heavens radiant with winter starlight, and
now and again the moaning of the northeast wind in the
wide chimney would act upon the fire like a bellows and
set it roaring.

My father never talked of going to sea again, greatly
as he missed his old life. He was much at Shields, looking after his interests there, and though he would sometimes take me for a walk, and occasionally not leave the
house for above an hour or two, for three or four days
together, yet he was not with me as mother had been, and
often I felt extremely lonely and dull.

We did not know many people in Newcastle. Most of
our friends were seafaring people and their families, who
lived at a distance, and every year thinned their number
by their removal from the neighborhood as the husbands
got employment in ships trading from other ports. No
doubt it was my own fault that I had not many friends.
My schoolmates had grown up and would have been glad
for me to come to their houses. There was no dearth of

companions and plain, homely amusements for me, had I
possessed the social disposition most girls are born with.
But my mother, during most of her married life having
had no other companion but me during her husband's absence, had kept me much at home, and this home-keeping
grew into a habit too well-rooted to be shaken by such
pleasures as I might have got by accepting invitations to
drink tea, or by carrying my work for an evening into a
circle where the conversation would be chiefly made up of
small-talk on subjects I cared nothing about.

Unhappily, the dulness that fell upon me after my
mother's death—the sense of loneliness, the lack of some
distinctive interest to keep my thoughts employed—was
not of a kind to be relieved by tea-drinking, and the simple
diversions of the social sphere to which I belonged. Much
as I loved canny Newcastle, I was tired of it. The spirit
of roaming was strong in my heart, and I felt sometimes
that if life was never to consist of anything bigger and
more suggestive than the streets I had traversed until I
knew every flagstone, I should be glad for the curtain to
fall that I might join my mother and take the peace of
the grave.

It happened one day in March—about three months
and a half after mother had died—that, being alone in the
house and feeling unusually dull, for my father had gone
away early in the morning to Shields, I resolved to go and
visit a Quaker widow named Mrs. Barnett, who lived at
Gateshead. She was an invalid, and had been a great
favorite of my mother; and it was because my mother had
loved her, and because I had not seen her since my mother's death, that I thought I would call upon her now. I
will give no further account of this visit beyond saying
that I sat with Mrs. Barnett till about seven o'clock, when,
the evening being gathered, and thinking it late enough
for me to be out alone in the streets, I bade her good-bye
and started to return to Newcastle.

Two bridges then, as now, spanned the Tyne betwixt
Gateshead and Newcastle; one a stone bridge (since replaced by a very fine piece of mechanism), and the other,
Robert Stephenson's noble, world-renowned structure,
called the High Level Bridge, which connects the rail-

road between London and Scotland. There is a footway
for passengers on this bridge, just beneath the elevation
which the trains traverse, and though I have crossed and
recrossed the structure some hundreds of times, yet I never
remember being upon it without pausing to admire with
ever fresh astonishment the wonderful majesty and solidity
of this astounding achievement of engineering skill, and to
look down at the river and the vessels lying alongside the
quay, dwarfed into mere toys by the amazing elevation.

I could not choose but stop a minute or two on this
occasion, for the night-scene of the dark river flowing a
long distance beneath me was extraordinarily fine and impressive. There was still a faint tinge of northern twilight upon the dark air overhanging the western side of
Newcastle, against which the buildings stood in massive
black groups, relieved by points of yellow light. On my
right the town of Gateshead lay in deep shadow. A curious atmospheric effect was produced by the smoke slowly
floating up from the further reaches of the Tyne upon the
light draught then blowing, and this, mingling with a thin
haze that hung low upon the water, created an atmosphere
that magnified the lights which swarmed like fireflies
along the river-banks. Every light was surrounded by a
glory of golden hairs, which shot into the surrounding
gloom, and melted in a thin, reddish haze that circled the
central flame like a nimbus. The rushing river, black as
ebony, was all a-tremble with the speeding of its own
current. In the intervals of stillness I could hear it gurgling far below round the gigantic supporters of the
bridge; it broke the ruddy reflection of the shore-lamps
and of the burning lanterns on the moored or anchored
vessels into a thousand flakes of molten gold, and in places
where the bend of it focussed the lamps into a mass of
light the water looked to be on fire. Here and there, to
the right, down along the river's side past Gateshead, a
body of dark red flame would gush up suddenly from the
orifice of some factory chimney, and wildly illuminate a
broad area of the smoky atmosphere with a blood-colored
gleam, in the midst of which could be discerned a vision
of crowded structures lifting tall chimneys into the void,
with many a glowing streak of fire among them, while the

sound of the throbbing of unwearying engines, the faint clinking of hammers, the muffled hum of furnaces, and the vibrating pulse of a ceaseless industry stole softly to my ears from the deep built-up shadows. The vessels at the quay-side loomed as dimly as phantom ships, with little floods of light upon their decks, and I could hear the sounds of a concertina—a thin trickle of music—played on board a steamer lying near the stone bridge.

There was something wonderfully solemn and mysteriously beautiful in the spectacle of the black coil of water marking its current by the breaking-up of the reflected lights in its inky breast, and something almost weird in the pulsing undernote of the ceaseless activities hidden away in the blackness, mingled with the distant hum and surging of life in the towns on either hand of me. Twice, while I watched, the gigantic fabric on which I stood trembled with the weight of a train passing over my head, and I cannot express the profound emphasis this near and thunderous sound of rolling dead-weight, the panting of the locomotive, and the suggestion of hard, prosaic, toiling life conveyed in the engine's shrieking whistle, gave to the silent darkness of the distant plains away out in the northeast, where the stars were shining wanly through the vapor which overhung the precipitous bed of the river.

Likely enough it was those far-off stars, putting into my head thoughts of the seas and lands over which they were shining, that brought my mind back to those roaming fancies which had been strong in me all morning. I resumed my walk home in a very dull frame of mind, thinking it a hard lot that women should be denied, not more by society than by nature, the freedom which men enjoy ; that I, a girl with as adventurous a spirit in me as any sailor could wish to have, endowed, as I am sure, with a full capacity for enjoying the wonders and beauties which voyaging carries you to, should be forced to stay at home, merely because I was a woman—because it was unfit that I should wander about alone, and because nature had not given me the muscle and the strength and the staying powers of a man.

As I approached our house, I spied a light in the parlor

window, by which I understood that my father had returned. On the servant opening the door I stopped,
smelling tobacco - smoke and hearing voices, and asked
who was with my father. The girl answered, a young
gentleman ; she did not know his name. I supposed it
was Mr. Fowler, and stole up-stairs to remove my hat, and
then returned and, entering the parlor, found the young
gentleman to be Mr. Fowler, as I had guessed. We shook
hands, and, after giving my father a kiss, I pulled a chair
to the fire and sat down.

" Where have you been, Jessie?" asked my father.

" Drinking tea with Mrs. Barnett, at Gateshead," I answered.

" Ay," he exclaimed, with a kind of twinge shooting
across his face, " your mother's friend. Well, I wish you
would go out more. You stay at home too much. It's a
job to get her across the street, Fowler, unless I go too ;
but I can't be always giving her my company, for my
affairs want looking after, and I'm bound to be at Shields,
if I have not a mind to lose what it has taken me forty-
seven years to get."

" You should go about, Miss Snowdon," said Mr. Fowler.
" You know, it is said that man wasn't born to live alone ;
and that's a saying truer of girls than of men."

" I should be very glad to go about," I answered, looking at him and laughing, " if there was anything to see.
But I've lived in Newcastle all my life, and am so tired
of the same shops, the same streets, the same river, the
same lamp - posts, that I assure you the only novelty I
can get out of the canny town is by not looking at it at
all."

" Hillo !" exclaimed my father, pulling his pipe from
his mouth and gazing at me with unaffected astonishment. " What story-books have ye been fingering lately?
Why, Jess, my lass, here's enough heresy on a sudden to
set all Tyneside lads a-praying for mercy on your soul !"

" Heresy or not," said Mr. Fowler, glancing at me with
his bright, dark eyes, " Miss Snowdon is right. One may
love a place heartily, captain, and yet grow so wearied of
it at times as to wish it at the—at—at Jericho."

I was in an aggressive mood, and there was something

in the way Mr. Fowler looked at me that was like an invitation to pour out my heart.

"Would you not suppose," said I, addressing him, "that my father, who has been roaming all over the world ever since he was a small boy, and whose love of change and of being away was so great that, in order to cure it, it was necessary for a mighty storm to arise and very nearly wreck him—would you not suppose, Mr. Fowler, that he would be one of the very first to sympathize, not with my dislike of the old town—no, no, I dearly love Newcastle—but with my weariness of a scene in which I have lived and which I have scarcely left for twenty years?"

"Well, that's brave," said my father, smiling at me. "She plumps out her age as an honest woman should. I've taken her three voyages, any way."

"Oh, be sure your father sympathizes with you," exclaimed Mr. Fowler. "What countries have you a wish to see, Miss Snowdon?"

"No countries at all, Fowler," answered my father, rising to empty his pipe-ash into the fire-place. "She wants to be at sea. Ever since she was as big as my thumb she's been craving to ship the tarry breeks."

This was not strictly true, but it was true enough to make me cast my eyes down and smile, with some color in my cheeks.

"Do you like sailors?" asked Mr. Fowler.

"Yes," I replied, "all sailors—as a body. I have always been fond of sailors and the sea."

"Had she been a boy she should have gone to sea ten years ago, with my blessing on her," said my father, resuming his chair and slowly refilling a pipe. "But it's a little hard upon the old man that the lassie should be telling you, Fowler, that I don't sympathize with her merely because she was born a girl, and because, therefore, she stops at home, as all girls do, or should, if they don't."

"Miss Snowdon finds Newcastle dull; she has had enough of it. She wants a change," said Mr. Fowler; "there's nothing unreasonable in that, captain."

"No, no, I don't say there is," answered my father, looking at me fondly. "But what change can I give ye, Jessie? You can't travel alone, and you wouldn't drag about a worn-out old man like me—a broken-down old seaman, who finds the journey to Shields quite as much as he relishes—would ye?"

"Let us change the subject," said I. "What led to it was my being obliged to excuse my love of stopping at home. Mr. Fowler, you will stay and have supper with us, I hope?"

"Certainly he will, Jessie," returned my father. "What have ye got to eat?"

I said I would go and see, and left the room, and busied and fussed in the kitchen, but was so full of self-consciousness as to do many things mechanically. All the time I was thinking, "They are talking about me upstairs," and I wondered what they were saying, and what would come of my blunt confession of dulness. As to Mr. Fowler, I could not imagine that any man should have a face and manner more to my liking than his. He was a thorough sailor in appearance, with fine dark eyes and brown hair, a tanned complexion, handsome nose, ivory-white teeth, and a well-proportioned figure. The charm of his behavior I could not express; it was in his voice, smile, movements—things not to be defined by the pen. The good blood in his veins—and this he got from both his parents—had survived the hard, tarry, rough training of the forecastle and cabin, and it informed his manners with a grace that was all the more relishable to me for owing everything to intuition, and nothing to shore-going conventionalism, and for possessing a salt-water freshness to be met nowhere but in ocean sailors who are gentlemen too.

In all this I am not anticipating, as the novelists say, for I had already discovered what I am telling you. My first impression—though it was caught from little more than a passing bow—was a pleasant one; but now I had seen him in a good light, I had been able to talk to him without crying, and had found not only my first impression, but what my father had said of his appearance, as true as the truth can be.

I made haste in the kitchen in order to get back to the parlor.

"Ay, here she comes," said my father, as I opened the

door, "with scarlet ears, no doubt. Don't look as if you believed we have not been talking of you, Jess. Fowler takes your side. He says you're bound to be dull, and has been rating me in proper quarter-deck fashion for leaving you so much to yourself."

"I'm not dull," I answered; "at least, you need not believe I am until I complain."

"Complain!" he exclaimed, laughing softly, but gazing at me very tenderly; "d'ye think women have only their mouths to complain with? Why, I've seen more 'growling' in a woman's face—I've seen more in the coil of her body, the stand of her as she hung in the wind with her back half turned—than she could have packed into twelve hours of grumbling with her tongue! But see here, my lass—what's to be done? Ye can't go about alone; ye don't seem to care for the society of your friends. Ye surely wouldn't have me apprentice you to the sea, Jessie?"

"If I had been a man," said I, laughing at the whimsical puzzlement in his face, "I would have been there long ago. But why am I to be a subject of conversation? What were you and my father talking about before I came in, Mr. Fowler? I did not wish to interrupt you."

"Why, of freights, registries, customs' duties, seamen's wages, charter-parties, and other romantic features of the life you so love, Miss Snowdon," he replied.

"That was it," said my father. "D'ye remember, Jessie, that Fowler was my mate in the old *Countess?*"

"Yes, very well."

"He's captain now. I've got him a ship. He's lord paramount henceforth, with the weather-side of the quarter-deck to himself, no watches to stand, and the privilege of coming and going as he pleases."

"I congratulate you, Mr.—I should say Captain Fowler," said I, making him a little bow. "When do you sail?"

"I have a month or five weeks before me ashore," he answered. "But why do you say 'captain'? Only naval men are captains. We merchantmen are masters."

"I can't call you master," said I, laughing.

"Nor skipper," rapped out my father; "there's the pity of it. A master's obliged to be called captain when spoken

5

to; I wish it were otherwise. And I'll go further yet, and wish that merchant-seamen were more sensitive in the matter of their own calling, and that they kept more within the professional lines chalked down for them. If they can't help being called captain to their faces, that's no reason why they should put it on their visiting-cards and have their letters addressed with it. There's nothing under the skies," he exclaimed, warming up, "that lowers the calling more in my eyes than the sight of a merchant mate or master aping, or being forced by the service he's in to ape, the dress of the navy people. Brass buttons may do very well for harbor-masters and yachtsmen, and the queen's livery would be a poor job without 'em; but what's a merchantman got to do with a uniform? It's the same with his title. What does he want to call himself an officer for, as if he was a policeman or a bailiff?—can't he stick to the good old sea-term of 'mate'? Imitation's a flattery ye can't mistake; and it makes my blood boil to think that there should be in the British merchant service a set of men capable, by their monkeyfication, not only to let people see that they're ashamed of their calling and would like to be mistaken for something else, but of making the navy folk suppose that all hands on our side are agreed that they're finer seamen than we are, and their service out and away superior. I respect navy men just as much as they respect me, and no more; but I'd rather be towed astern six hours a day for a fortnight in any kind of weather, Fowler, ye'd choose to name, than allow a navy man to flatter himself, on the strength of my waistcoat buttons, and the cut of my cap and conduct, that the white ensign is one jot better than the red. I'm called 'captain,' it's true, but, as I say, a man can't help that. Everybody's a captain nowadays, from the captain of a man-of-war down to the captain of a billyboy, and further down yet, to a captain in the militia. But whenever I speak of myself—unless I make a slip—it's as 'mister,' and whenever I had to give a name to my calling, I always wrote 'ship-master,' and was proud enough, too, of the title."

Here the entrance of the servant to lay the cloth for supper stopped my father's energetic protestings.

I need not linger over this particular evening, though, considering that it was the threshold of a new life for me, or rather, the first hint of a change that was to happen, I have good reason for brightly and clearly remembering it. No more was said about my dulness; indeed, for the rest of the time I listened a good deal more than I talked. It was a cold, raw night; my father bade me sit close beside him near the fire, and often would feel for my hand, and retain it for minutes at a time; Mr. Fowler sat opposite, and it was his conversation, his anecdotes of sea-life, his references to his mother and father, of whom he spoke with such manly, simple tenderness as no one could have listened to without respecting and liking the honest heart from which the words came, that kept me interested, and reluctant that so calm and pleasant an evening should come to an end.

My father made as good a listener as I, which was somewhat singular, as he seldom let a younger man than he tell a professional story without capping it by some salt experience of his own. Mr. Fowler tried to draw him into conversation, but it would not do. After supper he grew thoughtful, talking occasionally, to be sure, yet with an air of abstraction, the cause of which I might have suspected had it not better pleased me to watch Mr. Fowler's handsome eyes.

It was striking eleven when our guest rose to go. As my father shook hands with him, he said, "Now, Richard Fowler, you know your way here. If you come every night you'll not come too often. We want cheering up, and you're the lad to do it. You have a month or more of shore-life before you, and you can't devote your evenings to better purpose than sitting and yarning with an old man, who is all the more lonely," said he, looking at me slyly, "because his lassie's always gadding abroad."

"Only in fancy, father," said I, laughing.

"Ay, but fancy is a sort of fact too," he exclaimed. "If your heart is on the high seas, it would be idle to say that Jessie Snowdon is to be found in Newcastle-upon-Tyne."

Mr. Fowler thanked him heartily for his invitation. "I shall take you at your word. I shall be here very often," said he; giving me a look, to see, perhaps, how I liked that threat.

I said nothing, being pretty sure he would find no excuse in the answer in my face for staying away. He then shook hands with me and left the house.

My father returned to the fire, and stood with his back upon it, following me about earnestly with his eyes as I put away the spirits and made the table tidy. "So, Jessie," said he, a little sadly, "ye've found out that the life you're leading is a bit dull. Well, I believe it is—I believe it is. I often think of ye, my lass, when I'm away. The dear mother's going was a dreadful loss, and you must always continue to feel the want of her while your life goes on as it was before she died."

"I came home low-spirited," I answered, "and said more than I meant. It's my own fault that I am dull. I have friends if I choose to seek them. I am chiefly dull when you are away; for this house is gloomy without mother, and there is only the servant to talk to."

"I must pluck up my spirits a bit," said he, "and bring friends about us. There are plenty willing to come—mostly sailors. Ye like sailors, Jessie?"

I smiled.

"What d'ye think of Mr. Fowler?" he asked, smiling too.

"He's just a canny lad, father," said I, giving him a taste of the dialect he loved; "a very proper man."

There was a touch of warmth in this answer that was quite involuntary, though I noted its existence the moment I had spoken, by the expression in my father's face.

"Ay," said he, "I told you he was handsome, and as good a sailor as ever went to sea. I believe he'll get on—he'll do well. A few fellows of his kind about ye, Jessie, would clap a stopper on your dulness, wouldn't they—especially if you knew they all call ye bonnie, as Fowler does?"

"Bonnie!—did he call me that?" said I, feeling that the eyes I lifted had more pleasure sparkling in them than I cared should be seen.

"Well, no—he didn't say bonnie; he's a south-country man, and bonnie's a word not to be spelt out of any alpha-

bet that's to be found out of sight south of the Cheviots,"
he answered, looking at me thoughtfully; "but he said as
much as was proper a man should say to the father of the
lass he admires."

"But what *did* he say?" I inquired, feeling, after all,
that it was my father I was talking to, and so not much
minding what he should think of my curiosity.

"What *did* he say?" he echoed with a chuckle. "How
would ye have me spear up his meaning that was coiling
along the bottom of his talk, like eels under water? Can't
a sensible man make you know what's in his mind without
whipping it out in black and white? But I'll tell ye what
I'm going to say, Jessie—that it's time to go to bed. So
get me my candle and kiss me."

CHAPTER VII.

RICHARD FOWLER PROPOSES TO ME.

WHETHER the thought that Mr. Fowler and I might
grow to like each other, become sweethearts, and marry,
was in my father's mind that night I cannot say; but after
we had said good-night, and I was alone, I could not help
fancying there was a deeper meaning than mere hospitality in his hearty invitation to Mr. Fowler to visit us every
day, if he pleased, until he sailed. The night before my
mother died, as you will remember, he had spoken about
my being old enough to think of a husband, and had advised me to take care and not get stranded as an old maid.
He had never since referred to the subject; but it might
well come into his head on hearing me complain that I
was dull; and though I was sure it would grieve him to
the soul to part with me, I was equally sure that when he
came to consider he was growing old, that if he died before
I had a husband I should be alone in, and at the mercy of,
a world whose arts, rogueries, and customs I knew ery
little about, he would consider it his duty to endea~or to
settle me before he joined my mother.

These thoughts gave my mind plenty of occupation,

and I was as wakeful that night as I had been on that occasion when he said I ought to think of a husband.

When we met next morning at breakfast, I thought from his manner that he meant to talk to me gravely, and my heart beat quickly when I caught him looking at me steadfastly and anxiously. However, though he wore a very thoughtful air, his conversation was on light topics. After breakfast, while he was smoking his morning pipe, he said,

"I promised so-and-so" (naming the man) "to see him at South Shields to-day; indeed, I am to dine with him. I can't take ye with me, Jessie, for I should not know what to do with you. Yet, after what you said last night, I don't like to leave you alone again all day. I think I'll stop in Newcastle, and we'll go for a cruise together across the moor. We'll go and have a look at Jesmond Dene."

"No," said I, not caring that he should sacrifice his interests for a ramble that would tire us both without giving us much pleasure. "If you have an appointment, you must keep it."

"D'ye think so?" said he, looking brighter, for his heart was among the old captains he met at Shields. "It certainly wouldn't be polite to keep my friend's dinner waiting. Besides, if I go to Shields, I can bring Fowler home with me. I doubt if he'd come two days running unless I fetched him."

"I think," said I, feeling the color in my cheeks, "you must be in love with Mr. Fowler, father. You talk of him the last thing at night and the first thing in the morning."

"Which shall it be, Jessie?" he asked, laughing; "shall I stop at home and go for a stroll with you across the moor, or make for Shields and fetch Fowler along?"

"Do whichever will best please you," I answered.

We fenced a bit, but it could not last long. We both wanted the same thing: he to go to Shields, and I that he should go, that Mr. Fowler might return with him. The evening was always the dullest part of the day. Last evening had been rendered festive in comparison with others by Mr. Fowler's visit, and I longed for him to come again. He might not come, as father suggested, unless he were met and brought; and so, as I have said, after a little parrying and coquetting, we both had our way, and father went to Shields.

Well, Mr. Fowler returned with father, just as I hoped he would, and found me ready to receive him. I had never met any young man up to that time whose visit would have made me take particular trouble with my dress; and anybody, therefore, who knew me well would have reckoned the care I bestowed on my appearance to meet Mr. Fowler a bad or good sign, according to his views on falling in love. I was a whole hour in my bed-room, I believe, dressing myself and arranging my hair— a bold speculation of vanity, for I could not be sure that Mr. Fowler would come. I was in mourning, of course, but I looked the better dressed for that, for my hair was a fine match for crape, and my complexion lost nothing by its contrast with my dress.

A woman's pride in the memory of the prettiness she has outlived is the only excusable vanity I know; yet it makes me laugh, and not over gayly, to look back upon those maidenly buddings. A wife may love her husband dearly, and yet wonder that she should have taken so much trouble to please him before marriage. This wonder, however, will to some extent diminish when she reflects that marriage is only the rendering of the poetry of courtship into plain prose, in which many points are clear that before were lost in the music and the pretty jingling of the rhymes.

My father noticed the pains I had taken with my appearance in an instant; ran his kind, smiling eyes over me from top to toe very swiftly, and then cautiously peeped at Mr. Fowler, with a father's pride, to observe the effect my appearance produced on him.

There is no need for me to speak of that evening, nor of others which followed. Mr. Fowler remained ashore five weeks, and he came to see us pretty nearly every evening. He needed no pressing; he saw that he was welcome, and was glad to come and sorry to go. Whether I should have fallen in love with him had he not fallen in love with me, I do not know; but when it was impossible even for me, who had no experience in that way, to doubt that I had his heart, I gave him mine, and before the five weeks had run out we were as much in love as two young people can well be, though neither of us had made the least sign—that is, no sign beyond, of course, the meaning that stole involuntarily into our eyes and behavior.

Meanwhile, my father appeared to take no notice at all. There had been some shrewdness in his glances at me at the beginning, when the three of us were together, as if he saw what was happening; but in proportion as our love-passage must have become more plain to him, he seemed to grow more blind, and not only made no reference to the thing that was taking place under his nose, but gave it not the least imaginable attention that ever I could detect.

This troubled me, and I put it down to inconsistency. At first he was quite willing that I should have a sweetheart, lauded Mr. Fowler to the skies before ever I set eyes on the man, and then insisted on his coming to see us every day, as if resolved we should fall in love. And now, when what he had apparently desired had come to pass, and he could not help seeing that my head was full of Mr. Fowler, as his was of me, he shut his eyes, never mentioned the name of Mr. Fowler to me when that gentleman was absent, and paid no heed whatever to my manner in Mr. Fowler's presence—a manner, as I may suppose, a thousandfold more suggestive than that which had made him talk slyly and smile knowingly at the beginning.

On the day preceding that on which Mr. Fowler was to sail I was at home with my father. It was the afternoon, growing dark; a strong wind was blowing; all day long rain had been falling, and the look of the weather out-of-doors, the streaming streets, the gloomy, stooping, smoke-colored sky, combined with the groaning of the wind, were as depressing as a funeral.

I had been sewing near the fire, but, no longer able to see, I put down my work and lay back in my chair, full of such thoughts as you might guess would visit a girl who was in love with a sailor bound to sea next day, who in going would take her heart with him, and yet would leave her not a single memory of spoken love to solace her memory, as he would go without any other token than he had found in her manner to remind him that he had a sweet-heart in Newcastle.

My father, who had been poring over the *Newcastle Daily Chronicle* through his glasses, gradually "sluing" himself, as Jack says, in his chair to bring the firelight to bear upon the journal, until he had twisted himself into the most uncomfortable posture that can be imagined, at last threw down the paper, yawned loudly, and, facing the fire afresh, took a long look out of window, and then a long look at me.

"Are ye asleep, Jessie?" said he.

"No," I answered.

"This is agreeable weather," said he, "for a man not given to reading, who can't play the piano, who knows nothing about drawing, who's too old for carpentering, who's too impatient to bother over story-books, who hates writing letters, and who has only just settled down after forty-seven years of extensive knocking about. D'ye know, my lass, if ye were to get married, I'd go and live at Shields; at least," he added, thoughtfully, "I think I would. Newcastle's too far off from salt water to satisfy me now. Besides, my business lies at Shields, and the journey to and fro's a nuisance."

"You'd not like to leave the old home when it came to the point," said I.

"Well, I don't know about that," he answered. "I gave up the sea, which was an older home than this shanty," looking slowly round the room. "I'm getting rather tired of these curios. They're always here. When I come down to breakfast, there's that old shield and there are the models. When I come to dinner, there's still the old shield and the models. When it's tea-time, the old shield and the models are still there; and the old shield and the models are the last things I see before I go to bed. They want shifting. They'd look better at Shields. They're good enough of themselves; it's their setting that requires changing."

"The other day," I exclaimed, "when I said that Newcastle was a town one might love very well and yet be glad to get away from occasionally, you seemed quite sur-

prised to hear me speak so; and now you are calling the
old home dull, and wanting to give it up forever, and settle
in Shields."

"I said I've a mind to go and live in Shields when ye
get married, Jessie," said he.

"Well, I'm not married yet," I answered, yawning.

"No, that's true; but ye're not far off from it, though,"
he exclaimed.

On his saying this I sat upright and tried to see his
face, but in the changing play of the firelight it was impossible to decipher the meaning in it.

"Why, what do you mean, father?" I asked.

"What do I mean?" he echoed, in his hearty voice.
"Aren't ye in love with Dicky Fowler; and mustn't it soon
end in the parson giving you a charter-party, and sending
you afloat with Dick's colors at the masthead?"

"If you suppose," said I, very gravely, "that Mr. Fowler and I are engaged to be married, I can assure you that
not only has he not proposed to me, but that I have never
given him — consciously," I put in, resolved to be su-
premely honest—"an excuse to do so.   Do you imagine,
if he had offered me marriage, that I should not instantly
have told you?"

"Look here, Jessie," said my father, " you're a woman,
and I'm not going to pretend that I shall ever be able to
get at the truth in your mind if ye're resolved to keep me
walking round and round it.   Will ye give me a plain answer if I ask you a plain question?"

"Yes," said I, hesitating a little.

"Then, said he, turning round in his chair to face me
fully, " are you in love with Richard Fowler?"

"It's not fair to put the question so bluntly," I replied.
"If you ask me whether I like him, I'll tell you yes."

"Like—like !" mumbled he, laughing under his breath.
"Lasses don't *like* sweethearts; they *love* 'em.   Speak out,
Jess, like a bold woman.   Aren't ye in love with Dicky
Fowler?"

It was a question I would not answer with my tongue,
though I could not say no to it either.   He waited, looking at me as I sat silent, with my head hanging down,
and then said :

"Well, you mean yes. The lad'll make himself clearer than you when I talk to him. Ye know ye're both as soft on each other as a piece of wax is on the equator."

"Don't be so sure," said I, a little pertly, but very well pleased that he should have found us out, and confirmed not only my own conviction that I was in love with Mr. Fowler, but my hope and belief that Mr. Fowler was in love with me. "How do you know we're so soft as you say?"

"How do I know?" he answered. "If a ship heaves in sight, if a squall's coming along, if the vessel's off her course, how do I know? By looking, my lass, isn't it? Why, think ye, did Providence give me these?" pointing to his eyes.

"But you never seemed to take any notice," said I, letting him understand by this admission that he was right in his notion about my being in love.

"What was the good?" he replied. "I couldn't stop it, and I couldn't help it, had I had a mind to do either. Are ye fond of him, Jessie?"

He caught me prettily, for I answered without reflection, "Yes, father; but he doesn't know."

"Doesn't he? Is he fond of you?"

"He looks and talks as if he would like to be," said I.

"He is—I'll answer for him. He took to you the very first day he ever set eyes on ye, and when he said as much to me t'other day I was glad to hear him; for Dick Fowler, in my opinion, is an honest, well-bred English sailor, the fittest man I could wish to find to hand you over to— a lad proper to take my place by your side, though he'll give ye another sort of love than a father's. He's sure to be here to-night. It's his last night ashore for some months."

"Yes," said I, mournfully.

"If he comes I'll bring him to the scratch," said my father, somewhat gleefully. "When the wind's fair there is no use 'bouting ship every half-hour. If the lad's in love with ye he may as well say so, and set your mind at ease and his too. Waiting and hoping and expecting is a poor lookout for young folk. Better ye should come to business at once; strike a bargain, and be happy."

"You don't mean to say, father," said I, "that you intend to ask him to-night if he's in love with me?"

"I do," he answered, resolutely, getting up and peering at the clock, "if he comes."

"Then," said I, "when I hear his ring I shall go to my bedroom and stop there. And I shall never be able to face him again."

"Think not?" said he, mildly.

"I am quite sure," I replied, so confused and agitated that I hardly knew whether to cry or laugh.

"Never mind," said my father. "You leave him to me; I'll manage him."

"He will misconstrue your motive," I replied; "imagine that you want to be rid of me, and that you mean to get me married at any sacrifice, without regard to your self-respect."

"If I thought he was such an ass as that," he answered, "I wouldn't have him if he was heir to the British throne."

"But suppose he should tell you that he liked me very well as a friend, but that he had no other feelings towards me, and expressed his surprise that you should suppose he could fall in love with a girl in five weeks?"

"Don't you bother," said my father. "You leave him to me; I'll manage him. He's not been out in a hurricane with me for nothing."

I could only hope that he would change his mind, or that he was merely joking and did not mean what he threatened; yet he certainly spoke and looked as if he were in earnest, and the firelight disclosed a merry expression in his face as he sat with his eyes fixed on the glowing embers, and his lips moving, as if Mr. Fowler were before him, and he was going through the promised performance.

However, no more was then said on the subject; the afternoon passed; we were at tea when the house-bell was rung. I was sure the visitor was Mr. Fowler, and father guessed the same, for he instantly said, with his eyes twinkling, "Here's the laddie, Jessie."

"Now, father, you will not speak to him?" said I, rising.

"Certainly I shall," he rejoined. "D'ye think I'm afraid?"

"Then you'll see me no more to-night," said I, and I hurried away, hearing him call out as I left the room that I had better stop and finish my tea ; but what else he said I do not know, as I bounded up-stairs to be out of sight before the servant opened the front door.

It was an exceedingly awkward position for me to find myself placed in, and for the first time in my life I believe I was really angry with my father, and could have quarrelled with him. My bedroom door being open, I heard Mr. Fowler's voice plainly enough, and my father calling to him from the parlor to come in. I lighted a candle and sat down, feeling the bedroom very cold after the warm parlor, and I was half disposed to go to bed, so as to give my father no chance of getting me down-stairs should he seek me ; but when I looked at my watch I thought it would be a foolish thing to go to bed at half-past six in the evening.

Still, I was resolved not to go down-stairs, nor to meet Mr. Fowler ; a determination that vexed me so heartily, I could have cried with annoyance that my father's threat to "manage" the man should make it necessary.

I was too honorable to endeavor to hear what was said, which I might easily have done by stepping on to the landing, and putting my ear over the head of the staircase. I took a book, but was too cold and angry to read. My secret fear was that my father's blunt talk would make Mr. Fowler suspect I was a consenting party to this direct challenge to his feelings for me, and that it would end in his despising me. Even had he proposed to me, and come to talk over the marriage with my father, my absence while they conversed would have made my solitude uncomfortable enough. But he had not proposed ; not a word of love had ever been exchanged ; neither my father nor I had any right to suppose that he had the least degree of affection for me ; and yet there was my father down-stairs "managing" him—"making him come to the business"—and leading him, I dared say, to suppose that it was through my wish he was being "managed."

No girl was ever placed in a more mortifying position, and such a wretched time as I spent in that cold bedroom I hope never to pass again.

I had been up-stairs about three quarters of an hour, and was so cold that I was forgetting all about what they were discussing in the parlor, while I plotted how to reach the kitchen and warm myself there without being heard as I descended the staircase, when I was startled by a loud groan in the passage, followed by another, and then a strange kind of wheezing noise, which, but for the groans that had preceded it, I should have taken for suppressed laughter.

The groans were my father's, and, much alarmed, I ran to the door; but as I ran I heard a clattering on the staircase, and in bundled the servant.

"Will ye please come down-stairs, miss?" said she.

"What's the matter?" I exclaimed. But she ran off without giving me an answer, a piece of behavior that naturally increased my apprehension.

The fear that my father had in some way injured himself put my objection to meeting Mr. Fowler to flight. I could think of nothing but my father, and at once hurried after the servant.

Mr. Fowler stood in the parlor doorway, but I could see nothing of my father. Without so much as wishing Mr. Fowler good-evening, I asked, with a beating heart, where my father was, and what had happened.

"If you will come in and sit down," he answered, looking rather nervous, and yet with a kind of smile in his eyes, too, "I will explain."

I went in, my head full of my father, and never giving a thought to the reason that had sent me up-stairs and kept me there, looking anxiously round the room and then at Mr. Fowler.

"Pray sit down," said he.

"Must I sit down," I answered impatiently, "to learn what has happened to my father?"

"There is nothing the matter with him," he replied, bringing a chair. "I have more to talk to you about than your father."

I turned scarlet, for I saw through the trick in an instant. I was in a real passion, and he afterwards told me my eyes seemed on fire.

"He groaned and pretended to be hurt," said I, "merely that he might bring me down-stairs!" And then, seeing Mr. Fowler trying to smother a smile, I brought my foot down with a smart slap on the floor, biting my lip to check my tears.

"Now that you are here I hope you will stop," he exclaimed. "I have something to say to you. I sail to-morrow, you know, and shall not see you again for some months, if we ever meet again."

I knew that too well, and, angry as I was at the humbling trick my father had put upon me, I felt sure that, if I left Mr. Fowler at once, I should not be alone ten minutes without regretting my haste and wishing myself dead and buried.

I refused to sit, but he cooled me down by telling me that he had had no hand in my father's stratagem, and that the trick had only been played to bring me down-stairs.

"You cannot be angry with him," said he; "he loves you dearly. He thinks only of your happiness, Jessie."

"I know that," I answered, a little startled to hear him call me Jessie—for hitherto it had always been Miss Snowdon—yet finding such a music in the name as he spoke it as I had never noticed in it before. And meanwhile I kept biting my under-lip and feeling my cheeks burning, and dreading to speak for fear of saying something to increase the embarrassment I felt.

"Jessie," said he, in a quiet voice, "you know the sailor's character. I'd beat about and come slowly to the point if I had tact enough to do it well. But I can only speak straight, as they say, and come out plainly with what my heart's full of. I'll call you Jessie, for that's the name I think of you by, and it will make talking easier to me. I've loved you, Jessie—ay, from the very first day we met—when you were crying, and when death had made this hearty, cheerful old home dark. Over and over again I've been on the point of telling you that I loved you, but it always seemed too soon. I was regularly hauled off by the fear that you'd laugh at me, and say that you'd had no time allowed to know me, and that you had never given me a thought that would gladden me to hear. That might be true of you, but not of me; for I've known you ever since your poor mother died, though I was only a minute with you then, and all that time I've been going on steadily loving you. Well, I sail to-morrow, and I thought, this being my last night ashore, that I'd come over and see if I could muster up heart to put in a word for myself. Your father's a plain sailor-man, as I am. When I came in here and found him alone, I asked for you. This led to an explanation. He told me about his talk with you, and the reason why you ran away when you heard me ring the bell."

Here he paused, and presently—for I was looking away from him with my head hung—I felt his fingers creep over my hand and clasp it.

"What did my father say?" I asked, in a whisper.

"Why," he answered, "he said that if I told you I loved you, you'd listen and not be angry."

I could not help smiling; and he saw the smile, for he immediately added, "Was he right to say as much?"

"He ought not to have spoken to you about me," said I, still carefully keeping my face turned away.

"But I spoke first," said he. "I asked where you were, and that led to our talking. See here, Jessie—sit down, dearest; here's a chair. Now that you are here you must not go and hide again. Your hand is cold as ice." And he began to chafe it as tenderly as a woman would.

I sat down as he asked me. After what he had said, I could no more remain angry than I could have flown to the moon; indeed, I was as happy in my heart as I was before irritated and mortified. It could not have been otherwise, for I loved him as much as he loved me, and, after having wondered and wondered again whether I had his heart, here he now was at my side, holding my hand and asking me to be his wife.

We were alone for half an hour, during all which time I never once thought of asking where my father was. I then heard his footstep, and had just a moment to draw away from my sweetheart's arm, when he came in. He was smoking a long clay pipe, which he withdrew from his mouth and stood looking at us over, as though it were a telescope, while a broad smile wrinkled his weather-tossed face.

"Well, boys and girls," said he, "have you settled your affairs?"

I meant to assume an air of indignation, but it would not do. The moment he spoke and looked at me, I started up and threw my arms around his neck.

"Ay," said he, holding me, "this is but a farewell embrace, my lass. I know what it means. Well, I told you I hadn't been out in a hurricane with yon lad for nothing. There, get you gone to your seat, Jess. Dick, pass your hand along. She's a sailor's daughter—ye've won her fairly. Ye'll find her heart of oak, Dick, as she'll find you teak-built, copper-bolted, classed A1, and warranted to go to windward like a steam-engine."

And, cordially wringing the hand of my sweetheart—whom he insisted upon calling Dick, though my name for him was Richard, his proper name—he wiped his eyes, relighted his pipe, and sat him squarely in his arm-chair, as a man might who considers he has honorably discharged a very difficult but a very manly duty.

Nothing more was said about his ruse to bring me down-stairs, though there was an expression of self-complacency in the smile he occasionally bestowed upon me that made me suspect that scheme was often in his mind, and that he valued himself highly upon it.

It was not until I recovered my composure, until my calm mind gave back the perfect image of the happiness that had come to me, that my spirits fell with the thought that to-morrow Richard would be gone, and that many weeks would pass before we met again. This is the hardest part of being a sailor's wife or a sailor's sweetheart. When my mother kissed my father before he went on a voyage, it was always with tears—always, as she would tell me, with a foreboding that they would never meet again; and no woman who loves her sailor-husband can part with him without a fear and pain in her grief that cannot make a portion of leave-takings for other adventures which are not equally perilous. And how many are?

Richard held my hand, and we sat close together, opposite my father, who was giving my sweetheart some sound
advice on the behavior of ship-masters to their crews, and
the like, when the wind raised a melancholy cry in the
chimney, and the window-casements rattled as the moaning blast swept past the house. I alone of the three appeared to hear the sound; but presently my father,
breaking off in what he was saying, leaned forward and
peered at me, and said, " Why, are ye crying, Jess?"

This made Richard look at me too, and see the tears I
could not repress.

"What's the matter, Jessie?" he asked. " What has
saddened you on a sudden?"

"Have we been saying anything to vex her?" inquired
my father, looking puzzled and anxious.

I was reluctant to confess at first; but, after a little
coaxing, I told Richard I cried because he was going to
sea to-morrow.

"Ever since she was a mere hop-o'-my-thumb," said
my father, " she's been saying she'd never marry any one
but a sailor-man. And now she's beginning to find out
what that vow means."

"There'd be no grief in the vow if I could go to sea
too," said I, crying.

"When we are married I'll take you with me, Jessie,
sometimes," said Richard, " if your father will consent to
your going."

"Well, ye can wait till I'm dead," answered father.
"It'll need a bit of thinking over if her going is to leave
me alone like a frog at the bottom of a dry well, out of
sight of water, and nobody to give me a hand. Mind!
I'm not averse to wives going to sea with their husbands;
I'd have taken my poor lass regularly if she'd been willing.
On the contrary," said he, warming up, "and, as I may
say, quite the reverse, it's a pity more sailors' wives aren't
afloat upon the ocean than may be found there. To say
nothing of their being up to all kinds of mischief, getting
into debt, falling foul of perfidious people, and going to
the devil with them, just for the want of having their
husbands to look after them, it would be the saving of
many a husband if his wife went along with him. When

a man has his wife aboard, his ship's a real home; and when in harbor, instead of running loose ashore, bringing up at the grog-shops and song-shops, and hunting after pleasures which do neither his health nor his soul good, but which he's often forced to seek on account of the dulness of the cabin, and the want of some one to talk to aboard, he'd stay with his wife, and pass his evenings as a respectable man should. There's nothing like a wife to keep a man straight."

"Come, Jessie, dry your eyes," said Richard, pressing my hand. "My sailing to-morrow only signifies that I'm going a voyage just to see what sort of skipper I'll make. You must look upon this cruise as if your father had stipulated I must take it before I offered for your heart. You'll find the time roll along quickly—"

"It seems to me," interrupted my father, whose mind, while Richard was whispering, was evidently running upon what he had said about captains carrying their wives to sea with them, "that until sailors can send one of their own profession into Parliament, there'll be no chance of the nautical calling ever being understood by the public. Considering what a mighty population Jack makes, it's a sin that there should be ne'er a living man in the whole House of Commons capable of putting the sailor's case before the assembly in such a way as to make Jack, hearing the newspaper read out, see that he's understood. The nautical element in Parliament consists of naval men who understand their own service, but know nothing about ours, and who despise us; ship-owners who make it their business to keep Jack back and out of sight for fear of legislation making him a little less cheap, and a little better looked after than he is; and yachtsmen, very nice, well-meaning gentlemen in their way, I'm sure, but the most dangerous sort of people ye can find to meddle with the sea—worse even than Board of Trade officials; chaps with just enough of blundering ideas to make people who know nothing at all fancy 'em well informed; a sort of 'longshoremen with plenty of money in their pockets, who sit down on comfortable cushions in cabins like little drawing-rooms, with ladies playing the pianos behind the bulkheads, and with the smell of a first-class dinner in their noses, to write books about Jack's life in the forecastle, and instruct the world upon the art of managing him. I don't know much about Parliament myself, but I think if a berth was to be offered me there—if Newcastle, or Sunderland, or Shields was to turn to and send me to London to speak up for sailors—you might boil me alive, Dick, if I didn't go, old and nervous as I am, if only to burst up some of those fine-weather yachting master-mariners, as they call themselves on the strength of knowing how to take the altitude of the sun with a quadrant, who are using the name of the sailor as a mere peg to hang up a reputation for themselves upon— ay, you might boil and ye might then eat me, Dick, if I wouldn't go, if only to make one speech, to let the public know not only what sort of life Jack's is after his tow-rope's let go and he's well afloat, but also to tell that same public that in my judgment any man who ventures to give an opinion upon the marine calling—I mean the inside of it, the fo'ksle, salt pork, shot soup, wet weather, and drowning side of it — without having done sailor's duty, drunk and eaten with sailors, gone aloft and suffered with sailors, is an impudent fellow who ought to be put down as fast as ever public opinion can settle the impostor back to his two-inch level."

This explosion, to which Richard listened with close attention and many marks of sympathetic appreciation, appearing greatly to ease him, my father lighted a fresh pipe, and surveyed us with an inflamed, expanded face through a cloud of tobacco-smoke.

However, though Richard had listened and was very much impressed, neither he nor I was quite in the mood to carry on a discussion on Jack's grievances and political neglect, both of us needing for ourselves all the sympathy we might otherwise have bestowed on the sailor. Indeed, as the hour approached for my sweetheart to leave me, I grew so despondent that I could barely speak. To feel my hand in his, to meet his dark eyes full of tenderness, to know that he was my own love, and then to reflect that in a short time all this happiness would be eclipsed, and that for months we should be as much separated as if he or I were dead, were contrasts that saddened me beyond words.

Just before he left he asked me to give him a pair of gloves. I said, "Very well," thinking he wanted some token to remember me by; but instead of bringing him a pair of gloves, I took a locket that was shaped as a heart, and threading the ring with a piece of ribbon, kissed it, returned, and slipped it into his hand. My father pretended not to see, leaning his cheek on his finger and gazing steadily at the fire.

"This is more than I should have liked to ask for," said Richard, looking with boyish pleasure at the trinket. "But I want the gloves too."

Wondering that the locket did not suffice him, I fetched the gloves, and he put them very carefully into his pocket. He then rose to go. The moment he stood up my father left the room, saying he should be back in a minute. This gave Richard and me a chance to say good-bye as engaged lovers should, which was, no doubt, what my father intended. When he returned he found me crying on Richard's shoulder.

"Why, Jess," cried he, trying to put a cheery ring into his voice, though the sympathy in it deadened the note sadly, "does it take ye five minutes to say good-bye? Well, Dick, God bless ye! Take care of yourself, my man. Stick to the three L's, and ye'll come through it safe enough. You'll find Jessie and me waiting for you. She'll pluck up presently. It's her first trial in this way, and God grant she may never meet with harder ones!"

Richard came over to me—for I had left him—and gave me another kiss, and then went into the passage with my father, where I heard them talking. Presently the house-door was opened and shut.

"Now, Jessie," said my father, coming in and putting his hand on my shoulder, "ye mustn't take on, my lass. This time last night you were in love without having a sweetheart. Now you've got one—and a good one too. Give the matter another spell of waiting, and then you'll have a husband. If that's not sailing fast enough to suit ye, all I can say is, you'll have need to ship your patience aboard a very much bigger world than this."

I felt that fretting would be unfair to my father, so I dried my eyes and endeavored to talk cheerfully; but all

the time I was listening to the moaning of the wind, and
wondering whether I should ever see Richard again.

CHAPTER VIII.

MY MARRIAGE IS ARRANGED.

NEXT morning explained why Richard wanted my
gloves. Shortly before twelve o'clock there came a ring
at the bell, and the servant brought me a little parcel. It
was a small box. Inside was a letter from my lover, and
enclosed in the letter was a diamond ring.

The letter cheered me wonderfully. It was as full of
love as a true heart could put into writing, and I believe
I read it over twenty times before I could make up my
mind to lock it away as a sacred treasure.

Old people wonder that poets and novelists should always be dwelling on the old theme of love ; but I, for one,
should not wonder were I to live to be a hundred—that is,
if my aged mind could preserve the memory of the happiness my love gave me. The world can never weary of
hearing about the only passion that makes grown-up people like children in the delight that trifles yield them ;
that such magic gives to a ring, a letter, a bit of ribbon,
as converts it into a talisman by which the most prosaic
passage of existence is transformed into a tender and luminous idyl; that strews flowers for us upon a little space of
the road of life, and sweetens the atmosphere of at least one
stage of this pilgrimage with a fragrance which clings to the
heart for years, and often descends with it into the grave.

For the first two days I fretted a good deal, though secretly, after Richard, and then I grew reconciled to his
absence, and began to count the days when he should return. I was no longer dull in the sense that I had been
dull before. I had my sweetheart to think of ; and the
being engaged to him, and the waiting for his return, and
the thought of the joy our meeting would give us, occupied
my mind. There was something to live for ; life had a
new interest ; I could look out of the window without

wearying of the sight of the same old street and houses; and though I was as much alone as formerly, and even less disposed to call upon friends and procure their companionship, my loneliness did not weigh upon my spirits as it did.

Indeed, there is no cure for a moping girl like a sweetheart. To be sure, lovers are not always to be got; still, if parents, instead of spending their money on theatres and travelling and the like to cheer up their daughters when they grow dull and find no pleasure in home, would help them to get lovers, there would not be much moping in their houses. Young men are to be had, but mothers and fathers will not interest themselves; they thrust their own notions in the way, and block up girls' chances with objections. Nobody is good enough; and in the end Amelia, or Mary, or Maud marries somebody who is really *not* good enough.

I followed Richard's voyage in a way sailors will be amused to hear. My father had charts of the different ports to which my lover was bound; he took them one by one, and traced imaginary courses for me; and every morning when he came down to breakfast he would say, "Well, Jessie, what's the run been since this time yesterday, and where will Dick be now?" on which I would pretend that such and such a wind had blown, helping or retarding him, and, after calculating, I would make a mark on the chart. Richard and I afterwards compared these tracings, and it was wonderful to see how the real courses agreed with my imaginary ones.

I do not clearly remember the nature of that first voyage of his as master. He had to carry a cargo of coal to Cronstadt, then take a freight to some other port and wait for orders, and so on. But, be that as it may, when the first month was gone the days went by fast enough. I had several letters from him while spring was deepening into summer, and then in August came another letter to tell me to look out for him by the 28th. He was bound to Hull, which port he hoped to reach by the 22d. He would be detained there a few days, but I was to expect him in Newcastle on the date he named.

Now, not long before this letter arrived, my father had had a long talk with me about my marriage.

"I'm opposed to long engagements," said he. "Waiting is all very proper when you *must* wait, and can't help it ; but if ye *can* help it, then waiting's a mistake. D'ye think Dick'll be willing to marry when he comes home this time ?"

"If he isn't he'll be a poor sort of lover," I answered. "It's not for *him* to be willing. Shall *I* be willing ?"

"Come, Jess," said he, "let's walk straight if we're to walk at all. I take it that ye're both willing to marry at once ; and if that's so, then let's turn to and give the parson notice before Dick steps ashore, and so be making headway with the job."

"But who'll look after you when I go, father ?" said I.

"Who says you're going ?" he answered, smiling at me. "Isn't there room enough in this house for you and your husband ?"

"I thought, when I married, that you were going to give up the old house and live at Shields ?"

"Well, that was my intention," he exclaimed, gazing leisurely round the room with an expression in his face that was full of pathos to my eyes ; "but I've been turning it over, and doubt when it came to the point whether I'd have the heart to go. It's true, these curios would be the better for a different setting. I'd like to see yon foreign clay-stuff on another chimney-piece. There's no viewing the relievos, the best part of the vases, all that way up. Yet I doubt if I'd have the spirit to shift. The old house is still full of your mother, my lass, and there's never another building, I fear, the wide world over, that would give me such a sense of home as I get out of these rooms."

"It would be a happy arrangement for the three of us to live together," said I. "I should be at hand to look after you, and you would have Richard for company when he's at home."

"Then ye wouldn't be sailing away with him ?" said he, anxiously.

"No," I answered ; "I could not leave you alone, father."

He called me to him and gave me a kiss for that speech.

"Any way," said he, "these are matters we can settle afterwards. When d'ye say is Dick to be here ?"

"On the 28th."

"Well, we'll call it the 28th. Now, suppose I go to-morrow and request the vicar to publish the banns next Sunday?"

"No, no," I answered, laughing; "you must wait until Richard arrives to do that."

"Pooh, pooh," cried he; "you're always for waiting, Jess. If Dick wants ye he'll be glad enough to hear that the road's made smooth for him. And if not, the giving out of the banns'll not stop you from writing your name Snowdon to the end of time."

This, under the circumstances, was not a cheerful view to take, and I was grave enough as I answered: "It would not only be unfair to Richard to act without consulting him, but downright indelicate in us, father, and I shall strongly object to your making any arrangements until the three of us have talked the matter over."

"Now, look here, my lass," said he, talking to me with his finger raised to give emphasis to his words; "when I asked leave to manage your courting and bring Dick to a settlement of his feelings, you ran to your room, and I had to sham that I had broken a limb to draw you below. Ye see what came of my managing. That same night Dick offered to become your chief mate, as he had been mine—I beginning and you ending as his skipper—and ever since you've been a different woman; dulness gone, home no longer a prison, your old father supportable company, and life on the whole pretty flowery. Now, seeing that as I brought you snugly through that job, ye'll be wise to leave the settling of your marriage to me. You're not wanting in good sense, but when the heart gets foul of the intellect there's always a muddle; and if ye don't let me pilot you safe into Dick's arms, you'll stand to make a mess of the last and most exciting chapter of this romance."

"I can't help that, father," I answered, much too agitated by his talk of giving notice to the vicar to see anything to laugh at in his way of putting my position before me. "I admit that you brought Richard and me together that evening. But the banns must not be published — nothing must be said about my marriage until Richard arrives. Far better leave it to him. You have done all that you can, and all that you ought to do."

"Well, I don't agree with you," he replied. "If I don't know much about human nature, I've a good notion of sailors' nature; and if Dick's not a swab he'll come home pleased as Punch to hear that half the course to the altar's been sailed over in his absence. If I was a young man with a sweetheart ashore, nothing would suit me better, after seeing my owners, and rounding up the business of my voyage, than to come home and find the girl ready dressed to go to church, the parson waiting, the organ playing, and a well-freighted table in the back-parlor for all hands to fall to upon when the wedding-ring's shipped, and the vestry order-book's filled up. That's Jack's taste, and if ye don't find Dick of my mind ye shall boil me first and eat me afterwards."

But, argue as he might, I would not hear of his meddling with my marriage until Richard had returned; and, finding me resolved, he dropped the subject.

On the evening of the 27th I was at tea with my father when the bell rang.

"Talk of the de'il!" exclaimed my father, putting down the cup of tea he was about to carry to his lips. "If that should be Dick, now!" For we were at that moment speaking of him, and arranging to have supper ready for him next night on the chance of his coming.

I was instantly all of a tremble, to use the kitchen phrase, and stole with beating heart and quick breathing to the door to listen. The servant answered the summons, and the instant I heard the voice I flung open the parlor-door and ran into my sweetheart's arms.

It was a meeting to make amends for the long waiting. My father came into the passage, caught hold of Richard, and dragged him into the parlor. My joy at seeing him was the greater because he had come before his time, and on my side there was all the sweetness of unexpected happiness in our greeting. How well he looked! His complexion a little darker with weather than when he had quitted me, but the breath and spirit of the deep were upon his face; his dark eyes shone with pleasure; and as he stood grasping my hands and holding me out at arm's-length to view me, I thought a manlier-looking sailor never confronted a girl, that a gladder, franker smile never lighted up a lover's face.

"Ye're a day before your time, Dick," said my father, as they seated themselves, while I bustled about to get tea for my sweetheart. "Is that because Jessie had the end of your tow-rope in her hands?"

"Just that and nothing else, captain," answered Richard, laughing, and following me with his eyes. "We were loaded down to our chain-plates, but I made the old bucket creak as we hauled into these latitudes. The men thought me mad, for I carried a main-royal when in any other mood I should have had her under double-reefed topsails, and for nine hours before we made the land the water was pouring over the knightheads; it was up to a man's waist in the lee-scuppers, and you couldn't hear yourself speak for the roaring aloft."

"That's it!" cried my father, listening with gleeful sympathy and a beaming face. "Creak and hum!—those were my pleasures. Deliver me! how I once drove the old *Maria* up Channel! a real old Geordie, Dick, a tumbled-up brig, with a stump fore-topgall'nt-mast, and a boom fore-sail, and tops big enough to give a ball in. It took four men to steer her, and the sweat ran down 'em like oil. Blow! It was enough to flatten the nose on your face; but it was dead west, and I kept her under all plain sail until the North Foreland made me haul my wind. From abreast of Prawl Point to the Nor' San's Head we never touched a rope-yarn; and yet, with a gale of wind astern of her, I'm blessed if the old *Maria* would do more than four at the very outside!" and he burst into a fit of laughter.

"And what news have you for me, Jessie?" asked Richard, pulling a chair close to him for me to sit on. "What's happened in canny Newcastle while I've been away? Are you still as radical as you all were? And have the Tyne dredges beggared poor old Sunderland by bringing all the shipping further north?"

"If Sunderland don't mind, that'll be happening before long," said my father.

"You see I've come back safe," continued Richard,

whispering to me.   "Did you fret long, Jessie?   I think not.   Or is your prettiness like a sea-bird's feathers, which will take any amount of wetting without losing their soft-ness and beauty?"

"I fretted a little, but not much," I answered.   "And now that you're back I think myself silly for having fret-ted at all."

"What's that you're saying?" called out my father. "Are ye talking of your marriage?"

"No," I answered quickly, growing red.

"Dick," exclaimed my father, "do ye know that Jess yonder is the most impracticable girl any parent ever had to do with?   Ye'll hardly believe it—she pretends to know sailors' natures better than I do.   Not very long since I was for going to the parson and giving him orders to publish the banns.   Said I, 'If Dick's not a swab, he'll come home pleased as a newly paid fiddler to hear that the trouble of pricking off half his course to the altar, and of finding out his matrimonial whereabouts by the dead reckoning that's required in this kind of voyage, is spared him.'   But the lass wouldn't hear of it.   'No, no,' says she; 'stop till Richard comes home.   If ye meddle in this way without first consulting him, he'll think ye indelicate.'   If a man's to be called indelicate for wishing to save trouble to an-other who has duties to perform elsewhere, all that I can say is, the word can't be so bad as it reads, and that the dictionaries would be none the worse for a little overhaul-ing."

"I wish the banns *had* been published," said Richard, laughing, and looking at me.

"*There!*" shouted my father, with a face of triumph. "Hear *that*, Jessie!   Who's right now?"

All this was very distressing to me; and the very sense that any confusion I felt should be concealed made me blush and exhibit my embarrassment the more.   Yet when I raised my eyes to reproach my father with a look, I found his face so mirth-provoking, with the shining, merry tri-umph in it, that I immediately burst into a fit of laughter. It was the best thing that could have happened; it fur-nished an excuse for my red face, and threw a veil, so to speak, over my confusion.

"It's perhaps as well that you didn't see the parson, captain," said Richard, controlling his laughter, though the effort made his voice tremulous. "I fancy there's something to be done before they'll publish the banns. A man must live a certain time in the town where his sweetheart resides, is it? I don't know much about it, but I believe there's a ceremony of some kind to go through first."

"I forget," answered my father. "Jess'll tell ye, perhaps. Maybe you're right. I'm never surprised to hear of any fuss getting in the road of honest jobs like marriage. The British law's fond of impediments. It makes a sort of hurdle-race of life; forces ye to follow the course, but blocks every half-dozen fathoms of road with barricades, which ye've got to jump or scramble over as ye best may. What's more innocent than the birth of a baby, now? But look how the law pursues the father. First, he's got to dodge about in search of some one to take its name down; if he neglects this, the law brings him afore a magistrate. Then he's no sooner clear of that business, than down comes the law again with the vaccination papers. I say nothing of the christening. But, taking it all round, the law makes a baby a severe ordeal for a father, no matter how proud he may be of the little 'un."

He wiped his forehead with a pocket-handkerchief, and asked me to open the window wider. It was, indeed, a sultry evening, and, though my father rarely lost his temper, he easily excited himself. I hoped now he would change the subject, for, though I could not help laughing at what he said, or, rather, his manner of saying it, I was greatly mortified that almost the first words he addressed to Richard should be about our marriage. But he had no mind to let us off, for, after asking Richard where he was stopping, and hearing that he was at his old quarters in Shields, he said:

"If it's true that a man must live near his girl before he can marry her, ye'd better shift out of Shields, my lad, and come here."

"That's easily done," answered Richard, "but I'll not burden your house. Jessie will tell me where I can find a comfortable lodging."

"Don't call it burden," said my father, nodding towards his tobacco-jar that I might pass it to him. "You're not a ship, that you can reckon yourself at so much *burden*. Burden! Why, at what port did ye pick up with that word, Dick? Don't ye know that when you're married this old shanty's to be yours and Jessie's home? If ye're to be a burden as a guest, what'll ye be as a son-in-law? No, no, don't talk of *burden*. That's a worse word than *indelicate*. There's the tobacco. Ye'll find a pipe on the chimney-piece. But perhaps ye're right not to stay with us until you can't help yourself. I know nothing about propriety, but if I'm to learn, I don't want to find the lesson in the neighbors' small talk. However, Jess and you'll settle that. And now, how long are ye ashore for?"

"That depends. The owners, I dare say, will give me another ship if I drop the command I've just had," answered Richard, who, from the glances he frequently threw at me, I could see heartily enjoyed my father's manner and talk. And on any other subject I should have enjoyed it too, for there was such a note of heartiness and kindness running through his speech as you must have heard to appreciate, and it gave his language a significance quite impossible to convey in writing.

"Don't trouble yourself on that head," said my father. "I'll underwrite your getting a ship when you're ready to sail. But before you sail you've got to get married, Dick, and I'm for having that job over as soon as ever we can put our hands to it."

"What do you say, Jessie? I'm ready," said Richard, bending over me, with his hand on my shoulder.

It was impossible to look at my father's beaming face and remonstrate with him. My chief mortification now perhaps arose from the highly unromantic manner in which the sentimental subject of my marriage was discussed by him; still I was also much vexed by his hurried introduction of the topic, and embarrassed and confused by his saying before me what would have come from him properly enough in my absence. However, as I did not choose to leave the room, I thought it best to chime in with his humor, making myself easy with the assurance that Richard understood my thoughts.

"You will think that my father is very anxious to get rid of me," said I to him.

"He'll think nothing of the kind," interrupted my father. "What makes ye afraid of talking about your marriage, Jess? Is it not a solemn thing? Did ye ever take a step in your life fuller of meaning? If you think I'm in a hurry, there's Dick to tell ye you're mistaken. You say you're fond of each other, you tell me ye're pledged to each other; what's the good of wronging yourself and him too, by letting him suppose you're in no haste to wed him? If Dick was not a lad to my fancy, if I wasn't cocksure he'd stand to you through life, like one of Nelson's seamen to his gun, d'ye think I'd be talking as I am? Anxious to get rid of ye! No, no; he knows better than that. All I want is to see ye both happy. Sweethearts are not always quick to come to the point, even when their minds are o'erflowing with wishes for a prompt settlement. Love makes folks timid, afraid of misconstruction, uncertain—the de'il knows what besides. It's for interested outsiders like me to step in and say, 'Look here! I see what ye both want, and I'll show ye how to get it. Yon's a jeweller's shop full of wedding-rings; take your choice. Yon's a church, and there's a very respectable, nice old gentleman, dressed in a kind of bedgown, with colored trimmings, as the women say, down his back, waiting for your orders inside. Come along with me.' That is," he added, dropping his allegorical language with alarming suddenness, and staring at Richard intently, "*if ye're both in earnest.*"

"In earnest!" exclaimed Richard, clasping and kissing my hand. "I know my heart, and I know Jessie's. In earnest? I'll answer for it, captain."

"Then," cried my father, with such vehemence that his pipe snapped in halves in the clutch of his hand, "let's have no more nonsense. Let's talk reasonably, as grown-up people should, and fix the when and the how and the where now—out of hand. And if it's indelicate, according to Jessie, all I can say is, that when we've done with the subject, we must turn to and apologize to one another for ever having mentioned it."

CHAPTER IX.

THREE WEEKS PASS.

It ended, as might have been foreseen, in my father having his way, and before I left the room to give the servant a hand to get supper, not only was my wedding-day fixed, but my father had even named the friends he meant to ask to witness the launch, as he called it, and had arranged to go with Richard next morning and seek a lodging for him in the parish.

I had tried to oppose all this hurry, but feebly, I will own ; and I gave up when I found Richard against me. Indeed, I was as willing to be married soon as my father was willing to have me married, and I saw that Richard was more anxious and eager than either of us. It would have been stupid affectation on my part to hang back, and continue looking embarrassed, while my father and Richard were arranging the marriage.

And do not be surprised to hear that, as before, on the evening when Richard asked me to marry him, so now I felt in my heart that, angry as father's blunt candor had made me, he was right; that he knew my sweetheart and me better than we knew ourselves, and that he had given to our reunion the happiest significance it could take by settling then and there, even before my lover's kiss was dry on my cheek, when we should be married.

I know that, when I quitted the room to go down-stairs, I seemed to waltz to the sound of music ; my spirits were so gay, my feet appeared to dance as they moved ; and a looking-glass near the door gave me back a face so radiant that I would afterwards think of the joy of it as though it were another's face I had seen, or a painting of happiness incomparably imitated to the life.

Yet one thought came a little later on to depress me, and that was my mother's death. My marriage would not oblige me to discard my mourning, yet I felt that the sorrow I was never without when mother's dear image entered my mind would have been better served by the delaying of my marriage until, at least, the year was out. But then, I was going to marry a sailor. When once he left England, who could tell how long he would be absent? I could not persuade myself that, by at once linking my heart with his in wedlock, and putting up a wife's prayer for his safety, I should be wronging the love I bore my mother's memory, and the grief with which I mourned her. I do not doubt my father's thoughts went much in the same strain. His increasing years, my loneliness, the complaints of dulness I had freely spoken, his knowledge of the worth of the man to whom I was to be allied, were among the reasons why he would wish to speedily secure me such a friend as only a husband can be to a girl. He would think that the tenderest memory a man could possess for his dead wife could suffer nothing from the introduction into the year of mourning of such a passage of merry-making and happiness as the marriage of a child whom they both loved.

Our wedding-day was fixed for the third week in September, and for the present, at all events, I was no longer dull. Richard was with me every day, and we went on a whole score of excursions during those three weeks—as far as Morpeth, and Rothbury, and Durham. My father never accompanied us. He left us alone, and we were well pleased to be alone. But the sea was our favorite haunt—the sands and brown rocks of Cullercoats and Whitley, and, farther yet, to near St. Mary's Island.

September is a month full of beautiful seaside pictures. One day we have the breathless calm, with the vague, mysterious haze that brings the horizon to within a mile; a gray, sunless sky, a hard, brown strand, up and down which the white fingers of the deep creep softly; and here and there, where a hidden rock is, a little broken foam and lines of bubbles, which vanish quickly. The defined folds of the haze upon the near horizon are broken by a motionless cobble, the reflection of whose dark canvas streams in the sea under her. The voices of the men come across the water, with now and again the *thud* of a coil of rope thrown down, or the squeak of a sheave upon a rusty pin. In the haze the distant cliffs loom swartly, but there is an air of wonderful serenity upon the face of the rugged rocks which are clear to the vision. Every sound rising from the hidden town of Tynemouth, or from the little village of Whitley or Cullercoats, behind the brow of the cliff, comes with an edge, and yet with a mellow tone, that makes a kind of music in the air. It is now a steamer's whistle moaning in the mouth of the Tyne, or the voice of a hawker, or the jar of distant wheels. Out of the haze at sea from time to time steals imperceptibly forth the outline of a vessel. It is at first a shadow upon the gray mist, but as it darkens it grows defined; and then the shapely hull and canvas stand out firmly, and strike a wavy and sinuous picture twenty fathoms deep in the satin surface of the ashen water. These, and these only, are the seaward details of the haze which make the further reaches visionary. Yonder, perhaps, lies a buoy, with a faint inclination that denotes the set of the soft and breathless tide. Otherwise, between the shore and the folds of haze against which the vessels mark their outlines, that gather color as they draw near, all is a blank and dreaming space of water.

Another day we have the joyous summer breeze, with a bright sun stooping to volumes of white clouds sweeping up from the south, and checkering the leaping sea with acres of violet-colored shadows. The giddy surf shines like snow in the sunshine, and the tall and thunderous breakers in falling add to the white surface of foam which the dancing tide sets, like a big ship's wake, away to sea. Yonder, where the ground is shallow, the seas are breaking in curves, the froth of them, as they arch their crests, wheeling from the right to the left, like a flock of white wild-fowl. The wind is strong a few miles out, and the smoke from the funnel of the screw with the high iron bows, which heap the water in mounds of snow before her, is blown flat and flies low upon the waves. The sea-gulls scream as they hang poised, or slant their wings with exquisite grace to the stiff breeze as they swoop round into the wind's eye. Yonder is a handsome brig, making the most of this capful. Her sails stand like carven stone; the white canvas of her topsails skims along the deep blue of the glorious sky like the clouds which sweep stately over it. You can judge her speed by the sparkling vein she leaves upon the water; it dances down to the horizon, and the foam at her bows stands as high as her figure-head. Inshore the trees are tossing their arms, and the leaves as they fly glance like emeralds in the sun. The cliffs seem to open and close under the sweeping shadows of the clouds. The wind is as sweet as salt, and it reddens our cheeks, and the dance of our pulse shows that our blood confesses its purity.

And then another day we have what even Richard calls a gale, with a jagged horizon of black waves, whose rock-like forms are sharply cut upon the keen, windy ground of slate-colored sky. Along the gray firmament the clouds are driving with fierce speed; they come pouring out of the horizon like huge volumes of smoke, and the gale, which sticks to their skirts, rends and dislocates them, and as they pass overhead they stream out in rags and tendrils. Steamers and sailing-vessels, inward and outward bound, plunge with streaming decks among the boiling seas. The distant ships, which are finding a fair wind in this gale, that pipes like a boatswain's whistle through our teeth when we face it, carry a press of sail. They pitch majes-tically, and cataracts of foam pour their white brilliance at their bows as their sterns shoot high and black out of water, and their martingales harpoon the passing seas. Yonder is a little bark, beating for the mouth of the Tyne. She has just gone about, and as she pays off the gale strikes her full, and, deep as she is, yet the curl and wash of that big sea, which has shattered itself in a hill of snow against her and hidden her in a storm of flake and froth, lays her almost on her beam-ends. In fancy you can hear the scream and yell of the gale in her shrouds, and under the foot of her reefed topsails, as she rolls her spars to wind-ward. Under the cliffs the fine dry sand is blown along in puffs of powder, which take a glint of silver as they stream over the wet ground, which the breakers have made brown. The sea is thundering upon the beach in rollers like Pacific combers. Far as the eye can reach, the sands are strewn, as high as the line of the gleaming sur-face which the waves leave as they recoil, with masses of tangled weed, star and jelly fish, and strange fragments of old wreckage. Upon the huge projecting height of rock there, around whose solid forefoot the sand lies piled, the breakers are wreaking their fury, and the shock and thunder of the strokes may be measured by the upward rush of yellow spume, while the air around is saturated with salt rain, the moisture of which is sweet upon our lips.

Some people think the love-making that goes on before marriage the best part of the whole serious and solemn business. They may have found it so, and are honest to own it. I will not go so far; but I cannot deny that some of the hours betrothed sweethearts spend together, before marriage settles them down and renders moonlight meetings, appointments, and so forth unnecessary, come very near to being the happiest they are likely to get out of their passion. But to sit down and tell people how you billed and cooed with your husband when you were engaged to him, seems to me as impertinent and vulgar a piece of work as a woman could lend herself to. It is the merest parish chatter. At no other period in their lives do people talk more nonsense than when they are lovers, and going to be married—look at the letters read in breach of promise cases!—and, besides that, they often make ridiculous figures in the eyes even of their friends.

For this reason I pass over those three weeks which preceded my marriage, and come at once to the story of my wedding, and of the passage in my life which terminated in my going to sea with my husband.

As at my mother's funeral, so at my wedding, all the people invited were seafarers and their wives. My father took the whole management of the thing into his own hands, ordered the breakfast, wrote to the people whom he wanted as guests, and left me to look after matters which more closely concerned myself. I suggested that, since so many were to come, we might as well include one or two others whom I named.

"No, no," he answered; "they belong to the shore. We'll have no landsmen among us. Ye came into the world among sailors, my lass, and you shall be launched and christened with Dick's name among sailors."

But the marriage, so far as the church part of it was concerned, was to be quite private. There were to be no bridesmaids, nor any public fuss of that kind. Of the friends invited, only three, Salmon, Tarbit, and his wife, were asked to witness the ceremony; the others were requested not to come to the church, as my father thought that, if a number of people were seen entering in their best clothes, a crowd from the streets might follow. The breakfast was to be given at the Three Indian Kings, down on the quay, a hotel at that time kept by Tommy Dodds, as the skippers and owners who frequented the old house called him.

"Now," said my father, when he sat down to write the first of the invitations, "what hour shall I name for the breakfast?"

"Say half-past twelve," I answered.

"Ay," said he, "they'll be hungry by that time. Half-past twelve'll do. Salmon and Tarbit and his old woman can come back here with us after church, and then we'll walk down to the quay and receive the company. But I must make myself plain," said he, scratching his nose with his pen. "I must let 'em know it's half-past twelve in the afternoon, or they'll be bothering over the word breakfast, think I must have meant supper, and be ringing the bell here in the dead of night. For what," he continued, putting down his pen and lighting a pipe to refresh himself with a few whiffs before beginning the serious labor of writing, "should old-fashioned sea-captains like my friends know about wedding-breakfasts and the polite customs of modern society? Take Tarbit; he just drove up to the meeting-house in a cab along with the old housewife he was in tow of, and when the minister had done his job, they drove home, dined off a shoulder of mutton, and then went about their business; he to see after his vessel—for he was only mate then, and they were loading coal—and she to wind up the clocks, and set her house going properly. But we'll give 'em a taste of genteel life this time," said he, with a twinkling eye. "Tommy Dodds knows that money's to be no object this bout, and his orders are to put plenty of silver and jelly and flowers, and objects which impress the eye, upon the

table. Dick'll be thunderstruck. He doesn't know what's
preparing. There's to be the British ensign, the largest
that can be borrowed, at the end of the room where the
president's chair is—that is, where I'm to sit—and if I
could have seen my way to a little music, I'd have hired
a piano and a fiddle to give us a melody after every
speech, in the style of the Lord Mayor's dinners in the
city of London. But Dodds tells me he'd have to heave
a bit of the table overboard to accommodate a piano,
which would oblige me to request some of my friends not
to give me the pleasure of their company. I couldn't do
that, so I gave up the idea of the music, which," he added,
with an expression of simple sadness in his face, "is a
good thing to have happened after all, for, knowing that
when the time comes half my thoughts will be away back
in November of last year, and the other half with the
lass who's let go her father, and started on her own voyage, I doubt if I should have much heart to listen to the
music."

CHAPTER X.

I AM MARRIED.

I WILL spare the reader a particular account of my feelings, when, waking up one morning, I looked at my
watch, found that it was a quarter to eight, and that in a
few hours I should be Mrs. Fowler. I am not surprised
that female novelists should, as a rule, linger lengthily
over the emotions of their heroines on the marriage-day.
It is one of those times which no woman who has gone
through the experience is likely to forget. The feeling
that you are about to take a step that completely sunders
you from the past, that will give you a new name, a new
future, combines with the melancholy that will creep into
the gladdest hours when the old home and the old loves
are thought of, and produces feelings of which it takes
years to erase the recollection.

But a wedding is an exciting thing, and the business of
dressing, and the bustle and hurry of a score of prepara-

tions, leave the mind little leisure for the indulgence
either of melancholy or joy.

I had asked a Miss Ramsay, the daughter of a Newcastle ship-owner, to be with me and help me to pack up
for the little journey Richard and I were to make. She
had been an old schoolfellow, was about four years my
senior, was enthusiastic and amiable, had plumbed, as she
believed, the depths of unrequited love, and avenged her
blighted heart by printing, by subscription, a collection of
poems generally headed, "The Wounded Soul," and was
therefore a proper sort of person to be at my side at such
a time as this.

And here let me recall my marriage gifts. They were
the contributions of my seafaring friends, and did justice
to the liberality of their hearts and the accuracy of their
domestic views. Captain Salmon sent me—indeed, he
brought one in each coat-pocket—a pair of electro-plated
flat candle-sticks; Captain and Mrs. Tarbit an arm-chair;
Mr. Todd, a mate, a roll of fifty yards of yellow satin,
which I afterwards heard he had "looted" from the im-
perial palace at Pekin; Captain Robinson, of Sunderland,
a large umbrella—"fit for a hurricane," he wrote—which
I still keep as a curiosity, for its handle is like a cudgel,
and the whole fabric is strong enough to blow a ship
along. Others sent me various household utensils—such
as a Dutch clock, a pair of window-curtains, a handsome
coal-scuttle—"for the best room, from Ebenezer Duncan,
master-mariner"—and the like, all very useful, and showing hearty kindness on the part of people who, not having
the money to spend on costly elegancies, and being unper-
plexed by conventional ideas, sent me what they thought
a young wife would find of help when she and her husband came to furnish a home.

St. Nicholas's Church stood within five minutes' walk of
our house. As I was to be married in my bonnet, we had
arranged to walk there, mainly because, if the people saw
vehicles stopping at the entrance, they would take notice,
follow us in, and bestow upon the ceremony the publicity
we were anxious it should not possess. Accordingly,
shortly before eleven, my father, Miss Ramsay, and I
walked to the church, where we found Richard waiting,

talking to Salmon and Captain and Mrs. Tarbit. The clergyman presented himself, we placed ourselves in the proper order, my father close beside me, and old Salmon acting as Richard's best man, and the service began.

What I best remember of this is my anxiety that the clergyman should be quick and make an end. I was too fluttered to throw my heart into the prayers, and take note of what the clergyman read, as I should have done had I been there as a worshipper merely. The feel of the wedding-ring on my finger gave me a much clearer notion of what was happening than my responses and vows. However, the service came to an end at last; we followed the clergyman into the vestry, where I was kissed, complimented, and congratulated; and then, all being over, I put my arm into my husband's, and we went home, making quite a little crowd as we walked, and critically examined by all the boys whom we passed.

Were it to the purpose I might linger over the half-hour we spent in the old parlor before adjourning to the Three Indian Kings. I recall old Salmon standing up before me, and reminding me that he knew me when I was no bigger than that—pointing to the leg of a chair—and Captain Tarbit advising Miss Ramsay to bear a hand and follow my example, and quoting poetry to show the danger of delay: and Mrs. Tarbit smoothing her chin and surveying me with the most motherly, smiling, kindly interest; and my father—and Richard—

I paused a moment in the passage as we quitted the house. My trunk stood at the foot of the staircase, ready corded and labelled; a cab was to fetch it, and then call for us down on the quay and take us to the station, so that I should not return home; and, though we were to be away for only ten days, yet the feeling that I was a wife, that a new life had begun for me, made this taking leave of the old house as great a pang as if the separation were to be a long one, and I stood looking and looking, unable to enter the street, my eyes swimming.

"Come, darling," said Richard, taking my arm.

"What's keeping Jessie?" called out my father, who was on the pavement.

He peered in and saw me coming with my eyes full of

tears. He knew what was in my mind as though I had told him; and running in, he took me in his arms, crying in a broken voice—

"Nay, Jess, nay, my bairnie, ye're coming back again soon!" and then, looking round at Richard, he said, "Oh, Dick, my lad, every parting's bitter hard in this world! 'Tis her old home;" and, unable to say more, he turned his head aside and sobbed.

I took his hand and stood beside him, crying too, while the others, as well as my husband, drew away and left us together. I felt this little outbreak would do my father good, for I knew he had carried a full heart to church, and guessed his emotion there by his bearing, and the voice in which he had answered the clergyman, and his way of saying "Amen." He recovered himself presently, and giving me a kiss, and calling Richard, he said, "There, Dick, the pump sucks and our well's dry. Take his arm, Jess, and may the merciful God bless ye both and make ye happy!" and, pushing past us, he caught hold of old Salmon, exclaiming that, if we didn't make haste, the guests would be arriving and finding no one to receive them; and off we marched, I speedily recovering my spirits under the magical influence of my husband's conversation, and the fond pressure of his arm upon my hand.

It seemed strange to be walking to a fine breakfast—good enough, my father assured me, for a lord's nuptials—after my plain bonnet-marriage. For my part, I should have been glad to dispense with the eating and drinking, and drive straight from the church to the railway station. But my father had ideas of his own; he wanted to impress his nautical friends, and could see no reason, because he objected to a showy marriage—carriages, wedding-favors, bridesmaids, and the rest—why we should not wind up with a glittering feast.

We were received at the Three Indian Kings by Mr. Dodds, who conducted us to a room where we were to receive the guests. Here my father wanted me to remove my bonnet; but Miss Ramsay said no—it would be strictly in character for all the ladies to sit down in their hats and bonnets; and on Mrs. Tarbit joining in and saying that, not expecting to be asked to take off her bonnet, she had brought no cap with her, my father yielded, and followed Dodds out of the room to take a look at the apartment where the breakfast was laid.

In due course the guests arrived. They were all extraordinarily punctual, and came in a body, as though they had waited on the quay for everybody to be present before entering the hotel. They crowded round my husband and me, and overwhelmed us with congratulations. Some of them were strangers to me, but their north-country heartiness made nothing of that, and, after they had shaken my hand, I seemed to have known them all my life.

Had I been going to my execution instead of hand in hand with my husband to a feast that was to be eaten and drunk in our honor, I must have laughed at and with, and heartily enjoyed the talk, dress, good-fellowship, and cordial manners of my father's guests. They had spared no expense to do justice to the occasion by their dress. Mrs. Duncan, the wife of the master-mariner who had sent me the coal-scuttle for my "best room," was gorgeous in a noble satin gown, and a bonnet so embowered and heaped up with flowers and feathers, that in a picture it might have passed for some ancient Roman beast of the field going to be offered up as a sacrifice. I noticed Richard slyly smiling at old Salmon's tight black coat and high, stiff cravat, and at Captain Duncan's large shirt-front, as full of frillings and pleatings as the bottom of a woman's petticoat, embellished with what passed very well for diamond studs, the whole crowned with his brown, jovial, broad face, "shored up," as sailors say, with a shirt-collar whose iron-hard points lay close to the corners of his jolly, smiling mouth.

However, not much time was allowed us to admire one another. A waiter threw open the door, and we issued forth in a procession.

It was indeed an imposing scene. Dodds had done his work well. Not only was there the British ensign hoisted behind my father's chair, but the walls were covered with bunting, and the various colors brought out the wonders and splendors of the long table with fine effect.

"Where am I to sit?" called out old Salmon, running his eye along the table.

"Yonder," answered my father; "'twixt Jessie and Miss Ramsay; only take care ye don't get 'twixt Jessie and her husband."

"Well," said old Salmon slowly, and drawing a deep breath, as he rolled his eye over the flowers, bridal-cake, jellies, cold fowls, silver ornaments, and the other wonders of that table, "hang me, Tom Snowdon, if the Queen of England could wish to get married on a finer dinner than this. Breakfast, d'ye call it? Why, man, it's breakfast, dinner, and supper in one—ay, and ye may add lunch too, and then not be out."

This tribute—the offspring of appetite affected by dishes entirely new to it—delighted my father, and amid general laughter we took our seats.

Most marriage feasts are but dull affairs, yet I cannot but think that mine was made original and lively by the character of the guests. At the first going off there was a proper display of embarrassment; as the waiters came round with the dishes, our friends were a little too nervous to ask what they were offered, unless I except old Salmon, who, being a personal friend of the landlord, would look towards him as he stood at the door superintending the waiting, and sing out, "Is this good for an old digestion, Tommy?" or "Tommy, ye're an old hand; can ye recommend this, my lad?" which unusual calls not only kept my father laughing until his eyes were full of tears, but helped the others into an easier and more collected posture of mind.

"Is the fashion of drinking healths gone out, Snowdon?" exclaimed Captain Duncan, from the bottom of the table. "If not, I should like to take wine with Mrs. Fowler yonder."

"I don't know that it's gone out, Duncan," answered my father. "But stop a bit; we'll be doing that job in shipshape fashion presently."

"Tommy," cried old Salmon, "where did ye get that big ensign from, astern o' the captain's chair? Did ye find it aboard a wreck?"

Mr. Dodds, who seemed rather scandalized by these inquiries, went on instructing the waiters in a low voice, pointing, and apparently full of business.

"Shall I tell ye why Salmon asks that question, Snowdon?" exclaimed one of the guests, named Richardson, a little man with a red beard that stood out from his chin like the back of a perch.

"Because," cried old Salmon, who was not to be cheated out of the honor of the discovery—"I'm damned," said he, bringing his fist down on the table, "if Tommy hasn't viewed this ceremony as a case of distress, and hoisted that ensign union down!"

My father, the smile vanishing out of his face as if by magic, jumped up from his chair to look at the flag. It hung from a pole that was fixed in a kind of stand placed just behind my father's chair, and as the pole leaned away from the table, it had the appearance of a flag-staff on the stern of a ship. The top was a gilt crown, and it touched the ceiling, and the flag hung in folds from that height.

"Hang me, Dodds," cried father, looking up at the flag, as pale as death, "if Salmon's not right! Don't ye know which side of that flag ought to be uppermost? How came ye to make such a blunder?"

"Let him unship the pole and bundle the whole business below," called out Captain Robinson.

"Or take the flag down and hoist it afresh in such a way as to show we're not at all, no, not the least bit, in danger," piped little Richardson.

The ladies indulged in various exclamations: "How very stupid!" "How blind Mr. Dodds must be!" "Fancy the landlord of the Three Indian Kings not knowing how to hoist the English ensign!"

In truth, it was impossible not to see that the company accepted the union down as a very disagreeable omen. Even Richard looked concerned, though I begged him in a whisper not to be foolish, and to consider what sort of future ours was likely to prove if our destiny was to be at the mercy of a landlord's ignorance of flags.

Mr. Dodds, who was as red as the flag itself, and kept darting evil glances at Salmon, said it was Muffles's doing —who Muffles was I did not know—and offered to take the ensign down and hoist it properly; but my father refused to seat himself until it was out of the room. "If ye can't get it down-stairs, fling it out of the window,"

said he; "and if ye'll lash Muffles to it before ye pitch it
out, I'll lend ye a hand. Why, man, ye might as well set
up a skeleton in a glass case astern of me, as make me sit,
at my daughter's marriage, under the shadow of a distress
signal!"

After some trouble and several breakages, the flag and
the long pole were removed from the room.

"Don't bother yourself about such a trifle," sung out
Captain Richardson. "What are called bad omens are
only blessings spelt back'ards, Snowdon. Besides, a nautical blunder means nothing when committed by a landsman. Had a sailor been guilty of hoisting that ensign
union down I don't know but that I might consider there
was something in it."

"Ay," said his wife, "but no sailor would have done it."

"Just so," cried Tarbit. "It was Muffles. Now, who's
Muffles? Nobody knows — at least, *I* don't; and that's
why I say it's an accident that's not worth taking notice
of. Why, Snowdon, suppose you were asked to cook one
of those colored dishes," pointing to a jelly, "and ye were
to make a mess of it, which I dare say would happen, and
send it up green instead of yellow, and eating no more
like yon than a whelk eats like a potato, d'ye think Tommy
Dodds would call it a sign of bad luck if it came on to
his newly married daughter's table—"

"Forty year ago come next month—" interrupted old
Salmon, with his mouth full.

"Oh, never mind forty year ago come next month or
the month after," rejoined Tarbit, annoyed at having his
little speech spoiled. "Forty year ago aren't to the purpose. I'm putting a fanciful case. I say, would Tommy
Dodds consider a—what d'ye call it?"

"A jelly," said his wife.

"Ay, a jelly made by Tom Snowdon a sign of ill luck?
No, he'd consider it a sign of ignorant cooking; and that's
what Tom Snowdon must consider Muffles's distress signal
to mean."

I warmly espoused this view to encourage my father,
and Richard agreeing with me, and the others joining in,
my father presently recovered his cheerfulness, and no
more was said about the unfortunate ensign.

By rights, no doubt, it was my duty to be bashful and
fond, to blush when looked at or spoken to, to answer my
husband in whispers, and keep my eyes down, and smile
when he whispered to me.   Well, if that was my part, all
I can say is, I did not act it.   I chatted with everybody,
just as I should have done on any other occasion, ate and
drank and enjoyed myself, laughed heartily at and with
our sailor friends, and accepted the whole of the merry-
making as a piece of real humor.   Indeed, I had been so
accustomed to think of Richard all through the time that
went before our marriage-day as my own, that there seemed
but little novelty in reflecting that I was his wife, and in
hearing him call me so.   I was as happy in my spirits as
any woman could wish to be—proud that my friends
should see what a handsome lad I had for a husband, but
without any mind to let them guess by our behavior, as
we sat side by side, how fond we were of each other ; and
though now and again a shadow passed over my heart,
and sobered the smile on my lips, when I looked at
my father, and thought of him and mother and the old
home, the little darkness soon passed and left me merry
again.

The champagne brightened up the wits of the company
amazingly.   At first everybody had been shy, looking
with a kind of awe at the fruit and the flowers, and the
fine things upon the table ; but now everybody was talking.   I was greatly amused by a discussion provoked by
old Salmon asking Miss Ramsay in a loud voice, in an interval of silence, if she was married—apparently not having heard the piece of advice given her by Captain Tarbit before we came to the breakfast.

"No," she answered, blushing and laughing, and looking at me, for the silence made old Salmon's question em-
phatic and striking.

"A good job, too," said the old man, stooping so as to
bring his eye to bear on the inside of a wine-glass.   "Living single is one of the few bits of sense I come across
now and again in this generation.   It's uncommon enough,
too.   When it's gone—and it's going fast, for all the world
seems bent on marrying nowadays, thinking of nothing
else—there'll be but little of the old kind of sense, the

good sense that ye might ha' found when I was young, to follow after it."

"Why, Salmon," exclaimed Tarbit, with a serious face, while the ladies stared at one another, "that's a queer sentiment to let fall on an occasion like this ; I'll say nothing about pretty nigh all who hear ye being married."

"I can't help that," said Salmon, doggedly. "If ye'd all got four-and-twenty wives apiece, and if there were five hundred newly married young women as well as Mistress Jessie yonder—whom I've known ever since she was no taller than a Wellington boot—sitting at this table, I'd speak the truth. I'm too old to go against my conscience, mate. What I say is," said he, turning his head slowly so as to cast his eye around the company, "living single's a bit of good sense. If there's any gentleman here who thinks he knows better, let him speak up, and he'll find me agreeable to listen."

"Salmon talks out of spite. He knows he never could get any woman to marry him," cried Tarbit, laughing loudly; and this being severe, though very well merited, all we ladies joined in the laugh.

"There ye're out," retorted Salmon. "Had I married all who would have had me, there's ne'er an anchor that's lain fifty year at the bottom of the sea deader and more gone than I should have been afore I was aged thirty."

"What's your objection to marriage, Salmon?" asked my father. "D'ye know, it's not the first time I've heard ye talk against wedlock."

"My objection is," answered Salmon, "there's no good in it. I'll put men aside and take women. When a woman marries, all she does is to shift her duties from her parents to her husband, who, let him be good or let him be bad, 'll find her more to do than ever she had to lay her hands to at home. Take this young lady here," indicating Miss Ramsay, "and take your daughter, Tom. Let this young lady go on for the next ten years as she is, and let Mistress Jessie go on for the next ten years as *she* is, and then compare 'em, and ye'll say old Salmon knew what o'clock it was when he reckon'd there's no good in marriage."

"Why, what's the matter with you, Captain Salmon?"

exclaimed my husband, evidently not appreciating the drift of the old man's arguments.

"It's the jelly," called out Captain Robinson. "Jelly's not thought wholesome for retired master-mariners."

"I'm quite surprised at your language, Captain Salmon," cried Mrs. Tarbit; and another lady exclaimed in a very audible voice, and with many nods of the head, that for her part she could only hope that *all* gentlemen who gave up the sea did not leave it with such very strange ideas of good manners as Captain Salmon had.

"Marriage," continued the old man, talking deliberately and with a wooden face, and not in the least degree put out by the remarks levelled at him, "means expense, likewise responsibilities, also worries, to master the significance of some o' which is as high above my capacity as a royal yard's above the foot of the mast it belongs to. Ever since I've had to shift for myself—getting on now for so many years that Bob Tarbit yonder's a boy alongside of 'em—I've found it hard enough to manage for one, and keep *him* pretty comfortable. But if I'd married, instead of one, who's going to tell me there mightn't ha' been half a score—ay, and more than half a score—for after twenty years of married life there was old Dick Robertson mustered eighteen souls in his house—each one bringing troubles and vexations which ne'er a man in this world would consent to carry away for me, though I offered him all I had—"

"Ay," interrupted Mrs. Tarbit, "but how about your comforts? Who airs your linen?"

"Yes," cried Mrs. Duncan, "and who sees that the laundress don't cheat ye?"

"Who looks after your meals?" said another lady.

"And who minds him when he's ailing?" called out a fourth.

"It 'ud be a poor look-out for me, mistress," answered Salmon, fixing his eye on Mrs. Tarbit, "if I couldn't chuck an old shirt o'er the back of a chair when it wanted warming, without having to keep a wife to do that job for me."

Here Captain Duncan suddenly roared out "Silence!" and immediately afterwards Captain Richardson stood up.

"Snowdon," said he, "these breakfasts, as they're called, are novelties to me, shipmate, and so I hope you and the company'll excuse me if I'm out of order. Is it allowable for me to make a speech?"

"Ay, fire away, Richardson," answered my father; and every eye was turned upon the little skipper, amid a dead silence.

"Well, ladies and gentlemen," said he, "we've been having a long spell at this table, eating and drinking, and enjoying ourselves, and I think it's about time that somebody turned to and asked ye to fill your glasses to drink to the health of Jessie Fowler and her husband. Ye'll not want me to remind you that Dick Fowler's one of us, and that his lass is a sailor's wife as well as a sailor's daughter, to make ye pledge 'em in a hearty, old-fashioned English bumper. There's no calling to equal the seaman's, and there's no man who better deserves a handsome girl for a wife than he does." Here I saw old Salmon look steadfastly at poor Mrs. Tarbit. "Dick Fowler's got her; and just as when ye see a fine, new craft launched—her spring bold, her lines beautiful, her figurehead like a bit of poetry, and her colors English—it's not in human nature to help envying the skipper who has command of her; so are ye bound to look upon Dick Fowler as a man who's dropped in for an uncommonly big slice of good luck. I wish 'em—we all wish 'em—a prosperous voyage. They must expect to meet head-winds now and again, and occasional storms, as others have, in which they'll prove their seaworthiness and power of going to wind'ard. Ratching and lying-to's no hardship when ye're not in a hurry to fetch your port, and let us hope that many a long year must pass afore they're called upon to warp alongside, and discharge that freight termed by Shakespeare—who sometimes wrote like a nautical man—a mortal coil, which God Almighty puts aboard us all, and which it's our duty to unload in as good condition as we received it. That's all the speech I find I can make, ladies and gentlemen, and so you'll please to join me in drinking the health of Mr. and Mrs. Fowler."

All stood up, the ladies as well, and most royally saluted us, and scarcely had the deep-sea shout of the men, tempered by the women's voices, subsided, when a feeble pipe was heard tuning up, "Weel may the Keel Row," and looking, we were all amazed to observe old Salmon engaged in singing.

There was nothing very appropriate in the words of the song to the speech that went before it, but it was an air none of us could listen to without being eager for the chorus to come round, that we might all join in. A canny old song it is, and, though Salmon had but a broken voice, yet the circumstance of so old a man singing it gave the fine, hearty melody such a pathos to our ears as it could hardly have taken from the most accomplished vocalist; it was like old Father Tyne himself getting up and singing the air to whose measures his waters have flowed for generations.

We rang out the chorus nobly, and such was the effect of the inspiriting, endearing song upon the minds of the guests, that when it was over the whole party were occupied in shaking hands; and pleasant it was to hear the captains God-blessing one another, and exclaiming, "Glad to see ye, captain!" and, "Long life to ye, skipper, and to your lady!" and the like.

My husband returned thanks in a few words, and then up got Tarbit to propose the health of his old messmate and shipmate, Tom Snowdon—"a man he'd be content to go on sailing round the world with until the very rats gave up, and the ship's bottom was as thin as a sailor's shirt." But his professional compliments were interrupted by the arrival of Mr. Dodds to inform Richard that the cab was waiting outside the court. My husband, looking at his watch, said that if we were to catch that train we had no time to lose. The ladies embraced me, and the gentlemen shook hands with me, and by the time I came to my father I was nearly breathless.

"Keep up your spirits, father," I whispered, as he folded me to his heart, unable to speak. "Our separation is only for a few days."

He kissed and released me, and turned away to conceal his tears; and then, taking Richard's arm, I left the house, followed down the court by the whole of the company—for the Three Indian Kings stands at the end of a narrow passage off the quay. Our guests filled the pavement, and the people passing at the time, seeing a number of persons, the men without hats, around a cab, supposed that an accident had happened, and in a very short time there was a great crowd, all sorts of grimy faces poking forward and peering into the off window to have a look, and I could hear them saying, "Is onybody deed?" "Myek way for them as'll till us what's happened;" "It's arle reet, Tommy, it's nowt but a weddin';" until at last the cab drove off, my friends giving us a cheer, which the crowd caught up, so that we took our departure amid such a "demonstration of public sympathy and good-will," as the newspapers say, as would have done no mean honor to the nuptials of very much higher and mightier people than a merchant skipper and his wife.

CHAPTER XI.

I RETURN TO NEWCASTLE.

WE spent our honeymoon in London. My husband had made arrangements to take command of a vessel at a date that gave us only ten days, and what with a fog that twice in one week rolled down upon the city, and what with the shortness of the time and our ignorance of localities, which obliged us to consume hours in hunting about for places of amusement—many of which proved to be small enough treats in spite of the trouble we had to get to them—I cannot say I saw very much of London.

However, it was my first visit, and though Newcastle is a very busy place, and as noisy as carts and cabs, newspaper-boys, singing beggars, locomotives' whistles, fish-wives, and quarrelsome dogs can make it, yet the uproar of but a single thoroughfare in London so exceeded the combined discords, in their most aggravated form, of the northern capital, as we call it, that I was utterly distracted, and in a large measure deafened, and always felt, when I turned into a quiet street, as if I had been travelling three hundred miles, without stopping, in an express train.

We stayed at a little hotel out of the Strand, and nothing, I fancy, but the sort of triumph a person who has lived from childhood in the provinces feels on visiting London for the first time, could have surmounted the disgust with which I must otherwise have ever associated that trip to London, in consequence of the hotel we stopped at.

Our bedroom was small, stuffy, obscurely exhibited in the daytime by means of a kind of palpable yellow, foggy light that oozed through the narrow window, whose glass gave all sorts of angular distortions to the houses over the way. The private sitting-room was equally small and equally stuffy, filled with a smell of flue and faded upholstery, oppressive with the gloomy yellow atmosphere that hung in it, whether the sky outside was blue or black.

However, this melancholy hotel, with its mute-like waiters, its mysterious landlady, with sausage-shaped curls bastioning a small fortress of bristling cap, who was perpetually shaping herself out of the shadows in one corner to melt into thin air in the shadows in another corner; its dingy "boots" in a sleeved waistcoat, who made Richard's life a burden by continually lying in wait for him, armed with a hard clothes-brush, was good for us in one way—it drove us out of doors, and compelled us to see more than we should have been tempted to look at had our quarters been comfortable.

It is needless to say that we visited such places as Westminster Abbey, the Tower, and St. Paul's, the British Museum and the Monument, of which provincials know a very great deal more than Londoners. Richard amused me with a good illustration of this.

He fell into conversation with a gentleman whom he found in the smoking-room—a little, dimly lighted box at the back of the house, commanding an extensive view of the windowless wall of a tall house. The gentleman said he lived in London, and had called to meet a friend from the country. He then asked Richard where he lived. Richard told him.

"Ah!" says the gentleman, "you're a sailor, and are therefore about in the world. But, for my part, I never can understand how any man can find the heart to deliberately live out of London. You know what old Dr. Johnson said—it's the only place for a civilized being to live in?"

"Was old Dr. Johnson civilized?" asked Richard.

"Why, yes; the Johnson I mean wrote the great dictionary."

"Well," says Richard, "London certainly is a wonderful city. I took my wife to the Tower to-day. I believe those beef-eaters tell a good many lies. But it's a glorious old pile—the history of England in stone."

"Oddly enough," says the gentleman, "I never was there."

"St. Paul's is another noble building; but I like Westminster Abbey best. But do you think that recumbent figure of Mary Queen of Scots like her? It gives her a deuced ugly profile. It strikes me that Queen Elizabeth must have drawn the portrait from which that face is copied."

"The places you name," replied the gentleman, "are undoubtedly full of historical interest. I've often made up my mind to devote a day to them, and have a good look round."

He then launched forth into praise of the wonders of London, and wound up again by expressing his astonishment that anybody could be found content to live out of it.

"Pray, sir," says Richard, "in what part of London do you reside?"

"At Hammersmith," replied the other. "My wife thinks the air there good; but if rents would only come down, I'd draw nearer the Marble Arch."

"And how do you manage to pass the time?"

"Pass the time?" says the other, laughing. "I have plenty to occupy me, I assure you. I go to business at nine o'clock every morning, and seldom get away much before six. I go down to the city on the top of a 'bus winter and summer, ride back as far as the Marble Arch, and, for the sake of exercise, walk the rest of the way home."

"Then you devote your evenings, no doubt, to London life, sir?"

"Well, we have acquaintances in the neighborhood.

But the theatres and places of amusement are so far off that we rarely go to them. I'm glad to be quiet after my day's work, to smoke my pipe, read the papers, or in summer to kill an hour in the garden at the back of my house."

"And this," said Richard to me, laughing with all his might, "is what men call 'living in London!' There are hundreds and thousands like that man. They sneer at provincials, wonder how rational-minded people can live out of the great metropolis, and yet know less of their own city than Hodge, who comes up for two or three days once a year to attend a fat beast show. They get up of a morning, eat their breakfast, catch an omnibus, read a newspaper the whole way, sit in an office up an alley or at the top of a building till one, rush out for a mutton-chop, run back and sit until five or six, put on their hats, catch another omnibus, arrive home, clap on an old coat, seize a book or a watering-can, and call it 'living in London!'"

We were ten days away, and then returned to Newcastle. I was not sorry to leave London. I dare say I should have enjoyed myself with my husband as well, or perhaps better, anywhere else; but I was not particularly glad to go back to Newcastle. The glimpse of an outside world I had caught made me want more; and when I thought of Newcastle after London, the canny town seemed to shrink up; it seemed little more than a respectable village after the miles of metropolitan bricks and mortar I was fresh from.

My father gave us a hearty welcome. We arrived in the evening, and found a good supper awaiting us, a cheerful fire in the bedroom, and other signs of consideration as tender and acute as a woman's.

He hugged me when we met, he hugged me when I left the room, and he hugged me when I came down-stairs again. His heartiness and pleasure were, indeed, contagious. All the journey home I had been depressed, because, now that my little honeymoon was over, the thought that in a few days my husband would be saying good-bye came to me with cruel sharpness. But it was impossible to feel the cheery, hopeful influence of my father's glad and affectionate welcome and remain dull. Indeed, the mere sight of him, with his jolly, red, beaming face, kind eyes, and winning smile, was as good as a cordial, for he was not only inspiriting himself, but the thought he gave rise to in me was full of encouragement. I mean that he too had left his wife a score of times oftener than I meant that Richard should leave me; and yet here he was now, in good health, and not yet sixty-one years old, having outlived that same devoted wife, who had dreaded his going lest they should never meet more, as I now dreaded Richard's.

We sat down to supper and talked busily. I had much to tell father. He only knew London as a sailor knows a port; familiar with the riverside from London Bridge to Blackwall, but of London proper as ignorant as the cockney my husband met in the hotel. And he took great interest in my account of the places we had visited, and looked indeed as if he thought such experiences deserved a larger audience than he made.

"So, Dick," says he, "your wife finds London bigger than Newcastle?"

"Why, father," I answered, "you could almost extinguish Newcastle by dropping St. Paul's Cathedral down upon it."

"No, no, Jess, that won't do!" cried my father. "No, no, ye must draw it milder than that, my lass. What, St. Paul's Church in London smother Newcastle! Ye shall clap the whole of London on this little town's back, and, so far from Newcastle being smothered, I'll tell ye what would happen; she'd run away with the city! Bless your heart and soul, Jess, look at our factories along the Tyneside—look at our engine-works, our ship-yards! Why, there's power enough 'twixt Paradise and Hebburn —to go no further—to warp Middlesex into North Durham! Smother Geordie Stephenson's toon! Gan alang wi' ye!"

We sat up talking late, and that same evening we settled the arrangements which had been suggested before my marriage. For the present, at all events, I was to continue living with my father.

"There's no need," said he, addressing Richard, "to

talk of your taking a house for your wife either now or by-
and-by.   All that's mine is Jessie's, and all that's Jessie's
is yours and hers.   The corporation will be turning me out
of this shanty soon, I dare say, for I hear big talk of im-
provements ; but until we get notice to quit we'll call this
old roof home, and bide with it.   It'll be time when I'm
driven out to see how I shall relish the notion of going to
live at South Shields, as I've threatened again and again."

"Jess should come along with me but for you, captain,"
said Richard.   "But I'm better pleased to leave her here
than I should be to take her to sea, hard as saying good-
bye is.   The sea's not a fit home for a woman."

"Well, I won't say that," answered my father, shaking
his head.   "It's not so much that the sea isn't fit for
women as that very few women are fit for it.   Jess is an
exception.   She's a tar-bucket in petticoats.   Breek her,
and I'll engage she'd stow a main-royal—ay, and give the
sail a real harbor-bunt too—with any ordinary seaman ye
might pit against her.   But that's not it.   I can't let her
go all at once.   She must slip away from me by degrees.
When ye come home you must run her about—give her a
day here, a week there, so that I may get used to being
without her.   Then ye shall take her to sea."

"Jess, my darling," said Richard, "when I get command of a proper ship, you shall come.   But I'm not going to make a bargeman's lady of you by carrying you
away in some old Geordie, whose tiller is half-way down
the companion-ladder, and whose wash-streak is within an
inch of the water."

"Well, Richard," said I, "father knows I love him,
and you know I love you.   I will obey you both, but I
must be obeyed too.   I'll stop at home for the present,
but only on the understanding that by-and-by I shall go
to sea with you, and remain with you there until you give
it up."

He kissed me, and asked in a whisper if I supposed his
heart would not be a thousandfold lighter than it was if
it were arranged that I should accompany him this time,
and all times afterwards, to sea.   He also told me to remember that we had both given father to believe that I
should not leave him at once.   "And besides, Jessie,"

said he, "even if your father were willing you should accompany me, the *Phantasy* "—for that was the name of his vessel—"though a fair specimen of her class, has no accommodation fit for you."

However, as I had not hoped to go to sea with him, at all events, during the first year of our married life, I could not feel disappointed at his not taking me. Yet I never could have guessed, from the grief I had in parting with him as a sweetheart, what my sorrow would be when I came to say farewell to him as my husband. I lay awake that night, crying far into the morning, when he was sleeping peacefully at my side ; and when, in the feeble light of the dawn, I looked at his face, the bitterness of the approaching surrender was so strong upon me, that I felt as if I were acting the part of a faithless wife in not turning a deaf ear to my father's appeal for my companionship, and to Richard's desire that I should remain at home, and so link my life with my husband's in the only way which would give a true meaning to my marriage-vows.

CHAPTER XII.

MY HUSBAND SAILS.

WELL, the day came when Richard took me in his arms and said good-bye. I will not linger over that farewell. His voyage was to the Gulf of Mexico, and we should not meet again for weeks and weeks.

There is many a wife who will understand what I felt when the door closed upon him, and I stood like a woman bereaved by death, listening to the fading echo of his footsteps as he walked down the street with father. Such eclipses of happiness seldom befall others than sailors' and soldiers' wives, and of these sailors' must suffer oftenest. For soldiers carry their wives about with them ; they live in barracks, the State looks after them, and seldom anything short of war divorces them ; but with Jack, whether in war-time or peace-time, signing articles means saying good-bye to the wife and the little ones. And this is as true of the cabin as the forecastle, for it is seldom nowadays that one hears of a captain taking his wife to sea, not because scores of masters and mates would not gladly accept the privilege of having their wives with them, but because ship-owners, for reasons it would be worth hearing their explanation of, object to a custom that was once common enough ; as if, indeed, they suspected that the presence of their wives, by making the safety of the ship doubly precious, would render masters inattentive to their duties !

I do not say this is the ship-owners' argument, but it might very well be ; for it is quite of a piece with the logic that is employed by them against any suggestion to ease and render more tolerable the sailor's hard, toilsome, and perilous life.

When my husband was gone, I fell back into the old home routine—helped the servant, looked after the house, and did what I could to make father comfortable. My marriage then seemed more like a dream to me than a reality. Sitting alone sometimes in the old parlor, and looking back at the past, I could hardly believe that the wedding at St. Nicholas's, the breakfast and speeches at the Three Indian Kings, the trip to London, were all real. Nay, the sight of my very wedding-ring would sometimes puzzle me.

There was nothing strange in this. I might compare myself to the man whom a king found sleeping at the door of his palace, and who was made a monarch of for a day. His few regal hours only lasted long enough to persuade him of their unreality.

Even my father would sometimes look at me and say, " Why, Jessie, when I come home and see ye at work, and going on in the old way, it's difficult to believe that ye're a married woman."

"I don't know how I may look, father," I remember once answering ; "but if the past is only a bit of make-believe, as I sometimes think it is, I wish it had not left me yearning for the sight of my husband, and longing to run away from you and join him. It may not be hard to look like a wife, but it is hard to have the sorrows and anxieties and none of the happiness of a wife."

"Tut, tut!" said he, laughing and patting my face when I made that answer; "you're wifely enough, Jessie, and growing bonnier too. Perhaps Dick likewise will think his marriage fancy, come back, fall in love, and offer ye marriage again. If he does, then, by thunder! though there should be no need for a second wedding, we'll have another glorification, and Salmon shall give us 'Weel may the Keel Row' once more!"

But, whether it goes joyously or miserably, the time is bound to pass, and praise Heaven for it, say I. The months went along, and in due course, and much about the time he had told me to look out for him, Richard returned. This time he stayed six weeks with me. I will not stop this story to describe our meeting, nor the manner in which we spent those six weeks. His going the next time was rendered bearable to me by the voyage being a short one to the Mediterranean, and he was back again soon. He made two short voyages, and then went away on a journey that was once more to last for some months.

It was during his absence this time that a little boy was born to us. Indeed, had it not been for the state of my health, I should certainly have sailed with him. His first long absence had taught me to view a like separation with dread; but my condition set both him and father dead against my wishes, and finding that they would not listen to me, I gave up worrying them.

My baby came into the world about six weeks after his father had sailed. He was a most noble boy, with grand eyes and the sweetest face imaginable by any mother's heart. Before my marriage I had sometimes wondered when I heard people say that such and such a person was proud of her baby; there were too many babies, it seemed to me, to justify the least degree of conceit in a mother; and, though I was fond of children, of their company and talk, I had always thought a baby must be as hard a trial as could befall a woman who had not the means to obtain plenty of help in the shape of nurses, servants, and the like.

But my baby cured me of that mistake, and gave me a new education respecting the pride and love of mothers. Indeed, I question if there ever was a mother prouder of

her baby than I was of mine. As to father, he was forever stealing to the cradle to have a look, or standing over
me, and peering at my darling as he lay in my arms, or
begging me in the most moving terms to allow him to
nurse the boy. His delight and pride were, indeed, something truly remarkable. He would sit holding baby up
in front of him, the bairn lying fairly upon father's square
hands, and talk to him until his eyes grew humid with feeling, while I would stand by in an agony lest he should let
my precious one fall, and long for him to cry as an excuse
to take him.

People were constantly coming to see Jessie Fowler's
wee laddie, all invited by father. I well remember Captain Salmon's visit. My father came to tell me that the
old man was in the parlor, waiting to see baby.

"Bring him to the light, mistress," exclaimed Salmon
as I entered; "I've but one eye to see with. So! this is
Dick Fowler's brat; and Tom Snowdon's a grandad!
Well, the bairn's bonnie enough. Does he eat and drink
pretty well?"

"Ask him to dine with ye, and you'll see," answered my
father. "Eat and drink! If ye had the keeping of him,
Salmon, in less than a month your neighbors would be
missing ye and dragging the Tyne for your body. Did
ye ever see such a baby afore? In all your voyages into
distant parts did ye ever come across the like of that portrait of a holy angel?"

"Well, I don't know that ever I did," answered Salmon.
"But mind," added he, with the literalness of an aged
north-country man, "that mebbe, Thomas, because babies
are things I don't recollect ever having taken much notice
of. How's his health, mistress? Does he suffer much
from wind?"

"He'd not be a sailor's bairn if he didn't," said my
father.

"Well, see that his bowlines are kept well triced out,
and ye'll find he'll draw ahead right enough," said the old
fellow, rolling his eye upon the window to let me see he
had had enough of my baby.

Though I sadly missed my husband, I could not be dull
with baby. I was uneasy if I was out of his presence a

minute. It was my delight to talk to him about his father, ay, as gravely as if he understood me. I remember once being in my bedroom, sitting with my back to the door; baby lay in my lap, and I was tickling his cheeks and making him smile, and yet watch me intently while I told him that father was at sea, but that he would be back soon, and so on—thinking aloud, indeed, in the pretty delusion that baby was listening and understood me, and talking out of my innermost heart the one fancy that was always there—I mean, my husband's joy and surprise when I should put baby into his arms—I say, I was rambling aloud in this way, supposing myself alone, while baby lay still and smiling on my knees—as perfect a little shape as the hand of God ever moulded for the contentment of a mother's love—when something caused me to look around, and there stood my father, leaning over my shoulder and peering at baby.

"I've been waiting to hear Dicky answer ye," says he, meaning by Dicky the baby. "He understands you; ye may see it in his eyes. How d'ye make out his thoughts, Jess?"

I was somewhat ashamed to be caught, even by father, talking in such a rambling way, and looked to see if he was without his boots, for he had come in as quietly as a mouse.

"Oh, baby understands me," said I, putting my mouth to the little face on my knee.

"Ay, that's plain enough," answered my father, stepping round; "but how d'ye understand *him?* D'ye imagine he says things, or is there a meaning in him ye get at as nobody else could?"

I thought he was joking, but it was impossible on glancing at him to mistake his gravity and earnestness.

I answered that I was merely thinking aloud, and looking at baby while I tickled him and talked.

"No, no," he exclaimed, "I've been standing o'er ye a full five minutes. It was no thinking aloud, but a regular conversation 'twixt you and the bairn. Ye seem to forget that you waited for his answers and then went on again. What's the secret, Jess? How do ye find out what's passing in his bit mind?"

I burst into a laugh, which seemed to vex him. He looked at me anxiously, and said, " I'm not such a donkey as to suppose he can talk, or that he's yet capable of understanding English ; but ye'll never persuade me that he can't follow you, and that ye can't see into his mind and put his ideas into words for him."

Incredible as it may seem, he never ceased to believe from that night that I had the power of conversing with my little baby, and I afterwards heard that he would go among his friends and boast of my power in that way, overriding all incredulity by warmly and stoutly declaring that he had stood behind my chair, when I did not know he was in the room, and heard me conversing with the baby, that lay quiet and attentive on my knee, listening closely, and answering me in some mysterious fashion, as he might judge by the way I stopped and then went on.

I mention this to show the simplicity of my father's truly original character ; but I could tell of even simpler faiths in sailors' ideas of the relationship between mothers and their babies.

The time passed and brought me to a day which left only another fortnight for Richard to be away. Hour by hour my little one had expanded, intelligence brightening in his clear and beautiful eyes, and every day revealing some fresh, sweet baby-humor to draw him closer to my heart, if that, indeed, were possible.

But in a minute, as I may say, this star of my life was eclipsed, and within a fortnight of my husband's return.

I had left baby sleeping soundly in his crib, and was at tea with father, when my nurse rushed into the room with a white face to tell me that baby was choking. · I ran upstairs, followed by father, and, going to the crib, saw my little one in convulsions. But I did not then know what was the matter with him. He was black in the face and rigidly stiff. I told the nurse to run for the doctor, and, distracted with grief and terror, snatched up my child and held him to my bosom. My father stood by helpless and heartbroken. We neither of us knew what to do. It seemed an eternity before the doctor came. When he arrived he immediately applied himself to recover my poor child. But it was too late. Indeed, I cannot dwell upon this passage. Within an hour from the time that I had left my baby sleeping soundly and healthfully in his crib, he lay dead in the same little bed, and I was sitting by his side, stunned, tearless, heart-crushed by the intolerable blow.

I had felt my mother's death cruelly, but, beside this loss, it was as a snowflake falling on the hand compared to the searing of the flesh by a red-hot iron. One moment, as it might be, my heart was as glad and sunny as a spring morning, with thoughts of my husband's coming and of the treasure I should put into his hands—ay, even after I had hushed my baby and laid him down in his crib in that sleep in which the dreadful hand of death was to strangle him, I had hung over him a full ten minutes, lost in a glowing fancy of his father's delight when he should look upon the canny little face, and trace in it his own and the features of the girl whom he loved more than he loved his own life—one moment, I say, I was proud and happy beyond words in these musings, and the next my child was gone, my heart was bleeding, there seemed to be no light left in the world, and, instead of the old buoyant yearning for my husband's return, I looked forward to his arrival with a kind of dread, as if it were through my fault that our darling had died, and as if his love would hold me accountable for bringing him to a grave instead of to a cradle.

My father's grief at the beginning was bitter indeed, but he was too old a man to mourn long; the deaths of those he loved or knew were only as milestones to remind him that his terminus was not far off; and this was a consideration to temper his grief for the dead as though God's voice had spoken to him.

On the evening before the funeral he came to me as I stood looking, more like a stone figure than a breathing woman, at my beautiful darling as he he lay in his coffin. I had tried to pray, but could not. I could only stand and look, without a tear in my eyes, upon the restful face softly pillowed, with the golden hair shining upon the little head. My father came to me, I say, and took my hand, and stood looking too; but I never moved.

"Jessie, dearest child," said he, softly, "I would have

given my life to save yon bairn. The merciful God whose light is upon his little face knows it. But now that he is gone I would not have him back. He lies there safe. We know where he is, Jessie ; we shall always know while life is with us. Think what he is spared by leaving this world a child. Sin cannot touch him ; such grief as ye are feeling, my lass, can never come near him ; there will be no thankless toil for him, no disappointments, no perils ; no flying years which make men old before they feel they have lived, and which leave naught astern of them but a desolate sea, with here and there a bit of the wreck of some cherished hope mournfully tossing, and ahead of them a horizon full of the darkness of the coming night. Jessie, call up your heart and think a bit of what life means, and then look at yon bonnie sleeper, and ask yourself if ye would have him awakened ?"

He kissed me, and his kiss and tenderness set me crying as if my heart would break, and he led me away. His words went against the grain of my grief then; they fell like ice upon me, who was yearning for my lost one. Yet I have lived to know he spoke the truth, insomuch that though after twenty years I cannot think of my little one without dim eyes, yet if by speaking I could bring him from his grave to bless and love me, I would not say the words, but rather would give thanks to God for taking him to himself in the dewy, innocent hours of his life, and for making him an angel instead of suffering him to be a man.

CHAPTER XIII.

ELSWICK CEMETERY.

THIS time Richard was a week behind the date he had hoped to return by. The first mingled emotion of dread of and eagerness for his arrival, that possessed me when baby died, had been replaced by a passionate longing to have him with me, that he might share my sorrow and comfort me. When no letter came on the day I expected to receive one, I grew anxious, and as day after day the postman went by without ringing our bell, my anxiety grew insupportable. But on a Friday—making it six days past the date he had named—there came a letter from Sunderland, saying he would be with me next night.

Then again the old dread, if I may so term a sense I could not clearly define, seized me. Richard could not know that baby was dead; nay, I was not even sure that he had received the letter I sent him announcing our darling's birth. I now earnestly hoped that letter had never reached him, for in that case, whatever his hopes might lead him to suppose, he would have no fixed idea of there being a little one at home to greet him, and so the news of baby's death could not grieve and disappoint him as it would had he dwelt throughout his homeward voyage on the happiness in store for him.

"Jessie," said father to me on that Saturday on which Richard was coming, "d'ye mean to meet your husband in that crape?"

"Yes, father," I answered. "He would not like to find me in any other dress when he heard of our loss."

"Well, ye know best," said he, with the soothing tenderness of manner and voice he always addressed me with now. "But I hope to live to see the day when those black clothes'll go out of fashion. Death's made a deal more cruel than it need be by our custom of dealing with it. If I had my way I'd send all the mutes in the country to sea, and order all those objects called hearses, with their plumes nodding atop like scarecrows, meant to frighten respectable people out of the streets, to be converted into bathing-machines. I don't know, I'm sure," said he, lying back in his chair and looking up at the ceiling, "where we could have got such notions as mutes and hearses from. I haven't much acquaintance with the ancient Jews and Greeks, but I'd be willing to bet a pound or two that our hat-scarfs and gloves, and hired mourning countenances, didn't come from them. If they *did*, all I can say is, those people deserve to be the forefathers of the folks who now call themselves by their names."

He went on talking in this way, while I sat near the fire, straining my ear at every sound in the street. It was November, bitterly cold even for Newcastle latitudes, and

9

a strong wind was blowing, but this—Richard being ashore and safe—I took no notice of. It was two years and a few days since mother died, and getting on for seventeen months since I was married, and I could not help feeling with pain, as I now sat waiting for my husband's coming, how little I had seen of him during those seventeen months, and how being a sailor's wife was very nearly as bad as being a widow or a divorced woman.

Shortly after seven o'clock the door-bell rang, and in a minute I was in Richard's arms, weeping with uncontrollable emotion, and unable to speak. Resolved as I had been to school myself, to give him the welcome he would like, the struggle was of no use. The moment I saw him I thought of our baby, and broke down, crying grievously, and speechless.

We stood in the passage, and he was silent a moment or two, proving his surprise at my grief, and by that surprise his ignorance of the cause of it.

"Bring her in, Dick; bring her in;" my father called out. "Give her her way for a spell; she'll be the better for it."

My husband obeyed, still wondering, and, putting his arm into mine, led me into the parlor, too much concerned and surprised even to shake hands with father. He seated himself on the sofa, holding me close to him.

"What is it, Jessie?" said he. "What bad news have you had, my darling? What friend have you lost?" apparently noticing my deep mourning for the first time.

"Did ye get no letter from her at Pensacola?" asked my father, in a tremulous voice.

"One," answered Richard; "but there was no bad news in it."

"Nothing to tell ye that your wife was a mother, Dick?" continued father.

"No," replied my husband, quickly, and then stopping short and drawing me more closely to him, as though he now guessed all that could be told.

I raised my head from his shoulder and looked at him.

"I knew there was a little one to come," said he.

"He's come and he's gone, Dick," exclaimed my father,

solemnly. "God loved him too well to let him bide, even for thee, my lad. It's Jessie's grief. But her heart'll mend now that she has ye to talk to."

And, getting up, he pretended to seek for something, peering first here and then there, and finally left the room, that my husband and I might be alone.

If ever I had dreaded telling Richard of our loss, I had now no other sense of that fear than to reproach myself for having felt it. It soothed me unspeakably to pour out my heart to him as I sat nestling at his side, earnestly and tenderly watched by his loving eyes. For, in spite of my father's touching, simple, consoling sympathy, I had felt myself alone with my grief. There was only one person in the whole wide world who could truly share it, and he had been away when my anguish was greatest.

True it is that life draws a circle round husband and wife, in which the dearest and fondest relative makes but an intruder. The lawyers may call marriage a civil contract if they like; but for my part, though born and bred a Protestant, I hold that Church right which considers it a sacrament, and believe that no woman who has lost a child, and laid her head upon her husband's breast to weep there, but thinks of marriage as a covenant as sacred as the Divine love that appointed it for us.

I could not expect that Richard should feel as I did. He had never seen our darling, never beheld his beauty, nor watched, as I had, the gradual unfolding of the little bud whose bloom and promise had been nipped by the cold frost of death. Yet there was deep disappointment in his face, and such a sorrow as must arise in the heart of a man who could see with his soul's eye the love that had come and vanished in his absence, that had been as real as life and beauty could make it, and yet no more than a dream to him either.

However, before my father joined us, I had told him the story, had dried my eyes, and was talking to him about himself and his voyage, and smiling as he kissed me and told me to remember that we were together again.

"Yes," said I, "and we will remain together. You must take me with you next time. I am so lonely now— even with dear father—that it would break my heart to say good-bye .to you again, and to remain childless and widowed as I have been."

As I. said this my father came in. I believe he overheard the closing sentence, but he said nothing about it until much later on, when, the supper-things being removed, and we being gathered round the fire, which father had built up until it not only looked like a furnace but roared like one, he said,

"Dick, if ye have a mind to carry Jess with ye to sea next voyage, she shall go."

"Well, captain," answered Richard, "you know I have little heart to take her from you, and leave you alone in the old home. But.she is very down-spirited. Her health is not as it might be. I believe a few months at sea would make her hearty again; and as for me, there'll be no happier man afloat when I get her fairly aboard with me."

"What do ye say, Jess?" asked my father.

"If you can do without me, father," I replied, "I should like to be with my husband."

"Be it so, then," said he. "We'll have no more palaver. The thing's settled. There's no use in your stopping at home if your heart's abroad, and, as Dick says, ye want a change. Besides, the pleasure of being with him'll be meat and drink to your spirits. Where are ye bound next, Dick?"

"I sha'n't know till next week," answered Richard. "I heard this morning that the *Phantasy* is promised to Captain Gardner, and that there's a chance of my getting command of a pretty little clipper bark that was launched on the Wear not long ago by Laing. If so, my port will be Sierra Leone."

My father shook his head.

"The white man's grave, Dick."

"The climate's bad, I admit, captain, but we're not going to live there."

"Why, that's very true," said my father. "And I don't know, when all's said and done, whether it's worse than the West Indies, or the parts ye're fresh from. If ye go to Sierra Leone, Jess, ye'll have to carry a few dictionaries with ye. I hear there's nigh threescore languages spoken in Freetown alone. What's the name of the bark, Dick?"

"The *Aurora*."

"Another fancy name," exclaimed my father, again shaking his head. "Why don't they leave poetry to the navy folk, and stick to the old *Susannahs* and *Mary Anns* and *Jemimas* of my day? *Aurora!* How's a plain, able seaman to answer a hail with such a mouthful as that behind his teeth? I suppose she'll be having good cabin accommodation?"

"Sure," answered Richard.

"Wood or iron, Dick?"

"Wood."

"That's a good job," said my father, lighting a pipe and looking pleased. "Wood was meant by Providence to swim, iron to go to the bottom. If ye'd have said iron, I don't know whether that and Sierra Leone put together wouldn't have set me against Jessie's going."

"And what will you do, father?" said I, timidly, feeling almost conscience-stricken by the gladness his resolution to let me go gave me.

"Do?" he replied. "Well, it'll have to be a break-up. Another shifting job, and the last one, I hope, in this world. I'll go along to Shields and get ready a home for ye to settle down in when Dick and you have had enough of salt water."

He looked slowly round the room, letting his eyes linger, with a wistful expression in them, on the old curiosities which littered the side-tables and sideboard and chimney-piece.

"It'll be a bit of a wrench," he continued, "but it'll soon be over."

"Why do you wish to leave?" said I. "It would make me happy to feel as we sailed home that we were returning to this old house."

"Think a bit, Jess, and the answer'll come to ye. Here mother died. Here our little bairn died. Here ye were born, my lass, and here ye've lived all your life. Fancy me coming home and sitting alone in this room, hearing nothing but the wind, and the clock ticking, and the ashes dropping out of yon grate? D'ye think I could bear it, with all the past standing like a picture before me? No, no," said he, coughing to clear a sudden huskiness out of his voice; "when you and Dick go, I go. I'm not a fanciful man, but there'd come ghosts to this house after ye were gone that would keep me fretting as no wise heart will ever let itself fret. But don't ye mind about that," he exclaimed, with a sudden burst of forced cheerfulness; "I shall be right enough. You two take care of yourselves, and come back home safe. That's all ye need attend to."

Well, as you may suppose, it depressed me sadly to hear him talk like this. But then I also remembered that he had been a good deal away from me, sometimes never seeing me from breakfast to supper-time for days together, and that therefore he would not miss me to the extent he imagined; also that at Shields he would have plenty of congenial society to keep him interested and amused. Besides, for whom was I going to leave him? I should little have deserved the name of wife had I hesitated between him and my husband.

Next day being Sunday, we three went to church, and after service Richard and I walked to Elswick Cemetery to visit our baby's grave. That spacious burial-ground is tolerably well filled now; monumental stones stand thick under the shadows of the trees; and down the breezy open slopes—from whose summit you survey the Durham hills, with the Tyne at bottom winding its silver coil towards Blaydon and Newburn, and Wylam, immortalized in English story as the birthplace of George Stephenson—the soil heaves in billows with the furrows of innumerable graves. But in those days the cemetery was little more than garden-land, with here and there a grassy hillock, or the gleam of white stone amid the shady recesses, to denote its character.

Our darling's resting-place was marked by a little cross, with that sweet sentence, "Jesus called a little child unto him," carved on the steps. It was a bitter cold day; the northeast wind howled through the valley of the Tyne, and the flying sunshine flashed and faded upon the hills as the dark bodies of vapor swept across the sky. When my husband came to the spot where our baby lay, he stood looking a while without speaking, touched to the heart by the littleness of the grave and the sight of his and my name upon the cross, and the age of the lost one—"Five months and one week." He then took off his hat, and knelt down and said a prayer.

It would have moved a heart of flint to see this sailor, with his hair tossing to the wind, his hands clasped, his eyes fixed on the little cross, praying at the resting-place of his child whom he had never seen, whom he loved, yet could only think of as a spirit. Never did death appear to me so great a mystery and miracle as at that time.

CHAPTER XIV.

THE "AURORA."

HOWEVER, a change was now about to come, and the thoughts of it, coupled with the feeling that I should not again be separated from my husband, greatly helped my spirits. The dream of my childhood was to be realized at last; I was not only the wife of a sailor, but I was to live with him in a ship, traverse with him that measureless deep which ever since I could remember had wooed me with the voice of a magician, and behold some of those shining lands, those glorious blue waters, those rich azure tropical heavens, of which the fancy had haunted me like a dream of things seen in another state of life.

My father, having made up his mind to my going, viewed my departure with more spirit and firmness than I had dared to hope in him. He interested himself to secure Richard's appointment to the *Aurora*, and knowing the owners—indeed, having some risks with them—he easily and speedily obtained his end, and within a fortnight of my husband's return the command of the new bark was given him.

The date of sailing was fixed for the 1st of February, "a cold month for the North Sea and Channel," said Richard to me; "but once clear of the Land's End, Jess, every hour will carry us nearer the sun;" so that I had plenty of time to make all necessary provision for the

voyage, which I learned was to occupy a longer period
than I had supposed, for after discharging at Sierra Leone
we were to proceed, either with a freight or in ballast—I
cannot tell which, for one forgets more important things
than that in twenty years—to Cape Town, there to load a
cargo of some kind for home.

The bustle and business of making ready for a journey
helped greatly to draw my thoughts away from my recent
sorrow, and also prevented me from dwelling upon my
approaching separation from my father. He advised me
in my outfit, made purchases for me, and brought such an
experience to bear upon my personal wants as Richard
had no notion of.

A week before I sailed I went down with him and my
husband to where the *Aurora* was lying, to look at her
and inspect the cabin. She was alongside a coal-staith,
one of the most unpicturesque of inventions, and what
with that and her grimy surroundings, the bitter cold,
gray, cheerless day, the streaming, turbid river, and the
smoke-colored atmosphere, which rolled away in folds before the wind, my first impression, as we came upon her,
and Richard pointed her out, was anything but pleasing.

But I was undeceived when I got aboard, for then I had
the whole hull, so to speak, before me, and, raising my
eyes, could behold the beautiful, delicate fabric of spars
and rigging soaring into the leaden heavens, and re-echo-
ing in a continuous shrilling noise the voice of the freezing blast as it swept through the complicated tracery.
As I have said, she was a brand-new vessel, small indeed,
of within four hundred tons registered burden, as nearly
as I can remember, but as pretty a model as was ever
launched. She was painted black, with a narrow white
line running along her sides like a silver ribbon; her quarters were decorated with gilt scrolls; the copper on her
bottom, being new, shone like dull gold; her figure-head
represented a woman with a star upon her forehead, the
right hand grasping a torch ; but the beauty of this de-
sign could only be appreciated by noting the lovely curve
of the cutwater, and the stately run of the bowsprit and
jibboom shooting far in advance of the marble-like figure,
as though some giant were pointing out the road with a

colossal spear to the torch-bearer, who gazed steadfastly ahead.

We are building nowadays such hideous vessels—drain-pipes, as I have heard them called—shapeless metal fabrics, with huge up-and-down bows, small pole-masts, funnels close against the taffrail, and a broadside view as elegant as the back of a camel, that the mind instinctively recurs to the yacht-like and handsome models of twenty and thirty years ago. The *Aurora* was a real specimen of the shipbuilding taste of that age. She was the work of a firm who have furnished the merchant service with some of the handsomest wooden vessels which ever flew the red ensign.

"Come here, Jessie," said Richard, and he took me to the wheel; "now you see her," said he, looking at me to see what I thought.

From this point I commanded her full length, and though her decks were littered with what sailors call raffle, and the yards were braced different ways, while the surroundings, such as the coal-staith, the sullen weather, the gloomy river, and the perspective of the Tyneside prospect—never more unlovely than on a dark, wintry, smoke-discolored day—were all so many defraudments of her beauty, yet even I, bringing but a woman's eyes to her, could behold such points of honest, tasteful workman-ship, such harmony of proportion, such combination of strength and delicacy of bulwarks, spars, deck-fittings, and the like, as filled me with admiration, and I could not help exclaiming, "Oh, Richard, she is just a little sea-home to dream of! With all sail set and under a blue sky, what a lovely sight she will be!"

My father, who had not seen her before, was delighted with her. He peered into things no landsman would dream of noting, and accompanied his inspection with a running commentary of appreciative criticism.

"Finer sticks I never saw," he exclaimed, looking aloft. "There's nothing like bright masts for appearance—ay, and for wear. Give me varnish afore paint. Paint, I al-ways say, rots; the toughest fibre can't stand it, and it'll eat into oak itself like salt-water worms. Ye've got a spread of topsails there, my lad, that should make you fit

to take a comet in tow on a bowline. Ye'll need to stay
the mizzen-topmast forward a trifle; the lean of the lower
mast'll look the better for it. Jacob's ladders, I see.
Well, the boys should be grateful. Better them than topgallant ratlines, though I'm for shinning, and leaving
everything light and airy from the cross-trees. I'd never
fit those ladders under a thousand ton. I'm glad they've
given her the old-fashioned chains. The more spread the
better hold, say I. They're losing sight of the sensible
notions, and the less beam they allow, the further they
bring their dead-eyes inboard. That's why ye nowadays
hear of so many masts going over the side. A good roll
and away they go, like a man's pipe out of his mouth when
he tumbles down. Dick, I like your boats. As Jess is
going along, see that ye keep 'em all ready for getting
overboard. Don't be ashamed of having tackles ready for
the long-boat, and if your spare booms won't sit atop of
the galley, then lash 'em alongside ; don't build in your
long-boat. She's meant to save life when wanted, not to
be turned into a forepeak and lazarette in one."

Considering the *Aurora* was to be my home for I could
not tell how many months, it was very reasonable that I
should examine her closely, and follow all that my father
said about her with attention. She was flush-deck : that
is—for I must remember I am not writing wholly for sailors — her decks were a level sweep fore and aft, which
made her look longer than she really was. The little galley just abaft the foremast, the long-boat, and the lower
masts, alone obstructed the view. Some of her deck-fittings might have embellished the deck of a yacht. The
harness cask, for instance (where the salt meat for the
crew would be kept at sea), was girdled with bright brass
hoops ; the belaying-pins for the mizzen rigging were
brass ; the wheel was richly carved ; the cabin skylight
and companion looked to be of dark, polished mahogany;
a sand-white grating abaft the wheel hid the tiller-chains;
and each cathead was decorated with a gilt disk and rays
representing the sun.

Of course I should not have noticed these points but for
my father, who called them out, as if he read from a catalogue, as he went here and there, or hung over the fore-

castle rail. Though my knowledge of ships was tolerably
minute for a woman, it would scarcely embrace such features as these. But their being pointed out to me made
me the prouder of my new home, and as I stood a moment
at the companion before descending, and looked up at the
tapering heights which soared overhead, I remember feeling a longing for the time when I should see the white
canvas gleaming silent and full against the ocean heaven,
and hear the moan of the foam pouring from the knife-like
stem, and hissing and seething away astern upon the leaping and sparkling waters of the glorious deep.

The cabin was a small square compartment containing
five berths, one of which was tolerably large—occupying,
indeed, the whole breadth of the vessel under the wheel—
while it communicated by means of a door in the bulkhead with a smaller berth on the starboard or right-hand
side. The big berth was to be ours, and the little one
next it at our disposal to use as a box-room or dressing-
room.

"There are two drawbacks," said Richard. "First,
you'll feel the pitching here almost as severely as if you
were in the forecastle; and, secondly, you will find the
clank of the wheel-chains and the jar of the rudder-head
bothersome; but you'll soon get used to the noises, while
as to the pitching, you're too good a sailor, Jess, to take
notice of any frisking the *Aurora* may have a mind to
favor us with."

"Take notice of the frisking, d'ye say, Dick?" cried my
father, laughing. "Man alive! if the lads aren't smart,
you'll find her at the yardarm showing 'em how to pass
the earings! And keep her clear of marlinspikes and
dangerous tools of that kind, for if there's any sogering
done aloft, ye'll have her after the lubber, though he
should be shifting the dog-vane, and your crew'll not be
so numerous that you can afford to let your wife prick
'em one by one overboard from the mastheads."

I smiled as he shook his head and wagged his forefinger at me, as though I were veritably the terrible and
audacious nautical woman he made me out to be.

"Who will sleep there?" said I to Richard, pointing to
the berth next ours on the port side.

"The mate, Mr. Roger Heron," he replied.

"D'ye carry a second mate, Dick?" inquired my father.

"Second mate and carpenter," he replied. "More carpenter than second mate, captain, I expect; but, if a good seaman, better than either. He sleeps abaft the galley. There being no use for these two spare berths, I've given them to the steward, one to sleep in, and the other for his forks and plates."

"And a very good arrangement, too, seeing that ye'll have a lady passenger aboard who'll want looking after," said my father, prying about and examining the interior of our berth minutely, and evidently quite satisfied with all he saw.

After lingering here some twenty minutes, we returned on deck and went ashore; but even there my father stood running his eye over the vessel, scanning her narrowly aloft, walking to a place where he could see her "run," and taking note of every detail, from her bends to the royal-masthead, before we could draw him away. And then, coming over to where we waited, he drew a deep breath, and said:

"She'll do. She's proper to look at, and fit to remember and talk of. Jess, in your husband's hands she'll make ye as safe a home as ever ye found in the old parlor and bedroom. Don't ill-use her, Dick; don't drive her when she's willing to go. It seems a sin that such a hull should be made a coal-hole of; but ye can show your remorse by letting her have no more to carry than she's fit to hold. She'll look like a summer butterfly in fine weather on the water. And had I the pick of a whole year's shipping in this river—ay, and ye may chuck the Sunderland docks in too—there's ne'er a craft among the whole of 'em that I'd choose before the little sea-home ye've given to your wife to take her first voyage in with ye, Dick."

CHAPTER XV.

AT SEA.

THE day came at last when I was on board the *Aurora* for good. My luggage was in the cabin, I had said good-bye to father, and been held in his embrace until it seemed as if he would never let me go, and already the little bark, in tow of a tug, was courtesying upon the deep, whose breast in many latitudes was to rock me, as I supposed, for some long months before I should again set eyes on that brown and greenish coast that ran north and south upon our quarter as we followed in the wake of the steamer.

I stood leaning over the side, looking at the Tynemouth coast and light-house, and the pall of smoke that overhung Shields, and the line of cliff trending away past Marsdon Bay and looming vaguely in the haze. Glad and proud as I was to be with my husband, almost triumphant, too, in spirits, if I may say so, at this complete realization of my old dream, yet as I stood gazing I could not fight against the temporary depression that had followed my leave-taking of dear old father. I thought of him in his loneliness. Then, too, the sight of Tynemouth, and the summit of the Lawe in front of South Shields, revived the memory of that dreadful day of storm when mother and I watched father's brig making for the Tyne, and of the next morning, when I followed father to his bedroom and found mother dead there.

The wind was east, moderately fresh and bitterly cold ; the sea was ash-colored, and lively with little surges which poured in quick play past us as the bark swung over them under the strain of the great hawser. It was a true winter day, with a gathering thickness over the sea-line, and a pale sun, a blotch of yellow light, shapeless, in a dim and misty blue, across which a few steam-like clouds were rolling, and every fathom we measured

made the coast on our quarter and over our stern dimmer
and fainter in the grayish haze whose folds deepened as
we drew away.

The crew were standing about the forecastle waiting
for orders to make sail, and my husband and the mate
were pacing the weather side of the quarter-deck with
the regular pendulum step of sailors, every now and again
taking a look at the weather and then a glance up aloft.
I had already been introduced to the mate, whose name,
as I have said, was Roger Heron. He was the only man
on board introducible to me in the conventional sense, the
person next him in station being the ship's carpenter, a
man styled second mate in order to furnish him with an
excuse to stand his watches and relieve Mr. Heron.

When I bowed to the mate, on my husband making us
acquainted in the cabin, I thought that he was not a man
I should much like. He no more came up to my idea of
a seafaring man in appearance than an attorney's clerk
would. He was of a disagreeably pale complexion; there
was not an atom of *weather* in his face ; anybody might
suppose that he had lived in a cellar and worked by gas-
light all his life, instead of having confronted those suns
and storms which toughen the skin and bronze the cheeks.
His beard and mustache were a light red, his eyes a pale
blue and without steadfastness of gaze ; his hands, throat,
and neck were so attenuated as to resemble a consumptive person's ; there was not a single point in his appearance that gave me the least hint of that sort of heartiness
which distinguishes the real salt. His very dress was unsailorly, consisting of yellowish trousers, cutaway coat,
and a fragment of shirt - collar showing over a spotted
neckcloth. I thought, as I watched him and Richard
pacing the deck, that, if he was a sailor, the old traditions
which give the seafaring qualities to men like my husband and father—broad-shouldered, daring-faced fellows,
with a regular deep-sea swing in their walk, eyes full of
alertness, men who could *look* their calling without masquerading as Jack Tars in the least degree — were all
false.

By the time the land had vanished in the haze, which
had narrowed the horizon to within a few miles, Mr.

Heron left my husband, and bawled out some orders in a sharp voice. In an instant the crew were in commotion. Coils of rope were flung down, and presently might be heard the hoarse, peculiar notes of sailors hauling upon the running-gear, mingled with the flapping of canvas as jibs and staysails mounted the stays. Some of the hands then trotted aloft to loose the topsails (those were the days of single topsail yards); and while they were casting the gaskets adrift, tossing up the foot-ropes as they overhung the yards, the tug let fall our tow-rope, which was laid hold of by four or five of the crew, the cook and the steward (idlers, as they are rather ironically called, because they work all day and have all "night in," as Jack says) lending a hand to drag the ponderous hawser over the forecastle head.

I looked at the tug as she swept round and headed for the Tyne. She was a small, clinker-built boat, with thin, naked paddle-wheels, and a funnel like a pipe-stem; her skipper stood on the bridge, and her men hung over the rail watching us. She was the last link to connect me with home. As she swept past, the fellows aboard her waved their hands and called farewells to our crew, the foam roared out from under the paddle-boxes, and left a long line of water as white as milk in her wake, and the little fabric pitched and yerked at the swift, snow-crested seas which broke away from her bows in wild showers of spray, in which the misty, wintry sunlight kindled patches of radiance as many-tinted as a rainbow.

I watched her until she became a shapeless blotch upon the haze, and was then awakened from my thoughts by my husband putting his hand upon my arm.

"Have you given her your heart to carry back with her to the canny town, Jess?" said he, smiling.

"If you had been left behind I should say yes," I replied.

"Are you sorry our voyage has begun?" he asked.

"Sorry!" I exclaimed.

"No, no," said he, "you are not sorry. We are together, and I thank God for it. But I must see what those fellows are about," and he crossed the deck.

The vessel was full of business, the crew running about,

the mate in the waist and the carpenter on the forecastle
vociferating orders, fellows up aloft bawling down to
sheet home, and all hands hard at work. There is no
scene more confusing to a landsman than that of the crew
of a merchantman making sail upon their vessel. All
seems uproar and distraction, shouts below and above,
choruses rising in all parts, the decks littered with ropes,
the vessel heeling over, and the canvas raising a low thunder as it shakes its folds to the wind. To me, however,
who could witness to a large extent the order prevailing
amid the apparent confusion, and understand a great
number of the terms cried out by my husband and the
mate, the picture was full of color, interest, and excitement. Yard after yard was mast-headed, halliards belayed, tacks boarded, all hands tailing on to a rattling
chorus, sheets hauled aft, braces hauled taut, until the vessel was bending before the breeze under canvas as high
as her main-topgallant-sail. But she had now all the
cloths she needed, and presently the men had cleared up
and coiled the ropes away over the belaying-pins.

The bark was running swiftly across the water, a delightful quietness taking the place of the songs and the
shouts ; a fellow aft at the wheel giving the spokes a
turn now and again to meet the swing of the vessel, and
little more to be heard than the hissing and pouring noise
of water under the bows, and the smothered booming of
the breeze in the white and spacious concavities overhead, and the occasional creaking of the spars as the
under-run of the seas brought the bark leaning to windward. The haze completely obscured the coast, and we
might have been a thousand miles at sea.

I had been somewhat afraid that I should suffer from
nausea, for it was many years since I had been upon the
sea, and though when I had gone on those early voyages
with my father I was as little troubled with sickness as
he, I could not be sure that I should enjoy the same freedom this time. To test myself I went and stood right
aft, against the grating behind the wheel, where the
motion of the vessel would be most strongly felt, but, to
my great satisfaction, found that I was not one jot more
inconvenienced there than in any other part of the bark,

and that I was as free from all qualms as if I stood upon dry ground.

"Here's the *Aurora* under sail at last, Jess," said Richard, coming up to me. "What do you think of her? I've been watching you take her in, from the truck to the main-hatch, as if you were not only her skipper, but her builder and owner."

"You're quite mistaken," I answered. "Instead of admiring your bark, I've been waiting to see if I'm to be sea-sick."

"You!" he exclaimed, with a hearty laugh. "Why, just run below and take a peep at yourself in the looking-glass. Sea-sick! When a girl suffers from that 'long-shore complaint she surely has not rosy cheeks and bright eyes, nor talks and smiles as you do, dear. But what do you think of the little hooker, Jess?" and he cast his eyes proudly along the sweep of clean deck beautifully defined by the run and curve of the bulwarks, and then up aloft at the square, taut, handsomely cut spaces of canvas towering into the vague blue, with the main-royal-yard making a black line for an apex on which the furled sail lay like a fall of snow.

I praised her with the admiration I felt. "And is she not a fast sailer, Richard?"

"Ay," he answered, "a real Baltimore clipper. With the wind a single point free, and with nothing above a main-topgallant-sail on her, she's doing seven and a half knots as fairly as if she were driven by a propeller. See the men forward there, looking over the side. They don't want a book to explain the meaning of that white race"—pointing under the arching foot of the mainsail at the foam that was churned up and flung out by the passage of the vessel.

He was determined I should admire her as he did, and told me not to be afraid, but to catch hold of his hand and lean over the weather-rail, and look at the vessel's hull as it swept through the gray and foaming waters. It needs a sailor to show you how to admire a ship. He could not have posted me better, for, propped up and held by him, I overhung the rail, where I could see the glossy side of the bark as far forward as the fore-chains, with a

10

space of her bright, gold-like copper brought up out of the water by the inclination of the vessel, its refulgent surface contrasting with glorious effect with the creaming swirl of the froth that swept past in a giddy sparkle and convulsion of leaping surges, while insensibly my eye, wandering from the symmetrical, eager, bounding shape of the hull, from which every now and again the head of a sea would break away in a smoking rain of crystal particles, followed the ebony lines of the shrouds and backstays to the yellow, leaning masts, in which the pallid sunshine trembled in points of fire, until my gaze rested upon the swollen, distended cloths doing their work as steadily as shapes of carven marble.

"Beautiful!" I exclaimed, feeling my face flushed with the magic and spirit of the windy, speeding, rushing scene, and by the steady pouring of the winter breeze. "Now help me down, Richard."

And down I came, saying that I only wished father were here to see it with me.

"After forty-seven years, he'd tell you he had seen it once or twice too often," replied Richard, laughing. Indeed, my husband was always laughing; there never was a lighter-hearted man. "And now, Jess, what do you say to going below and getting your cabin shipshape? If you want any help, call the steward. I must keep on deck."

"What time do we dine, Richard?"

"What! are you hungry? Come, your father would be glad to hear that," said he, looking at his watch. "You have another hour yet. There'll be no dinner till half-past one."

Although the deck had a strong slope, and the dance of the bark was exceedingly lively—for such sea as there was ran at her weather-bow—I found I could keep my legs with the utmost ease, and refused the hand that Richard extended to help me to the companion. This was my first visit below since we had quitted the Tyne, and I stood awhile at the bottom of the steps, holding on to the brass handrail, and looking at the cabin that was to answer, in a sense, to the old parlor at home. The doors lay over at angles, intersected by the swinging trays; there was much noise of creaking bulkheads, and even through the closed skylights I could hear the voice of the wind pouring out of the hollow of the great spanker, that, viewed through the skylight glass, resembled a huge white fog-bank against the sky.

My husband, unknown to me, had had a couple of long boxes fitted up, one on either side the skylight, full of shrubs and ferns, together with two globes of gold and silver fish; and, simple as these additions were to the furniture of the cabin, I cannot express how greatly they brightened it, and qualified the severity of the plain, strong bulkheads, and the solid deck overhead pierced by the mizzen-mast (that vanished, as it seemed, through the carpet) and the square table, and the row of hair-cushioned lockers.

The experiences of most women who make a voyage include a stewardess, or, at least, some person of their own sex to wait upon them. I was without that luxury, but I did not miss it nor want it. I was very well able to make my bed, to fill the locker with the dresses and warm clothing I immediately required, and to attend to my wants to my own complete satisfaction. I found in the spare berth next to ours some hanging shelves full of books, an arm-chair and table, more ferns, a small harmonium, and various other things, all due to my husband's anxiety that I should be comfortable.

Now, I could not help smiling when I saw that harmonium. I was then, and still am, ignorant of music, in spite of my having learned the piano long enough at school to ruin the teacher's temper for life. I liked it, but had no ear for it, was never able to sing in time, nor to remember more than a few easy airs like "Weel may the Keel Row," and "Annie Laurie." I was sorry Richard had not known this, as it would have saved him the expense, poor fellow —and I say "poor fellow," for he had only a mate's savings at that time to come upon—of spending twelve or fourteen pounds upon what was as useless to me as a Jew's-harp or a bagpipe. I was not ashamed of my deficiency. If he was ignorant of it, it was because the subject had never come up between us. Could I perform on a fiddle, I believe I should boast of it, for a fiddle is a difficult thing. But everybody can play the piano. It is ridiculous to go on calling it an accomplishment. It has long passed that point, and is now high among the nuisances. I have heard the jingling in cottages whose tenants pay half a crown a week for rent, and air their linen out of their bedroom windows; and will any one doubt, when missis leaves the house, that poor little slatternly Sall or Sukey of the kitchen does not steal up-stairs from her friends the black beetles, and, sitting down to the yellow keys in the front drawing-room, regale her soul with operatic selections?

I spent the hour before dinner in the cabin, or sleeping-berth, as I should call it, to distinguish it from the cabin, making the little place comfortable for myself and Richard. The poorness of spirits with which I had come away from saying good-bye to father was fast yielding to the happiness I felt at being with my husband, and at sea with him, and to the sense of freedom and buoyancy of pulse and brain excited by the sweeping wind and the gay and rushing dance of the bark along the water.

Dinner was nearly ready by the time I had done my work, and while I stood brushing my hair in front of a little swinging glass, courtesying and bobbing in order to see myself, for the action of the vessel that swung the mirror one way forced me another way, my husband came in.

He stood watching me dodge the glass, and laughing at me. "But how well you keep your feet!" said he. "You poise yourself upon this tumblification as if you had wings."

"You talk," said I, "as if you expected to find me rolling about on the deck, helpless as a bucket, and moaning for the steward. If I were a sufferer in that way, my dear, you would not catch me here, much as I love you."

"Have you looked into that spare berth there?" said he.

"Yes," I answered, "and have seen the books, and the table, and the arm-chair, and the little harmonium."

"And what do you think of the ferns and the fish in the cabin?" he asked. "Don't they make it more cheerful for the shore-going look they give it?"

"Certainly they do," I replied. "But what made you buy the harmonium?"

"Why, for you to play on," said he. "A piano would have bunged the berth up, and there's no room for one in the cabin. A harmonium is not so cheerful an instrument as a piano, I admit—I always keep on fancying it's Sunday when I hear one played; but it's better than a concertina."

"But where's the music?" said I. "*I* have none, you know."

"Music!" cried he. "Dash my buttons! I never thought of that. Can't you play by ear, Jess?"

"Not a note," I answered.

"Well, well," said he, looking very rueful. "What an ass I must be, to be sure, not to have thought of bringing a bale of music along with us! Here have I been counting upon sitting and listening to your playing when it's Heron's watch on deck, and now I find, through my blunder-headedness, that it would be all the same if that old organ there had no works at all inside it. But never mind," said he, looking as if he would console me; "I dare say we shall make shift to come across some odds and ends of music at Sierra Leone, enough to keep us going till we get to Cape Town, where they're more civilized."

"Come, Richard," said I, "I'll not deceive you any longer. If all the music that was ever written was on board, I could make nothing of it. I can't play a note."

"Can't you, indeed, Jess?" said he, looking half pleased and half surprised.

"Not half a note. I've heard of A sharp and B flat, and C something else, but it would take me all the way from here to Sierra Leone and back again to find them out, and then I dare say I should be pointing to the wrong keys."

"Why, then," said he, bursting into a laugh, and catching me round the waist, "I'm not an ass, after all, for not having shipped any music. But, Jess, since the instrument's there, you might as well turn to and make out a tune—grope at it until you have it right—just to astonish your father when you return. You'll be able then to boast that there's no finishing school in the world equal to the sea. Only mind, when you do sit down to that

hurdy-gurdy, how you work it.   The shopman, when I
asked him to explain the operation, cautioned me against
working the bellows without letting the steam blow off
by pulling out those hat-peg looking gilguys; otherwise,
said he, 'thor may coom what th' I-talians caal a boost-up,
maistor.' "

At this moment the steward knocked at the door to tell
us that dinner was ready.   I followed Richard, and found
the cabin looking very hospitable, with a white cloth upon
the table, black-handled knives and forks, strong tumblers,
plates of the old pattern (little Chinamen with their heads
on one side, crossing bridges, etc.), fiddles, as they are
called, to save the crockery from tumbling off the table,
and a smoking joint of roast beef, with vegetables.   The
presence of the steward to wait upon us gave quite a
grandeur to this little repast.   However, I was not sorry
to find that he only loitered to take the cover off the beef,
which done, he went up the companion-ladder, "to see
after the pudding, Jessie, in the galley," said Richard.

"When does Mr. Heron dine?" said I.

"After us—that is, when I go on deck to relieve him,
for I can't trust the carpenter alone until we are clear of
the Scillies," he answered.   "On the high seas it will be
turn and turn about, one day with us, the next day after
us.   What do you think of him?"

"I can hardly say.   I know nothing of him yet," said I.
"Is he a good seaman?"

"You mean by that that he doesn't look like one," he
exclaimed.   "Nor does he.   By the cut of his jib he'd
pass better for a grocer's assistant than a shellback.   But
he holds a master's certificate, which counts for something,
though not much; and I don't know why he shouldn't
turn out a decent mate."

"And what sort of crew have you, Richard?"

"There again you have me, Jess.   New brooms sweep
clean, and I make no account of the first rush or two.
They and I must be shipmates a little longer before I can
answer your question.   They are all strangers to me."

We went on talking in this way about the bark, and the
men, and the voyage, and then of home, Newcastle, my
father, whereabouts in South Shields he would rent a house,

and so forth ; but all the time I was taking notice of my husband's vigilance, of his constant glances at the telltale compass that was secured to a beam over his head, of his manner of darting a look through the skylight, and the expression of close attention that came into his face at every sound upon deck. The steward arrived with the pudding.

"What's the name of it ?" said Richard, eying it narrowly.

"The cook calls it a baked dam—I mean, a baked jam roly-poly," answered the steward, a short man with bow-legs, a camlet jacket, and a sour face, decorated with a long, bright strawberry mark along the right cheek ; but as active as a monkey, and so steady with his limbs that a dish or a swinging-tray was not safer than when in his hands.

CHAPTER XVI.

THICK WEATHER.

WE had finished eating as much as we wanted of the pudding, which proved to be very good, when we heard the mate's voice hailing the forecastle sharply and loudly. My husband probably caught the words, or, if not, took in the import of the shout from the tone in which it was delivered, for he instantly sprang to his feet, seized his cap, and ran up the companion-steps.

Curious to understand the reason of the mate's loud call and my husband's hurry, I put on my jacket and hat and went on deck. The crew were running about, hauling up the mainsail, and dancing over the coils of rigging which had been flung down ; Richard, standing close to the wheel, was shouting out orders, and the mate stood on the forecastle, overlooking the sea, and shaking his fist at some object out there, while he vociferated with his other hand at the side of his mouth.

The weather had been hazy enough when I left the deck, but now a dense fog had suddenly rolled down and enveloped the sea. The bark had been thrown up into

the wind, which, though it had not freshened, had force
enough to make the sails rattle violently ; and to these
harsh and thunderous sounds were to be added the
jerky, disagreeable pitching of the vessel, that was now
almost head to sea, and the voices of the crew singing
out as they hauled, and the steam-like folds of vapor
which, by obscuring everything, introduced an element
of uncertainty, and almost of fear, into the confusion.

I stood in the companion to be out of the way, and,
looking in the direction in which the mate stood bran-
dishing his fist, I could just make out the shape or shadow
of a large ketch or keel, or of some vessel of that description, staggering upon the seas under the full pressure of
her dark sail, but obstinately steering the course which
had very nearly brought us over her.

"Why don't you shift your helm?" I heard Mr. Heron
roar out, amid an interval of silence in the singing of our
crew, with so much passion in his voice that it was as
hoarse as a raven's—a complete croak, and a very ugly
one too.

A sort of "boo, boo, boo!" whether words or laughter
I could not distinguish, came from the swiftly melting
outline upon the fog. In a few seconds the dark shape
vanished, leaving the *Aurora* head to wind, chopping furiously at the seas which came running at her out of the
thickness, all her sails aback, her way stopped, and in what
a Yankee would call a quandary.

However, there was not wind enough, fortunately, to
make the situation a critical one. By dint of letting go,
and brailing up and flattening in forward, and squaring
away aft, the bark was made to pay off.

"Get the mainsail stowed, and keep her under topsails
and foresail only until the weather clears," called out my
husband to the mate as he came aft.

These orders were repeated, and the men went aloft to
furl the canvas.

Richard looked pale and vexed. He paced the deck
close to where I stood in the companion without taking
any notice of me. The mate in the gangway gazed with
a scowling brow at the seamen on the mainyard as they

rolled up the sail and tossed the bunt to a chorus. Presently my husband called him.

"Mr. Heron!"

"Sir?"

"How long has this fog been upon us?"

"About five minutes before you came up from dinner," answered the mate.

"Was that vessel we nearly ran down in sight before this smother rolled up?"

"I saw nothing of her, sir."

"Ay, but I am asking was she in sight?"

"The lookout man spied her," answered the mate, visibly struggling with his temper, "but never reported her, believing her to be crossing our bows, and further off than she was, and that I saw her."

"What is his name?"

"James Snow."

My husband seemed to make a mental note of it, and then continued:

"But where were your eyes, Mr. Heron, not to see her?"

No answer.

"And when this fog came down, why didn't you call me?"

Another pause, and still silence on the part of the mate.

"And how came you not to shorten sail in readiness for this thickness, which you must have seen coming along, instead of keeping the vessel under a topgallant-sail, and shoving into it at the old rate of speed?"

Mr. Heron made no reply.

"Well," said Richard, quietly, "this is our first voyage together, and pretty nearly the first hour of it. I hope you'll not require me again to tell you to keep a bright lookout, and see that others keep it too, and to call me when your experience as a seaman instructs you to guess that I should wish to be on deck. I want no driving in thick weather in the North Sea, sir."

As the mate made no excuse, I concluded that he had nothing to say; certainly I had a right to suppose this from the look on his face, that was warrant of more than one sharp answer, had he had any good reason to give for

his negligence. My husband did not seem to notice that
I stood near enough to overhear what he said, for which
I was sorry, as the mate was perfectly conscious of my
presence, which would necessarily give a reprimand such
as he had received more significance than it needed as a
professional monition; so much is there, on occasions of
that kind, in an audience of even one person. In a few
minutes he went below to get his dinner, and I joined
Richard as he paced the deck to and fro, from abreast of
the wheel to the mizzen-mast.

As a sea-picture of a peculiar and impressive kind, I can
imagine nothing to surpass the appearance the bark presented as she dragged along, with spars inclined and decks
dark with humidity, through the white, vaporous void that
encompassed her. The mist was so thick that nothing
above the crosstrees was visible; the bowsprit vanished
a few feet forward of the gammoning; and the figures
of the two men stationed on the lookout, standing close
against either cathead, loomed indistinctly, and like motionless forms of bronze, amid the woolly density that
seemed to boil up out of the wind. The breeze blew
sharply, and with a most bitter, biting edge in it, out of
the fog, that lay so close to the sides of the vessel that
the water was out of sight a fathom or two distant, and
an effect, striking and beautiful, was produced by the
waves, which, as they came rolling towards us, formed themselves upon the pallid thickness as though there was no sea
beyond, and the surges only began when their shapes were
to be seen. The moist atmosphere had already darkened
the centre cloths of the sails, and the black standing-rigging gleamed like oil. All the crew were on deck, looking over the side or pacing sharply to and fro. Their
various attire—some in pilot-cloth, some in yellow oilskins, some merely in shirts, sou'westers, and canvas trousers, with sheath-knives lying upon their hips, together
with the various casts of faces—one dark-bearded, another
fair as a Scandinavian, one of them a mulatto, and others
again bronzed and ringletted, with the high cheek-bone,
the attenuated features, the gleaming, restless eyes, full of
a subdued mutinous spirit, which I have somehow learned
to associate with American seamen—gave a peculiar im-

pressiveness to the picture of the fog-soaked bark, that seemed, as she went ploughing through the short seas, flinging them from her in glass-like curves, which flashed into foam as they struck the water, and dropped seething and hissing astern, to be groping her way like a creature of instinct through the blinding smother that had suddenly rolled down over her.

"You should go below, Jessie," said Richard; "you'll get wet through here."

"I don't mind that," I answered. "If a fog is to confine me to my cabin, I should have stopped ashore. Richard, I was not born to live in a glass case."

"Did you hear me rate Heron just now?" said he.

"Yes," I replied. "I stood in the companion. How could I help hearing?"

"I wonder what your father would think of such a trick as this mate played me?" said he, subduing his voice, but looking to right and left over the side, and peering with bent eyebrows ahead into the fog all the time he spoke. "He must have been keeping a queer kind of lookout not to see the vessel, that was visible, by his own confession, from the forecastle. Then, again, it was his duty to report this sudden fog to me, that we might not drive through it, in such a thickly navigated sea as this, at seven or eight knots an hour. He says we were in it five minutes before I was aroused by his hailing the forecastle. Another ship's length and we should have been into the vessel; sunk her, perhaps, and sustained damage enough to compel us to return to the Tyne. That would have been a nice beginning of our voyage!"

"You rated him warmly, Richard," said I.

"Not more warmly than he deserved," he replied. "Although you know a good deal about the sea, Jess, you don't know all; and one thing you are never likely to know, though you should come to be able to build and rig a ship, and that is a master's responsibilities. If any disaster had befallen us through that vessel, the Board of Trade lawyers would have dropped upon me, made out that it was my duty to have been on deck, and that I had no business to be eating my dinner in the cabin whether I knew the fog was over us or not, and, finally, have robbed me of my certificate for three or six or twelve months, which to ninety-nine captains in the hundred means ruin. Its having been Heron's fault would not help me. A sea-captain is not supposed to be human, Jess. He must never sleep, never eat, never leave the deck; though even any amount of supernatural qualities of endurance won't save him if his ship comes to grief after all. His own act and the act of God are much the same thing. The act he wants is an Act of Parliament, to give him the rights which the meanest scoundrel of a landsman has when he's arraigned for an offence. Heron will find me a pleasant shipmate enough while he does his duty as a good seaman, and gives me the help he is paid to render me; but if I find that he's crawled aboard through the cabin windows, I shall have to ride him down, Jess—I shall indeed."

"Don't be too hard with him at first, Richard," said I. "Give him time. He knew you were at dinner with me, and thought, perhaps, you would not like to be disturbed."

He burst into a laugh.

"Oh, Jess!" said he, "only get command of a ship, for you'd make one of those skippers a man would like to sail round the world with."

Somewhat abashed by his laugh, I said that I did not want Mr. Heron to dislike him.

"Neither do I, Jess," said he, with another merry laugh, looking at me fondly; "but if Heron's a sailor-man, dear, he'll not dislike me for telling him he's wrong when he *is* wrong; and if he is *not* a sailor-man, why, then it will be all the same whether he dislikes me or not."

The fog was a great annoyance, as it robbed the fresh, steady breeze that blew of half its virtue by forcing us to jog cautiously along under very little more canvas than we should have exposed to a gale of wind. My husband had the log hove repeatedly to ascertain the progress of the vessel through the water, and was constantly running below to consult the chart that lay spread on the cabin-table under the skylight. What, however, was to be feared more than shoals and the like was a collision. We had already very narrowly escaped one, and any moment might bring us the shock of the iron bows of a steamer burying themselves in our side, or find ourselves foul of a sailing-ship, locked yardarm to yardarm, with spars and blocks and gear tumbling about our heads.

The worst of a fog in frequented waters is, that whether you heave to, or go on steaming or sailing, or bring up (supposing the bottom lies near enough for your anchor), you are pretty nearly equally badly off. If there be any choice in several evils, I think to keep on moving is the safest course, for when your vessel is under command you have a chance, if a very small one, of dodging the object that looms suddenly upon you out of the fog; but at anchor, or hove to and at rest, if the vessel will not clear you, you cannot help her to do so: come she will, and you must receive the blow, and make ready to jump aboard her or go to the bottom.

Dinner appeared to have improved Mr. Heron's temper, or he may have had time to digest my husband's reprimand and get some good out of it; for when he arrived on deck again he showed himself very alert, bawling out to the men forward to keep a bright lookout, running first to one rail, then to another, and bending over and peering ahead and around him.

This went on until I was tired of seeing nothing but what resembled clouds of steam sweeping athwart our decks, and I was beginning to feel my jacket and dress very heavy upon me with the damp, and to suspect that the feather in my hat would need a good deal of curling to make it presentable, when the fog brightened all around, producing the same kind of effect upon the sight that would be got by your coming with closed eyes out of a dimly lighted room into one brilliantly illuminated; and, so suddenly that it seemed like a stroke of magic, the bark danced out of the dense mist into clear air, bright wintry sunshine, a pale blue heaven mottled with sweeping cloud similar in appearance and color to the fog we had escaped.

I have seen some fine contrasts upon the deep—many effects of moonlight and sunlight, and distant storm; but I can recall nothing comparable to that solid body of fog, standing up as compact and cleanly defined as the side of a cliff upon the sea, stretched right across the horizon east and west, completely blotting it out, as though the end of the world was there, and if you went to the edge you must fall over; the mass of vapor taking from the sunshine the sort of radiance observable on gunpowder smoke, or, better still, on a cobweb—a sort of shot-silk lustre, not unlike the pearly streakings inside an oyster-shell—while this side of it, and laving its base as though it were a coast or an iceberg, were the running waters, breaking into short flashes of foam, sparkling giddily in the sunbeams, and making the eye reel with the tumultuous radiance.

Directly ahead of us, on a line with our flying-jibboom, was a collier brig, deep in the water, swarming along stiff as a church under a press of rusty, ill-fitting canvas. How long she had kept that distance from us—whether she had passed us in the fog, or whether we had been slowly gaining on her in such a manner as to show that had we exposed another cloth, or had the fog not lifted when it did, we should in all probability have run over her—it is impossible to say. As it was, she was so close that a stone might easily have been cast on to her deck from our fore-castle. The moment her people spied us they showed the most amusing consternation. An old man in a black sou'-wester, and a white beard that made him look like a ring-faced monkey, jumped on to the taffrail, and roared at us in the richest Blyth brogue that was ever shed by human lips hailing from that port; while the fellow at the tiller ran it hard down, and stood against it with his back curved, and his legs away from him, like a man keeping a door shut against a crowd. The black-faced crew hopped about in all directions, and the old coal-sacks which served the brig for canvas rattled like linen drying in a strong breeze, as the deeply laden craft slowly came round into the wind.

A shift of our helm sent us past in safety. I stood looking at her as we went by. We were deep in the water too, yet when I leaned over the rail to watch her I could see right down on her decks. She took me back in fancy to the Newcastle quayside, and brought up the whole picture of the Tyne there before me as though we were sailing up it—the towering High-Level bridge, the old keels poling or "powing" along, the grimy, crazy buildings on Gateshead side squatting upon the water's edge, and all the thousand-and-one features of a scene which I had never thought on so tenderly as I did now that every mile we measured was leaving it farther and farther behind.

There is no uglier vessel than a real old north-country Geordie or coalman, with the run of a sugar-box, boom-foresail, stump topgallant-masts, and bows like the side of a bucket; and for that very reason, perhaps, there is none to my mind more picturesque. The name of this deep and wallowing tub was the *Richard and Ann*, of Blyth, and whenever I think of the first day of that voyage of mine with my husband, there comes before me that old brig, with her apple-shaped bows splashing and bobbing and ducking, like a Dutchman taking a bath: one mast leaning aft, the other forward, every rope as black as coal; a boat bottom-up, lying upon the main hatchway, surrounded by several heaps of coal; and the three or four fellows—among them the cook, in a red cap —who composed her crew clumsily sprawling about as they obeyed the orders of the skipper, who had seized the tiller, and sent the fellow who had been holding it to help the others to trim sail.

If she was not from the Tyne she was from some port close to it, and as I watched her dropping astern, falling off and slowly gathering way as her canvas filled, standing up in such bold relief against the wool-white, compact body of vapor beyond that she looked like a carving in ebony mounted on marble, I thought with a little touch of sadness of the many times she would have voyaged and returned to the well-loved coast which we were leaving before we should find ourselves again in these waters with our bowsprit pointing for a north-country port.

CHAPTER XVII.

NIGHT IN THE NORTH SEA.

HOWEVER, I was speedily aroused from these reflections by the brisk orders shouted upon our own decks, the movements of the men, and by the fine, shining, windy

afternoon we had run into out of the fog that had been
hanging about us like the night itself. The sea was clear
to its farthest confines, with several vessels in sight ; but
though I went to the compass and looked earnestly in the
direction where the English coast lay I could not see the
merest shadow of it.

The *Aurora* was now to have all the sail she could
carry, and the little vessel rang with the shouts of my
husband and the mate, the hoarse voice of the carpenter
forward, and the chorussing of the crew. Yard after
yard was mastheaded, and gave its expanding canvas to
the wind. The different orders, the gradual leaning-down
of the bark under the increasing pressure, the roar of
foam speeding past, so exhilarated me that I felt I should
like nothing better than to go among the crew and pull
and haul with them to their songs. I heard Richard say,
" Give her the main-royal, Mr. Heron ; we must make up
for the fog," and forthwith a young seaman sprang into
the shrouds, and presently the light sail swelled out like a
balloon in the grasp of the clewlines, and a faint shout of
"Sheet home !" came down from the giddy height.
"Overhaul your clewlines !" bawled the mate. A quick
song resounded along the decks, and the sail was set,
crowning the stately central edifice of canvas with an
apex as light, graceful, and beautiful as a wreath of moon-
lit cloud hovering on the summit of a snow - covered
mountain. Another order, to set the fore-royal, crowned
the vessel with all plain sail ; and leaning down until the
seething foam alongside was within reach of the arm, and
flinging up the spray forward in whole clouds of rainbow-
tinted smoke, the noble little bark swept along like a
steamer under the lordly pile of white canvas which soared
into the heavens from her shapely hull.

Had I been the most disconsolate woman alive, the
magic of that buoyant windy speeding must have set my
heart leaping. But not being disconsolate, but, on the
contrary, happy to be at sea, happy to be with my husband, and falling a little pensive only when my thoughts
were carried back to Newcastle, I stood enjoying the scene
with such prodigious relish that now and again I would
catch some of the crew, who passed me to drag on a rope

here, or to coil down and clear up there, staring and then looking at one another with a grin.

The color of the water had changed. It was no longer gray, but a clear, gleaming, deep-sea green, the surges hollow and well defined, here and there a long stretch of foam rising and falling, while over it there lay an afternoon sky of winter blue, with squadrons of light clouds sailing athwart it, blowing up out of the sea into the greenish tinge of the heaven of the horizon, like puffs of smoke from artillery at work behind the ocean-line. The vessels in the distance stretching along the flashing and trembling and hurrying surface gave the finishing touch to the fine picture of free, eager, and sweeping movement conveyed by the onward-rushing fabric on which I stood, the racing surges, the flying forms of the clouds, and the keen, swift pouring of the ice-cold steady blast that hummed in the rigging as though there was a band of music somewhere about.

Richard went below for a few minutes, and Mr. Heron came to look at the binnacle compass, near to which I was standing. I asked him what he thought of the *Aurora*.

"She's a nice little ship," he answered, barely glancing at me, and then fixing his eyes again on the card.

His manner was very awkward and short; but I then put it down to nervousness.

"I wish we could keep this wind for a few weeks," said I; "our voyage would be a quick one."

"Yes, you are right; it would," he replied.

"I may guess by your accent, Mr. Heron, that you are not a north-country man," said I with a smile, willing to persevere in speaking amiably and in a friendly way— partly, perhaps, from the feeling that it was the best apology I could make for having been a listener to the reprimand my husband gave him.

"No, I'm not a north-country man," he answered; and, casting his eyes aloft, he went along the deck, and bawled out for a couple of hands to lay aft and get a small pull on the weather-royal and topgallant braces.

I will not say those sails did not want trimming, but it looked very much as though he had given the order as an

11

excuse to get away from me. His shortness of manner, which came very near to rudeness, did not greatly annoy me ; he perhaps thought he had a right to hold off from any conversation with me, after what Richard had said to him in my presence as to minding his duty and keeping a bright look-out ; but as I watched him walk forward, and took note of the cut of his clothes and his unsailorly appearance, I heartily regretted that my first voyage to sea with my husband should not have been made in company with a mate more in keeping than Mr. Heron was with those notions of sailors I had got from association with my father and with my father's marine friends.

I began now to feel the effects of the steady pouring of the cold wind against my face. I had that sensation of drowsiness which most persons get who come fresh to the sea and remain long in the strong air. There was more work for me to do in my cabin before I could consider everything arranged and in proper order, and I went below, but rather for the sake of shelter than with the idea of working. However, I put my hands to a few things, taking good care not to touch my husband's table, on which was spread a number of instruments for purposes of navigation, books, papers, and the like ; and then, feeling tired, I sat down in the arm-chair in the spare cabin, and fell sound asleep like a baby.

When I awoke, my eyes opened on Richard standing at the door and looking at me.

"Why, Jessie, my darling," said he, "if you're sleepy, why don't you turn in regularly, and have a good nap?"

"No, I'm refreshed and wide-awake now," I answered, getting up and taking hold of his arm to steady myself, for the deck sloped like the side of a hill, and the vessel was jumping as though she were a horse in a steeple-chase.

"Then," said he, "if you're awake, come on deck and see one of the grandest sights the sea is ever likely to offer you."

"What is it, Richard?" said I, as I followed him.

"Stop till you're on deck, he answered.

The moment I lifted my head above the companion I saw it. Well, it was not a whale, nor a ship on fire, nor any wonder of that kind; it was nothing more, indeed, than a sunset; yet so magnificent a one that I cannot believe the like of it was ever before seen. It would have most gloriously served a painter as a background for a picture of the Day of Judgment.

A bow, that looked to be of brilliant burning gold, was arched over the horizon from the westward of northwest far into the northeast quarter, the loftiest point or keystone of which would be about fifteen degrees high. From this wonderful bridge of streaming fire there depended a number of clouds, dark at the base, but shot in their upper parts with vivid orange, sapphire, and emerald streaks; they hung vertically, and amid them, as if suspended in a mighty flaming cage, his lower limb touching the water, was the sun, a vast red shield, with the dark surface-spots looking like little clouds. The blood-red incandescent mass heaved and swelled and throbbed amid its own glowing atmospheric folds, though the effect produced upon the eye was that of an orb of molten metal palpitating in the throes of its inexpressible ardency. Slowly floating athwart the vertical pillars were a quantity of soft white and delicate rose-colored clouds; but above them there was spread as far as the zenith a vast crimson haze, which resembled steam rising from the burning ocean and taking its hue from the conflagration on the sea-line, through which the clouds, as they came rolling up with the wind, passed in slate-colored shapes, their shoulders only catching the sunset glory, and giving it back in a dull brick-red. Everywhere, save directly under the sun, the sea was a hard, dark, wintry, windy green, racing headlong in foaming surges, along which the *Aurora* was bounding with a roaring noise around her, her slanting masts exposing a surface of canvas that brought the foam to leeward, with every *send*, as high as the scupper-holes, through which it flashed in white streams, like jets from a force-pipe.

"I always thought it was necessary to go very much higher north than this to see such a sunset," exclaimed Richard, gazing at the beautiful sight with admiration strongly expressed in his face.

The glorious scene so affected me that I could only look

without speaking. It brought up all the old fancies which had haunted me in my childhood—visions of a still blue sea, sun-bright islands, dusky figures, and all the riches of a tropical vegetation; and, one idea leading to another, it recalled the queer curiosities in my father's old parlor—the ivory junks, the shield, the tomahawk and spears—until memory grew so strong that this wind-swept sea, this rushing and thunderous bark, and yonder space of effulgent firmament, appeared no more than one of those dreams I dreamed when I was a little girl, and nothing real but the old parlor in which I seemed to be sitting, beholding those visions which, when a child, had made me crazy to be at sea and view the spacious world.

Presently the splendor faded away. A hollow flush lingered in the west, the green water took a darker color, the vivid flashing of the froth grew wan and vague, and looking into the east I spied a star winking bleakly among the clouds there.

"Now that the curtain has dropped, we'll go and take some refreshments," said Richard, grasping my hand; and down we went for a cup of tea.

When I returned on deck again I was in no hurry to leave it. The wind was full of frost, yet somehow it did not affect me as the same degree of cold would have done ashore—whether because of the salt in the sea-air, or because of the bracing properties of the wind, I cannot say. The night had come down very dark, but, now that all daylight was gone out of the sky, the stars shone brightly among the clouds, some of the larger ones burning with a sharp, clear, greenish tinge, others with a faint pink, while beyond them the black heights glittered with the silver dust of myriads of tiny orbs.

It was my first night at sea for many a long year. I was young when I went on those voyages with my father, and had not sufficient intellect to observe with full delight the mysteries and beauties of the sea and sky; but now I brought a more matured mind to this contemplation, and everything I looked at wrought upon me like a revelation.

Richard could not understand what pleasure I found in holding by a backstay, full in the streaming wind, and watching the vessel and the sea; nor could I explain.

The feelings which possessed me were not definable in words. It was not only the dark vision of the bark, rushing like a phantom over the black coils of water; the pallid gleam of the bed of froth thrown up by her, laced here and there with the mystic radiance of phosphorus; the mystery of the boundless, desolate ocean leaning its vast shadow towards the twinkling stars of the horizon, its hollow surges echoing back the wailing voices of the wind, and making its mighty presence heard and felt, rather than seen, by its effortless lifting and poising of our deeply freighted vessel, and by the tumult of its trampling and turbulent surges away out in the gloom; nor the resonant visionary spaces of canvas melting in the darkness as they soared towards and seemed to become a portion of the driving clouds; nor the wild minstrelsy that rang through the straining shrouds and rigging; nor the deep-voiced thunder of the bow wave pouring away in a roar from the keen stem, and stretching far enough out in a seething, whirling mass to leeward to give me the clear configuration of the vessel's hull on that side on the white and shrieking swirl—it was the *spirit* of the whole that held and subdued me, a magic as undeterminable as the spell of a dark, beautiful, and passionate eye; born, indeed, of the wild, hurrying, foaming scene, but informed by a thrilling sense of mystery that owed its inspiration to something I could not have explained by pointing to the stars and the speeding phantom of the bark, and the black shadow of the clamorous waters.

By this time the regular sea discipline prevailed on board, the men having some hours previously been mustered and divided into watches. The darkness and silence along the decks greatly added to the impression produced upon my mind by the hoarse roaring of the wind aloft, and the seething noise of breaking and rolling waters. Forward there was not the least sparkle of light to be seen; nevertheless, I could faintly distinguish the outline of the lookout-man as he moved about the forecastle, and follow the arching foot of the fore-course as it curved transversely across the deck, by observing the stars glitter and disappear as the bark ran up and swept down over the ocean surges. Aft, however, the cabin lamplight lay softly upon the skylight, and a pale, luminous haze hung like a fog about the binnacle, abaft which a man stood grasping the wheel with both hands.

The "officer" of the watch was now the carpenter, a powerfully built, square-shaped man, who was stumping the deck near enough to the skylight to catch the radiance from it, and to exhibit a figure that looked in that uncertain light more like the body of a giant, with his legs cut off at the knees, than a properly proportioned human shape.

"Now, Jess," said my husband, coming up to me, "I can't allow you to be frozen to death on the very first night of our voyage. I am going below for a biscuit and a glass of brandy-and-water. Come along, Jessie."

This was the third time of his trying to break in upon my deep enjoyment of the dark, phantom-like picture, and I yielded.

"I could understand your admiring the bark," said he, as we went below, laughing as he spoke, "on a fine, warm, moonlight night. But it's as dark as a pocket. There's nothing to see; the thermometer is at freezing-point, if not below it. It's a night to make a man think of warm blankets, not of the wonders of the deep."

"All I can say is, I enjoy it," said I. "By-and-by I shall get used to it, no doubt, and perhaps be wondering, even more than you do, at the delight it first gave me. But while it is fresh I must have my way."

"Ay," said he, smiling, and speaking lovingly, "there's no fear, Jess, of your not having your way with me. Only don't let Heron and the men guess that you are the real skipper, or they'll be refusing to turn to to any orders but yours. That won't do *yet*, though, at your present rate of sailing, there's no telling how soon you'll be sending me aloft with the slush-bucket, while you hunt after the sun and make experiments with the nautical almanac."

I asked where Mr. Heron was.

"Where every sensible man would wish to be on such a night as this, in his watch below—in bed," he answered.

I was nearly telling him of the rebuff I had met with in my effort to be polite to that gentleman, but held my peace on reflecting that it would but needlessly embitter my husband against his mate, and lead to a common ill-feeling little to be desired on shipboard between two men forced to live together and act together.

We sat talking at the table in low tones, that we might not disturb Mr. Heron—for if there is one rule more rigorously insisted upon and observed at sea than another, it is that quietude should be maintained when there are sleepers near; and at last, when the steward came to say that four bells had been struck, and to ask if he should turn down the bright cabin-lamp that swung from a stout central beam, I considered it about time to go to bed.

"Get to sleep as fast as ever you can, Jess," Richard said; "I shall be up and about pretty well all night. "There'll be no regular dreaming hours for me till we've cleared the Lizard."

So we bade each other good-night as tenderly as if we were not to meet for a month; he went on deck, and I to our berth.

This berth was fitted with two good-sized bunks, or sleeping-shelves, one fixed above the other. Richard had given me my choice, and I chose the bottom one; first, because I should not have to climb to enter it, and next because, if I rolled out, I should not have far to fall. They had more the appearance of coffins than of beds, and, though they looked fresh and clean with their white coverlets and furniture, mine seemed, even to me, who was at sea as much for the love of it as to be with my husband, and who found a nameless charm in the roughest detail of a ship, but a poor substitute for the capacious English bedstead that filled one side of my room in Newcastle.

I very well remember undressing myself that first night at sea. My husband had praised my easy step on deck when the ship rolled, and, to speak the truth, I considered my sea-legs as good as his, though he had been at sea for years when I had no water nearer to me than the Tyne; but our berth was right aft, under the wheel. Here the least heave of the vessel was to be felt; and as the bark was now plunging under a press of canvas along a sharp head sea, her motion was sometimes so extravagant in that extreme end of her, that, poise and steady myself as I would, I was incessantly "fetching" away, as sailors say, forced into a sudden rush, first in the direction of the door, then towards the bunks, holding tight to such clothing as I was removing when thus impelled, or darting to and fro with my hair in one hand and a brush in the other.

As, however, I did not suffer in the least degree from nausea, this jumping and sweeping of the deck caused me no further inconvenience than to delay me somewhat and make my legs ache. At last I turned down the little lamp that swung from a bracket near the door, leaving it dimly burning for my husband, and crawled into my bunk, where I lay some time shivering between the bitter cold linen sheets, until my teeth chattered in my head. Indeed, the cold of those sheets was ten times keener to me than the frost of the wind on deck, and I heartily wished they had been of good thick muslin, such as I should have bought. But Richard had notions of his own: he was resolved I should go to sea as a lady, and reckoned that I should be but half-furnished for that condition if I was without linen sheets.

However, after a while I found myself growing warm, though little disposed to sleep. It seemed to me, as I lay listening, that that berth must be the noisiest that was ever built. I could hear the seas sweeping in muffled thunder under the counter of the vessel, as her stern chopped into the hollows, and the harsh jar of the rudder on its braces, and the shock that the blow of every billow communicated to the wheel-chains. The bulkheads creaked continuously, the beams and strong fastenings groaned like a chorus of wounded men, strange sounds came from the cabin beyond, and the air was filled with faint, laboring noises from the hull of the ship. Above all this, ringing steadily through it, was the booming of the ocean blast as it swept through the darkness on high, mingled with the thin and scattering echoes of trampling surges, and the seething of foam, faint as the pouring of a cascade heard at a long distance.

All this went on for some time, and I could gather from the thrilling and humming through the wooden fabric, her convulsive jumps, and the angle of her inclination, illustrated by the slope of the lamp and of some clothes hanging against the bulkhead, that my husband was hotly pressing the bark, making, as he was no doubt right in doing on a clear night, the most of a fine breeze that enabled him to lie his course, and which would carry us well forward on the road to the English Channel.

But I was pretty sure this driving would not last; and presently I heard the sound of ropes flung down upon the decks, followed by calls and the voices of the watch, as they hauled upon the running-gear. They were shortening sail, and the bark's movements grew easier. Soon afterwards the door was opened, and Richard came in. His shaggy coat glistened with fast-melting snow-flakes, and his face sparkled with drops of wet. He moved about quietly, putting on a suit of oil-skins and a sou'wester, taking for granted that I was asleep. Thus equipped, he came to my bunk to peep at me, and perhaps steal a kiss, but drew himself up when he saw my eyes wide open.

"Hillo! I thought it was your watch below, Jess," said he, drawing back for fear that his damp clothes should chill the atmosphere near me. "Can't you get to sleep?"

"I must wait till I grow use to the noises in this berth," I answered. "Every nail has a shriek, every piece of timber a groan, as if they derided the roaring of the sea outside, or were afraid that it will manage to reach them after all."

"I feared that," said he, looking around, as though he would stop the noises if he could. "But you *will* get used to it. The sea is Jack's nurse, and this is the song she sings when she rocks him to sleep."

"I wish the cradle moved more quietly, then," said I. "Is it raining, Richard?"

"Ay, there's a handful of sleet about. But now get to sleep, Jess. You're not nervous, my pet, are you?"

"Nervous!" I exclaimed, a little indignantly.

He laughed, pulled off his sou'wester to give me a kiss —the foremost flap or thatch of the elegant head-dress being very obstructive to tenderness of that kind—and told me that, if he found me awake when he looked in again, he should suppose I really was nervous.

"Very well," thought I, Irish-like, "whether you find me awake or not, you shall think I'm asleep."

He then quitted the cabin, but whether he returned

again I do not know ; for, on opening my eyes after closing them, the sun was flashing brightly on the scuttle near
my bunk, and, looking at my watch, I found that it was
half-past eight, proving that I had slept without stirring
for a full nine hours.

CHAPTER XVIII.

"ALL IN THE DOWNS."

I DO not remember that we sighted any land until we
were abreast of the North Foreland.　Our expectation of
making a good run was defeated by a strong southerly
wind, that forced us to the eastward, and it was not until
the fourth morning after leaving the Tyne that we picked
up the Margate coast.

But this fourth morning was very fine, the wind extremely light, and, although coming in faint puffs from
the east-southeast quarter, as mild as the temperature of
a spring morning.　I had, of course, passed through the
English Channel before, when I went a voyage with father
and mother to the West Indies ; but on that occasion my
father had steered his ship to the eastward of the Goodwin Sands, and kept so wide an offing that the English
shores were but little more than a cloud upon the distant
water, while in the Straits of Dover we seemed to be mid-
way betwixt the pallid films which on our port hand indicated the Calais, and on our starboard hand the Dover,
cliffs.　But now, by my husband taking the Channel to
the north and west of the Goodwins, we had the land—to
use the nautical phrase—close aboard ; and when I came
on deck after breakfast on that fourth morning, I felt as
if I had been transported into an early summer.　The
water, which was of a delicate blue, though discolored
here and there where it was shallow, lay softly heaving
in folds, like a silk carpet gently shaken, while within a
couple of miles of us stood the snow-white cliffs of the
North Foreland, the cream-colored lighthouse on its summit clearly defined upon the azure of the northern sky.

The early sunshine streamed full upon this beautiful stretch of coast, and the searching brilliance flashed up the ramparts of chalk into the dazzling whiteness of foam. Much as I love the rugged browns and greens of our Northumberland and Durham coasts, the black-fanged rocks, around which the surf coils like the salival froth in the jaws of a hound, the masses of gray, honeycombed, pebble-shaped blocks of stone which litter the beach in places, and the storm-swept aspect of the whole of that low, long, powerful range of cliffs that grimly confronts the gales and surges of the gray, tempestuous North Sea, I own that there is a majesty of strength and beauty, of light and shadow, in the stretch of coast between the North and South Foreland, and onwards yet past the giant heights of the Shakespeare cliffs, to where the land leans down and leaves visible the green fields and gardens, and the distant swelling plains of Kent and Sussex, that is not to be found betwixt Tweedmouth and the Tees.

It was like sailing in a yacht along the soundless swell of the Channel waters to look up at the white and glittering canvas — the light sails only yielding to the mild breathings of the morning air—and then at the sparkling sea in the east, and then at the brilliant cliffs which slowly revealed their towns as we floated by, rhythmically swung by the noiseless heaving, whose respiration was marked by the cadence of the canvas as it came in against the fire-streaked masts and swelled out again.

I thought of Tynemouth as I looked at Broadstairs, and saw the windows of a row of seaward-gazing houses filled with flashing stars, and the line of foam upon the yellow sand, and the short, rickety pier standing black upon the water and against the snow-like cliffs, with a cluster of fishing-boats—not unlike our north-country cobbles—rolling upon the swell that ran towards them in shadows of violet laced with the silver of the sunshine.

My husband joined me and stood at my side, leaning over the bulwark-rail. The men were scattered about, at work on some of those scores of jobs which a vessel when at sea finds for her crew to do ; two of them in the fore-top, and I could hear their voices, as they spoke to each other or hailed the deck, hollowly thrown back and down

by the topsail; another perched like a monkey upon the
flying-jibboom end, outside the fore-royal stay; another
at work on some chafing-gear in the main rigging, and so
on.   Mr. Heron, who had charge of the watch, walked
quietly to and fro in the gangway, glancing at the men,
and sometimes coming aft to peep at the compass, but
apparently taking no notice whatever of the shining
stretch of coast scenery to which my eyes were chained.
So light was the air, that the smoke from the galley chimney went up as high as the foretop in a straight line and
then arched over like a feather, and floated away as languidly as a puff of tobacco-smoke in a room.   A few
ripples broke from the stem of the vessel, and bubbles as
brilliant as prisms passed slowly along the side and veered
astern to join the short oily surface of wake under the
counter.   Betwixt us and the Goodwins, whose sands
could be clearly seen lying in a long, yellow line a hand's-
breadth this side the horizon, framed in a thin setting of
surf, were a couple of deep-laden colliers, striking their
shadows into the sea, and sending with every roll a sound
like the discharge of musketry from their dark sails.
Within musket-shot was a small empty cask, over which
three sea-gulls were hovering, their radiant bodies, poised
with inexpressible grace upon their tremorless wings, reflected in the water under them like flakes of suspended
quicksilver; and at intervals, when a complete hush fell
upon the bark, I could hear the melodious moaning of the
surf that tumbled in a line for miles, from the foot of the
lowering Foreland to the fine, pallid, amber-like thread
over our starboard bow that denoted the Ramsgate pier.
    "I'm afraid we shall have to bring up," said Richard
to me.   "There's a haze drawing up in the south, with
every appearance of a calm behind it.   I hope this draught
will let us fetch the Downs, though."
    "Are the Downs in sight?" I asked.
    He pointed right ahead.   "Do you see those black specks
yonder, which will turn out to be vessels when we approach
near enough to make man's mighty handiwork visible?
That space of water where those craft are is the Downs."
    "And is that the place where black-eyed Susan came
aboard?" said I.

"Ay," he answered, "the very identical spot where sweet William,

'Who high upon the yard,
Rock'd by the billow to and fro,'

spied her. There must have been a breeze of wind blowing that day, Jess. And what did sweet William do when he cast his eyes below? Why,

'The cord slides swiftly through his glowing hands,
And quick as lightning on the deck he stands.'

He couldn't have been quicker if the mast had been going overboard. It's a wonder he did not break his neck in his hurry. Fancy calling the topgallant - backstay — it must have been a backstay that sweet William came down by—a cord! Yet it is a good old song, with a true flavor of salt in it, got, no doubt, from the number of forecastles it has found its way into."

"I cannot imagine," said I, "that there is any prettier coast scenery than this in the world."

"Wait until you've seen Sydney Bay," said he, laughing, and eying the white cliffs with a little contempt too. "You'll not greatly value chalk after beholding clusters of green islands set in silver water that is gloriously fringed by a shore beautiful with South Sea vegetation, while pretty houses gleam among the fairy-like verdure, and the soft sky is all a-quiver with birds more richly plumed than anything of the kind you ever saw in a milliner's shop. Some of these days we may make a voyage together to those parts. But this won't do, Jess, this won't do!"

And forthwith he began to whistle for the wind, and presently walked over to Mr. Heron.

It was not hard to guess that neither of them much relished the notion of bringing up. Nothing sailors dislike more than having to handle their ground-tackle after the anchor is fairly at the cathead, and the voyage begun. My hope, however, was that the failure of the wind would oblige us to anchor. I wanted to see all I could. Once we got upon the Atlantic we should not sight land for days and days, unless we caught a distant glimpse of

Madeira or the Canaries; and as I knew that Deal lay opposite the Downs, I determined, if we came to anchor there, to coax Richard to take me ashore.

He did not long remain talking to Mr. Heron. I asked no questions, and therefore at that time could not positively declare that he disliked the mate or distrusted him as a seaman; but already I had noticed that they spoke seldom to each other. Indeed, a more unsociable man than the mate I could not imagine. When his watch below allowed him to dine with us, he would sit at table, never speaking unless addressed, and whenever I accosted him, even to say good-morning, his reply and manner were invariably short, as though he would have me to know that he neither required nor returned civilities of that kind, and preferred to be left alone.

However, I presumed that so long as he obeyed orders and did his duty there was nothing to be said. I was quite aware that it is unjust to judge sailors by the rules that are applied to landsmen. I have met men so austere, gloomy, even sullen in their deportment, that you would have supposed them really bad-hearted people; yet in spirit and feelings they were good, kind men, and their manners were merely the result of harsh discipline in their youth, of long hours of loneliness spent in the cabin and the night watches, and of a career passed in association with unruly crews and tyrannous masters. Yet, with every disposition to make what is called allowances for Mr. Heron, by supposing that his early training had been at fault, or his later experiences harsh, or that he might have anxieties upon his mind of which no stranger could arrive by conjecture at the character, I own that the more I saw of him the less I liked him, and recalled, with something of self-flattery, the accuracy of the judgment I had formed of him at first sight.

The faint stirring of the air, for it was little more, continued; and the bark crept forward with a motion as imperceptible as if some submerged power were languidly drawing her. I could tell, however, by the slope of a buoy which we passed, that the tide was with us. By twelve o'clock we were abreast of Ramsgate; and, on looking through the telescope, I could see people walking on the pier and on the top of the cliffs. The picture was a very pretty one. Here, as at Broadstairs, the windows caught the sunlight and shone like flames; the white cliffs stood with singular brilliance upon the blue water, and some smacks in tow of their boats, their reddish sails waving upon the swell—while the tiny clink of winch-pawls, and the thread-like voices of men, and the grind of the oars in the thole-pins stole from them—furnished a foreground of delicate color and quiet sea-life to the sun-bright English marine-picture of the cliffs and the town.

I looked up at our moonlike, finely cut, and well-set canvas, and thought with pride that if people were viewing us from the heights there, they must be admiring the beauty of our bark. Then I reflected how little they conceived of the life aboard her; of the young wife making her first voyage with her husband, watching the houses and the church-top standing up among them, as though the vessel were at rest, and that town was only a part of a panorama of the coast, that was being uncoiled and wound along, as one has seen it on a stage. Indeed, I was only reviewing an old fancy in this; for many a time have I stood at Tyne-mouth or at Shields, and gazed at distant passing sails, and imagined the life aboard—pictured sailors on the forecastle viewing the distant land and talking of home; women leaning over the bulwarks, their eyes growing dim as there arose memories of the dear ones in the graveyards of the old homes they might never behold again; of the pleasures, struggles, trials, the poverty, the marriage which led up to their being at sea, sailing away, never again, perhaps, to set foot on that soil from whose rugged northeastern coast I stood watching.

Here now was the picture reversed: I was upon the sea, bound on a long voyage, and wondering if the people, whose figures I could discern through the telescope, were watching us and speculating on us as I used on distant vessels. Indeed, there is no symbol of life more touching and suggestive to me than a vessel outward bound, passing the towns and villages of the coast of her native country, as she pushes her way towards the great deep. Who can tell the freight of heartaches she carries? the fears, hopes, tears of the human souls in her, which quicken her inanimate fabric, and make, as I have thought, a very shape of instinct of her? One wonders what the fortunes of her people will be, and what her own success in the struggle with the cruel and capricious ocean, whose colossal might she, a mere toy, is about to wrestle with; and follows her with deepening interest as she sinks below the sea-line, and the topmost of her white canvas glimmers an instant, like a waning star, upon the far-off blue circle, ere it vanishes.

I was aroused from the revery by Richard's unpoetical announcement that dinner was ready; but I sat with impatience through the meal, and was glad to get on deck again. The sun was westering fast by the time we had neared the Downs, and there was scarcely a breath of air to be felt. The sea lay heaving like molten glass, with a haze upon it that shut out the Ramsgate cliffs, though the low, flat land abreast of Sandwich was visible, growing distinct and clear as it trended our way towards Deal and the South Foreland. By what magic the bark crept along I do not know. We owed much to the tide, no doubt, and yet, when even the sails hung up and down, and the water was like oil over the side, I took notice of our motion by the passage of now a piece of seaweed, now a jelly-fish, now a piece of wood covered with green weed, floating by no faster than a snail's crawling. Indeed, what with one tide against us when there was a little wind, and another tide with us when there was no wind, it had taken us nearly all day to fetch our present whereabouts from the North Foreland, a distance of about ten marine miles.

"Do you mean to anchor?" I asked Richard.

"Yes," he answered. "We shall have to bring up. It's a great pity. I am never easy until I get the Scillies astern."

"Don't say it's a pity, Richard. It's just what I have been wanting. I should like to go ashore and see Deal."

"It will be dark soon," said he. "No use going ashore in the dark, Jess."

"Then you'll take me to-morrow morning?" said I.

"Certainly not," he answered, "if a breeze of wind springs up before the morning comes."

"Then I must hope it will remain calm all night," said

I, with a glance round at the sea, the breathless and beautiful placidity of which was equal to anything I had ever seen on a summer's evening, though, now the sun was low, there was an edge to the air that might well remind us winter lurked very close at hand.

The men were set to work to get the cable-range along, ready for bringing up. We were on the threshold of the historic anchorage, and I gazed with great interest at the twenty or thirty vessels which were lying there windbound, widely scattered indeed, yet looking to be in a group, too. There was scarcely a rig that was not represented, from the ship of twelve hundred tons—an American, black, tall, with lofty, tapering spars, terminating in skysail-poles—down to the little dandy, loaded to her waterways with salt or clay or tiles. It was a fine picture in the evening light. The sky was a bright crimson in the west, for there was not the tiniest cloud to add a reflected color to the streaming fires of the sinking luminary, and against this magnificent background towered the South Foreland, dark with its own shadow, sweeping in a line of gloomy rocks to Walmer Castle and the houses of that town, down to the flat level, on which were grouped the picturesque roofs of Deal, faced by a long shelving bank of shingle, on which a number of fine luggers were lying high and dry. The farther ships and the sea that way had the sunset glow upon them, and the water there was hung with a pinkish haze, amid which the vessels were rolling softly upon the long, silent swing of the swell, their spars streaked with the red light of the orb that was concealed from us, and their hulls and decks flashing up in sparks as the swaying of the fabrics caught the light upon the glass of the scuttles or upon the brass of the binnacles. But on our side all was steeped in the gray of the evening shadow; already the east wore the velvet darkness of the fine night, stars brightening upon it, and upon the waters the yellow lanterns of the Goodwin light-vessels were flashing and fading.

My husband said something to the mate, who instantly bawled out, "Hands, shorten sail! Clew up the royals and topgallant-sails! Aft here, some of you, and get the mainsail hauled up!" The bark was alive in a breath;

12

ropes were flung down, blocks squealed like rats as they soared aloft, and, amid the songs of the sailors and the deep rumbling of heavy yards descending the masts, the canvas fell in festoons. "Stand by to let go the anchor!" and, after a pause, "Let go!" Clank, clank! skirr, skirr! and the brief spell of silence was broken by the crash of the mass of iron striking the sea, and the roar of the cable as it rushed through the hawse-pipe. Then all hands went to work upon the sails again, letting go staysail and jib halliards, brailing up the spanker, and singing at the top of their voices; in the midst of which the bark slowly swung with the tide, bringing the dark line of coast and the lights of Deal, which were now twinkling like a galaxy of fire-flies hovering in a mass over a point of tropical shore, upon our port or left-hand side, and in a few minutes the little vessel lay, held by the bight of her cable, gently and slowly swaying upon the swell that came along in dark folds full of broken starlight out of the darkness in the southeast.

I was very well pleased to be at anchor, and felt, indeed, as if this were seeing life. To be lying in the Downs, the most famous piece of water in the world, with the historical town of Deal opposite, and the prospect of going ashore in the morning, was making a voyage to some purpose. This was seeing the world, beginning with England. Nothing would have pleased me better than to have anchored off some fresh town every morning as far as the Land's End, and then come back and worked our way down the Channel in the same way along the French coast. But this would have been yachting. Our cargo wanted despatch; and my husband, as he walked about the deck, giving orders and looking round the sea, showed many marks of impatience and disappointment at this compulsory stoppage.

Presently the men came off the yards, after rolling up the canvas; and, with a riding-lamp burning brightly on the forestay, and an anchor watch set, the bark lay at rest, her decks quiet, the stars glittering through her rigging, and the nearer vessels standing in shadows upon the dark water. My husband lighted a pipe, and walked up and down with me. We could hear the surf washing on the

Deal shingle, also the faint strains of a band of drums and fifes, and once I heard a clock striking. But these were the only shore sounds audible. There seemed to be more life upon the water, where the vessels lay at anchor; and first here and then there a concertina or a fiddle would strike up, or it would be the reedy echo of a strong male voice singing, followed by a chorus; while from the darkness in other directions would steal the metallic pulsing of a capstan, the harsh jangle of chain cables dragged along, mingled with cries, and the striking of bells upon the larger craft. There was no moon, but the stars of the first magnitude burned with fine, powerful, blue or green or white fires; and there was a constant play of meteors, which made me think of some mighty hand flinging silver dust over the black heavens.

"If sailorizing consisted of nothing but this," said Richard, "we should have more of your sex signing articles and swinging their hammocks, Jess."

"Is there any prospect of a breeze before the morning?" I asked.

"I wish I knew," he answered; "and yet February is not the month for calms of this kind either."

"Well, the more I see, the more I shall be able to tell father," said I. "It is something even to have brought up in the Downs."

"A very great deal, in the sense of delay," he exclaimed. "Do you hear the drums and fifes, Jessie? It sounds as if they had marines at Deal. Who's that walking in the starboard gangway?"

"It looks like the mate," I replied.

He was silent, and then said in a smothered voice, "I wish I had a livelier mate. What is this fellow? A poet? He seems to be always dreaming."

"Is it that he won't forgive you for reprimanding him, or is it that he is naturally morose, and can no more help his character than I can help the color of my hair?" said I.

"Both, I dare say," he answered; "but there's one thing that does not please me, though. He and the carpenter seem on good terms. There would be no harm in that were the relations between him and me what they should be and would be if he were a smarter and pleasanter man.

But it's a bad sign when a mate looks for friends forward, even though the chum he selects has charge of a watch."

"What's the carpenter's name, Richard? I have never yet heard it."

"Thomas Short."

"A good name for such a figure. I suppose Mr. Heron finds something congenial in the character of that man. Certainly, as far as behavior goes, there seems but little to choose between them. The carpenter looks more like a ship's figure-head than a human being. Is he a good sailor?"

"Oh, he knows the ropes," he answered, laughing. "However, whether they like it or not, I'm master, and I believe they'll not have much trouble to find that out. Ah, Jess," said he, stopping to strike a match, the flame of which burned without a tremor in the perfectly still air, "young fellows when they go to sea are all mad to become masters; but they little know the difficulties and anxieties of that post. It is not only that a man must be weighed down by the heavy responsibilities committed to his sole care in the shape of precious human lives and valuable property; he must know human nature, be able to deal with the dozen different types of character which every ship's crew holds; and, hardest of all, while knowing that nothing must be left to chance, he is so much at the mercy of chance—for what other name can you give to that capricious element?" pointing over the side— "that every fathom of water he measures is like the fling of a coin — if heads, all right, he wins; if tails, good-night!"

He spoke with a little air of depression, partly bred by the delay that vexed him, and partly by the train of thought into which he had talked himself. Indeed, he was but a young man, and, for the reason also of his being a good and able seaman, thoroughly sensible of the heavy obligations of his post. Only landsmen who have been much at sea as passengers can understand something of the life of the captain of a ship. They will remember lying in their berths, listening to the crashing of the seas outside and the heavy groaning and straining of the laboring fabric, and thinking of the man in whose hands their lives lie, standing in streaming clothes upon the black and storm-swept deck, with vigilant eye and brave heart, ready for any emergency, searching the tempestuous night lowering upon the froth-covered deep, and watching his ship, as faithful to his duty and as sleepless — though many long hours may have passed since he closed his eyes—as the magnetic card that glimmers like a glow-worm under the eyes of the helmsman. They will remember the generous glow of admiration and respect that warmed them towards him when, the long voyage being over, all the perils of the deep escaped, the coast, that their hearts have long been intent upon, looms up with the sunshine upon it right ahead, and the old or the new home is in sight at last. But even such seasoned voyagers as these know but little of the truth; for they do not follow the shipmaster into his cabin, and see him poring over charts and intricate calculations; their ears are not at his mouth to catch the hundred anxieties inspired in him by the weather, the conduct of the crew, the efficiency of the mates, the length of the voyage, the expectations of his owners.

However, I was determined my husband should not long remain depressed; and, as I had a hearty, laughing, cordial nature to deal with, it did not take me long to set him talking light-heartedly, so that when we went below —he to take his nightly allowance of one glass of brandy grog, and I to nibble a biscuit—his spirits could not have been better had we been in the Atlantic, prosperously bowling along with the trade-winds shouting in the rigging.

CHAPTER XIX.

A SMALL DISAPPOINTMENT.

It did not remain calm all night; but there happened what was as unserviceable as if the air had kept breathless, and that was a westerly wind; a mild breeze indeed, soft, sweet, and genial, as if the month of May were coming along with it, but dead in our teeth; so that, had we

got under way, we should have to keep 'bouting ship, a
tedious job even where there is plenty of room for long
boards, but disgusting to a ship's crew when it has to be
performed repeatedly, and perhaps in the eye of a current
that brings the vessel regularly back to her old starting-
place.

When I left the deck it was perfectly calm, and the
sea like a looking-glass full of stars and the red points of
the riding-lights on the vessels about us, and of the flashing lanterns of the light-ships; and I had no notion that
there was any change until I went on deck in the morning, and felt the mild west wind blowing.

Well, it was such a scene as might have made a French-
man in love with the sea; for, first, the water was blue,
throbbing and sparkling, full of little surges with white
crests, like flocks of floating sea-gulls; then in the south
the sky was beautiful with a net-work of spray-like clouds,
as if the silver azure had been inlaid with feathers of
pearl. The early sunshine streamed full on Deal and the
green country beyond, and gave an exquisite distinctness
to the distant Ramsgate coast, while the near gigantic
headland of the South Foreland stood up as though surveyed through a magnifying-glass. The breeze had
thinned the shipping in the Downs, all the eastward and
northward bound vessels having got away before daybreak; but at least a dozen remained, and a bright show
they made upon the glittering blue, most of them, like
ourselves, with a fragment of canvas hoisted, to ease the
strain of the tide—that washed in foam past us, and ran
away in a wake—upon their cables.

I found Richard, who had left our cabin long before I
awoke, on deck watching the men washing down. He
knew what was in my mind, for almost his first words
were, "When a woman wants her way she'll get it. Jess,
I believe you're capable of outweathering the weather itself. I suppose it's decided that we are to take a run
ashore after breakfast?"

"Yes, dear," said I, very affectionately; "quite decided. I want to see Deal."

"Well, it'll be a break for you. There's a long stretch
of sea before us; so trot down, and tell the steward to

bear a hand with breakfast, that we may get ashore and look at the hats and bonnets in the windows before a change of wind comes."

I did not want bidding twice.

"Steward," said I, "please get breakfast at once, as the captain and I are going ashore."

"Breakfast at once!" he exclaimed, looking at me sourly out of his little pantry, where he stood polishing a spoon. "I doubt if the cook's got the galley fire lighted yet, mum."

"Oh, yes, he has," said I, "for I saw the smoke. Be as quick as you can." And I entered the berth, that the man might have no excuse to argue the point. Indeed, what with Mr. Heron, and the carpenter, and this steward, whose name was John Orange, any one would have supposed that the person responsible for the crew, whether crimp, owner, or shipping-master, had made a point of furnishing out a ship's company by selecting the gruffest and worst-mannered men he could find.

To economize time I dressed myself ready to go ashore; but on entering the cabin found the steward leisurely laying the cloth. His impudence made me angry, and I exclaimed, "If you are not more active, I'll prepare the table myself; and if Captain Fowler asks me why I'm doing your work, I'll tell him."

"Why," he answered, falling back a step, and extending his arms in an attitude of expostulation, "the cook says the water in the coppers ain't even warm yet."

As the men would shortly be going to breakfast, I knew this statement must be false, the excuse of an ill-tempered man, who was annoyed because his routine was temporarily deranged. Determined to take the matter into my own hands, feeling, at least, that I was as much mistress in this cabin as I should be in my own house, I went on deck, and walked boldly to the galley.

This was a small house, fitted with a cooking-range and boilers, and entered by a door on either side the deck, travelling in grooves, so that the weather-door could be kept shut when the water flew over the rail. Attached to it, aft, was the carpenter's berth, where he kept his tool-chest, slung his hammock, and had his meals, a mercy for which I was deeply grateful, for had the man lived aft and joined us at our table, the cabin must have been unbearable. The cook was lord of his galley, and it was by his favor only that the crew were allowed to dry their clothes, or light their pipes, or come in "for a warm." He was variously referred to as cook, or "Drainings," or sometimes as "Old Slush" and "Doctor;" but his real name I never knew. He was busy with a swab when I put my head in and asked if the steward had told him we wanted breakfast at once.

"Yes, mum," he answered, staring hard to find me so close to him, for I had never before quitted the quarter-deck.

"He says he cannot hurry, because the water in the coppers isn't warm," said I.

"Warm!" he shouted, resenting this as a professional attack. "Why, it's biling! Warm! I'll give him ten shillings down if he'll turn to and wash himself in it. Warm! but what's the coppers got to do with the cabin? Yon's the capt'n's hot water," said he, pointing to a steaming kettle. Then, sinking his voice, he exclaimed, "Ay, it's John Orange. I've been shipmates with John Orange afore. John Orange is a man who doesn't mind telling a lie." Then, bursting out again, "If he'll come and wash himself with what's in them coppers—never mind about it's being the men's tea—I'll put ten shillings of as good money as ever he handled into his pocket."

I went aft again, surveyed, as I passed along, very critically by the crew, who wondered what I was doing out of my own latitudes, and met Richard, who asked me, with some surprise, what I had been talking about with the cook. I explained, telling him that I did not want him to be troubled with such matters, and that I looked upon the steward as my servant, whom I was quite able to take in hand, sour as he was.

"And so you shall take him in hand," said he, "but first let me show you how to do it."

I followed him into the cabin, where, looking around him as if amazed to find nothing ready, he said, "Where's the breakfast, steward?"

"I'm getting of it, sir," said the steward, looking a bit

frightened, and putting some bustle into his movements.

"Getting of it," cried my husband. "Why, you lazy, skulking swab, you! Getting of it! You've had twenty minutes to do it in, and here's only the cloth laid! If the breakfast is not on the table in ten minutes"—pulling out his watch—"I'll log you for insubordination; I'll turn you out of the cabin into the forecastle and make a *boy* of you. Getting of it!" And here he dosed him with a whole broadside of marine abuse, calling him scaramouch, soger, and such like quarter - deck names; and, though employing no term unfit for me to hear, utterly overwhelming the steward, who probably little suspected my husband's capacity of putting his contempt and anger into words such as a nautical man would fully appreciate the force of, and who, after muttering something about its being the cook's fault, bolted up the companion-ladder.

"If it's to be a struggle for mastery between me and those under me, they'll find me tough eating for their teeth, though they had the triple grinders of a shark," said Richard, breathing quickly. "Why, what kind of a crew have they shipped for me?" he continued, pacing the cabin quickly. "Are we among Yankee Irishmen, disguised as mates and stewards, or among English seamen? If we go on in this fashion we shall be having a mutiny before we're out of the Channel. Insubordination in a *steward!*—the most useless hand aboard a ship! —a breek'd chambermaid! A creature with nothing to do but to polish plates and to look out for *lurches* as he comes along with the dishes! A nice beginning!"

I felt as indignant as he, and felt it the more because I was afraid that, taking the mate on one side and the steward on the other, my husband's temper might come very near to being ruined. I remembered my father saying that even one skulking, grumbling hand is enough to imbitter a captain for a voyage, and make him disliked by the crew, by forcing him into severity and even tyranny. Ship's companies are, unhappily, only too willing to listen to abuse of their skipper, and take their tone from the language of those among them who hate him. Even a steward, little as Jack esteems the holder of that post,

by going forward and talking among the men, may excite
disaffection and ill-feeling towards "the land of knives
and forks," as the sailor calls the cabin.

However, I kept these thoughts to myself, and, the
steward having put breakfast on the table within the pre-
scribed ten minutes, we were presently on deck, waiting
while a couple of seamen jumped into one of the quarter-
boats and got her alongside.

I had caught hold of the man-ropes, and was in the act
of putting my foot on the short gangway-ladder that had
been thrown over, when Richard exclaimed, "Come back,
Jessie! Below there! Get the boat hooked on again.
Mr. Short, send some hands aft to hoist the boat. Smartly
now! We'll make use of this slant."

I left the gangway, much surprised.

"The wind has shifted, and will let us get away, Jess,"
said my husband. "I am sorry you should be disappointed; but, depend upon it, it's all for the best."

I was not so disappointed as he supposed. Certainly I
should have liked to inspect the salt, quaint, sparkling
town that lay grouped behind the white foreground of
shingle; but my spirits had been damped by the little
trouble in the cabin and the reflections it had given rise
to; and, besides, the mere circumstance of my husband
speaking as if glad to escape the excursion reconciled me
to the abandonment of it.

The wind, blowing very regularly all the time, must
have shifted at the moment that I was about to enter the
boat; yet not so suddenly but that my husband's vigilance noticed the change at the instant it happened. I
walked aft to be out of the road, and sat down on the
grating to watch the process of getting under way.
The westward-bound vessels in the Downs were as alert
as ourselves, and already from some of them came the
clanking noise of revolving windlasses, as the crews hove
short before running aloft to make sail. When our boat
was hoisted all hands went forward to man the windlass,
and I remarked the steward's gloomy face among them.
Mr. Heron stood between the knight-heads, the carpenter
heaved with the men, and my husband paced the quarter-
deck. For some moments the resonant clank, clank of

the windlass pawls went on with no other sound along
the decks, but then a hoarse voice broke into a song,
which, at regular intervals, was taken up by all the men
in a chorus, the hurricane note of which must have been
distinctly audible at Deal. Their song was "Across the
Western Ocean"—a melody full of plaintiveness, as many
of the sea-working choruses are, or *were*, for the steam-
engine has taken their place, and the anchor now comes
up to the humming of cranks and piston-rods. I wish I
could convey the inspiriting effect produced by first the
long-drawn hoarse solo and then the storming chorus, the
metal windlass pawls clanking rhythmically through the
ocean song, combined with the picture of the bark heaving softly upon the flashing blue of the streaming waters,
her masts soaring into the light morning azure, and the
whole framed with the rocky heights of the South Foreland and the low-lying plains of Deal and Sandwich on
the one hand, and on the other the vessels getting under
way, with here and there a steamer stretching along
this side of the red-hulled light-ship, and leaving behind
her a long trail of smoke that came floating towards us in
a clearly defined line, its shadow tossing under it upon
the sea.

As a rule, the mate, whose post is forward when the anchor is being weighed, will inspirit the men by such cries as
"Heave, boys!" "Up with her, cheerily!" "Heave, and
raise the dead!" "All together, my lads!" and the like,
taking advantage of the pauses between the solo and the
chorus to employ these hearty and encouraging invitations. But Mr. Heron remained silent, merely looking on.
Indeed, he would have passed for a passenger, and a steer-
age passenger, too, instead of a mate full of responsibilities and business, as he stood in the eyes of the bark,
moving now and then just to steal a peep at the cable
over the bow.

Presently he reported the cable hove short; on which
Richard gave the order to loose the sails. All hands left
the windlass, and then began the bustle I described when
the tug left us off the Tyne. The necessary canvas having been set, the windlass was again manned, a hand came
aft to the wheel, and in a few minutes the mate bawled

out that the anchor was a-weigh. This meant that the
anchor was off the ground, easily guessed by me, who,
looking at a little schooner anchored on a line with the
light-ship, saw her slowly glide away to the left.

The moment the bark lay down to the breeze that was
slowly freshening and coming very raw and chill with
the eastering of it, she felt the impulse, and, meeting a
little sea, broke it into foam, like the Chinaman's method
of taking the oath with a saucer, to show the honesty of
his intentions, and, with a short spring, settled herself
down to her work. It was as good as going ashore to me.
I should have liked to see Deal, but I hugely relished
what was now happening too. I heard my husband tell
Mr. Heron, when the mate came aft, not to spare her, that
there was twenty-four hours' reckoning to make good,
and that he must show those hookers the road, pointing
to the vessels which had got under way with or before
us, and were swarming along in a body, crowding canvas
fast, and illustrating their sailing qualities in a way that
made the scene as gay as a yacht race. But after we had
got our tacks down and rounded the South Foreland we
were soon among them and drawing ahead like a roll of
smoke. Only one match we had, and that was the big
American. Her anchor had been catted when ours was
still on the ground, and accordingly she was very nearly
abreast of Folkestone before we had hidden Deal behind
the Foreland ; but when a shift of helm enabled our men
to slacken the lee-braces, bringing the breeze about a point
and a half abaft the beam, so that every stitch of canvas
upon the bark was holding wind and pulling honestly,
and the little vessel began to *speak*, piling up the white
water in front of her, and slanting her masts as a race-
horse slopes his ears when in full career, I soon saw that,
let Brother Jonathan drive as he would, he was bound to
come astern presently.

The sea has few livelier experiences to offer than these
unpremeditated races. I have heard of a race lasting
from the southwestern skirts of the Bay of Biscay to the
Cape of Good Hope, the vessels being in sight of each
other all the time, and as the mornings came round sometimes one being astern and then the other, until at last

the passengers aboard the two ships grew so excited that they would make bets, writing with chalk on black-boards which could be read with the telescope, and, in consequence, some hundreds of pounds changed hands when the ships finally arrived at Melbourne within two days of each other.

We passed the other vessels, which were mainly deep coasters, so easily that they provoked no interest in me outside their picturesque appearance and those speculations as to their missions, the people aboard, and so forth, which no craft of any kind ever encountered my view without exciting; but it was nice to beat the Yankee, which was a fast ship, and made a very lordly object with her high black sides, elliptical stern, and cotton-white canvas towering and shining and tapering as high as the royal-mastheads, with the naked skysail-poles pointing above them like flag-posts.

"I am sorry, for your sake, Jess, that we could not take a run ashore," said Richard, coming up to me as I stood looking, with a binocular at my eyes, at the noble range of Dover cliffs as we were passing.

"Never mind, dear," I answered. "I am heartily enjoying this. It's a greater treat than a walk through Deal."

"I can tell you now," he continued, "that nothing but your wish to go ashore would have made me entertain the notion. I doubt if I could have been easy away from the bark with Heron in charge of her."

"Is your opinion of him as low as that?" I exclaimed.

"I don't trust him," he said, shaking his head. "I'm sorry, for he may be well-meaning. But I go beyond his seamanship, and doubt his principles. If it's a mere prejudice on my part, his conduct, if he goes on well, will remove it. Then there was another consideration; a couple of men would have pulled us ashore, and been left in charge of the boat. Suppose, after having seen enough of Deal, we had walked down to the beach and found the boat, but no men? Sailors have a knack of running away. I don't say this would, but that it might, have happened. It would have involved more delay, and much trouble and anxiety. These thoughts were in my mind when I told you at the gangway that our remaining aboard was all for the best. Still, I am sorry that you should have been disappointed," said he, fondly. "I want my little wife to enjoy her first voyage with me."

"And she is enjoying it," I replied. "Don't say another word about my being disappointed. I was never happier, Richard."

And, indeed, I felt as I spoke. Even had my husband's professional anxieties been greater than I supposed them, my not being able to master their significance would to a large extent have prevented me from sympathizing with him ; I mean to such a degree as to suffer in my own spirits from the responsibilities that weighed upon him. My notion was that much of his anxiety and his short fits of foreboding were due to his being master, and to these being very early days, when the sense of his professional obligations would be sharp. I said to him, as we stood talking and looking at the coast and at the American vessel ahead, " When we are once fairly out at sea, Richard, and the life on board settled down into steady routine, your mind will grow easier ; you'll take Mr. Heron as you find him, and cease troubling yourself with the man, outside his bare duties."

" No doubt, Jess, no doubt," said he, smiling, but not speaking very heartily either ; which set me thinking whether, no matter how clever a wife may think herself, she is likely to understand her husband's business half so well as he understands it himself.

But it was impossible long to possess any other thoughts than those purely excited by the brilliant, gay, and beautiful scene through which we were now sweeping. Although we were heading for the middle channel, our course gave us a good view of the land ; and we had the coast in sight as far as Dungeness. Through the glass I could distinctly see the towns of Dover and Folkestone, and the hard, wintry green of the country trending towards Dymchurch and Romney, with now and again a windmill, a church spire, and the like. The water was a pale blue down to the very point where it melted into surf, and here and there upon its trembling, luminous surface I could see some little brown vessel, a lugger, a cutter, creeping close along inshore. I gazed earnestly at the land, for Richard told me that when we were clear of Dungeness we might not sight the coast again, and that knowledge made me find a peculiar fascination in it.

Indeed, this leave-taking of the shores of the old home is one of the sad moments of the voyage out. You feel, in truth, that the journey is fairly begun, and that the mighty problem of the deep is before you, for the vessel on which you stand to solve. You think, before you set eyes again on the green or white or brown coasts, of the changes which may take place, of the friends who may die in your absence, of the few who will remember you when you are away. But, whatever may be your mission, whether you are leaving home for good, or for pleasure, or on business, and for a time only, the fading coast of your well-loved country will move you as a faint, reluctant farewell, almost as tender as the kiss and the tears of those from whom you have already parted. The sea is before you, like life itself, full of uncertainty, and you feel, as you turn your eyes from that quarter of the deep on which the last film of the English coast has flickered and vanished, and look into that spacious surface of sky and water towards which the bowsprit points, as a child feels when it leaves its mother for the first time to descend into the great amphitheatre of life, and join in the struggle there for bread.

I was aroused from these thoughts by my husband calling my attention to the American ship we were overhauling, but so slowly as to make the contest of speed fairly exciting. The other vessels which had got under way with or before us were some distance astern, making a lively picture of the sea in that direction as they swarmed along, heeling over to the breeze, all of them with a brilliant tremble of foam at their cutwaters, and the smaller ones tossing, and occasionally flinging up the surges in showers of spray as they plunged in our wake and quarters; but Jonathan—though not quite holding his own, was trying his best to do so—was evidently "working up his old iron," and had no mind to be passed by the little clipper bark that was crawling up to him in a smother of froth that might have been taken for the base of a water-

spout. We could see his crew giving a drag here, a small
pull there, getting the watch-tackle on to the foretack,
tautening and setting the canvas in such a way that not a
foot of the white cloths but was adding its weight to the
general strain.

But it would not do. Though she was half as lofty
again as we, and light, though stiff enough for sailing
well, and apparently in good trim, there was nothing in
her to stop the beautifully modelled hull of the *Aurora*
from showing her the road. As the breeze gathered
weight we improved our pace, and it was a sight to look
over the side and watch the rush of the white water spinning past in hissing whirlpools with an angry roar. Yet,
as Jack says, "we held on all," and so did the Yankee.
All that was done was to send the royal halliards over to
windward. I could not have better realized our rate of
sailing than by observing the manner in which both the
Yankee and ourselves picked up a large three-masted topsail schooner. The long and gleaming wake that poured
out from under her counter made her look to be running
like a race-horse; yet we passed her as if she had been in
stays or hove to, and I saw her crew staring at us as we
swept along, as if they believed the race between the
ship and the little bark was something more than a casual
encounter and contest of speed.

"Look at that old chap in a tall hat!" exclaimed Richard, laughing. "His mouth's wide open, Jess. What
does he think? that we have a bailiff or a police-officer
aboard, and that our business is to nail the American for
a debt, or for having a criminal among her dunnage?"

"There comes something to make us feel insignificant,
Richard," said I, pointing to a magnificent ocean steamer
that had crept up unobserved by us to within a mile and
a half on our weather-quarter. She was the biggest vessel I had ever seen, and I forgot all about the American
ship in looking at her. It was wonderful to view her
speeding along, with not a fragment of canvas upon her
short masts, propelled by a power that, being hidden,
made a miracle of the flying stately shape; the gilt tracery
about her shapely iron stem threw out dull flashes, which
were repeated like echoes in the glass of the scuttles along

her dark-green sides. She came along with the speed and silence of a cloud-shadow, with a short height of steel-bright waters under her bows, seemingly fixed there, and a thin glittering ribbon of a wake, no longer than a thirty-ton yacht would throw off, following her as though she towed a band of silver cloth. Yet, if her manner of passing us materially qualified the sense of speed inspired by our own rushing motion, our vanity might have been consoled by the interest our vessel appeared to excite among the crowds of people who gazed at us, many of them with glasses at their eyes, from her fore and after decks. In our way, no doubt, we were as fine a sight as she, and some might think finer ; for, to my mind, the steamer never yet was built, no matter how noble and lordly the fabric, that could approach, in beauty, picturesqueness, and majesty, a handsome sailing-ship, leaning before a steady breeze, whitening the deep and green and windy waters over which she passes like a column of snow-like vapor, and looking as perfect a detail of the mighty deep as a giant albatross or the little petrel that seems born of the foam of its surges.

By the time the steamer was abreast of us, we were abreast of the Yankee, whose skipper, coming to the rail, shouted through his nose that he guessed if there was room in this gutter—meaning the English Channel—for studding-sails, he wouldn't mind losing an hour or two in giving us a lesson in the art of towing. This quarter-deck defiance was re-echoed by his men forward, who fired over their forecastle rail several specimens of American humor at our crew. But we were passing them fast, being to windward, and taking the wind out of their sails, and could listen without anger to their derisive shouts. Gradually the big black vessel settled astern, while the great steamship, her hull full of sunshine and the merest stain of faint gray smoke oozing from her low, squab, powerful-looking funnel, drew ahead ; and by the time the latter had dwarfed herself into a toy in the far distance, we had laid the Yankee's jibboom flush with the sea, and were slowly sinking her courses.

13

CHAPTER XX.

ON THE ATLANTIC.

MY husband proved a prophet when he told me to take a good look at the Dungeness coast, as there was a chance of our not sighting land again. Towards the close of the afternoon the wind shifted into the northeast, the bright, spring-like weather vanished like wax before fire, dark clouds came rolling up, and the horizon grew thick all round. Old Winter was awake again, and, as if angry at having been caught napping, made his presence felt by several hard squalls full of hail-stones, which rattled upon the deck like buckets of duck-shot emptied from the tops, together with a wind so piercing that nerve and bone ached in torment with every blast of it. Happily, the breeze which stormed up before dark into very nearly half a gale favored us, and we drove along over the short, angry Channel sea under double-reefed topsails and fore-sail.

This change from the mild sunshine and soft southerly breeze of the Downs to an arctic temperature, a rough and foaming ocean, a mirky, near horizon, and an atmosphere constantly darkened by heavy discharges of sleet and hail, was a good illustration of the vicissitudes of the sea. Richard said to me that it was worse than Cape Horn, because there, cold as it is, you have the whole Pacific to move in, while the icebergs—the one danger—can be smelt when they can't be seen; but here it was not only bitterly cold, but the sea was narrow and crowded with shipping, so that to keep clear of collisions and to come through the thickness safely, a man had need to possess as many eyes as a peacock carries in its tail.

I could stand a deal of weather, but the deck was now become something above my womanly endurance. I therefore remained below for some hours; but, wearying of my own company, I thought, just before the night settled down, that I would go and have another look at the sea, and accordingly wrapped myself up warmly and mounted the steps, but got no farther than the companion. One glance round was enough, for the cold was as if some one had nipped my cheeks with a pair of pincers. The bark was the most desolate-looking object that could be imagined. The decks were dark with wet, and, as she plunged, flying masses of green water constantly broke over the forecastle, and came hissing in small white torrents along the lee scuppers. Her slender bands of topsails, gray with the moisture, waved to and fro under the hard wintry slate of the sky, along which there were rolling masses of cloud, in color and motion like the smoke that breaks in coils from a factory chimney when the furnaces have been newly fed; and over the topsails the naked spars and yards swayed heavily, looking as black as ink, with here and there a tracing of snow that gave a very sharp and clear finish to the picture of frost and gloom.

Two men were on the lookout, gleaming in oilskins, holding on tightly, and now and again stooping as the bursts of water flew over the rail; the rest of the watch hung in a group to leeward of the galley, where they found some shelter from the wind; and a rugged mob they made, in their black or yellow sou'westers, which gave a peculiar whiteness to the faces of those whose complexions were pale, and in shaggy coats and oilskin leggings, as they stood beating their arms upon their breasts to put life into their frozen fingers, and stamped upon the deck with their heavy sea-boots. It is at such times as these that one sees what the sailor's life is, and how much truth there is in the romances which represent him as always, more or less, smoking, drinking, fiddling, singing, yarning, and acting as if the sea were merely a merry playground, and there was nothing to do but sit down and let the soft winds blow him along.

I peeped around the companion to get a glimpse of my husband, and saw him walking up and down the weather side of the deck, while the mate stumped the lee side. They were both muffled up to their noses. Richard, in-

deed, in his sou'wester, the flaps well over his ears, com-
forter, oilskins, sea-boots, and mittens, which swelled out
his figure to twice its ordinary size, looked the picture of
one of the old-fashioned North Sea pilots, completely cor-
responding in his appearance with the traditions which
represent those sturdy mariners as going dressed in stock-
ing-net and linen shirts, two thick waistcoats, shag jacket
and pea-coat, woollen stockings, fearnaught trousers, and
long boots!

But two minutes' exposure was enough for me. I hurried below again, removed my mufflers, and, taking a
book, sat cowering over the cabin stove, listening to the
groaning of the hull and to the long-drawn, mournful,
and depressing moaning of the wind and the seas.

We carried this weather with us the whole way down
Channel. I saw very little of Richard, for I rarely left
the cabin, and he hardly entered it, except to take his
meals, which he despatched with such expedition as to
leave me no time to converse with him. Not a light was
to be seen at night, the sea being shrouded in a dreary
haze, which a squall would at intervals close right round
us, leaving nothing visible but a few fathoms of the turbulent surges, over which the bark wildly plunged as she
foamed along her course.

Whenever I hear of the anxieties of shipmasters, I
always think of that run down Channel. Even in clear
weather a man wants all the wits God has gifted him
with to carry his vessel safely through those waters; but
in such weather as we had the tax upon the brain and
attention is altogether beyond words. It is true that by
this time we were a long way to the westward of the
Goodwin Sands and the dangerous shoals of the Dover
Channel; but an error of compass, a deceptive current, a
small inaccuracy in the dead reckoning, might easily
bring the loom of the coast darkening the haze close to
us, not to mention that horrible risk which thick weather
and strong winds engender—I mean collision, than which
there are but few deadlier marine perils, and certainly
none that is so incessantly happening. My husband afterwards told me that during that time he was as often on
the forecastle as on the quarter-deck, not choosing to

wholly trust to the men, but keeping a lookout for himself, and peering into the daylighted mist, or the gloomy folds of the night, until his eyes reeled in his head.

However, every hour of sailing carried us nearer to the open ocean, and on the third morning after leaving the Downs, when I awoke, I found the sun shining and my husband standing at the side of my bunk, waiting to tell me that we were clear of the English Channel, and that the whole Atlantic was under our forefoot.

I little thought, as I lay still a short time, while Richard moved about the cabin, changing his clothes, and talking to me, that this same morning would be memorable in the annals of our lives as introducing the first of those troubles which were to culminate in that great misfortune which it is my main business in writing this homely narrative to relate. Let me here be a little particular, for I am about to enter on the beginning of what that noble, honest writer, Defoe—prince of writers, as I think him, for style, art, pathos, and absolute freedom from sentimentality; whose residence at Gateshead makes us Tynesiders think of him as one of ourselves—would maintain to be a truly surprising, strange adventure.

When my husband left the cabin, I rose and dressed myself; but not till then did I know that I had overslept my usual time of rising by an hour, so that when I entered the cabin I found breakfast ready, and Richard at the table waiting for me. The mate also joined us, emerging from his berth, where he had been having a "wash-down," as Jack says, after having kept the deck since four o'clock. I always felt a constraint in his presence, and hard as I sometimes tried to master it, for the sake of the peace and good-will I desired for the cabin, I never succeeded; nay, I believe my very efforts in that way gave emphasis to my dislike by making him feel my anxiety to conceal it.

"What sort of weather have you, Mr. Heron?" said I. "I have not yet been on deck."

"Fine," he answered. "A pleasant breeze and a clear sky."

"We deserve a clear sky," exclaimed Richard. "A few days of thickness in the English Channel is enough to make a young man's hair white. No wonder shipmasters look old at a time of life which is called a man's prime ashore."

"Yes," said Mr. Heron in his short way, "the sea's full of worry, and mates have their share of it too, sir."

"I ought to know that, and I freely admit it," answered Richard, heartily. "At sea there is very little to choose between the responsibility of the mate and the master. It is one load, with two pairs of shoulders to support it. When both backs are in good accord and pull together, each man gets but half the weight."

Mr. Heron looked at him under his drooping eyelids, and then went on eating his breakfast without answering.

"In large ships," said I, "one hears of third and even fourth mates."

"I have heard of fifth mates," exclaimed Richard, laughing. "But that's when midshipmen are carried, and when the owners are anxious to cultivate premiums. How does Short get on with the men, Mr. Heron?"

"Right enough, so far as I can tell, sir," answered Mr. Heron.

"I notice that you and he are well disposed towards each other, and I am glad to see it," continued my husband, looking, I thought, somewhat attentively at Mr. Heron, who kept his eyes upon the table, unless he lifted them up— when the whites of them would show like a man praying —to glance through the skylight. "Were you shipmates before this voyage?"

"No," he answered, "and I don't know that we're particularly well disposed. Though ship's carpenter, he's second mate too, and I treat him accordingly."

"Well, I say I'm glad to hear it," exclaimed Richard. "I like mates to be on good terms with each other, always providing that their talk and thoughts keep clear of the lee scuppers and leave the quarter-deck sweet for their captain and themselves."

I looked at Richard as he said this, not quite guessing what was in his mind. He was not speaking in the tone and manner a man will employ who wants to give a lesson or a warning by means of strong, broad hints; and yet I could not doubt that that was his intention, remembering, as I did, his reference some time before to the intimacy between Heron and Short. When I glanced at the mate his eyes were upon me, but he immediately dropped them.

"It's an old notion," continued my husband, in a light manner, "that English soldiers and sailors dislike men as officers who are not gentlemen. This may be true of the army and navy, and I believe it would be true of the merchant service were more gentlemen to be found in it, so as to educate Jack into distinguishing between the cad and the well-bred man. But a good seaman without manners will always stand well with the forecastle; and, considering the disposition on the part of working-people to drag down to their own level the men who have risen from among them by their own abilities, I want no better testimony to the seafaring qualities of a sailor than to hear of him mixing familiarly with a crew, and yet holding them well in hand when his duties call him up to take charge of them. If Short has the men's friendship in the forecastle and their respect on deck, he's a good man, depend upon it."

"Yes," said I, rather illogically, but rendered aggressive by the mate's manner, "particularly as he has a very unprepossessing appearance to contend against."

"Oh, that means nothing at sea. There's no beauty on the ocean; it's all under water among the mermaids," said Richard, laughing, but winking at me, too, as much as to say, "No more of *that* argument, Jess."

"I can't tell you what's thought of Short by the men, sir," said the mate.

"And what sort of a crew do you find them, Mr. Heron?" continued Richard, still preserving his light, open manner. "They appear fairly smart to me—all but James Snow, perhaps, who'll be none the worse for the wigging I gave him for not reporting the vessel that day off the Tyne."

The mate took a little time to reply, as if considering within himself the manner rather than the matter of his rejoinder, and then said, "I think you'll find there will be trouble among them soon, sir."

"What makes you suppose that?" inquired Richard quickly, yet without sharpness or eagerness.

"I understand there's talk going on forward that some of the men who shipped as able seamen are not fit for their work," answered the mate.

"You understand; from whom, pray ?"

"From Mr. Short."

"Oh ! have *you* noticed anything in that way, Mr. Heron ?"

"Ever since I became mate," answered Mr. Heron, "I've made it a rule never to take notice of what goes on among the crew until the matter's brought aft. If there's any grumbling, it'll find the road to this end of the vessel fast enough."

I cannot tell what immediate impression this speech made on Richard, but its effect upon me was to lead me then and there to believe that the mate was a rascal, that he hated my husband, that he meant mischief, and was with the crew in any disaffection then brewing.

"Well," said Richard, "as you say, Mr. Heron, there will be time enough to trouble ourselves when the men bring their grievances aft." With which he changed the subject, talking to me about the Channel scenery we had missed, the beauty of the Isle of Wight viewed from the sea at sunset, and so on.

Presently Mr. Heron quitted the table, and withdrew to his berth. I looked at my husband, and was about to speak; but he put his finger to his lips.

"Softly, Jess," said he, in a low voice ; "though the man is not altogether an ass, he has long ears, and when nature bestows those appendages on the human animal, she never omits to supply him with the principles which go to the proper using of them. I see through him, and the view is not made more cheerful by his appearing not to care whether I see through him or not. Meanwhile, all is well, and you have nothing to worry yourself about, Jess. If it is to be a contest between Heron and me, take my advice, and stake your money on the bigger man ;" and, giving me one of his cordial smiles, he drew himself up with an air of half-humorous pride, and laid his hands upon his broad chest. He spoke almost in a whisper, for Heron's berth was very nearly opposite to where he sat.

The arrival of the steward made me leave the table.

This fellow, though he had no capacity whatever to infuse anything resembling civility into his demeanor, had bestirred himself somewhat since that morning in the Downs when my husband rated him ; yet I never cared to be in the cabin when he was fussing about, and was always uneasy at table when he hovered near.

"Are you going on deck, Jessie ?" said Richard.

I answered "Yes," as it was fine.

"You'll find the air keen, so keep moving about. I shall lie down for an hour or two."

I wrapped myself up, and, ascending the companion-ladder, emerged into a bright, rippling, blue-and-white scene of heaven and sea. I went to the side to look, for this was the great Atlantic Ocean which I had traversed, when a little girl, in the voyage I took to the West Indies with father ; but the majesty of whose boundless horizon —the vastness of which was magnified by the thoughts of the mystery of the wondrous leagues upon leagues of water lying behind the clear blue line against the shelving sky— could not affect me then as it now did. A fresh breeze was blowing, but there was little sea, though there followed in the wake of the bark a long swell, which, as it swept under the vessel at regular intervals, gave an indescribable grace and beauty to her motion.

She was under all plain sail, and was running along lightly and without noise ; but very fast, it seemed to me, as I stood gazing at the passing clouds of foam which revolved under the surface of the water, and at the streaks and bubbles and the hundred exquisite milk-white configurations which were conjured up by the keen stem as it tripped through the fountain-like surges, and sent them scattering in showers of sleet and snow on either hand.

There was nothing in sight, though to windward the shoulders of the pearly clouds rising above the horizon might well have passed for the canvas of line-of-battle ships bearing down with regal stateliness before the wind. The morning was an extraordinarily exhilarating one, full of health, of the frosty sweetness of an ocean breeze, with nothing to taint its heaven-born purity for thousands of miles of flashing silver sunlight, of dark-blue water, the whole forming a sparkling setting for the bark that

swirled along with the merry strains of the breeze in
her rigging, and her decks like lace-work, with the jetty
shadows of the shrouds and backstays.

***

CHAPTER XXI.

MUTINY.

YET, in spite of the joyous inspiration of the day, I found
myself secretly anxious, and even depressed. When I
came to consider the matter, I could find nothing in the
mate's words to justify my foreboding, for, after all, my
husband was captain ; he could break the mate, and send
him forward, or put him under arrest if his conduct ne-
cessitated an extremity of that kind ; and I knew enough
of Richard's character to guess that discipline was not likely to fail for the want of resolution and courage on his
part to enforce it.

And yet, reason as I would, I could not ease my mind
of the worry in it. There was a weight on my spirits such
as might be compared to the feeling a person has when he
awakes in the morning to a trouble which he cannot determine until his full senses have come to him. That, I
say, was the sort of feeling I had. I could not imagine
anything unhappy or distressing likely to take place, and
yet I felt as if something evil were in the air, and would
be upon us by-and-by.

When one fairly gets into this sort of posture of mind,
a fine day only makes the depression worse. I remember
father once saying that a man belonging to a vessel he
commanded made several attempts to jump overboard in
dark, foul, miserable weather, but never had the heart,
as he told his shipmates, who took his threats as a joke ;
yet when the weather cleared up, and the day was beautiful as a dream, he tossed his hat down when nobody was
looking, put his hands together, and went overboard, shouting, "Thank God for this release !" The bright sun and
the happiness of the shining scene were too much for him ;
it was like ridiculing his misery ; whereas a dark day and

drenching rain would have made him think nature understood his troubles, and took his part against life.

But this carries me too far. All I want to say is that the fine morning did not find me in the spirits to enjoy it. I looked and saw what was to be seen, but my eyes were not those I had in the Downs, nor in the North Sea when the fog rolled away.

Mr. Short—he was called "mister" when he had the watch—was on deck, straddling along the weather side, with a large junk of tobacco in his mouth, the juice of which he would politely discharge by stepping over to the lee rail. The crew were variously employed on deck and aloft, and seemed to be working very quietly. As I looked at them, I thought of their forecastle, and wondered what sort of place it was, how the men passed their time in it, and the like.

I would have given a great deal to inspect it, and was in the mind there and then to go to the scuttle and ask leave to take a peep. But it was out of the question. I never doubted that I would be respectfully treated, for a sailor must be a ruffian indeed if he is not chivalrous to women. But, apart from the fact that the forecastle is Jack's bedroom, the sailor is a man who does not like people to come and peer at him in his quarters, as if he were a caged animal, a new and strange object lately caught; and that consideration would be sufficient to stop me, even could I have been sure of overriding the dozen objections my husband must certainly have made.

However, I grew tired of walking about alone, and not choosing to go to our berth for fear of disturbing Richard, I went up to Mr. Short, whom I had never yet spoken to, hoping that his gruffness was all outside, and that he would tell me about the life forward, and talk to me in that sailor fashion which is one of the charms of the genuine seafaring character.

I have already described this man's figure as resembling that of a mutilated giant. The suggestion was completed by the length of his arms, his hands being very nearly on a level with his knees; huge knotty brown hands, which hung down as he walked, without swinging; the fingers curled up, as though they grasped a rope, and the palms stained to the complexion of walnut juice with tar and toil. His face was slightly pitted with the scars of small-pox, which gave a finishing touch to its grotesquely rugged character. In each ear he wore a gold hoop of the size of a small wedding-ring. His eyes were deep-set, and black as polished jet beads, the whites, or what is called the whites in most eyes, being of a kind of orange color, somewhat paler, as though the balls were congested. He was dressed in a thick, well-worn coat, flannel waistcoat, round the collar of which was hitched an old black silk neckerchief, and a fur cap that, by compressing his thick hair, caused the lower portion of it to stand out over his ears and at the back of his head as a piece of inflated elastic does when compressed between the fingers and thumb. Though he had more the air of a seaman, in spite of his singular appearance, than Mr. Heron, I own that my old notions of the typical tar, the broad-shouldered, narrow-hipped salt, who rolls along in flowing trousers, with his bronzed and jolly face framed in a circular tarpaulin, had been as rudely shocked by him as by the mate when I first saw him. But life on shipboard easily accustoms one to the oddest-looking associates, and by this time my familiarity with Mr. Short's appearance had robbed it largely of its power of impressing me as something tremendous in its way, and more fit for a fair or a travelling show than a quarter-deck.

He saw that I meant to speak to him, and, as I approached, made one or two feints, as if to look at the compass or exchange sides ; but, finding me coming, he made a stand at the mizzen rigging, and seemed to be suddenly absorbed in the contemplation of the maintop.

"It is strange," said I, as genially as I could, "that we should have been a week at sea without having spoken to each other. What do you think of the bark, Mr. Short ? Does she come up to your expectations ?"

He glanced at me hurriedly, clearly embarrassed to find me talking to him, and, grasping a backstay, began to writhe his body about, while with his other hand he twisted his fur cap first over his nose, then on to the back of his head, affording me a sight of an immensely thick silver ring on his middle finger and a wrist embossed with a mass of tattooing in red and blue.

"Ay, she comes up to my expectations, mum," he answered; "she's dry, and she's fast, and she knows how to go to wind'ard."

"Is the forecastle a comfortable one?" said I.

"Good enough for sailors, though I'm not often in it," he answered, looking away from me.

"Do you mean that it isn't comfortable?"

"I mean it's good enough for sailors who go to sea to become dogs, and don't reckon upon getting more nor kennels to lie in," he replied, raising his voice as if he wanted the able seaman at the wheel to hear him.

"Do the men sleep in hammocks or in bunks?" I asked, hardly knowing whether to go on talking, and putting the question merely for the sake of saying something, though a peculiar glance from him convinced me that he suspected a direct motive in these inquiries.

"Why, there's a mixture of both," he said. "Was ye never in a ship's forecastle!"

"Never."

"Well, I wish that had been my luck," said he, with a short growling laugh, and another glance at the wheel. "My acquaintance with rats and cockroaches would be smaller if that had been the case, and my arm 'ud have been saved a good deal of weariness in trying to clear the weevils out of soft and mouldy bread, that there's ne'er a hog but 'ud toss up and smell to, and leave for sailormen to get plump upon."

"Surely that is not so here?" said I.

"No, no; the provisions are good enough; there's nothing to be said against the provisions," he answered. "Ye were asking questions about ship's forecastles, and I'm answering of 'em, mum."

I thought to myself, if I continue conversing with this man, he will presently say something that would make Richard angry with me for courting. Yet, I did not like to draw away abruptly either; so I said, "I know sailors are treated ill in some ships, but they cannot be thought to fare badly in a new, sound vessel, commanded by a kind and able master, and supplied with as good provisions as can be found at sea."

"I don't suppose they can," he answered, looking away

from me again ; " that is, if ye reckon that nothing more's wanted to make 'em happy and comfortable. However, as I don't live in the forecastle, I can't tell 'ee what's said and done there. I take things as I find 'em—for ye see, it's no part o' my duty to look out for what don't consarn me. And so I agree with you, mum, that our men ought to be satisfied with the provisions, and the vessel, and the kind and able captain as commands us all."

Enough had now been said to determine me to say no more ; and without ado I left him and resumed my walk on the after part of the deck.

Though I knew no more about the sea than what I had gathered from listening to father and his friends—whose conversation on that subject was more educating than any professional manual I ever heard of—I was well aware that it is frequently the misfortune of shipmasters to find themselves associated with officers perilous as subordinates and disagreeable as shipmates. But I could not but suppose it was seldom that two such mates as Heron and Short —for I must call this carpenter a mate—came together under a young captain. Short was a man whose character was not so hard to master as Heron's. In most ship's companies there will be found some growling and cursing old seaman, full of mutiny, who resents every order given to him, looks upon the lightest duty he is told to discharge as a stroke of malice on the part of those above him, and who will sit through a whole watch below abusing the captain. This sort of man is given to prophesying that such and such things will happen—things which he knows *must* happen in the ordinary routine of discipline on shipboard—but over which, when they occur, he will triumph in such exclamations as—"There ! I told you so. I knew it 'ud come ! We're only here to be rode down. It's lucky flogging's out of fashion, or I reckon some of us 'ud be feeling for the skins on our backs, and wondering what's become of 'em," and the like.

I was pretty sure that just such a man as this was Short. He had the face of a growling, sour character, full of rebellion and dislike of superiors, no matter whether they were good or bad ; and though powers were intrusted to him, and he was placed in the position of one of those people whom he would have hated had he been a forecastle hand, yet his nature was not to be altered by the change, so that in his watch on deck he took charge of the bark with the same sullen, rebellious feelings he would have had had his lot been cast among the men. I suppose I brought a woman's shrewdness to bear upon him, and read him through as most women who can use their eyes and have no prejudices to blind them, can read through men. But here I stopped. I mean I could not carry my perception further than the man himself; for my knowledge of forecastle life was too slender to enable me to guess that a character like Short may prove a firebrand among a crew, and set all the rough passions of the rude seamen smouldering, and yet be too clever to give the captain a chance of stopping the mischief; most mutinies being started and ripened by incendiary whispers confined to the forecastle, and by a behavior on deck which disarms suspicion.

Forgive me for dwelling on these mates; if I do so it is because I consider that they were at the bottom of the heavy troubles that afterwards befell us.

I say I believed I could understand Mr. Short; but Mr. Heron puzzled me. Here, at least, was a man of some education; the holder of a master's certificate, with professional interests which could be ruined by misconduct. And yet nothing was more certain than that, although England was only a week astern of us, he hated my husband, was unwilling to aid or second him, and, what was darker and more ill-advised yet, had apparently taken no trouble to conceal from Richard that he was on very close and intimate terms with the coarse and, I will say, the brutal man who kept watch and watch with him.

Well, had you been aboard, and seen me walking up and down the deck, with my face full of thought, you would have supposed I was captain, and had all the responsibilities of that post on my head. As my eye sometimes rested on the ugly, powerful figure of the carpenter, I would say to myself, how much would I give if father were here to take that man in hand! I had every confidence in Richard as a resolute, skilful sailor; but then I could not but think of him, too, as a young man, lacking those stern, unbending qualities which old seamen know so well the use of in their dealings with unprincipled or skulking or mutinous characters. I imagined my father on deck, going up to Short, and having a good look at him, and then giving him one of those doses for which our old Tyneside skippers were famous in their day, throwing all policy overboard, not troubling himself with consequences, but taking the shortest cut at the man, and never removing his hand from his throat, so to speak, until he had got him into port.

All this while the bark was quietly sailing along, heaving with stately grace over the long blue folds of water which chased her, lifting into the azure those gleaming heights whose white beauty and softly graduated proportions I was never weary of admiring, while the men went on with their work; and nothing disturbed the silence but an occasional call from one of them, or the creak of the blocks in which the tiller-chains travelled, or the steady tramp of the mate as he paced to and fro, while the shaling noise of the water alongside seemed to accentuate the stillness, and resembled the blowing-off of steam from a pipe heard at a distance.

Presently I guessed it must be near noon, first, by seeing the men drop their work and go into the forecastle for dinner, and secondly, by the arrival of my husband and Mr. Heron, each armed with a sextant.

"Well, Jess," said Richard, coming up to me, "how have you been getting on?"

"Very well," said I. "I sha'n't perish for the want of fresh air."

"Have you been on deck since breakfast?" he asked.

"Yes," said I; "conning the ship, as you call it, and keeping a bright lookout while you were sleeping."

"But aren't you cold, dear?" said he, with concern. "Why, you must take care, Jess, or you'll overdo it. But perhaps the company was to your liking?" added he, with a glance at Short. "You haven't been flirting with that old beauty, I hope, while I've been snoozing?"

"Does he look like a man who can talk prettily?" said I, laughing. "He is an ogre, Richard, fit for the Christmas pantomime at the Tyne theatre. What evil genius prevailed when the mates and rancid Mr. John Orange were chosen for the *Aurora?*"

"Has he been saying anything to offend you?" said Richard, quickly, and the expression in his eyes grew hard, like a flame when you concentrate its rays.

"No, no," I replied, quickly, too. "I am speaking of his manner."

"Now, Jess, don't notice him. Short is not a man for you even to be civil to. He and Heron are a pair of sea-dogs, only one's more of a mongrel than the other. I'll endeavor to sicken them of me before we reach Sierra Leone, and then, maybe, we'll be able to furnish our cabin and quarter-deck with cheerfuller company."

So saying, he crossed to the side where Heron was standing, and began to ogle the sun through his sextant.

While he was thus employed, I amused myself by watching the ordinary seamen waiting for the cook to fill the mess-kids. The better to see I drew as close as my fear of the cook's language—something had crossed his temper—would suffer me to approach. The kids stood outside the galley door, and the cook filled them by spearing up the bits of beef out of the coppers, and shaking them off the prongs into the kids. One of the ordinary seamen expostulated with him for not taking the kids inside instead of shaking the meat off in the cold air, while every now and again the cook in his wrath would threaten the man's face with his fist; so that from where I stood all that I could see was the ordinary seaman leaning forward eagerly, and abusing the cook, and then recoiling as a naked arm, terminating in a clenched fist, shot out, and then pressing forward again and falling back afresh as the arm and fist went in and out.

At the same time I took notice of a man—a dark-bearded, pale-faced fellow—standing in the forecastle with nothing but his head showing above the hatch. I concluded that he was waiting for the arrival of the dinner; but when the ordinary seamen had carried the kids below, and I had walked aft, I noticed, on looking forward again, that the same head had reappeared, and that the man steadily watched us.

14

Mr. Short had quitted the quarter-deck, and was walking to and fro abreast of the galley. I could not see that he took any notice of the man, whom he approached close in his walk.

"Make eight bells!" called out my husband, meaning by that, that it was noon by the sun.

The carpenter walked over to the bell and struck it. It was more like a preconcerted signal than an ordinary piece of discipline, for, while the last stroke was vibrating, the man whose head had been fixed in the scuttle raised himself and stepped on deck, and, the moment he was up, there appeared another man and another, following fast, as if to a cry of "All hands!"

Richard had come across to speak to me, and was saying something, when, seeing me looking with surprise at the unusual movement forward, he turned his eyes in that direction.

"*Now*, what is it?" said he to himself, almost under his breath; and, stepping to the skylight, he put down his sextant and returned, looking for a few moments very steadfastly at Mr. Heron, whose gaze was fixed on his sextant, as if reading it off, and who did not appear to observe the sudden gathering of the crew.

The carpenter, after striking the bell, entered his berth, and I lost sight of him. It was clear that the crew had assembled for some other purpose than that of merely breathing the air and looking at the weather; but they kept us in suspense for some minutes, while they hung in the wind, talking one to another, and gazing our way with a certain irresolution.

"What are all hands doing on deck? What do they want, Mr. Heron?" exclaimed Richard.

"I'm sure I don't know, sir," answered the mate.

(I'm sure you *do*, then, thought I. What did you mean by saying at table this morning that there was likely to be trouble among the men?)

Richard waited, and then turned on his heel, evidently with the intention of taking up his sextant, and going below. The crew, observing this, made a movement, and came aft in a body. My husband was standing near the cabin skylight, and the men halted a short distance abaft the lee gangway. I was struck by a something in their manner that implied a reckless enjoyment of the business in hand. There was no longer anything irresolute in their bearing. They were of the average type of the merchant-man's crew, rather above than below the average, I should have supposed, there being two men whom I have before described as reminding me of American seamen, who, in their blue dungaree trousers tucked into half-Wellington boots, narrow hips, thin, athletic figures, as elastic as a steel blade, and dark, bearded faces, gave, when among the others, a kind of finish to them, like a drawing-master's "touching-up" of the crude sketch of a pupil. In all there were seven of them, counting four able seamen, two ordinary seamen, and an apprentice; the fifth able seaman being at the wheel. There was another pause when they came to a stand, and the picture at that moment often recurs to me; first, the men, some with their arms folded, all with their faces turned our way, and their jaws working as they gnawed in the fulness of their feelings upon the pieces of tobacco secreted in their cheeks; then my husband, waiting for them to speak, his face pale, but full of firmness; just beyond him the mate, toying with his sextant, and stealing glances rather than honestly looking, sometimes biting his under-lip in such a way as to show his upper teeth, though all his biting, and the grimacing that came of it, could not conceal an expression of satisfaction; forward was the cook, with his head out of the galley door, and his face full of curiosity; and lurking at his elbow was the steward, though it was plain, from the trouble he took to conceal himself, that he did not wish us to know he was listening and looking; while all around was the deep blue sea glittering with the flashing silver of the breaking surges, along which the bark, inclined by the fine, gay wind, and lifting a tower of white cloths to the sky, was quietly and swiftly sailing, making the shadows of the little company of men upon her decks sway like pendulums at their feet as the swell slowly lifted and slowly sank her.

"What do you want, my lads? Why have you come aft?" said Richard, in his usual voice, finding that the men only stared, without speaking.

One of the seamen, in blue dungaree and half-boots, a fellow named Isaac Quill, advanced a step, and letting fall his arms, which he had held tightly locked upon his breast, said,

"We've come aft to complain that the vessel's short-handed."

"How short-handed?" said Richard. "The articles provide for five able and two ordinary seamen, and a boy. You have two idlers and a working second mate besides. There are thirteen men in this small bark. Is not that complement enough for you? What do you mean by short-handed?"

"That would be right enough," answered the man, speaking defiantly, "if the five able seamen as signed were *all* able seamen. But if a vessel of this here tonnage is to be worked by three able seamen only, helped by five men who are no better than boys, and with a second mate that's not expected to go aloft onless the torps'ls are to be reefed, I say, as one of them three, that if I'd ha' known what was afore me, I'm cussed if I'd ha' gone to sea in the bark."

"The same here," said the other man in half-boots.

"Who are the inefficient men?" said Richard.

There was no answer.

"Look here!" exclaimed my husband, with some color in his cheeks. "If you have a grievance, let me hear it. If *sogering's* your game, you're in the wrong ship for that kind of skylarking. Who are the inefficient men?" he added, raising his voice.

"Well, Jim Snow's one," replied the spokesman of the men.

"Snow, do you mean to tell me that you don't know your duty as a seaman?" exclaimed Richard.

The man answered sullenly, "Quill and the others say I don't. It's not for me to know."

"Have you ever had occasion to find fault with that man, Mr. Heron?" said Richard, turning to the mate.

"He was the man who failed to report the ketch in the fog," responded the mate.

"I know that. But what are his other faults?"

"There's scarcely been time to find out," said the mate.

"You've had as much time as the men. And, if you

have seen nothing, and if I have seen nothing, what should Quill and Cutter there see to bring them here?" exclaimed Richard. "Send Mr. Short aft, one of you."

Nobody offered to move ; but the apprentice, who was a great strapping lad of eighteen or nineteen, with whiskers, named Anthony Moore, put his hand to his mouth and bawled out, "Mr. Short, the cap'n wants ye !" on which the carpenter at once came out of his house. He was munching, as though he had left his dinner on a sudden, and showed no surprise at seeing the crew gathered in a menacing manner in the gangway.

"Mr. Short," said Richard, "the men are complaining of inefficient hands among them. Quill, there, says that two of the five able seamen are worthless. So far as I have noticed them, one appears as good as another. Mr. Heron professes not to have had time to make discoveries," he continued, with a contempt he took no pains to conceal. "What have you seen ? Is this complaint a reasonable one?"

The carpenter looked at Mr. Heron and then at the men, and said, "I doubt that some of them are not up to much."

"Name them," said Richard.

"Jim Snow's one, isn't he, my lads?" exclaimed Short, addressing the men. "And then there's Dan Cock and Micky Craig."

"Ay, that's it, Mr. Short," answered the men in a chorus, the fellows charged with inefficiency themselves saying, "Ay, that's it."

The mere fact of the carpenter running over the names proved that he and the crew were one in this business. But worse still was it that two of the three men—the third man being at the wheel—who were represented as inefficient, took the accusation of Quill in good part, without a protest, as if the subject had been rehearsed, and they were to play the part of worthless seamen. This alone was ample condemnation of the whole proceeding as an insincere, wicked conspiracy ; for such is the feeling among sailors in the matter of their rating, that no honest man, knowing himself to be equal to his duties, would stand by without indignantly expostulating, should his shipmates call him useless to the captain before his face.

If this was apparent to me, how plain must it have been

to Richard! He was very pale again, but his face was as hard as stone, and nothing but an occasional fluttering of the nostrils and a sharp fire in his eyes gave warning of his temper.

"How this has been brought about," said he, "I don't yet know. Maybe I shall find out. But I see through your meaning, and therefore decline to hear another word upon it. So, now go forward."

One or two men made a movement, as if their habit of obedience were stronger than their mutineering humors; the others stayed where they were.

"That's no answer to our complaint," said Quill. "We signed articles for five able seamen, an' it turns out there are only three. I'm not going to work in a watch in which I'm the only capable sailor-man; and, as the whole thing's wrong, I'm here to tell you, for myself and the others, that, if we're not to have our rights, we shall refuse duty."

"Your rights!" exclaimed Richard. "You shall have your rights, depend upon it. Go forward, do you hear?"

"What's your answer?" said the man named Cutter.

"Why, that you're a gang of loafing vagabonds—a pack of idle ruffians, whom I'll make such an example of yet that you'll remember Captain Fowler while you have breath in your bodies! That's my answer!" shouted my husband, with both his fists clinched, no longer able to control his passion. "I've sailed with worse men even than *you*, and have seen them beaten. I'll match you, Quill! I see through you!" and he made a movement as if he would fall upon them.

I bitterly deplored this outburst of temper. He could do no good by calling the men hard names. Far better had he reasoned with them coolly, for, though nothing should have come of his arguments, yet he was bound to have had their respect by keeping cool and talking temperately. Indeed, I was more frightened by seeing him lose himself in his passion than by the attitude of the men. I stood at the after-end of the skylight, a picture of fear, I make no doubt; for, indeed, when my eyes quitted the faces of the crew, and I looked at Richard, and at the mighty and lonely expanse of waters, in the midst of which our little bark was sailing, the only object probably for leagues and leagues, the helplessness of our situation rushed upon me, and I realized, in all its nakedness, the horror of a mutiny at sea.

"Ye may bully and threaten as much as you please," responded Quill; "but all such talk is no answer to our complaint."

"What do you want the captain to do?" said Heron, breaking silence for the first time, but speaking with an air of indifference that he did not take the least trouble to conceal.

"We want the bark to have her proper complement of working-men," answered Quill.

"Well, you'll have to wait till you get to Sierra Leone," said the mate, talking like a man who was playing a part, too.

"No, we won't," said Cutter. "We mean to put back. There's Mr. Short to bear witness in our favor; and, before we make the English coast, ye'll have found out that we're speaking the truth, sir."

"There'll be no putting back," said my husband, speaking, to my great relief, with moderation, though with intensity. "We're bound to Sierra Leone, and to Sierra Leone we'll go."

"Then the cabin will have to work the ship, for I'm damned if the fo'ksle will," said Quill, folding his arms and lurching about on his legs to the rolling of the vessel.

"You've said it, and we'll see. Go forward, now!" said Richard.

Cutter was about to speak.

"Go forward!" shouted my husband, laying his hand upon the breast of his coat.

Whether the gesture frightened them or not—to me it was horribly significant—I cannot tell; but this time they obeyed, and, going in a body to the forecastle, disappeared down the scuttle.

"Who's gwine to relieve me here?" sung out the fellow who was steering, a mulatto named Dan Cock.

"Keep your place," answered Richard. "Have you no sense, man?"

"No; I can't keep my place; I'm one ob de crew," he answered. "If nobody come, I most let go de wheel—I most, so help me, sah! Eight bells hab gone—my trick's up, sah! Wid dis wedder helm she'll fly right into de eye ob de wind—ay, sure as I stands here—and den look out for de spars." And, as he said this, he made as if he would let go the wheel.

I stood close by, and thinking he was about to quit his post, I took hold of the spokes. He drew away a pace, and stared at me with his mouth open, then took to his heels, ran with all his might to the forecastle, and jumped down the scuttle like a water-rat in a river.

Both Short and Heron stood together at the skylight looking idly on; but neither of them offered to take the wheel from me. Though I had not held a wheel for years, yet I had steered my father's vessel so often, to amuse myself, during the voyages I took with him, that the act came to me very easily now. Moreover, such was the trim of the bark, that, with a slight weather helm, she steered herself, and I had nothing to do but to keep the wheel steady and watch the card. However, I was not to be kept at this work long, for, when the mulatto ran forward, my husband called the steward. The man came out of the galley, walking very slowly, with an acid face.

"Go and take the wheel," said Richard.

"Take the wheel!" cried the man, trying to look as if he thought my husband was joking. "Me?"

"Yes, you! Aft with you, now."

"I can't steer," said the steward.

"Well, you must learn. Go and lay hold of the spokes," said Richard, with his voice tremulous with the temper that was again mastering him.

"It's no part o' my duty to steer," exclaimed the steward. "I didn't ship for that sarvice. There's no seamanship expected of me. Ye may send me aloft, and ye can make me turn to in all-hands work ; but ye can't oblige me to steer."

Whether he was within his rights in this I do not know.* My husband turned from him, and addressing the mates, said,

---

* He was not. It is true that no seamanship is expected from a steward ; but there can be no doubt that he is bound to obey any order the master may give him as though he were a common seaman.—*Editor.*

"Am I to expect any support from you? Let me know at once."

"You have no right to challenge me, sir," answered Heron. "I've disputed no orders as yet."

"And you?" said Richard, turning upon Short.

"Oh," answered he, with a heave of his back, "I've shipped to do certain work, and I'll do it. Only I didn't bargain upon this mess, cap'n, and I'm not going to do the duty of a whole ship's company."

"Then go and relieve that lady at the wheel there."

The man took a moment to think, turned on his heel, and came with a leisurely shuffle to the wheel. I joined my husband.

"Mr. Heron," said Richard, who was pale and deeply agitated, as if beginning for the first time to realize the meaning of the trouble that had come upon us, and, above all, the monstrous unfairness of it, "what part are you playing in this mutiny?"

"No part at all," answered the other, sullenly.

"If you are with the men you are against me. Is that so? Let me know, sir." And I, who had put my hand on his arm, as an appeal to him to restrain his passion, felt him trembling like a freezing man.

"You have no right to speak like that, sir," said the mate in a low voice. "I'm not forced to wear my mind inside out. Time enough for you to find fault when I refuse your bidding. Give me an order and I'll execute it."

There was something so contemptible in this reply, that it must have fallen cool upon the hottest man's passion. Nothing in life was clearer than that this man was on the side of the crew—not because he believed in their trumped-up grievance, not because he cared one jot about them in any way, but because his desire was to see my husband thwarted and troubled, and because he wished to jeopardize, if he possibly could, Richard's professional character and chances, without endangering his own interests. There was, indeed, no other way of accounting for his conduct. Beyond the reprimand Richard had given him at the beginning of the voyage, nothing that I knew of had passed between them to account for the mate's dislike of him.

He might have been jealous of my husband's position, for he was the elder by several years; or his character was sufficiently base and resentful to be set smouldering by even so small a professional circumstance as the reprimand he had received; but, whatever the cause was, there he stood, professing duty with his tongue, but looking dislike, and even hate, with his face, and scarcely concealing his satisfaction at the heavy and perilous embarrassment that had come upon his captain.

My husband stood looking at him for two or three moments without speaking; then, with a changed manner and changed voice, told him to go aft and hoist the ensign, union down, at the peak; and, as he gave this order, he stooped to look under the foot of the mainsail at the sea that way, and afterwards swept the horizon to windward, but there was nothing in sight. I did not like to speak to him. The distress of his mind showed so visibly in his face, that I could hardly bear to look at him. He walked swiftly to and fro athwart the deck, biting his under-lip and knitting his brows; then, in a sudden, passionate manner, hurried forward, gained the forecastle, and closed the top of the hatch in such a way as to imprison the whole of the crew who were below.

CHAPTER XXII.

THE MEN ARE RELEASED.

As he returned, he looked into the galley, and addressed some words, with a violent gesture of the arm, to the cook, and then rejoined me.

"I have them now," said he. "They tame wild beasts by keeping them without water; and those scoundrels shall lie there till thirst brings them to their senses. You see what I have done?" he called out to the mates.

"Yes, sir," replied Heron.

"Understand—both of you—that that scuttle is not to be touched without my orders!"

They answered at once, "Ay, ay, sir."

After a little the mate went below; but my husband continued walking athwart the deck, with his arms locked upon his breast, while I stood beside the skylight watching him, greatly agitated by what had taken place, and wondering what we should do. The bark, as I have said, was under all plain sail. The cloths offered an immense surface ; and, as I looked at the white and glistening spaces, a feeling of terror possessed me when I thought of what must happen if the weather grew boisterous and the men refused to return to their duty.

Presently Richard's eye lighted upon me. He stopped, and, forcing a smile, said, "Your old dreams of the sea never included a business of this kind, did they, Jess?"

"No," I answered. "How has it all come about, Richard?"

"I know no more than you," said he. "But I have no doubt whatever that the mates are at the bottom of it. They have found some rascally hands in the forecastle—Quill, for instance, and that yellow devil who ran away from the wheel just now; and the carpenter, taking his cue from Heron, has encouraged them to grumble, while they in their turn have influenced the rest. The whole thing is vamped up. The men who pretend not to be equal to the discharge of able seamen's duty are merely acting a part agreed upon."

"I felt that as I listened to them," said I.

"Did you note the behavior of the mates? Short actually chimed in with them. Heron, who is more unprincipled, was more cautious. But, depend upon it, he took care to let the crew tell by his manner that he was as much against me as any of them."

"It seems so unreasonable, so monstrous," said I, "that a whole crew should turn like this, so early in the voyage, upon a captain they have nothing to say against. Even were it true that some of the able seamen are bad sailors, it would be a grievance no honest man among them would hold you responsible for."

"When sailors *are* rascals, there's no kind of rascals worse," said he. "This is not the first time a ship's crew have mutinied without just reason ; and I have even heard of a second mate turning out to be the promoter of the rebellion; but never in all my experience and reading have I come across such a thing as both mates — nay, every living creature aboard a vessel—combining against a master who has done them no wrong, and where there is no complaint to be made against the ship. Am I to assume that Heron is paying me out for the talking-to I gave him in the North Sea? But what is the use of conjecturing? Here is the thing right under our noses. How am I to cope with it? Oh, Jess, I wish you were at home! I wish you were safe with your father! Your presence unmans me. Your precious life weighs against the resolution I ought to have to deal with these villains."

He was deeply moved, and looked at me with sorrowful eyes and a face full of bewilderment. I was equally moved to hear him speak in this manner; for, as he knew how great was my love for him, he might well suppose that I could desire no greater glory than to share in his difficulties and perils, and that nothing could shame me more deeply to the heart than to believe him capable of supposing I thought only of my own safety when he was in danger.

Maybe he read what was passing in my mind, for so I interpreted his smile, that was like a recognition of my thoughts. But he was too much troubled to dwell long upon any one point of this sudden calamity. He kept on saying, as if to himself, "Both mates against me! Not a living creature honest enough, among a company of twelve men, to admit that I am being cruelly ill-treated! It is incredible! Who would believe it? Why, if the mates and the seamen had all been convicts, they could not prove more dangerous scoundrels to go afloat with. Our very lives are not safe!" and, as he said this, he laid his hand on his breast.

"What have you there?" said I.

"Nothing, Jess, nothing," he answered, letting fall his hand.

"Why not tell me?" I exclaimed. "Is it a pistol?"

"Yes," he replied, with a little hesitation; and a darkness came into his face as he said, "Thank God, Quill went forward when I told him. In another minute I must have shot him."

"Oh, Richard," cried I, clasping my hands, "for God's sake do not carry such a horrible temptation to your passions about with you."

"Hush!" he exclaimed, looking in the direction in which the carpenter stood steering. "I am one to twelve, and I know my men. Say no more about it, Jessie;" and he spoke so sternly that the protest I was about to repeat died away on my lips. I had guessed by the manner in which he slapped his breast, when he bade the crew go forward, that he had a pistol there; yet I was not so certainly convinced but that the confirmation of my suspicion affected me like a violent blow, bringing home with unbearable emphasis the character of our peril, by giving me to see how he had prepared himself for it.

His glance happened to fall upon his sextant, that lay upon the skylight. He instantly took it up and said, "I must go below to work out these sights. They had utterly passed from my mind. Stay on deck, Jess, till I return, and should the steward or cook approach the forescuttle—that little hatch there, just before the windlass—call to me through the skylight." So speaking, he left me, just going to the binnacle, and saying something to the carpenter, and looking up as he spoke, as though referring to the quantity of canvas on the bark, and then narrowly scanning the horizon to judge of the weather, and also to see if there were any vessel in sight.

It seemed strange indeed to me to be walking the deck as if I had command; for this was the feeling given by the responsibility to keep watch that my husband had put upon me. I knew what he feared was that the cook or the steward might in his absence sneak forward and liberate the men; who, should they be let loose in this way, were very likely to be hurried into extremities by their rage at having been battened down in the small forecastle and threatened with hunger and thirst, if they did not return to their duty. Accordingly, I kept my eyes closely fixed on that part of the vessel; but all the while I was wondering how this unhappy and dangerous business was to end, whether any good would come of my going to the men, and endeavoring to make peace, and, above all, how we should manage, far out as we were

in the Atlantic, and without a man to trust to, even
among the four who had not directly mutinied—*i. e.*, the
mates, steward, and cook—if the crew continued obstinate
in their refusal to work the vessel.

My imagination, always most active when I was least
thankful for its suggestions, painted that darksome interior forward for me, and, though I do not know what
sort of appearance the inside of the forecastle presented,
I could easily figure a sort of gloomy cave, dimly lighted
by an oil lamp, the whole made resonant by the wash and
hollow thunder of the bow wave, as it roared from the
cutwater, and picture the faces of the crew, pallid as
ghosts, in the sickly light, as the men sat up on their
chests, and conferred upon what was best to be done now
that they were imprisoned, and there was no chance of
obtaining provisions, unless they turned to.

It was a strange imagination to come into my head;
but the mere thought of the crew would inspire it when
my mind went to them from the beautiful, sunbright,
breezy picture of the bark, and the glorious expanse of
curling, sparkling, yeasty sea.

Presently, turning my head, I noticed Mr. Short standing squarely at the wheel, and steering with a dogged
face. Little as I relished addressing him after his manner
when I had before accosted him, I fancied that something
might come of an exchange of words with the fellow;
and, as I could command the forecastle as well from the
wheel as from the skylight, I walked aft.

"This is a very unhappy business, Mr. Short," said I.
"What is the cause of the men mutinying in this manner?"

"You heard their answers to the cap'n, mum," he replied. "They say there aren't enough good hands among
'em."

"But is that really the case, or is it a mere pretense to
give my husband and Mr. Heron and yourself trouble?"
I said.

He turned his eyes slowly upon me as much as to say,
"Don't bracket *us* with your husband; that's a kind of
sop that won't do here!" and exclaimed, "Some of the
men aren't up to much. Yet not much good can come
of their striking. The ship must be worked, if we don't

want to be drownded, an' it's hinconvenient enough to me, mum. Here am I fetched off my dinner afore I'd taken three bites at it."

I was about to offer to hold the wheel while he went for his dinner; but instantly thought, No! if he offers to release the men, I shall be unable to leave the wheel to call my husband. So I said, "Shall I tell the steward to bring your dinner here?"

"Thank ye, mum, I can wait," he answered gruffly. "I suppose there'll be an end o' this job presently, and then somebody'll relieve me."

"Did you ever hear of a crew mutinying so early on a voyage as our men have?" I asked.

"Ay," he replied, "scores of times. Why, pretty nigh every day ye may hear of crews refusing to man the windlass, and that means that they mutiny afore they begin the voyage."

"But not without some grievance—something to justify them in refusing to go to sea?"

"Oh, if they think themselves short-handed, they'll mutiny fast enough," he answered, with an unpleasant grin. "A good many sailors 'ud reckon our men very patient for waitin' so long afore they come aft with their troubles."

"I have heard of mutinies, but was never in one before," said I; "but if I thought the men—even in stories about mutinies—mad, what must I think of the reality when I see this vessel as good as deserted, left to the mercy of the weather, with all the crew confined in the forecastle, bound to perish if the bark should founder, and yet apparently valuing their lives so lightly, that in order to bring us all into danger they have to invent a grievance?"

"Well, that's what you say," he responded, insolently; "but I, who'm no more than a fo'ksle hand, though I'm styled second mate and carpenter, and who knows more about the life forrards than ever you can, am not going to call the men liars right off 'cause they come aft and makes a statement. I'm not with them, and I'm not against 'em. I've got nothing to do with it. But if, as you say, they're willing to lose their lives rather than do the ship's work, don't ye think folks ashore would take that to signify that their grievance must ha' been pretty real to make 'em agreeable to go to the bottom sooner than let them in authority have their own way?"

If this, thought I, is a specimen of the logic this sealawyer uses in his conversation with the men, small wonder that they mutiny; and, as the meaning behind his reply grew clearer to me, I felt more than ever persuaded that much, if not all, the present mischief was owing to the mates, who, finding the crew willing, as, unhappily, most merchant seamen are, to hunt about for grievances, had quietly stirred them up into their mutinous and menacing posture.

I was now startled by the noise of heavy thumping forward. It lasted several moments, and when it ceased the cook came out of his galley, and, looking my way, roared out that he was so-and-so'd if he didn't believe the men were suffocating. The knocking was repeated, and I ran to the skylight, and called Richard. He came on deck at once; but had no need to ask what was the matter, for on his head emerging from the companion he heard the knocking plainly.

"Ah!" he exclaimed, "they are coming to their senses, are they? Mr. Heron," he cried, putting his head down the companion, "come on deck, and bring the handcuffs you'll find on the table in my cabin with you."

The mate arrived very promptly, holding the handcuffs.

"Now," continued Richard, taking the handcuffs from him, and looking at him sternly, "am I to reckon upon your support?"

"Certainly," answered Heron, who was very pale; and I was not surprised that he should be so, for there was something of real desperation in my husband's manner, such as might easily have persuaded the cowardly, unprincipled fellow before him that any hesitation *now* might cost him his life.

"Then follow me," said Richard, and strode hurriedly forward, the mate going after him, and making, I thought, with his narrow shoulders and 'long-shore clothes, but a poor figure beside my husband. When they reached the forecastle, Richard stooped over the hatch, without touching it, and called out, "Below there! have you had enough of this? Are you tired?"

I was too far off to catch the answer, or even to hear the faintest murmur of it; but a reply was made, for Richard called out again, "I have more patience than you! I can beat you at this game! Are you willing to turn to? If so, say so, and I'll let you out. If not, stop where you are—for we're bound to Sierra Leone, and there we'll go; and if you can do without air and water and provisions till we get there, good—you shall have your way."

Here the men answered again, on which my husband said, "Very well; I'll open the scuttle, but Isaac Quill must come up first. If any man offers to follow without my leave I'll shoot him. I'll put a bullet through his head the moment it appears. So mind yourselves!" And there was a ring in his voice that could have left them in no doubt of his determination. He then opened the top of the scuttle; but when Quill stepped forth my husband with a quick movement closed the hatch again, and before Quill could gain his sight, blinded as he was by coming from the darkness into the streaming sunshine, the handcuffs were on his wrists, and he was standing like a felon.

All this I could plainly see from where I stood. My heart beat violently. I never knew what was going to happen next; what dreadful tragedy might spring from Richard's desperation on the one hand and the men's undisciplined passions on the other.

My husband now said something to the mate, who, taking Quill by the shirt-sleeve, came along the deck with him. Heron's lips moved as they approached, as though he spoke in a very soft voice to Quill; probably he said something to encourage him, or to excuse himself for taking the part he was now playing. They went down the companion, and on peering through the skylight I saw the mate open the door of the berth occupied by the steward. Quill entered. The mate then shut and locked the door, and brought away the key, that dangled between his thumb and forefinger as he walked forward to rejoin my husband.

Certainly this behavior was consistent with his assur-

15

ance to Richard that he was willing to do what he was told, and I drew some comfort from it; for I hoped that, now he saw Richard was a resolved man, not to be vanquished without a hard and it might be a bloody contest, he would fall readily to his duties, withdraw his sympathies from the men, and give us no more trouble this side of Sierra Leone, where, no doubt, my husband would find some means of getting rid of him.

Meanwhile Richard remained standing at the scuttle, with his hand in his breast, waiting for the mate, and not addressing the men under the hatch. When Mr. Heron joined him he took the key and put it into his pocket: and then, leaning his head to the scuttle, he called out,

"If I release you will you turn to and give me no more of your growlings and your lies about being weak-handed?"

The answer was inaudible to me, but evidently satisfactory, for without another word Richard threw back the top of the scuttle and exclaimed, "Very well. Tumble up and return to your work and we'll say no more about it. The past shall be the past. Let the man whose trick it is go aft and relieve the second mate at the wheel."

He then, followed by the mate, slowly returned along the main-deck, coming to a stand near the winch abaft the mainmast, and facing the forecastle to view the men.

CHAPTER XXIII.

MORE TROUBLE.

THEY came up one by one, looking very dazed, and rubbing their eyes. The routine aboard the *Aurora* was the same as in most merchant vessels. The watch who were relieved at eight o'clock in the morning had the forenoon watch below, but all hands were kept at work on deck in the afternoon. It was past noon, and consequently quite in order that all hands should be on deck; but, whether because they were sullen, or because their sense of routine had been capsized by the spell of mutiny, they stood in a body near the windlass, not offering to scatter and fall to their various jobs.

Richard, observing this, said something to the mate, who called out, "Whose trick is it at the wheel?"

Dan Cock, the mulatto, answered, "It's Ikey Quill's, sar. Him was to reliebe me at eight bells."

"Who relieves Quill?" exclaimed Richard.

"Me, sir," answered Gray, an ordinary seaman.

"Then lay aft, Gray, and take the helm," said Richard.

I saw the man give a hurried look round at his mates, but my husband was watching him, and perhaps he missed the encouragement he sought in the faces of the others. He came along the deck and took the wheel from the carpenter.

"Now then, look alive, my lads! get about your work," sung out the mate.

"We should like to know what's become of Quill first," said the seaman named Craig, one of the men in the port watch, who pretended to be inefficient, and who had listened complacently when Quill had called him useless.

"If you want to know, he is locked up as the ringleader in the mutiny," answered my husband. "Turn to now without another word. I have kept my promise, and liberated you on the assurance that this trouble was over. Be as honest to me, men."

"Ay, but there's no use saying the trouble's over while Isaac Quill's locked up, because it isn't," responded Craig, with as much defiance as was shown before my husband had them under the hatch.

"Come, come, enough of this for to-day," said the carpenter, who had gone forward and stood near the galley. "If Quill 'll promise to turn to I dessay the cap'n 'll let him out."

"Quill's one of our best men, and if we're weak with him, we'll be no good at all without him," answered Craig.

Had my husband been properly supported by his mates, this argument would have been impossible, because the three of them would have gone among the men and tumbled them to their work without ado; but the seamen very well knew that their captain stood alone.

"Don't you hear what Mr. Short says?" exclaimed Heron. "If Quill will promise to turn to the captain's pretty sure to let him out."

"He promised to turn to afore the scuttle was opened —he promised with the rest of us; and the first thing the cap'n does is to lock him up!" shouted Ralph Green, an ordinary seaman.

"Don't you mean to turn to?" said Richard.

"Not without Quill," two or three voices answered together.

Here, then, were we as badly off as before—nay, worse off; for before, the men's grievance was but a sham one, whereas now it was real—I mean, that they felt that Quill's imprisonment was unjust to him and them, after the promise my husband had made them to give them their liberty if they agreed to turn to; and that Quill's detention would unquestionably weaken their working strength by one good hand.

My husband must have taken this view of it, for he stood for a little space staring at them, and then walked aft with a look of indecision mixed up with the anger and disappointment in his face. I observed the mate and the carpenter follow him with their eyes, as if they took close note of his hesitancy, and I felt heartily annoyed, for that reason, that any hint of embarrassment should appear in his manner.

The men hung together upon the forecastle, talking, while now and again a laugh broke from them, but they showed no disposition to go to their work. Every moment I expected to hear the man at the helm call out for somebody to relieve him, as the mulatto had done, and for the same reason; but probably his being at the extreme end of the vessel prevented him from seeing what was going forward, or maybe he had not the colored man's mutinous audacity.

Richard came to a stand at the skylight, and I went round to him.

"Is not this maddening?" said he. "It's enough to make a man give up. What chance have I with such a crew and such mates? They want to drive me back—but they'll not do it."

"Be advised by me, Richard," I exclaimed, "and release Quill."

"What! that pirate—that ringleader! he'll go among the others and breed another mutiny right away!" he cried, with his face very dark.

"Yes, but you promised him his liberty if he agreed to go to work, and he did agree. You're bound to keep your promise."

"To the others, but not to that dog. If I had not taken him unawares there would have been a fight. I had made up my mind to have him in irons."

I continued urging him to release the man. He argued with great warmth, but gradually yielded, and said, "I am willing to keep my promise, but dare not. I must not let those villains enjoy such a triumph. It would destroy the little that remains of the miserable command I have."

"I should not mind that," said I. "I would risk the result. Tell the men that you have thought the matter over, and that you will keep your promise and let Quill have his liberty in the faith that they will act honestly and fulfil their duties as seamen. What else is to be done, Richard?" I added, imploringly. "They are unanimous, and are all against you, as you say, and must master you if you don't shift your ground. And what then is to become of us?"

This appeal moved him more than all my other arguments, by making him believe I was concerned for my own safety, which was just what I wished he should suppose, as I knew that I had but little chance of getting at him by any other kind of entreaty.

He looked affectionately at me and said, "Ay, Jess, I must never lose sight that I have your safety to answer for—a precious trust, indeed." And without another word he left me and went some distance forward, where he hailed the crew.

"Since you tell me," he exclaimed, "that in your opinion my promise to Quill ought to stand as well as my promise to you, I'll let it stand. I'll meet you as you meet me. If you're reasonable, I'll be reasonable; if not, you'll find me the devil. This is not my first voyage as master, and whether as mate or as skipper I've never sailed with a man who would not be glad to join me again as shipmate. What this mutiny's about I don't know. I'm no Yankee, no hazing bully, but an English seaman who's been through the mill like yourselves, and would be the first to right you if I thought you wronged. But what I can't see I'll not believe in. The complaint you brought aft is not an honest one, and you know it. Those men who signed articles as able seamen can do able seamen's work if they like; and if they refuse and put their duties on other men's shoulders, then I'll serve them as they deserve, punish them for fraud, and give them boys' pay. You know I can do it, and I will. That's all I have to say; and now, Mr. Heron," said he, turning to the mate, "you can go aft and release Quill." And he handed him the key.

Though I heard every word of this address, I was too far off to judge accurately of its effect upon the men, but I thought from the manner in which they received it, and the silence they preserved when Richard concluded, that its influence was good.

The interval between Heron's disappearance and return was a long one—suspiciously long, for he had nothing to do but open the door of the steward's berth and tell the man to come out and go forward. At last he arrived, and Quill followed, with the handcuffs upon his wrists.

At the sight of those irons I glanced at Richard, for it seemed a terrible blunder to expose the man, with his arms pinioned, to the crew, who were all eagerly looking. Was this a stroke of the mate's malice? Richard speedily settled my doubts on that head by savagely turning on Heron.

"Remove those handcuffs! What do you mean by producing the man pinioned? Didn't I tell you to *release* him?"

"You said nothing about the handcuffs," answered the mate.

"Take them off!" shouted Richard, with a violent stamp on deck.

The mate obeyed the order, but very ostentatiously, and with many needless flourishes, taking care to pose himself and Quill that all hands might see what he was doing. When he had removed the manacles he flung them down, causing them to ring out, as if he invited the attention of the crew to them, that they might see there was no deception. Richard controlled his temper with an effort that left his face crimson. He was in too great a passion to address Quill in a speech ; he waved his hand and said, " Get forward now and go about your work," and then told the mate to pick up the irons and carry them below. The mate did so, swinging the irons in his hands as he walked to the companion.

Richard waited until he recovered his self-control, and then called Mr. Short to him.

" Who has charge of the deck ?"

" Mr. Heron, sir," answered the carpenter.

" Well, as you are on deck, go and turn the crew to at once, and send a hand aft to haul that ensign down."

The carpenter left us, with a show of bustle, and began to call about him.

" Come along to the cabin, Jessie, and get some dinner," said Richard. " Unless the cook has mutinied, there should be something ready for us by this time. I don't want the crew to think I'm watching them. It will appear as though I had confidence in them if I leave the deck."

So we went below, nor can I say that I was sorry to leave the deck. There was no pleasure for me in the magnificent expanse of glittering sea, and in the freshness and glory of the steady, singing breeze, and the bending blue of the heavens, with the shadow of mutiny lying darkly upon us. I felt as if my nerves had suffered a sudden violent wrench when I reached my berth and stood brushing my hair and preparing to join Richard at the table. Indeed, a mutiny at sea is one of those formidable incidents which cannot be understood even in the most powerful and lifelike descriptions. To gauge it, you must live in it, have your safety concerned by it, watch the faces of the men, hear their talk, observe their defiant postures and the increasing boldness of their manner, and reflect, while you note those things, upon the proverbial recklessness of the seaman's character, the unlettered and undisciplined classes from which the maritime ranks are recruited, and the sailor's notorious incapacity of realizing, when at a distance from land, the punishment his captain has the power to procure for him when the ship arrives in port.

But I did not want Richard to know that I was "upset," to use the word that best expresses my state of mind; so, pulling myself together, I entered the cabin with a smile, and found him seated at the table, waiting for me to join him, before carving the piece of brisket which the steward had placed before him.

"Did you hear the men singing out just now?" said he. "The wind has drawn ahead, and they have been trimming sail. Their songs seemed to have the old ring. Pray God this trouble is over for good!"

"The mates are more to blame than the men," said I. "They never gave you any real support. I have the worst possible opinion of Mr. Short, Richard. I am sure he has been talking to the crew, and angering them against you."

"But are they not a pack of scoundrels, to be led into mutinying without a cause?" he answered.

"Yes," said I; "but if they considered that the bark is big enough to deserve another hand or two, and spoke to the carpenter, and the carpenter agreed with them, they would easily be made mutinous by his encouragement, and arrange among themselves to invent a grievance, by saying that some of them are inefficient."

"That's about it," said he; "you've hit the cause, I'm sure. But still they are rascals. And, bad as Short is, I consider Heron ten times worse."

"I look upon Short as a grumbling, riotous seaman by nature—a man who loves mischief," I replied, "and who will make mischief wherever he is. But Heron, I consider, is actuated by spite and dislike of you, and by anxiety to thwart and imperil your interests. Why, I cannot imagine. But there is no good in speculating upon the principles of a rogue. I hope to goodness you will get rid of them both at Sierra Leone."

"Trust me!" he exclaimed; "and perhaps before."

"How before?"

"Not by throwing them overboard," said he, with a laugh, his natural cheerfulness breaking out. "But I ex-

pect before long that Heron will find himself in the plight
from which he released Quill just now. If the game he
is playing means anything, it must mean this : if the crew
compelled me to put back, he would go to the owners,
represent the fault to be mine; that I had not the power
to control a crew; that they laughed at my authority;
and make out, in a word, that I was not fit to have command of a vessel. Mud thrown in this way sticks; for,
you see, the return of the ship would cost the owners
money; and loss of money always makes the loser willing
to hear complaints against the man who had charge of the
losing venture. Perhaps the fellow might hope to be appointed in my stead. It is impossible to tell what hopes
agitate such a brain as Heron's. You see he is cautious
not to do anything that would enable me to charge him
with insubordination, or with conniving at the intentions
of the crew. But my time will come. He is sure to give
me the chance I want. And now," said he, smiling, "what
do you think of sailors? Is your affectionate esteem for
them as high as it was?"

"You are talking to a sailor's wife," said I.

"Ay," he replied, "to a sailor's wife, who has seen a
crew battened down for mutiny and threatened with famine, and her husband slapping a pistol over his heart, and
menacing the Jack Tars with blood and thunder; and all
in the first week of the voyage."

"I would no more judge of sailors by the specimens we
have on board," said I, "than I would judge of the morals of Newcastle by looking for them in the police court.
But, oh, Richard, I hope you will turn all these men away
when we get to Sierra Leone. It's as far from that town
to the Cape as it is from England to Sierra Leone, and to
have to travel all that distance, with the mates and Orange
and the crew, would be more—indeed, Richard, it would
be more than I could endure."

"Jess," he replied, "you are in my hands; leave me to
manage. Neither the mates nor Orange nor the crew
shall trouble you." And then, to divert my thoughts, he
talked of home and of father, and how much I should
have to relate. "After all," said he, "you are seeing
ocean-life as sailors see it; sounding its perils, and find-

ing out that there are other dangers than those of fire and
tempest. And something more you're seeing; and that
is, the obligations, the troubles, the difficulties of the poor,
unfortunate British shipmaster—a man who, let people
think as they will, is out and away in a more unfriended
condition than the 'common sailor,' as Jack is called,
whom everybody pities and thinks an ill-used and neg-
lected man. For if the common sailor goes wrong his
pay is stopped, or he is locked up ashore for a short spell,
that is, if he doesn't cheat the law by deserting; and,
when his punishment is over, he begins again, and is no
worse off than he was before. But if a skipper goes
wrong, he is ruined for life; nobody will employ him;
he is unfit for shore-work, and if he has a wife and children they must all go to the union together. However,
for one thing let us be thankful, Jess," said he, smiling,
"and that is, that this mutiny took place on a fine day.
Had foul weather come along when the men were under
hatches we might be mourning the loss of some excellent
spars."

<hr />

CHAPTER XXIV.

A LITTLE BREATHING-SPACE.

THIS conversation brought us to the end of our meal,
and Richard went on deck to let Heron come below to
his dinner. I entered my berth, not meaning for the present to leave it; but, growing anxious to see how the crew
were behaving, I put on my hat and cloak, thinking that
I should have enough of the cabin when the darkness
came.

I found the mate at table, sitting, with squared elbows,
before the salt beef, and waited on by the steward, who
favored him with more attention than he gave us, though,
if a ship's steward is anybody's servant at all, he is the
captain's. I passed by without taking any notice of him,
but not without a feeling of deep regret that the breezy,
wholesome, plain little interior, radiant as it was at that
time with the hearty, cheerful afternoon sunshine stream-

ing down through the skylight, and bright with the ferns
and gold-fish, should count among its occupants so disagreeable a person as Mr. Heron, and that my ill luck should
associate me with a man to whom it was impossible to be
civil, and with a steward whose morose character made it
distressing to me to speak to him.

But, no matter! I thought, as I went up the companion-
ladder; our port is not very far off; and the days pass
quickly. Richard will get rid of all these odious people,
and the memory of this wretched, anxious time will only
sweeten the rest of the voyage. These were my thoughts,
I say. Could I have but seen a few weeks in advance of
me! Why, there was not a man on board who would
have taken more trouble to drive Richard back to England than I. Not a man who would have been comparable to me as a mutineering spirit to excite the crew into
taking the charge out of my husband's hands and sailing
the ship home.

It was past two o'clock. Isaac Quill, grasping the
spokes of the wheel, was the first object that confronted
me when I arrived on deck. Any artist, on the lookout
for a figure to strike the eye in the painting of a mutiny,
would have been quick to seize upon this man. I have
described his thin face, his gleaming eyes, his narrow
hips, and the piratical cut of his trousers, squeezed into
half-boots. But no written description could convey his
air of complete recklessness, the defiance and insolence of
his posture, as he hung in a kind of floating way to the
spokes, his cap pushed back, the wind tossing his hair
upon his forehead, and his mouth and jaws moving as he
gnawed upon the tobacco junk in his cheek. And yet he
looked a smart seaman, a dexterous hand at the wheel,
anyhow, as even a landsman might have guessed, by noting how he would give a twirl to the spokes, as if by
instinct knowing when the vessel needed it, seldom looking aloft or at the compass, and yet making the wake follow him in a line as straight as a ruling upon paper.

I threw a hurried glance along the decks. The men
were scattered about, all at work, and as quiet as mice.
Two of them sat on a sail, stretched along the weather
side of the main-deck, stitching at it; there was a spun-

yarn winch going on the forecastle, and there was a hand
on the foreyard, but what doing I cannot say.   The recent
revolt seemed like a dream when I looked at the men, and
noticed how quietly they did their work.   The breeze had
hauled ahead while we were at dinner, but only by a little ;
it held free, and blew from a point that gave the bark her
best sailing chance.   There was too much of it for a fore-
topmast studding-sail ; indeed, the gaff-topsail, foreroyal,
and flying-jib had been taken in, which left the little vessel as much canvas as she wanted.   She lay down until her
covering-board was close to the sea ; but the water was
smooth ; there never had come a better time for testing
her qualities as a clipper, and she behaved as if she knew
she was being watched.

It was like flying.   There was little noise, for there
were no billows to crash through, and the swell was too
long-drawn for her to break ; there was but a thin streak
of foam on either side of her, no more than what a finely
lined screw-steamer would make in a calm.   Her speed
was best to be judged by looking over the counter, and
fixing the eye on any revolving flakes there, and watching them run away.   And yet, though the sea was smooth,
it was merry, curling in silver-crested dark-blue lines which
the whistling wind would sometimes catch and blow up
in little bursts of prismatic smoke ; in the southwest quarter the sun set it on fire, and all that way it lay trembling,
as if it were molten quicksilver bubbling.   The fore and
main tacks groaned, as they labored like giants to uproot
the solid planking to which they were confined ; the
canvas stood round, hard, and smooth as polished meer-
schaum ; from the mainmast-head, where the little red
dog-vane flickered like a tongue of flame, to the dark
dead-gold of the copper to windward, where the white
water lined it with an ivory setting, the *Aurora*, as I
viewed her on that sunny, windy, wintry afternoon, made,
I thought, one of the fairest pictures which the cunning
of man ever contributed to the sparkling blue canvas of
the deep.

We were not alone ; far out to windward, faint as a
white shadow, with her bulwarks just showing above the
water-line, was a full-rigged ship, heading to cross our

weather quarter, with studding-sails aloft, and the clew of her mainsail hauled up. I took up the glass to look at her, and Richard, coming to my side, said quietly in my ear, "She is too late. Two hours sooner, and we should have had that ship bearing down to learn the meaning of our distress signal."

"But the mutiny is over," said I.

"Ay, it seems so; fairly crushed out. The men have their senses again. Yet look at that pirate at the wheel! If there is to be more mischief, his hand will have the brewing of it."

"There would be nothing to fear from him if the mates were loyal," said I.

He muttered something under his breath—indeed, I think he bestowed a sea-blessing on the mates—and saying, as he looked at the ship, "She'll be able to make out our colors shortly; she may as well have our name to carry home with her," he called Moore, the apprentice, aft, and in a few minutes the bark was further glorified by a string of brilliant bunting, denoting her number (it was Marryat's Code in those days) streaming from the peak.

"Now, Jess," said Richard, "if you want a job I can give you one. Keep your eye on the ship and see if she answers."

This I did, but a quarter of an hour went by without any sign being made aboard her. By that time, however, she was well on our quarter, and from that point our colors were distinguishable, for I spied a long thin flag stream palely from her mizzen-royal-masthead.

"She has hoisted a color, Richard," I called out.

He took the glass and peered at her. "The answering pennant!" he exclaimed. "She has made out our number. In a few days your father will know that in such and such latitude and longitude the *Aurora* was spoken, proving that Jessie Fowler was afloat up to that hour."

Ay, thought I to myself, I hope he may know that, but I should be sorry were he to know more.

A whole week passed away, during which everything went on quietly. I watched the men as closely as I durst when I was on deck, thinking I might be able to see more

than Richard had eyes for, and asked questions of him
about them; but there was nothing to cause the least uneasiness, nor had Richard any complaints to make. The
carpenter I saw little of, and never addressed; he kept in
the gangway when he had the watch. It somehow happened for the most part of that week that when I was on
deck he was off duty; so that, I say, I had small opportunity of observing him.

Mr. Heron, of course, I often met. His manner was as
offensive and unsociable as ever it had been; but since
he did his work, was fit to look out for a change of wind
when he had command of the deck, and was very dexterous at figures, with such a thorough knowledge of navigation, every branch of it, all those things which combine
to make it a science—astronomy, geometry, trigonometry,
and so forth — as left very few men his masters, I say,
since he did his work, Richard left him alone. And yet,
so far as his practical seamanship went, I am persuaded
there was scarcely a keelman or collier mate then afloat
who, without knowing more about the sun than that it
rose in the morning and set at night, would not have
beaten this mathematical Mr. Heron out of sight. A man
may have the art of the sextant in perfection, and yet be
no more fit to take charge of a vessel than a linendraper's
assistant would be to have command of an express locomotive engine.

But he would answer the purpose, Richard said to me,
well enough until he could be got rid of, if he kept himself to himself, and gave the men no secret encouragement
to become rebellious. Indeed, in a sense his sulkiness and
sullenness were really convenient, for we did very well
without his conversation, and I may say, for my part, that
I never liked him so well as when he was away.

So, day after day going by without any recurrence of
that violent passage of mutiny I have just related, made
us in a manner forget it. It seemed to have been no more
than an extravagant burst of temper on the part of the
men, for which they were now ashamed. It is true they
never showed any great willingness. There was never
visible among them any of that hearty activity which
distinguishes a good and contented crew; they behaved

as men who could not overcome their resentment, but who would not allow it to control them, either. I pointed this out to my husband; but he was quicker than I, and had noticed it sooner.

"My notion is," said he, "that they are bottling themselves up because they mean to give me the slip at Sierra Leone. They have had some pay in advance, and, as the voyage to that port is a short one, they'll lose little by running. However, if they go on as they are, I may think proper to check their hopes in that way. I doubt if a ship's crew is to be picked up by wishing for one at Sierra Leone."

"If they wish to desert, let them," said I. "We don't want any more mutinies."

"What!" he exclaimed, laughing, "and be buried for a few months in the 'white man's grave,' eh, Jessie? to arrive home and find your father in a high mourning hatband, under the impression that we are dead and gone! But we'll see; we'll see. Only let things go on as they are, that's all."

Well, for that week there was every promise of things going on as they were. And what was equally to our purpose was a fine, steady sailing breeze that kept the *Aurora* humming day and night, so that on the morning of the 14th of February Richard came into our berth, where I was lying sound asleep in my bunk, and put his hand on my shoulder to tell me that old Father Neptune, knowing I was coming, had prepared a pretty valentine for me, and that I must get up and see it. He would not explain until I was on deck, and then, pointing on the port beam, he said, "There it is!" and, looking, I spied a mere fragment of haze that was no more than a tiny smudge upon the horizon.

"What is it?" said I.

"Land!" he answered.

"Land!" I exclaimed. "Pooh, Richard, you're mistaken. It's the top of a cloud. It will disappear in a minute."

"A bad lookout for the people on it if it does," said he. "Why, my dear, it's one of the Canary Islands— Palma."

This assurance made me gaze at it earnestly; but, though I took the glass, I could make nothing of it. It was just a film, a mere wreath of smoke, whether I looked at it with or without the glass.

"I'm sorry it is so far off," said I. "Were it some miles closer there is no valentine I should have better liked to see."

Still, though it was but a mere shadow, the circumstance of its being land made it extraordinarily interesting to me; and had it been the port to which we were bound, nay, had it been a fragment of the coast of England, I could not have stared at it more intently, nor found more to move me in it. Indeed, after you have been at sea some days the very whisper of land being in sight runs like a thrill through the heart. I cannot explain why there should be any magic in what resembles a piece of blue thread hovering over the water-line; but such is the fascination that everybody will run on deck to have a look. Even the sea-sick passenger will crawl from his berth to peer over the rail; the monotony of the sea life is broken; there is eagerness in the people's faces, a cheerfuller note in their voices; there is a general brightening; and yet the cause of it all is no more than a little hazy blotch in the corner of the sky, so vague that only a navigator's eye would look out for it and know what it was. In a short time it is on the quarter, and then it fades out like the blur of your breath upon a looking-glass.

"And that is land?" thought I; and never before did my mind so fully compass the magnitude of the deep as when I turned from that mere speck, which indicated an island thirty miles long, to the world of blue and speeding waters round us, which on all sides met the sky, as though it were as boundless as the firmament that arched over it.

CHAPTER XXV.

A HURRICANE.

WE were now upon the verge of the parallels where the northeast Trades usually begin to blow, though, like other winds, they are capricious, and are certainly not always to be found in one place. At dinner that day Richard said he believed that the breeze that was then blowing would carry us into the Trades, in which case we might look for a fine run to our port, as already the distance covered by the *Aurora* was nearly equal to steam— as steam *then* was—the average having been over two hundred miles for seven days continuously. Indeed, he was in excellent spirits; the continued quietude of the crew, the fine weather, and the noble progress of the bark all helped him to recover his old buoyancy of mind.

Heron dined with us, and my husband, in his good temper, talked to him as if he would have him know that the past was the past and forgotten, and that on his side he was anxious there should be nothing but smooth water in future before them. But it would not do; the mate's sulky, morose manner was impenetrable. He answered in monosyllables, gave no help to the conversation, seemed to make nothing of Richard's obvious well-meaning, but, on the contrary, to behave as if it annoyed him, and as though he wished the ill-feeling between them to be undisturbed; and, finally, quitted the table the moment he had done his dinner, like a man in an eating-house, who has been sitting with strangers.

I find myself constantly coming back to this wretched creature; but I dwell the more on him because, though I am perfectly convinced there was not the least taint of madness in his mind, there was something so offensively odd in him as to make him a character worth drawing with care. And I heartily wish, for the sake of shipmasters, that it was in my power to give them hints, out

16

of my husband's experiences, how to guard themselves
against association with unprincipled and ill-mannered
subordinates. But, unhappily, at sea men's characters appear when it is too late to get rid of them. Steam has
diminished, if it has not extinguished, this trouble, by
making voyages short; but in sailing-ships which perform long voyages the danger may still be found. Masters find themselves with men under them whose good
behavior they could have guaranteed at first sight, but
who turn out rebels and rascals when the vessel has fairly
started, and who multiply the perils of the ocean by risks
which have terminated, and do and will again terminate,
in dreadful tragedies.

By this time, you may suppose, we had left winter far
behind us; every hour added ardency to the sun, and
took something away from our shadows at noon. The
fresh wind had kept us cool, and prevented me, at least,
from noticing in the daytime the gradual change in the
temperature, though I felt the sleeping-berth warm at
night, and those linen sheets which had kept me shudder-
ing in the North Sea were now become very grateful.

But on this 14th day of February the wind failed us.
I was below in my berth looking over some wearing apparel, and noticed that the deck was rapidly losing its
slope. I went on with my work, examining this, folding
that, with my mind full of thoughts of home, of my dead
child, of my father, of my first meeting with Richard,
and our marriage-feast at Tommy Dodd's, for memory
grew busy when I took up anything that transported me
in fancy back to Newcastle. Presently the door opened
and my husband came in.

"Phew!" he exclaimed, throwing down his cap, and
mopping his forehead with a pocket-handkerchief, "here
are the dog-days upon us at a bound. I've come for a
thin coat; this is too heavy;" and he pulled off the coat
he wore.

"The wind is dropping," said I, going to the little scuttle and opening it, for all through the week it had been
to leeward, with the foam sometimes over it, "and giving
the sun a chance of making himself felt."

"It isn't so much the sun," he replied, "he's too near

the sea to make himself felt. It's a complete change of temperature—though better than frost and snow, Jess. Bah! confound the wind! I had pinned my faith to its running us into the Trades."

"Perhaps this change is a forerunner of the Trades?"

"I should be willing to think so," said he, "but, unluckily, there's a gale of wind coming first. Look at the barometer there! That's a serious drop to take place in two hours."

"It will be my first gale this voyage, if it comes," said I.

He went away, and by-and-by I followed him, taking, however, another peep at the barometer before quitting the cabin, and noticing that the mercury continued steadily to fall. When I gained the deck I found a breathless calm, and the bark languidly rolling upon a light swell from the northwest. There was something very sluggish and thick in the motion and aspect of the sea; the color of it was indefinable—a sort of yellowish blue, if you can figure such a compound, as if a sediment of pale mud had risen and mixed with the azure water. This effect was produced by the sky, over which there was spread a haze that reminded me of the Newcastle sky when an easterly wind sends the smoke from the factories along the river's side drifting over the town. About a stone's-throw astern were a shoal of porpoises heading into the north. Some were very big fish, and looked like young whales as they curved their gleaming backs along the water, like rocks showing and vanishing amid the folds of the swell. They rose and sank with curious regularity, as though they were attached to a wheel revolving just under the surface. Now and again one of them jumped clean out of the water, revealing the whole of its clumsy, massive shape, and fell with a mighty splash that left a broad surface of foam behind. These uncouth ecstasies, I observed, frightened the others, for after every display of the kind there was an interval of some minutes before the black bodies reappeared.

The lighter canvas had been taken in, leaving nothing exposed but the topsails and foresail, which swung softly as the vessel gently leaned with the movement of the sea. The temperature was that of a warm bath. I had not felt, or at least noticed, the change in the cabin, but when I

came on deck it was like emerging into steam ; I mean as
regards the warmth. The sun was still within two hours
of his setting, yet there was a sharpness in the heat of his
light such as is not commonly found so high north of the
line as the parallel we were then upon ; and this, too, in
spite of the veil-like atmosphere which clipped the luminary of his rays, and circled him with a very pale, faint,
silvery halo like what frames the moon when she betokens
wet.

I noticed my husband constantly directing uneasy glances
round the sea, and a peculiar something in his walk betrayed
the anxiety in his mind. I was no weather-prophet, yet,
even had I been ignorant of the indications of the barometer, I should have thought this calm, and the appearance
of the sky, and the blurred sun, with his wild-looking ring,
very ominous.

Few things are more impressive than the gathering of
a tempest at sea. On shore and under shelter the hush
that falls before a storm, when distant sounds take a
strange note, and the lightest chirrup of a bird seems out
of place ; when you may hear upon the dry leaves the
patter of heat-drops falling from a sky that does not seem
to have lost all its blue, though the shadow of the storm
is upon it—I say, even such a hush on shore will subdue
the mind, and disturb it with a restless feeling of expectation. But at sea this expectation is tenfold heightened by
the sense that, let the tempest burst when it will, and prove
what it may, it must find you shelterless, the only object
for hundreds of miles, perhaps, upon the surface of the
ocean, and that, when it comes, it may come with a sudden fury, with the shrieking of wind and amid the smoke
of flying water, dismantling your vessel with the first
thunderous outfly, and disarming you of the only weapons
with which battle may be given it.

But these would be a landsman's fancies ; no sailor
would let them disturb him. And yet, as I looked at our
crew, I thought I could catch the older hands among them
lifting their eyes from their work to sweep the sea-line
slowly and anxiously. They had fallen afresh to the various occupations from which they had been called away
to shorten sail ; but the recent work had left them with

crimson faces and streaming foreheads. Most of them
had kicked off their shoes and flung aside their jackets, and
their muscular, brown arms, naked to the elbows, and their
bare chests, disclosed by the open shirts, gave them a character of roughness and wildness I had never before noticed
in them in the same degree.

Presently my husband hailed the carpenter: "Mr. Short,
tell the cook to get the men's supper ready by five."

"Ay, ay, sir," answered the carpenter, in his growling
voice, and went in a sprawling manner to the galley. The
cook, swabbing his forehead on his arm, put his head out
in a kind of wondering way, looked at the sun and then
around him, and vanished again.

At two bells, Mr. Heron, who was now on deck, and to
whom Richard had given certain instructions, ordered the
men to knock off work and go to supper. Probably they
found the interior of the forecastle too hot, for most of
them ate the meal on deck, sitting on the stocks of the
anchors, on the heel of the bowsprit, on the coamings of
the hatch, with pannikins of steaming black tea in one
hand, and sea-biscuit in the other.

Meanwhile, not a breath of air tarnished the burnished
surface of the deep; but the sun, though still well above
the horizon, had lost his halo, and struck a very sickly reflection in the sea, like layers of lengths of dull brass hori-
zontally sinking and snaking in the swell. But over against
him, on the right-hand side, I observed a darkness, as if
the night had mistaken the road and gone round to the
wrong side of the world.

"Do you see that, Richard?" I exclaimed, pointing to
the gloomy appearance.

"See it, Jess!" he answered, with a smile; "why, I've
been watching it gather during the last half-hour."

"But what makes the darkness? I see no clouds,"
said I.

"Because the atmosphere is too thick," he answered;
"but the darkness is nothing else but clouds. How steadily the swell runs from the northwest! That is where the
storm will come from."

"You seem to be ready for it," said I, looking aloft.

"Not quite ready yet," he answered. "Let those fellows refresh themselves first, and get their smoke ; they will find me considerate, for we want no more trouble."

"So far things have gone well, Richard."

"So far, as you say. How I miss such a mate as I should like to have—as I ought to have!" said he, looking with a little frown at Heron, who was moodily gazing at the sun. "There is no speaking to that fellow. If I ask him what he thinks of the weather, he answers like the nigger —'I tinks de same as you do '—and *how* he answers you can imagine. I wish," he continued warmly, though in a subdued voice, for we were near the helmsman, "he would offend me outright—do something to justify me in breaking him—no ! I wouldn't send him forward ; he'd be too dangerous among the men—in sending him below and keeping him there."

"Patience, Richard, patience !" I answered, laying my hand on his. "We are fifteen days distant from England. You'll be able to— Oh, did you see that flash of lightning ?" I cried, breaking away from what I was saying with a start, for my eye was on the darkness while I was speaking and thinking of what I was talking about, and the gloom changed with startling suddenness into a mighty blue glare.

Just then three bells were struck. My husband walked away from me.

"Mr. Heron, turn the men to. Get the foresail and fore-topsail furled, and close-reef the main-topsail."

The mate repeated the order at the top of his voice, and the crew instantly became active. Had I been their captain, I could not have watched them more anxiously and vigilantly; but there seemed no skulking, no hanging back. Richard followed them out of the corner of his eye, but appeared to take no particular notice, leaving them to the mates, and walking up and down the deck. All hands buckled to the foresail first. There were men enough to clew up the topsail as well, for, as any sailor will suppose, the fore clew-garnets and leech-lines in a calm hardly required the whole force of our ship's company, which included the carpenter, cook, and steward. My knowledge of what I may as well call practical seamanship enabled me to appreciate this point. It really meant that the men were resolved upon letting Richard see that they thought themselves weak-handed, and I cannot express how depressing and vexatious it was to note this after the tranquillity of the week, and to see Mr. Heron looking quietly on, instead of calling to the men to distribute themselves, and clew up both sails at once.

When the foresail was hauled up, all hands went on to the yard to furl it. I counted them, and made out ten men on the yard, Short and Quill taking the bunt, while the cook and steward swung on the yard-arm foot-ropes, and held on, rather than worked. The sail having been furled, some of the men went into the top to wait, while the others clewed up the topsail. Ours were single topsails. Meanwhile the darkness in the northwest quarter was deepening and widening, and the sun, that was now only a few degrees above the horizon, looked like a great blood-stain upon the sky there: the orb had lost his shape, and resembled a mass of hazy, crimson, liquid fire oozing out of the firmament, as though, just where he was, there was a rent in the platform of the heavens, through which the fiery stuff was draining. The sea heaved as sluggishly as oil, and I could taste a strange, strong smell upon the air, such as you meet with upon the sea-shore at low water—a smell of marine weeds and salt mud and fish-spawn. There was no more lightning, but the deepening darkness—the gloom of haze-hidden clouds rather than the evening shadow that was to be looked for in the east—gave warning that a dreadful and heavy change was not far off.

My husband called to the mate, "One watch is enough to furl the fore-topsail. Let the starboard watch lay aft, and close-reef the main-topsail while there is no wind. Tell them to bear a hand, or the smother will be upon us before they're off the yard."

The mate repeated this order almost word for word. The men ceased their songs, and a voice—I could not tell the man who spoke—sang out, "Each topsail takes all both watches, and if there was more idlers they'd be welcome."

"Who was that?" exclaimed Richard, walking hastily as far as the mainmast.

There was no reply.

"Lay aft the starboard watch only, and close-reef the main-topsail!" shouted my husband.

Not a man moved. They had been clewing up the fore-topsail before, but now they stood with the ropes in their hands, looking idly aft, while the men in the foretop hung over the edge, staring down with a grin.

"Mr. Heron," cried Richard, turning his face, red with passion, towards the mate, "here's mutiny again, in the face of a storm that may dismast and sink us. Give me your support. Why do you stand staring there? Follow me, and show the starboard watch the road aft!"

"I can do no good," answered the mate, never offering to stir.

"Do no good!" shouted Richard, clinching his fists; "why, you never try to do good! You're as lazy, mutinous, and worthless as the worst of them. Will you give me your help or not?"

"The men are the best judges," said the mate, in a loud voice, so that all hands might hear. "They say that one watch can't stow that topsail, and I suppose they know their own strength."

My husband was at his side in a bound.

"Go below!" he cried, pointing to the companion.

"What am I to go below for?" replied the mate, recoiling a step, and raising his arms.

"Go below!" shouted Richard.

The mate hesitated. In a breath my husband had both hands locked in the collar of the man's coat, and the knuckles of his thumbs buried in his throat, and in that manner dragged him along the deck to the companion. The sight made me feel sick—not the sight only, but the dread of worse to follow, and then the shock of the suddenness of the thing. My heart beat deliriously, and yet I kept a watch upon the crew. I feared they would rush at and fall upon my husband, and I stood—weak woman as I was, and with a swooning feeling on me too—ready to throw myself between him and the first seaman that should approach.

They dropped the ropes, and drew together on the starboard side, the better to see, but made no attempt to rescue the mate. My husband dragged his man along as he would an empty sack. There was no contest. Had Mr. Heron been a giant, the peculiar manner in which Richard had grasped him must have rendered him helpless. A cry broke from me when they approached, for I now saw that Heron's face was of a dark purple, and his eyes half out of his head; but before the sound had fairly escaped me, Richard had got the mate to the companion, and, turning the man's face round, threw him down the steps, following himself.

"Now, then, my lads, let's get this torps'l up," cried the carpenter, in a voice that seemed to say, the fun is over, so let's turn to; and once more the men began to sing out; and, when the canvas was clewed up, all hands went aloft as before, with the exception of Mr. Short.

Just then my husband returned from the cabin. The verge of the shadow in the northwest seemed to be over our mastheads; the sun had disappeared in the thickness, and darkness was coming along fast. I could hardly distinguish Richard's face. He looked at the fore-topsail-yard, where all the crew were, and then round at the weather. Seeing Mr. Short in the waist, he called him to get the binnacle lamp lighted, and, while the carpenter attended to this, Richard let go the main-topsail-halliards, and the heavy yard ran down the mast with a loud, rumbling noise.

Meanwhile, up in the gloom forward the men were chorussing, as they first reefed and then rolled up the sail; but it did not seem to me that they hurried themselves. Yet, when they had turned to after supper, they had gone to work as men who were conscious that despatch was necessary, and many of them certainly had appreciated the perilous appearance of the sky, as I judged by the looks I had seen them cast at the sun. At any time the reappearance of the old mutinous spirit would have been alarming and disheartening, but it was peculiarly so now, in the very eye of what appeared to be an approaching cyclone. I say that, what with the malignant blackness in the northwest, and the dusky scowl that had settled upon the face of the heavens, added to the passage of violence between my husband and the mate, the mutinous posture of the men, as conveyed by their determination to

execute the captain's orders in the manner that pleased
them best, made our situation at that time formidable
enough to quail the most heroic heart in the world. Only
a short time before, Richard and I had been congratulat-
ing each other on the improved behavior of the crew, and
our freedom for a week past from all anxiety on that head;
and now, here they were, defying my husband's orders, the
ship's company weaker by the loss of the mate, and a dangerous storm gathering in our skirts.

But my husband showed no weakness ; he paced the
deck quickly, waiting for the men to come off the topsail-
yard, and glancing aloft at his spars, which, with the exception of the main-topsail and fore-topmast-staysail, were
denuded of their canvas. Presently the crew began to
lay in and get into the rigging. It was so dark that their
forms were barely distinguishable as they descended the
shrouds. Suddenly a wild flash of lightning blazed up
over the sea in the midst of the northwest darkness, and
revealed the conformation of the sky to some degrees this
side the zenith, lighting up and throwing out the dense
masses of vapor, which, to our eyes, and before the sun had
vanished, had looked a flat, gray surface, owing to the
thick haze that underhung them. I strained my ear, but
could not catch the least note of thunder. A silence as
of death was over the sea. The heaving of the vessel was
not sufficient to flap the heavy folds of the main-topsail;
and aloft all was still, unless it were now and again the
faint clank of a chain, or the straining of a belayed rope
upon the sheave of a block. The air was stagnant, so
heavy as to be respired with difficulty. Now and again,
where the hidden folds of the dark swell ran, there
would faintly gleam a space of phosphorescent light that
seemed to imitate the pallid play of the sheet-lightning
over the sea in the quarter where the storm was growing ; and, as the bark slowly and softly dipped her sides,
rays and circles and beautiful configurations of greenish light would dart from her into the gurgling blackness, and look like creatures made of fire sporting in her
shadow.

"Now then, men, tally on to those reef-tackles ! Bear
a hand, so as to be off the yard before the wind comes !"

called out Richard, in a voice that rang loudly through the silence.

As he spoke, a heavy drop of rain splashed on my face. I made a movement towards the companion, but paused, dreading the heat of the cabin, and wishing, also, to behold the storm break, and see with my own eyes what was to come of it. Richard took no notice of me. Indeed, he could no longer see me, for I stood in the shadow of the port-quarter boat. I dare say he would forget all about me at such a time.

Only a few drops of rain fell, but the marks of their moisture on the deck, where the haze from the cabin lamp made the planking visible, were as large as five-shilling pieces. The men were on the yard, knotting the points in the second reef-band, when, looking away into the sea on our beam—for in the dead calm the bark had swung broadside on to the swell, with her head to the south and west—I saw the storm coming. The darkness was equal to midnight; indeed, it was like being in a vault; but the storm made itself visible by an amazing appearance in the corner of the heavens out of which it was rushing. The clouds appeared to have divided, and left a narrow, sharply arched aperture, illuminated by a constant play of pale sheet-lightning, that irradiated the orifice without penetrating the ponderous masses of cloud on either hand of it; but what most impressed me was the surface of dull, gloomy, phosphoric light immediately under the aperture —a faint, wild-looking radiance, similar in character to the light that would be thrown by oiled paper surrounding the globe of a lamp, as though the hurricane were sweeping through the orifice in the clouds and tearing up the sea beneath it.

"Down, for your lives, men! Down, for your lives!" roared my husband. "Never mind the sail!"

I heard the thunder of the hurricane and the seething of the crushed sea, as though half the ocean were boiling, long before its fury struck us. It was one of those moments which can never be forgotten by those who have lived through the like of it: first, the overpowering blackness over us, and in the southeast a very sea of liquid pitch overhead, in which the spars vanished at the height of a few feet from the deck; a breathless calm on one side —so breathless that the very swing of the pendulum-like swell seemed to have come to an end, as if the onward-rushing storm had paralyzed the life of the deep for leagues before it; and then, in the northwest, the pale sheet-lightning, that seemed to open and shut, like the winking of an eye; the wild and dreadful light that swept outwards from the base of the cloud-opening, and the white water glimmering like wool in the blackness, and advancing towards us with frightful rapidity; and, above all, the roar of the approaching tempest, that boomed through the stillness with the fast-growing thunder of artillery, bearing down upon us with the speed of an express train.

Suddenly my husband rushed up to me. "Is that you, Jess?"

"Yes," I answered.

"For God's sake, mind yourself!" he cried. "You'll be drowned where you are!" and he dragged me to the companion, in whose shelter I stood, crouching and holding on to the rail, while he sprang aft to the wheel, shouting out some order at the top of his voice.

Immediately afterwards the hurricane struck us. I have no words to describe its fury. There is nothing in language to convey the mad shrieking, the deafening thunder, the crushing power of that terrific outfly. Over, over, over went the bark, heeling down till I could hear the water to leeward pouring like mountain torrents over the high bulwark-rail—over yet, until the angle of the companion forced me with it, and I felt the blood rushing into my head with the sharpness of the inclination of my body; while the water, white as milk, was washing to leeward within reach of my hand, and the darkness was blind with foam that flashed along as thick as an Antarctic snowfall. What is there to liken the roaring of that wind to? It was not only the ear-piercing and distracting yelling and whistling and shrieking of the furious blast, as it tore through the rigging of the prostrate bark. It roared with a distinct thunder of its own along the sky. Some of the foam-flakes torn out of the sea struck me in the face, which smarted as though a pistol filled with small shot had been fired at me.

On a sudden there was a loud report overhead. For the moment I believed that a cannon had been fired near us; but, observing that the vessel righted somewhat, I understood that the main-topsail had blown away. Yet the bark still remained half under water, perfectly motionless, indeed, for the hurricane had levelled the sea as flat as a board, and there was no time yet for the surges to rise. There was no lightning nor thunder, nothing but the mighty raving of the wind, and an ocean like a plain of snow. I held by the companion-rail, veritably half stunned by the tremendous uproar, barely protected from the gale and the drenching masses of flying spume, yet with enough sensibility left to feel prepared for the worst; for it appeared as if the bark would not right, in which case I knew she must founder. But, after a little, I noticed that the horrible slant of the deck decreased, and at the same time the hurricane appeared to veer and pour its howling weight and shrieking spray against me. To protect myself, I made shift to close the weather companion door, and crouched behind it, less inclined than before to go below, for of all the horrors my imagination when young had depictured, from reading narratives of disasters at sea, nothing had ever appeared to me more awful than the being locked up, so to speak, in the cabin of a sinking ship, and to be active and sensible for some time after being under water.

Indeed, this thought rushing into my head now put me in mind of the mate, whom I supposed my husband had locked up in his berth, and I should certainly have gone below, and endeavored to release him, had I not discovered that the bark was paying off—that is, slowly turning, so as to present her stern to the wind, and becoming more upright each moment, as she brought the hurricane farther aft. Whether this was due to the topsail bursting and blowing away, and to the fore-topmast-staysail stoutly holding, I cannot say; but it was like a reprieve from death to feel the vessel recovering herself, and getting upon a level keel, until her decks were horizontal once more, and she was flying like an arrow upon the wings of the hurricane, with the water gushing in torrents from her scupper-holes.

The speed at which she was urged diminished the weight of the wind upon us, and my impression at first was that the tempest was slackening its fury. But I was undeceived the moment I endeavored to quit the shelter of the companion. Indeed, but for my tenacious clutch of the hand-rail I should have been blown down the ladder as a piece of paper is caught up and whirled away by a gust of wind. What the velocity of that hurricane was I cannot imagine; but we were certainly sweeping before it at not less than twelve knots an hour, robbing it therefore of the amount of weight that would be expressed by that speed; and yet such was its might that no man could face it, no man could withstand it without holding on with both hands. It was as though a solid wall of stone pressed against the body. The ocean was a vast bed of foam, and there was a peculiar thickness and numbness in the *feel* of the motion of the hull that made us seem to be driving through a sea of mud. The spray that was ripped out of the water flew over the taffrail in showers, and, being full of phosphorus, rushed like shoals of fiery darts along our decks and overhead through the rigging, and vanished in the pitchy blackness beyond the bows. At short intervals a flash of lightning, that was sometimes an emerald green, sometimes golden, like sunlight, and sometimes a deep crimson, illuminated the tremendous scene of storm with its blinding splendor, laying bare the boiling ocean to its farthest confines, and revealing the monstrous shapes of dense black clouds hurled along, and revolving and scattering as they flew; but if ever thunder followed, it so mingled in the hellish bellowing of the storm-fiend as to make an indistinguishable part of the astounding and terrifying raving.

I remained standing in the companion, hearing no sound of human voices, and dimly perceiving in the pale reflection cast by the binnacle lamp the figures of the two men at the wheel, one of whom was my husband. The sea was now beginning to rise, and the bark to plunge heavily upon the under-running surges. Yet for half an hour we held on, rushing forward as madly as the storm itself, shrouded in the flying foam, deafened by the roaring of the hurricane, and dazzled at intervals by the picture of

the tempest and the driven bark flashed up in red or
green or yellow by the lightning that scarred the pitchy
night with jagged lines of fire, reaching from the zenith
to the remote horizon.

At last my husband shouted out some order from the
wheel. The blast carried his voice forward, and after a
little the figure of a man, leaning and staggering and
crawling and clutching, made his way aft to take the
place of Richard, who advanced and called to the men
to stand by to brace the main-yards aback, and heave
the vessel to.

If this was to be done at all, it was wise to do it before
the mountainous sea which the hurricane promised arose.

"Man the fore-topmast-staysail downhaul! Are you all
ready? Then let go the halliards!" Crack! The instant the sheet was slackened away, the sail split into
fragments, portions whirled up like the froth itself into
the darkness, and I heard the whips rattling upon the
stay as though they were firing volleys of musketry from
the forecastle.

"Never mind the staysail! Lay aft to the braces.
Wheel there! Put the helm down! Bring her to steadily."

We had now a repetition of the first experience; for
as the vessel presented her bow to the hurricane she lay
over until her decks seemed up and down. However,
this time she kept her lee bulwarks above the water;
but we had the whole force of the tempest in our teeth.
Its fury appeared redoubled, as though this sudden stopping and standing at bay of the vessel it had been blind-
ly hurling before it had driven it mad outright. Thus
we lay, rising and falling upon the surges, which were
momentarily growing fiercer, with the lee decks full of
water, the foam of the boiling sea alongside on a level
with the bulwark rail, and the whole black night full
of such dreadful thunderous sounds as no one who has
not been hove to in a cyclone can imagine the like of.

CHAPTER XXVI.

A HEAVY SEA.

I WENT below to change my wet clothes, and also to escape my husband's observation, as I was pretty sure he would be angry if he found me on deck. It was about half-past seven. The cabin, in spite of the hurricane, was close and oppressive ; the steward had lighted the lamp, and the way it swung was a pretty strong hint of the character of the sea that was already running. Indeed, it was now impossible to keep a footing. I had to watch carefully before letting go to make a dash for the nearest fixture, and worked my way to my berth by clawing along the edge of the table like a parrot along his perch.

The sounds here were of a different nature from those on deck, but more distracting if possible, consisting of a violently harsh chorus of creaking, grinding, and groaning noises, accompanied by the dull roar of seas striking the vessel, and the bellowing of the tempest, which resembled the rolling of heavy peals of thunder heard in an underground room. I had to sit in my bunk to change my clothes, and how I managed I cannot tell. I remember pausing repeatedly to follow with a quick-beating heart the giddy and overpowering rolling and pitching motion of the bark, for the hurricane, having tossed up the waves, had got, so to speak, a grasp upon the sea, and was rapidly swelling the billows into the height of cliffs; and our berth being in the part of the vessel where her pitching was most to be felt, the fearful headlong movements, the dizzy, sickening soarings, and the long, swift falls scared me at times to such a degree as to give me real trouble to collect my senses.

But, as I have said, I managed to exchange my wet clothes for dry ones, and was sitting in my bunk, holding on tightly, with something of stupefaction in my mind, when Richard came in.

"How long have you been below, Jess?" he called out, in such a cheery voice that the tone of it acted upon me like a cordial.

I told him.

"You are better below, you are better here," said he, adapting his postures to the heaving of the deck with such ease, his arms hanging by his sides, as at once convinced me that, however proud I might be of my sea-legs in fine weather, he was very much my master when it came to a storm. "Have you had tea, Jess?"

"No, indeed," I answered, "and I have never thought of tea. This is a fearful storm, Richard. Only feel how the bark pitches and rolls! It's enough to make me fear that it will all be over with us soon."

"Over with us!" he cried. "Has the gale blown all your courage away? Over with us! What would your father say if he heard you? I'll allow that this storm is fierce enough in its way; but do you think the *Aurora* is not a match for it?"

"Well, when she lay down before the first blast, I believed we were all as good as dead," said I. "I was very nearly running below, and letting Mr. Heron out. It seemed cruel not to give him a chance for his life."

"I am glad you didn't," said he, quickly.

"Have you *really* locked him up?" I asked.

"Yes, really. He is in his berth, and I have the key," he replied.

"But how is he to get his meals, Richard?"

"Don't trouble yourself about him, Jess. Leave him to me. Do you know that my mutinous fo'ksle beauties have cost me a whole topsail, which would have been saved had they obeyed my orders? But now that that impudent rebel, Heron, is out of the road, the men may come to their senses again." And here, changing the subject, he added, "I'll tell the steward to get some tea. If there's not hot water, then we must find something else to refresh ourselves with." And then, looking at me anxiously, he said, "I was sorry, Jess, very sorry, that you should have been a spectator of what took place between Heron and me. God knows, I am not fond of violence, and would have kept my hands off him if I could. But

17

what mortal creature could endure such gross disobedience? He refused to help me to deal with the crew, and gave a direct countenance to their mutinous conduct in the face of a storm which he knew, as well as I, would be a hard one. Let him thank Heaven I did not pitch him overboard! I was in the temper to do it. But I always knew it must come to my locking him up. Our lives and this vessel are too precious to be at the mercy of an unprincipled coward who draws mate's pay, and gives the men to understand that he is with them and against the captain. He can do no harm where he is—but it will be my turn when I get him ashore. I shall remember him."

All the time he was talking he was busy in putting on dry clothes and oilskins.

"Are you going on deck again?" I asked him.

"Certainly," he replied. "I must take Heron's place, and relieve the carpenter. Besides, do you suppose I could rest quiet below in such weather as this?"

And, as if to emphasize his words, the bark at that moment was swept skyward with such headlong, breathless velocity that I felt as if rushing upward in the car of a balloon, and I observed a look of expectation and even of dismay in Richard's face as he stood waiting while we sank into the roaring hollow with a crash of the counter that shook and boomed through the straining fabric as though the bark had struck the ground.

"Don't let this dance trouble you," said he; "the little hooker is only enjoying herself—tossing her heels because she is a trifle bedevilled just now. Can I get a kiss without capsizing?"

And with a little staggering run he threw his arms around me, pressed me fondly, and, bidding me tell the steward to call him when there was something to eat on the table, he left the berth.

When I saw the steward he said the cook had raked the galley fire out, and that there was no hot water to be had. There was such an air of satisfaction in the way the fellow told me this that I was sure he did not speak the truth; but I let it pass, first, because the condition of the decks would not suffer me to go forward and see if the galley fire was out, and, secondly, because I knew if the man lied, and Richard detected him, there would be more trouble, more hard words, more ill-feeling, to increase the stock that was already much too big.

So the "tea" that evening consisted of a bottle of brandy, cold water, a piece of salt beef, and a dish of sea-biscuits. These things were placed on the swinging trays, for the rolling and plunging of the vessel was now tremendous indeed, and so convulsive was the motion at times that nothing, even with the fiddles, would stand upon the table.

The steward went on deck to tell Richard that supper was ready—for it would have been more supper than tea even had the brandy-bottle been a teapot—but came back to say that the captain could not leave the deck, and that I was not to wait for him.

It was quite proper that he should desire to watch his vessel at a time like that, but my imagination, confused and excited by the distracting heaving of the bark, found something alarming in his resolution. Not long before he had said he would join me ; and now he could not leave the deck. Had matters grown more serious since he quitted the berth? Well, you would have sympathized with my fears had you been below with me in that cabin ! In addition to the frightful roaring of the night outside, and the soul-subduing sweeping and whirling of the vessel upon the mighty Atlantic surges, which the furious hurricane had swelled into monstrous acclivities, there was always the thought of the mate locked up in the berth behind me, brooding over his feelings, hating my husband, probably in possession of the sympathies of the whole of the crew, who would consider him a victim in their cause.

I could not eat ; I had not the least appetite, which in a sense was fortunate, as I doubt whether, without assistance, I should have been able to help myself to the food upon the trays, which oscillated with such violence that their lee rims were often hard against the deck. Any effort on my part to seize them must have ended in capsizing their contents. But, besides this, the moment I rose to my feet I required both hands to hold on with.

The steward remained in his pantry, with the door

closed, refusing, no doubt, to take any notice of me unless I called him, abiding by the old sea-maxim, "that
it's a good dog nowadays that'll come when he's called,
let alone coming before it." Fortunately, not being in
want of any supper, I could manage to do without him.

The being alone with my apprehensions, and hearing
nothing but the dreadful storm raging outside, and the
groaning and straining of the laboring, deeply freighted
bark, became unbearable at last. I am sure the cabin is
the worst place to be in, in a gale of wind at sea. On
deck you see what is happening ; but in the cabin your
imagination paints it. You don't know what is doing ;
every furious heave seems to threaten destruction, and,
bad as the real situation may be, your fancies, fed by
the straining sounds around you, and the muffled crashing and trampling of the seas outside, make it ten times
worse.

I felt that I must go on deck, if it were only for a minute, to have a look round ; and having, with very great
labor and much risk of losing my hold, and being dashed
against the bulkheads, regained my berth, and wrapped
myself up in a good waterproof cloak, the hood of which
protected my head, I crept and groped along to the companion-steps and mounted as high as the level of the
hatch.

My body intercepted the light flung upon the ladder by
the cabin lamp ; and it being pitch dark, and the weather-
door of the companion closed and the top drawn over,
obliged me to move very cautiously ; which was assuredly
a very fortunate necessity for me ; for had I immediately
stepped out of the hatch without taking proper care, I
should have been blown overboard or carried away into
the lee-scuppers, which were full of water, and stunned,
and perhaps drowned.

I do not say the gale was more furious now than when
I left the deck ; but whether it was owing to the peculiar horror which the awful blackness of the night gave
to it, or that I had somewhat lost the recollection of its
fury by having kept below, it seemed to me that the roaring noise the storm made in the sky as it thundered through
the darkness was greater than when it had first struck us ;

while, as to its fierceness, though I did but show my nose above the hatch, it instantly stifled all power of breathing not less completely than had I buried my head in sand or a feather-bed.

However, by dint of keeping my body in the shelter of the companion, and turning the back of my head to the wind, I managed to survey the sea to leeward, and judge by what I could faintly decipher of the shape and spars of the bark, and by hearkening to the ear-splitting shrieking of the tempest in the rigging, of the fury of the dark and bellowing scene amid which our little vessel was laboring.

I was only able, I say, to see the ocean to leeward ; but, though the windward show would make the more terrific spectacle, yet there was something to keep me breathless in the sight of the mountainous outlines which swarmed with vivid fires, while here and there, as the crest of some gigantic sea broke, the surface of foam fell and rose upon the rushing acclivities like a vast space of flaming turpentine. The bark lay under bare poles, and was, therefore, without way ; yet every time a sea rolled her over she swung into the roaring hollow with a force that sent immense bodies of foam spreading half-way up the enormous surge that rushed away from her ; and in the glimmering light of the snow-like masses, mixed with the hellish sparkle of the phosphorus, I could clearly trace the outline of the vessel as far as the fore-chains, and see the lee rigging blown out into semicircles and the gleam of water washing in the scuppers. At intervals, which seemed almost regular, there would come the shock of a sea striking the bark on the weather-bow, or on the beam, and making every fibre of her tremble, immediately followed by the splashing and tearing sound of a volume of water smiting her forward decks ; and every time that the receding surge forced her masts to windward, the yellings and shriekings and whistlings in the rigging grew fivefold wilder.

Suddenly a figure came sliding down out of the darkness abreast of me, easing himself down by slackening away the bight of a rope round his waist.

"What are you doing here, Jessie? My dear girl, you should be below. There's nothing to see. You'll be

washed overboard," exclaimed my husband, whose face I
could not in the faintest degree discern.

I descended the ladder by a few steps to make room
for him in the companion, for it was impossible for me to
speak so as to be heard outside that shelter.

"It is not very pleasant to be below alone on such a
night as this," said I. "If we are to perish, I don't want
to be drowned like a rat in the cabin."

"Perish! nonsense!" he cried, heartily. "The bark's
making noble weather of it."

"Why didn't you come down to supper, then?" said I.

"Because I don't want to leave the deck," he answered.
"Have you supped?"

"No," said I. "Who could sup on the brink of the
grave?"

He laughed outright.

"Why, Jess! this won't do. Is this your love of the
sea? Is this consistent with your old devotion to Jack
and his calling? Come, I'll give you five minutes, and
see if my taking a bite won't encourage you to imitate
me."

Putting his arm round my waist, he fairly lifted me off
my feet, and in a few moments had me seated next him
at the table.

"Jess," said he, as he dodged the swinging trays, and
with wonderful dexterity took what he wanted from them,
"you mustn't mind a gale of wind. We're not aboard an
old sieve; we're in as brave a little hooker as was ever
sent afloat, and, depend upon it, she'll show the scars of
many a worse bout than this before time knocks her into
a sheer hulk."

"It's my being alone, listening to the roaring and the
straining, and thinking of"—and here I nodded in the
direction of Heron's cabin—"that makes me nervous,"
said I.

"I can quite understand it," he answered. "But here,
eat this piece of beef, and first put your lips to this tumbler."

"Only feel how the vessel pitches, Richard! I never
pretended to be brave. Father himself would be nervous
were he forced to sit here alone and listen," said I, not

liking him to think me frightened, and yet feeling that it would be silly to pretend that I was not alarmed.

"When you've done your supper," said he, "go and turn in, and when you wake the sun will be up and all the wind gone."

"I hope so," I exclaimed.

"It's not only weel *may* the keel row, but weel *shall* the keel row, Jess, now that I have you to look after and carry home safe. There's an old song that says, 'Oh, pilot, 'tis a fearful night; there's danger on the deep.' And what says the pilot? 'Fear not, but trust in Providence!' Ay, Jess, trust in Providence, but give me a wee bit of your faith, too, sweetheart." And then, after a pause, "What troubles me more than this storm is my main-topsail. A good sail lost through that—" And here, doubling his fist, he shook it at Heron's cabin-door.

Meanwhile he was eating heartily, holding on to his plate at one moment, and then letting it go to use his fork, turning often to look at me with an affectionate and encouraging smile, and so cheering me by his light-hearted manner that under his influence I felt like another woman.

To remember him as he sat by my side in that heaving, staggering, thunderous, groaning and complaining cabin is to recall a true picture indeed of an English sailor. The gale had reddened his cheeks, and his eyes shone like diamonds. Upon his face lay little patches of salt crust, that is, brine that had hardened into crystals when the salt water dried. His oilskins sparkled with wet. I could not question but that such frightful weather would fill him with anxiety; yet I did not discover the least hint of any feeling of that kind in his face and behavior. Whenever the vessel gave an unusually heavy plunge, he would laugh and say, "That's the way to test copper fastening, Jess!" or "While she creaks she holds," or "Thank God, we're afloat in good wood! If this were an iron tank now, one of those metal baths with water-tight compartments, warranted to break down and fill at a pressure of one hundred pounds, eh, Jess?" until he almost persuaded me that the hurricane was little more than a moderate gale, and that we were as safe in this raging sea as we were when at anchor in the Downs.

"Now," said he, jumping up, "you'll turn in and go fast asleep. It's early, I know; but there's too much noise to read; you are not in the humor to practise on the harmonium; and there's nothing to be seen on deck. Nor do I want my pretty wife to let the wind blow the beautiful white teeth out of her mouth, which the gale comes hard enough at times to do. One kiss, Jess—so! I shall come below in about half an hour, and shall expect to find you snugly tucked up, and away in lands where there are no gales, no salt beef, no night watches, and no infernal mutineers."

I obeyed him, though it gave me no pleasure to go to bed. I would much rather have sat up all night in the cabin. However, I could not but reflect that, if our situation was as dangerous as the furious running sea and motion of the bark made it appear, Richard would not have told me to undress and "turn in;" and this consideration, backed by the cheerful influence he had already excited upon my mind, went a long way to encourage and support me.

But I should have had to be weary indeed to have fallen asleep soon amid the distracting noises in my berth. I was fully used to the ordinary sounds, and was no longer disturbed by them; but here now was an uproar very new indeed to my experience of the *Aurora*. The worst part was the blows of the seas under the counter. Some of the concussions were so furiously violent that I would start up, expecting to find our part of the fabric split and opening. The grinding of the rudder, too, was as if it would tear away the stern-post. On the lee side there was a perpetual gurgling and washing and roaring of water, which softened its notes as the stern of the vessel was thrown up, only to thunder forth again amid a whole storm of creaking and rending noises as the counter swooped into the trough of the sea, and buried the after-part of the hull as high as the taffrail.

All this was bad enough, but it took a new edge from the thought of the mutinous crew, of Mr. Heron a prisoner in his berth, of my husband alone, so to speak, in his ves-

sel, surrounded by men who hated him; and then there
would arise the scene of violence I had witnessed, the
dark and swollen features of the mate as he was dragged
along, and the looks of the men as they stood idly in a
crowd watching the struggle. How long I lay awake I
cannot say; for above a couple of hours certainly. Yet
my husband, in spite of his promise, never came to the
berth. I then fell into an uneasy sleep, from which I
constantly started, instantly wide-awake and listening to
the warring sounds around, and feeling the wild heavings
of the vessel, until at last I settled down into a deep slumber, and do not remember waking again until I opened
my eyes in the morning, and found that it was nearly nine
o'clock.

CHAPTER XXVII.

WATER-LOGGED.

WHETHER the gale had abated or not I could not say;
but the motion of the bark seemed steadier; a heavy but
regular lateral rolling, as if the sea were on the starboard quarter. I dressed myself quickly, being able to
keep my legs with comparative ease, and deeply grateful in my heart to find the daylight abroad and the vessel
alive.

I found the cloth laid for breakfast, and the steward,
looking out of his pantry, asked if I was ready for the
meal. I answered, "Yes, if Captain Fowler was. I would
go and see," and went on deck, climbing the companion-
ladder very easily.

On emerging, I found the gale had broken, though the
sky had a most loaded and dismal appearance, and a very
heavy sea was running. The weather side of the quarter-
deck was dry, and Richard was pacing up and down it.
He saw me as I advanced, and, taking me by the hand,
helped me to reach the mizzen-rigging, to which was
seized a square of canvas that had served him during the
night as a protection against the wind. I had no eyes but
for him at the beginning. He looked worn-out, pale for

the want of rest, while the salt in the hollow of his eyes gave a positive ghastliness to his face.

"Have you been on deck all night, Richard?" I asked.

"The whole night," he answered. "There is no sun yet, Jess, nor is the wind all gone; but I promised you a great improvement of weather when you awoke, and you see I'm not a false prophet."

"But could you not have taken some rest? Could not the carpenter have kept watch? If this goes on you'll fall ill," said I.

He laughed and answered, "My dear Jess, in other voyages I have never left the deck for one hundred and twenty hours—five days and nights. One night is nothing. If I look wearied it's not for the want of sleep, but for the want of a trustworthy crew."

He then asked me how I had slept, and bantered me in his loving way upon my timidity; though, presently growing grave, he said, "Though I am quizzing you, my jokes are not very honest. At midnight the hurricane was at its height; it was blowing the hardest storm that ever I was in. Thank God, we have outweathered it! The *Aurora* is a glorious little vessel. Look aloft! With the exception of her topsail she has not lost a ropeyarn, and her bottom's as dry as when we left the Tyne."

"I'll look at her presently, Richard; but I must think of you first. Do you mean to come down to breakfast?"

"Yes," he replied. "Is it ready?"

"The steward is only waiting for orders to put it on the table."

He went to the companion and bawled to the steward to get breakfast at once, then returned to me.

I had now the heart to look around me, and a more grandly gloomy scene I had never beheld. The vessel had been got before the wind, and was running with the gale on her quarter under close-reefed topsails and a reefed foresail. The main-topsail was brand-new canvas, and, as I might suppose, had been bent early that morning in the room of the sail that had been blown away. I could see nothing amiss aloft. All the running gear had been hauled taut, the yards trimmed, everything done to make her look shipshape, and had she just come out of dock she could not have been in better condition. And yet, in spite of it all, the brave little bark had a strained and driven look as she was swept upwards and rolled heavily forwards by the swelling surges which followed her. The ocean was a very dark green, whitened with the creaming of huge spaces of foam left by the breaking seas, which were of enormous bulk, as might be supposed after such a hurricane as had blown during the night; but the *Aurora* was sweeping over them like a petrel, sinking into their hollows until the foresail flapped and came into the mast in the stagnant trough, then borne skywards with her bowsprit pointing to the clouds, and the whole length of her deck sloping like the side of a hill to where I stood, while the surge under her forefoot broke into a wilderness of dazzling foam, and her canvas swelled into iron-hard convexities, and the howling of the storming blast in her rigging mingled with the swelling roar of the mountainous billows which chased and caught and hurled her down into the hollow again.

The tempestuous appearance of the sea was deepened by the surface of dark cloud that underlay the sky, along which a rush of sulphur-colored scud was sweeping with astonishing rapidity. The atmosphere was, however, exceedingly clear; and I could see the water-line to the farthest circle, and mark the seas rising and falling against the clouds in dark outlines, which looked like ranges of mountains perpetually shifting their places.

"Are we holding our course?" I asked Richard, as we descended into the cabin, after Mr. Short had been called to take charge.

"Ay," said he, "and making noble progress. A few days of this would do wonders for our latitudes."

This was good news, and, added to the gale having broken, and the barometer promising better weather yet by-and-by, put me in good spirits. Richard entered our berth to refresh himself with a wash and remove his oilskins, and when he rejoined me, and we sat down to breakfast, I told him he looked recognizable at last, and like the husband I was accustomed to see.

"But how," said I, softening my voice, and nodding in

the direction of the mate's cabin, "does Mr. Heron manage for meals? How is he fed?"

"Oh," said he, in a low voice, too, "at the usual hours for meals I give the key to the steward, who carries the food that's required to him, and then brings me the key. He fares as we do. I make no difference, though at first I had a mind to put him on bread and water."

"Is it lawful for you to keep him locked up, Richard?" I asked.

"Yes," he replied, "and in irons, too, if I choose. Of course, a master is answerable for what he does; but his first duty is to bring his ship safe to port. Heron refused to obey my orders. He connived with the crew when in a state of mutiny. He has therefore imperilled the discipline of the ship, and been guilty of what the law calls a misdemeanor — a mild term for scoundrelism. Consequently, I am holding him in safe custody until I can hand him over to the proper authorities when we reach port. Don't be alarmed, Jess," he added, laughing; "there's a good Act of Parliament behind me."

"But why must you lock him up, Richard? Won't he stop in his cabin with the door unlocked?" said I, pursuing the subject, not because I supposed he had no right to imprison the mate, but because, now that I could give the matter some earnest thought, it distressed me to feel that my husband should consider himself obliged to act the part of jailer, and give the men forward reason to believe him tyrannical.

"I wouldn't trust him," he answered. "He'd take the first opportunity to slip out, sneak forward, and lodge himself in the forecastle; the men would refuse to give him up. I could do nothing, except get a broken head by jumping below and trying to haul him out; and there he would remain, exasperating the crew against me, until neither your nor my life would be worth the value of this biscuit. No, Jess; leave him to me. I know the people I have to deal with."

This reasoning was convincing enough, as you may suppose, and taught me to perceive that in some things my husband was a good deal longer-sighted than I. I therefore changed the subject by asking him how Mr. Short behaved now that his friend was locked up.

"The hurricane has kept him straight so far," he answered. "He was on deck the greater part of the night, and was sometimes in a real stew, coming up to me and saying, 'Good Lord, what weather, sir !' and swearing that he never saw such a sea before, and that it was big enough to swallow up an island, let alone a ship. And he was not far out. At midnight it was blowing two hurricanes in one, and old Sunderland deserves to be immortalized in marine story for having turned out spars capable of outweathering such a storm."

"The sea is still very heavy, Richard."

"But nothing to bother one while it will let us run," he replied. "It remains squally, though," he added, looking up, for a sudden gloom had fallen upon the skylight, and in a few moments the glass of it was lashed by a heavy fall of rain.

Just as the rain ceased and the skylight brightened, a pair of clumsy, clattering sea-boots descended the companion-steps, followed by the long, awkward, muscular body of Mr. Short, who, without quitting the steps, leaned forward his head, cased in a fur cap, from which the wet of the recent squall streamed like the drainings from a soaked swab, and exclaimed, in a hoarse voice,

"There's a wessel on the lee bow that looks to be waterlogged, with foremast and mainmast gone, and a color flying in what's left of the mizzen-rigging."

My husband, hearing this, jumped up, and at once followed the carpenter on deck. I made haste to finish my breakfast, and then ran on deck too.

I turned my eyes upon the quarter of the sea over the lee bow, but some moments passed before I made out the vessel, owing to her having nothing but her mizzen-mast standing, and to her obliteration by the huge surges which swelled between her and us. She was a long way off; but the squall that had swept over us had already gone clear of her, and left the horizon visible, and when she was hove up and poised an instant on the crest of a sea she stood out with singular distinctness against the dismal, leaden background.

My husband came to the mizzen-mast, near to which I was standing, to steady the telescope upon one of the belaying-pins on the rack-hoop. From this point the vessel showed plainly under the reefed foresail.

"What is she, Richard?" I asked.

"Why," he replied, talking with his eye to the glass, "she is a large bark, timber-laden, apparently, and water-logged. She's a Dane—for that's the Danish ensign in the rigging—red with a white cross. My God, how she rolls! the seas break over her like the smoke from the foot of a cascade. I can see nobody aboard—and yet that ensign makes me think she can't be abandoned."

He gave me the glass, and motioned to the men at the wheel—there were two hands steering. "Let her go off a point—so! keep her steady at that now."

One shift of the helm brought the wreck just over the lee knighthead. I levelled the telescope, but our bark was pitching and courtesying so heavily, one moment settling her bows into the trough until the foam of the bow wave was washing as high as the forecastle rail, and then soaring up, until her bowsprit looked to be at right angles with the horizon, that I could not manage to cover the object with the lenses at all.

The watch on deck took no particular interest in the wreck. They were scattered about the vessel, variously employed, and sometimes turned their heads to have a look, but there was nothing of that eagerness which most sailors put into their behavior when a distressed vessel heaves in sight, and when there is a chance of their coming across fellow-beings whose lives are in deadly peril. Perhaps my prejudice exaggerated this peculiarity in them; yet their demeanor was certainly one of surly indifference.

We were sweeping towards the vessel with great rapidity, urged at intervals, as defined as the swing of the pendulum, by the regular send of the heavy seas which chased and overtook us. My husband pointed the glass afresh. He worked away in silence for a while, finding great difficulty in keeping the wreck covered, then suddenly called out,

"I thought so! There's a whole crowd of men aboard! Here, Jess, hold this glass. Mr. Short, get the foresail hauled up. Get it done at once. I shall stand by that ship! Her poop is filled with men!"

His voice rang out in his excitement, and I felt my heart beating wildly.

"Man the fore clew-garnets!" bawled the carpenter, going forward.

The men dropped their work, and tailed on to the ropes, but without singing. The foresail bellied out as the tack and sheet were eased off. In a few moments it was lying snugly enough in the bunt-lines, leech-lines, and slab-lines.

"Never mind about stowing it!" shouted my husband. "Lay aft to the main-braces, and stand by to heave the vessel to;" and, running to the companion, he called to the steward to hand him up his speaking-trumpet.

The only shipwreck I had ever seen in my life was the one off Shields, on that day of the gale when mother and I waited for father's brig to heave in sight. That had affected and overpowered me to a degree I could not express in words, and yet distance had softened the horror of it, and it was without that peculiar kind of dreadful melancholy which is given to disaster by the wild and lonely ocean. The wreck we were rapidly approaching was something, therefore, to come very much more sharply home to my sympathies. She looked to be a vessel of about seven hundred tons, but submerged to half-way up her bulwarks. There never was in this life a more dismal picture of a wreck. One would have said that nature had gone to work to complete the painting in such a manner as to make it incomparable for finish. The gloomy, squall-laden sky darkened the ocean with its stooping shadow, and the mangled and tumultuous scud that swept across it seemed of themselves true images of distress. The heavy, swelling sea, over which the strong gale was howling, tossed its olive-colored waters in endless ranges of rushing mountains; while here and there the brown shadow of a squall veiled a segment of the angry circle with a haze of rain, against which the crests of the surges, as they rolled roaring into foam, flashed out with the brilliancy of sunlit snow. And in the midst of this most desolate, storming scene lay the wreck, rolling heavily, but without the least capacity to lift with the seas, which, in consequence, poured their fearful flood of glass-clear green water over her, completely hiding all but her poop, and

smothering her in froth, out of which would fork the only
remaining mast, bearing its square ensign, that streamed
like a flame from the shroud to which it was seized ; while
at intervals the whole drowned and beaten fabric would
vanish behind the brow of the surges which ran between
us and her, and nothing of the wreck remain in sight but
the fractured head of the mast.

We were now close enough to distinguish the people
aboard. I endeavored to count them, but could not succeed, as they were all huddled together right aft, lashed
one to another, and to the rail abreast of the wheel and
the skylight. I made out eighteen, but there were more.
They were all of them men, and to this hour I have but
to close my eyes to see them. How is it possible for
people living ashore, who have never witnessed such a
sight, to realize it? The memory of an expression of
frightful despair upon a single human face will live in
the heart like a pain, and there are minds which never
can get rid of it. But here was a whole crowd of men—
I have said eighteen, maybe there were twenty-four or
twenty-five—ash-colored in the darkness of the leaden
heaven over them, and in the shadow of the death that
hovered among them, watching us with straining eyeballs,
motioning to us with wild, imploring tossings of the arms
and compressions of the hands, suffering and horror in
every countenance, lashed to one another, and clinging to
one another upon a surface of planking over which the
water welled as high as their waists at times, while on
the main-deck it was a boiling smother of froth which
every few minutes would be extinguished by the green
folds of a mountainous sea rolling over that part of the
wreck, and bending her down until the fragment of
naked mizzen-mast was nearly level with the roaring coils
of water on the lee side.

When we were within hailing distance of her my husband gave the order to put the helm down and lay the
main-yards aback. I could not but take notice of the little will with which our seamen worked. They swung
the yards with the air of men who resented this heaving-
to, as a job the captain had no right to put them to ; and
I could hear them muttering as they hauled upon the

braces without singing, darting evil glances at my husband, who stood with the speaking-trumpet in his hand, intently watching the wreck.

The wind seemed comparatively moderate while we were running before it; but now, when by putting the helm down we brought it upon the bow, I was surprised by its violence. Indeed, it still blew a gale, and the bark rose and sank upon the towering seas, pitching furiously, lying heavily over under her topsails, while the water flew over her forecastle in sheets, and, by soaking the waist and filling the scuppers, gave the little vessel back her storm-tossed appearance. My husband, holding on to a backstay, put his trumpet to his mouth, and roared through it to know if there was any one aboard who could understand or speak English. Three or four of the poor creatures immediately raised their arms.

"There's no use attempting to lower a boat in this sea," shouted Richard. "All that we can do is to stand by you until the weather moderates."

A voice came faintly up against the gale, "For God's sake, don't leave us, sir."

"No, no; we'll not leave you," answered Richard.

Here something else was said.

"What do you say?" bawled my husband.

The merest flicker of a voice replied; but it was impossible to catch it. The wind was thundering in our ears, and dead against the voices of the miserable crew; besides, being buoyant and with canvas on her, the *Aurora* was getting fast to leeward of the wreck, that lay like an anchored raft in the trough of the sea.

I stood watching the crowd of men, with my heart wrung by their misery, helplessness, and suffering. That faint cry, "For God's sake, don't leave us, sir," rang in my brain like a voice from the other world. As we slowly drifted ahead of them I could see their white faces, turned our way, following us, like spirits without voices to supplicate, but more passionately imploring in their silence than had they filled the gale with their cries. My husband came up to me.

"Is there no way of delivering them at once?" I cried.

"Not at once," he answered. "We have no boat that

18

would live two seconds in that sea. Mark its power!"
and as he spoke the *Aurora* was thrown up until the inclination of her deck positively seemed vertical, and then,
as she swung into the hollow, with her rigging full of the
wild and piercing notes of the storming wind, the liquid
acclivity that had poised her ran in thunder from her
side, blotting out the heavens to many degrees above the
horizon with its emerald-green volume.

I was about to speak, when Richard, taking me by the
arm, hurried me into the companion, telling me to wait
until the coming squall had passed; and scarcely was I
under shelter, when the rain came along like a mass of
gray vapor, plunging upon us with an outfly and fury of
wind that seemed as frenzied as the first of the hurricane on the preceding night. It made as much noise as
hail, tearing upon the decks and lashing the hollow companion as if every drop were a good-sized bullet; and I
watched it blowing along the sky in whole clouds dark
as smoke, whirling in the shape of gigantic corkscrews.
It veiled the deep as effectually as a fog, and truly wondrous was the sight of the huge green seas rushing out
of the weather circle it left clear around us, and then
vanishing to leeward in forms as polished and lucent as
glass, streaked with long, expiring stretches of foam.

When the squall passed, and I looked for the wreck,
she was to windward, and apparently half a mile or more
astern.

"We are leaving her, Richard," I exclaimed, as he
came round from the lee side of the mizzen-mast, where
he had sought shelter.

"I have her bearings," he replied, looking greatly
bothered and distressed. "I'll 'bout ship presently.
"But," he added, under his breath, as though thinking
aloud, "I have a ruffianly crew."

He left me and went and stood aft, gazing at the water-
logged hull. The watch on deck, three of them—two
being at the wheel—stood under the lee of the galley,
for the most part looking aft and talking, and in every
posture and movement most visibly expressing mutinous
discontent. The carpenter walked in the weather gangway. My husband was probably too much engrossed

with thoughts of the poor fellows on the wreck to notice his own men's idleness, or that Mr. Short never started them on the jobs they were engaged on before they hove the bark to.

For about ten minutes nothing was done, and we went on drifting steadily to leeward; the wreck grew smaller and smaller, yet I consoled myself with reflecting that the poor fellows would never suppose that we meant to desert them so long as they could see that we kept our main-topsail to the mast.

Suddenly Richard came forward.

"Wear ship, Mr. Short," and he called to one of the two men at the wheel to go forward and help the others.

"Wear ship, my lads!" echoed the carpenter.

None of the men moved; but Quill called out, "We'll get the vessel on her course, but there's no use beatin' about for them furriners. We're short-handed as it is, and if we're expected to boxhaul these yards about in a gale of wind, say the word, and we'll give up."

I omit the abominable profanities with which he interlarded this speech.

"Do you mean to tell me, men, that you refuse to help me to stand by those unhappy fellow-creatures of ours?" cried my husband, pointing astern, and appearing staggered and confounded by the seamen's inhumanity.

"They're not the only fellow-creatures who're in distress," answered James Snow, insolently. "Why don't ye give the chief mate his liberty? The only wrong he's done is to own that our complaint of being short-handed is right."

"Ay," cried Gray, one of the ordinary seamen, "it's easy enough to feel sorry for a lot o' bloomin' Dutchmen. Charity begins at home, says I."

"I order you to wear ship!" exclaimed my husband. "Do you refuse?"

"We'll put the ship on her course, sir," answered Quill. "But we never shipped for life-boat sárvice; that's hextry duty. And who's going to drive to wind'ard agin this sea and wind? It'll take us months. Leave them men for some other wessel to rescue."

What could my husband do? It is all very well to

talk of discipline on shipboard, when you are backed by
good officers, and when you know that some among your
crew would prove sound men could they be drawn away
from their mutinous shipmates.   But my husband stood
alone.   The whole ship's company, mates and men, were
against him.   There was not a living creature aboard the
vessel willing to speak up for him, or to remonstrate with
the others for their inexcusable revolt.

He turned from them, and walked aft again, and stood
looking over the taffrail, apparently watching the drowning vessel, that was scarcely distinguishable as she rolled
among the seas, though, as I guessed by his keeping his
back to the crew, he wished to conceal his face, which,
judging by the glimpse I had caught of it, only too plainly exhibited his dismay and distress.

I joined him, for I could not bear to see him standing
there, so helpless and lonely in heart and purpose, as I
knew he felt, so distracted by that dim and distant vision
of human anguish which his cowardly crew refused to let
him approach and assist.

"Bear up, Richard!" I exclaimed, taking his hand and
keeping my voice low, being mindful of the presence of
the seamen at the wheel; "if the men *will not* obey your
orders you must submit.   We must pray to Almighty
God that some other vessel will presently sight that
wreck and take off the men."

"Ay," he answered, in a broken voice, "and there is
something more to pray to God for; and that is, that he
will give me power to carry you safely through the perils
which those villains forward there threaten to bring about
us.   I cannot tell what intentions they have; but nothing
yet has occurred that looks darker and more dangerous
than this refusal of theirs to stand by those poor creatures yonder.   It *must* be because they do not want me
to take on board a number of men whose gratitude would
be proof against corruption, and who would stand between us and the miscreants who compose my crew.
Is that it?   Oh, Jess, were it not for you, I would not
value this situation, perilous as it looks, at the snap of a
finger.   I thought there would be no happier man afloat
than myself when I had you with me; and, instead, your

presence in this hellish company makes me so wretched that all my nerve seems to have gone overboard, and I feel as if I would be glad to exchange places with any dying man among that poor forlorn crowd there !"

I could have cried to hear him speak like this. But he stood in need of all the resolution and fortitude he could command ; so I held my peace, but kept by his side, watching the rolling bodies of dark-green water where the wreck was, and thinking, with a real heart-sickness in me, of the feelings of those poor, unhappy Danes when they perceived that, in spite of my husband's promise to keep by them, we were leaving them to their fate.

"We can't keep at this," exclaimed Richard, at the end of a few minutes, during which he had been lost in thought, with his arms tightly folded upon his breast. He went forward.

"Men," he shouted, "do you still refuse to help me to stand by that wreck ?"

"We're too weak-handed to be watching and beatin' agin a gale o' wind," answered Quill.

"Release the chief mate, and we'll stand by the furriners," cried Snow.

"Man the lee fore-braces," exclaimed Richard. "Wheel, there, put the helm over." And he added, clinching his hands, "If ever distressed sailors were murdered, those men yonder are ! Their blood is on your heads ; and there is not a man among you that shall dare call himself an English seaman after this !"

"Dan Cock'll not mind that, for one !" shouted Moore, the apprentice, referring to the colored hand ; and the others laughed as they went leisurely over to the braces.

In a few minutes the yards were trimmed and the foresail set, and once more the *Aurora* was heading along her course on an almost level keel, though rolling heavily, and plunging like a wild colt in a gallop, as the heavy following sea swung her up and shot her forward, smothering her bows in foam when her counter was hove so high that it was like peering down from the edge of a cliff to look over the taffrail. I watched a squall, dark as a thunderstorm, sweeping up towards us from the quarter of the ocean in which the wreck would be, though by this time she was not to be seen by the naked eye. I could perceive the long, slanting, fog-like streaks of the rain swallowing up the horizon, and follow the headlong rush of its course by observing the swift advance of the line of white water which it hurled up as it came, like a play of strong surf upon a length of coast. It was an image of the storm-fiend triumphing over its victims, whom we were abandoning, and casting the dark, death-like shadow of its whirring and clamorous wings over them. ·

The picture of that sunken, surge-swept deck stood up before me, with the rapidity and clearness of a vision beheld in sleep. The miserable crowd cowering before the lashing and soaking rain—yet ever bending their white faces and haggard eyes, all as one man, in the direction in which they had last seen our vessel—the agony of expectation that made them deaf to the howling of the squall which introduced a new note into the weary booming of the gale and the ceaseless crashing of the seas—I say, in my mind's eye, I saw it all: the dying crowd, the staggering, drowning hull, the regular coil of the mountainous waves over the stricken and beaten and foundering fabric, followed by the wild boiling of foam upon the decks!

"Come, Jess, hurry below before the rain comes!" said my husband; and he had just time to hand me to the companion, when the squall was upon us, and the whole scene of sea and sky lost in the rolling and revolving clouds of flying rain, while the shrill shrieking of the blast in the rigging seemed like the voices of the perishing crew, borne as a bitter curse to the ears of the inhuman wretches who had refused to allow my husband to succor them.

CHAPTER XXVIII.

THE SHADOW OF DANGER.

WELL, this incident was but an adventure of the deep, and, having related it, I will say no more about it, though it left such an impression upon my mind that, to this moment, I see the wreck and her crew as plainly as when I

beheld them from the deck of the *Aurora*. I come now
to stuff of a different fibre—to our own shipwreck, indeed,
and to the dreadful and astonishing perils we encountered,
until our deliverance from all the misfortunes which befell us in the *Aurora*, and after we had quitted her.

The hurricane, as you know, terminating in a steady
gale of wind, blew us along, under reefed topsails, all that
day and night, giving us a famous run in the twenty-four
hours ; for, besides the speed of the bark, we had the impulse of the seas, which, catching us so rhythmically that
you might have counted, say, twenty between the rise and
fall of the vessel's counter, without being one over or
under, for a dozen times together, ran us forward almost
as fast as the wind itself with every heave, so that, although
the wind failed us at about ten o'clock next morning, yet,
when Richard came to calculate his observations at noon,
he found that our run since twelve o'clock on the preceding day was a little over two hundred and eighty-eight
marine miles, or a full twelve knots an hour. We then
had a short spell of calm ; but at about two in the afternoon there came a light air from the eastward, which,
freshening up, drew into the northeast, and within an
hour of the first of the puff we had the Trades strong on
the beam, royals set, and a fore-topmast-studdingsail out,
and the bark leaning down with dry decks, and the hot
yellow sunshine sparkling in her masts and in the brass-
work and the glass, while the foam sped away from under
our counter, and danced in a line of snow upon a sea as
bright and beautifully blue as the soft heavens over which
the Trade clouds were sweeping in scattered wool-white
shapes.

If all had been well with us aboard, there would have
been but little to complain of as regards the weather, so
far. The hurricane was indeed frightful ; but we had
come through it unharmed, and it did us good by leaving
a gale behind which blew us fairly into the Trades. We
had made a fast run, and Richard talked of fetching Sierra
Leone early in March.

But not only the behavior of the men, but the circumstance of the mate being imprisoned in his cabin, cast a
gloom upon us, which was not to be cleared away by pros-

perous breezes and swift sailing. I speak of myself particularly. I was never easy in the cabin, either when
alone or with Richard. If ever I was disposed to laugh,
my merriment was immediately checked by the reflection
that the mate was locked up in that berth just over against
us, and would hear me. There was no freedom. We had
to converse in low voices, and the idea that Mr. Heron
could hear all that was said acted with such constraint
upon my husband, that I would, again and again, catch
him about to speak, and then stopping and considering
well what he was going to say before uttering it.

Talking to him in our berth on one occasion, I said,
"Why not see the mate, lecture him well, and offer him
his freedom and a promise of forgiveness if he will go to
his work again dutifully, and withhold all sympathy from
the men."

"It's too late," he replied. "Why, we shall be arriving at Sierra Leone presently. Besides, I *don't* forgive
him. He is a rascal, and I'll have him dealt with as he
deserves."

"Then can't you get him out of the cabin?" said I.
"The odious steward made it uncomfortable enough before; but now that the mate is boxed up, like a spy in a
cupboard, listening to all we say, it is positively unbearable."

"Where can I put him, Jess? In the hold? It's full
of coal. In the forecastle? There's nothing he and the
men would like better. In the lazarette, where there is
no light and no air, and where any rats the *Aurora* may
have shipped at Sunderland would be very glad to welcome him?"

"Have you seen him since he has been under lock and
key?" I asked.

"No," he answered, "and I don't want to see him."

"How do you know that he is properly fed, or that he
may not be ill?"

"Why," said he, laughing, "by his keeping quiet. If
anything were amiss in that way he'd soon make his wants
known. Those 'long-shore scow-banks are not a diffident
body of people."

As you now see, it could not be helped. My husband

had chosen to lock his mate up, for the reasons you have read, and there was no other place but his own berth to confine him in. But the thought that he was there, listening—imprisoned by my husband, who could release him if he chose, hating us so that the very sound of our voices would be detestable to him—made the cabin quite intolerable. I only used it for meals; for, when I was not on deck, I occupied the little spare berth, and sewed or read in it, and I never passed through the cabin without feeling as though there were a ghost at my heels.

It was a great pity, for it was a pleasant little cabin. When the sunshine lay on the open skylight, it was full of radiance that rippled in tiny billows upon the polished bulkheads; the wind-sail kept it breezy, and there was room to move about; whereas the sleeping-berth was small and close, lighted by a bull's-eye, and ventilated by a little scuttle that was, fortunately, to windward in the Trades, so that I was able to keep it open, for, had it been to leeward, the sweltering atmosphere caused by the fierce sun beating upon the deck overhead would have rendered the box of a place uninhabitable.

Meanwhile, there were no more open acts of mutiny among the men—I mean, there were no more collisions between my husband and his crew—though one very nearly happened two days after we had sighted the Danish wreck, by Dan Cock, the mulatto, who was in the port watch, that my husband now had charge of, saucily answering some order that was given him. He stood just before the main hatch, and my husband went up to him and told him to repeat what he had said. Richard afterwards told me that he was in the temper to have strangled the colored man, and Dan Cock probably witnessed this intention in his face, for, shrinking away, he said he didn't want to be impudent—he was willing to do his work—and so my husband left him. This was very fortunate, for, had Richard struck the man, the others would certainly have rushed in to defend him, and I dare not think what deeds of violence must have followed; for if ever men were possessed by the devil, the *Aurora's* crew were; indeed, our forecastle was like a house filled with inflammable goods—the least spark would have set the seamen on fire.

But though there was no open revolt, yet as the time
went past Richard's anxiety deepened, insomuch that,
over and over again, he would lie awake a whole watch
below, weary as any man could well be, yet too nervous
and apprehensive to close his eyes.   He was full of fore-
bodings, though unable to give shape to his fears.   On the
day preceding the dreadful trouble, the relation of which
I am about to enter on, he came below, after keeping the
deck four hours, and, sitting down at the table in our
berth, leaned his face on his hand without looking at me.

"What particularly troubles you, Richard?" I asked
him.   "Have the crew been worrying you again?"

"Not more than they usually do," said he.   "How glad
I shall be when we make our port, Jess!   I feel to be
growing light-headed for the want of sleep."

"You should take things a little more easily," said I.
"So long as the men keep their mutterings to themselves,
and do the ship's work, we may fairly say that all's well."

"Why, yes, we may say that," he replied.   "It's the
feeling myself to be alone among these ruffians—the man
who ought to be at my side, helping me, locked up—and
the second mate more friendly with the crew than ever
Heron was—it's these things which make me anxious.
But it's the lot of every shipmaster to be anxious.   Don't
let my manner weigh with you, dear.   You're quite right
to say that, while things go on as they are, all's well."

"Ay, Richard," said I;   "but your anxiety is not of the
ordinary kind.   You have misgivings which make no
part of the usual sea-life.   I wish you would talk to me
unreservedly.   First, any shirking or glossing over of
your troubles only ends in leaving me gloomier;   and,
next, if you do not take me into the very heart of your
confidence, what opinion can you have of me as a
wife?"

"Indeed, Jess," said he, smiling at my warmth, "I talk
to you as I would talk to no other human being in this
world.   Since you will have all that's in my mind, I'll
answer that my opinion of the men is so low—they have
shown such an utter want of principle and honesty in their
conduct—that I believe them capable of any crime that
can be imagined.   To be afloat with such men, and to

have you with me among them, is surely enough to account for my manner."

"But do you think they mean to do you a mischief?" said I.

"No," he answered; "I won't say that. My anxiety lies in my thinking them *capable* of doing us a mischief."

"But suppose them resolved, Richard, what form could their mischief take?"

"I can't answer that," said he. "I do not know. But there are many forms."

"Will you name one?" I exclaimed.

"No," he replied, "I won't name even one. I'm not going to fill your head with horrors."

"But they must have some sense of the law," said I. "They may play, as it were, round the brink, where they can be defiant and safe too; but they are not likely to do anything to risk their necks."

"There's no use in theorizing about them," said he, speaking as though he felt the subject ought to be dropped, for my sake. "There is nothing more exceptional than to find a whole ship's company turn upon their captain, even when they have substantial reasons for mutinying; for there are always one or two cautious or honest men who will hang back and refuse to come into so awkward and dangerous a muddle as a mutiny. But here is a whole crew mutinying without cause. There is no hanging back; they all pull together, and the mates are with them. I have thoroughly overhauled my conduct, but can find nothing to justify their behavior. I am no bully; I have endeavored to treat them considerately. When I reprimanded Mr. Heron, I spoke quietly. There is no cursing and swearing, no bouncing in me. The provisions are good. The hands who profess to be incompetent are as able as the others of whom no complaint is made; and though I will not deny that the crew is, on the whole, small, considering the vessel's tonnage, there are enough seamen to work her, and the number is up to the average. Therefore their grumbling and mutinying merely mean that they are a gang of unprincipled vagabonds—as if the forecastles of a dozen ships had been searched for their worst growling loafers to furnish out a

complement for this vessel. Ashore, these men would be
pickpockets, thimble-riggers, the scum of the rogueries
which haunt the east-end streets of London, and hang
about police courts and race-courses. They have brought
their principles to sea, and call themselves sailors. But I
am no easier in their company for that. They feel themselves a long way off from the law, out here, and I must
watch them closely, Jess, until I can get the police aboard."

There was not a word of this that could be contradicted.
However, he had said as much as he intended, and would
answer no more questions, believing he had gone too far
already, and that it would end in my thinking that the men
were only waiting for an opportunity to murder us both.

Well, the next day the Trade winds, that had swept us
nobly down to the parallel where we then were, failed us,
though we were still to the north of the equatorial latitudes, where they usually terminate—that is, when you
are sailing south in the North Atlantic. Whether this
was owing to our being well to the eastward I cannot say;
but if there be any foundation in the theories of the
people who have written explanations about these Trade
winds, then the vast hot continent of Africa has much to
do with the capriciousness of the breezes, gales, and tor-
nadoes which are encountered by vessels when they get
within a few hundred miles of those broiling coasts.

It was the hottest day we had yet had. The morning
temperature was not so extreme, because the lingering
wind kept the deck cool under the little awning that was
spread aft; but after dinner—that is, at about half-past
two—it was simply roasting. Suffocating as the cabin
was, it was as bad on deck. In the sun, whatever the
hand touched burned the flesh as though it were hot iron.
The pitch in the plank seams was as soft as putty; a kind
of bluish haze floated upon the decks, like the vaporous
exhalation that hovers over marshy soil early in the morning. There was a faint swell upon the sea, but the water
was like polished steel — of that very color, indeed; an
ashen gray, shot with a bluish light—not the merest film
of a cat's-paw darkened it, not the least wrinkle or fibre
of motion tarnished the breathless quicksilver of the huge,
faintly breathing circle. The heavens were stainless, too;

a deep, most beautifully tender African blue, a wonderful concave of glorious azure that kept the loveliness of its surpassing hue down to the water-line, where, I have observed in northern climes, the finest blue will lighten until it becomes very nearly white. Almost overhead stood the sun, a burning, fiery eye; one would have said the orb was a gigantic magnifying-glass, in which was concentrated the heat of fifty flaming luminaries. The bark gently leaned with the swell, but I took notice of a certain parched aspect aloft, a baked and dusty thinness in the appearance of the canvas, whose white cloths shone with the brilliancy of chalk, and a worn look in the running-gear, and even in portions of the standing-rigging, such as old rope has.

About fifty feet distant on the port quarter was a black, leaf-shaped object forking out of the gray, oily surface, and motionless as we were. I thought it was a bottle at first; but looking at it again, and seeing that it was not a bottle, nor, indeed, anything resembling the waifs one meets at sea, I called Richard's attention to it, and asked him what it was.

"Why," said he, giving the thing a careless look, "it's the dorsal fin of a shark, Jess. I'll bring him under the counter, where you will be able to see the beast, if you can endure the sun for a minute."

He called to the steward to hand him up an empty bottle, and, going to the taffrail, threw it overboard. The bottle made a little splash, and the black and gleaming fin advanced swiftly through the water, looking very much like the back of a negro's hand, with the fingers together. The refraction of the light soon rendered the fish discernible, and a monstrous creature he was, a full fifteen feet. If I vividly remember him, it is because, no doubt, I saw him on a day I am never likely to forget. His back, that was just under the surface of the water, was as black as if it had been newly coated with tar. There was not a point of him that had not a chilling deadliness of suggestion in it, from the shovel-shaped snout to the long, malignant barbed tail, the upper barb shooting out and curling up far beyond the other.

"Did any man ever see a more ferocious-looking brute?" exclaimed Richard, gazing with real awe at the monster, for he had never supposed the fin he had lightly glanced at belonged to such a fish as this.

The shark floated up to the bottle and smelled it, giving it a little shove with his square nose, as if to test its nutritive qualities or its flavor; meanwhile casting up its bright and evil eyes at us with so much horrible sagacity in the expression of them that I instinctively caught hold of Richard's arm and shrank back.

"Look, Jessie!" cried my husband, "dash my buttons if he's not going to bolt the bottle!" and, peering over, sure enough I saw the fearful creature slowly turn over, until his belly, colored like the inside of a mussel-shell, gleamed under the water; his huge jaws opened, disclosing a tremendous battery of teeth, and the bottle disappeared.

"After that," exclaimed my husband, "I'll believe anything Jack chooses to tell me about what's found inside a shark."

The fish rolled over again, and the black fin came above the surface; but he now stayed under the counter, peering upwards as if asking for another bottle.

Michael Craig, an able seaman, was at the wheel, but though a shark is always an object of curiosity, even to an old sailor, and though Craig could have seen the fish by stepping back without letting go of the wheel, I observed that he never so much as turned his head while Richard and I were looking at the shark and talking about it, a circumstance than which I know nothing better to give you an idea of the sullen, sulky deportment of the men, and how they stood off, so to speak, from my husband, as though he were a tyrant, and had found them a hundred reasons for hating him.

The calm lasted through the whole afternoon. The heat of the sun was so fierce that the image of the poet, when he speaks of the very deep rotting, seemed to be realized as I cast my eye over the boundless, breathless, thick and stagnant ocean; and it was with a feeling of real gratitude that I saw the roasting orb—a globe of blood-red fire—sinking behind the sea, kindling under him in the water long crimson flames, which waved with the swell, and filled one side of the firmament with a haze of dark-gold light, in which the horizon vanished as though a fog were there. When the sun was gone the night soon came down, for there was but the briefest pause of twilight, and then the air fell cool, though the decks kept their heat for a long time in spite of the dew, which lay so thick that the starlight crusted the bulwarks and portions of the planking and the skylight and companion as though they had been powdered with diamond dust.

CHAPTER XXIX.

THE DESTRUCTION OF THE "AURORA."

My husband had the first watch—that is, from eight till twelve. I remained on deck with him until eleven, dreading the close cabin. There was something very beautiful and seductive in the huge leaning space of hushed black waters, and the fascination of it was strong enough to keep me lingering, even had the sleeping-berth been cool and inviting. I walked or sat with Richard all the time, talking much of home and of that loss of ours that had made me eager to come to sea, that I might be with my husband. Never before had I so felt the wondrous magic of a deep night-calm upon the ocean. The stars of the first magnitude shone richly, and yet with a blandness in their sparkling, and dropped little wakes of silver light in the ebony surface under them. Once a beautiful sunbright meteor leaped out of the folds of darkness and floated swiftly athwart our mastheads, making a wide circumference of light around it, as though it were a little moon. Here and there the swell was haunted by a faint flash of phosphorus, that deepened to my humor the mystery of the spacious arena of gloom and silver stars and soundless deep. At times the canvas murmured softly aloft, or there would steal from the bows the muffled sob and wash of water as the bark rolled. Above all, the air was deliciously cool, so heavily dew-laden that, as the sails floated in and out, I could hear the moisture patter in little showers.

But at eleven o'clock it was high time to go to bed ; so away I went, wondering if Richard would find me asleep when he came below at midnight. Everything was quiet in the cabin, and the lamp burning dimly. The berth was very close, and yet not so oppressive as I had feared. I put my face to the open scuttle, and stood a few minutes looking at the small circumference of starlit sky which that aperture made visible. I then went to bed, and presently fell asleep.

I have some recollection of Richard coming to the cabin when his watch was up ; but he was always very quiet in his movements, and never disturbed me ; so, if I looked at him, I immediately fell asleep again.

As I afterwards calculated, I had been sleeping about an hour and a half, when I had a nightmare. I dreamed that I was at home in Newcastle, sitting with father in the old parlor, when, in some mysterious way, possible only in dreams, the room burst into flames. We tried to get out, but the door was locked. The fire caught my father's clothes, and in an agonized voice he told me to open the window, as his hands were burned off. But I could not move. The flames roared around me, and the smoke grew denser and denser, and I felt myself to be actually suffocating when I started up, covered with perspiration, with all the horror of the nightmare upon me.

The bracket lamp was alight, but what was the matter with it ? It burned with a hazy dimness, and the berth seemed full of fog. There was a disgusting flavor of poisonous fumes in my mouth, and I drew my breath with so much difficulty that the suffocation I felt in the nightmare was as strong upon me now that I was awake as it was in my dream.

I sprang out of my bunk, and I suppose this action thoroughly aroused me, for I then perceived that what I took to be fog was smoke, impregnated with a smell of burning as well as with the unspeakably nauseous fumes I have mentioned.

Richard lay in his bunk sound asleep, and breathing heavily. He was in his trousers and waistcoat, completely dressed in all but his coat and boots, for he seldom took off his clothes now when he lay down. I grasped his arm and shook him. As a rule, he was a very light sleeper, up and with all his senses about him at the first touch or call ; but, though I shook him roughly, he only muttered, and coughed in a choking way, and never opened his eyes. Indeed, he seemed to be stupefied. The smoke in the berth perceptibly thickened, and I felt that I should suffocate if I remained another minute in the place ; and the dying feeling, as it were, filling me with a kind of frenzy, I grasped my husband again, shrieking out that the bark was on fire, and in a few moments he opened his eyes with an expression of amazement that instantly changed to one of indescribable horror.

"My God, Jessie !" he cried, battling for his breath, "what is this ?"

He jumped on to the deck, and flung open the door. The cabin was as full of the sickening, fog-like fumes as the berth, but, mercifully, the vapor was not denser there than it was with us, otherwise we must have been strangled as we stood, by the first in-roll.

"Where are your clothes ?" he cried. "Collect what you can immediately !" And while I dragged down my dress from the peg on which I had hung it, and grasped the rest of my wearing apparel, which I had folded and laid together on the top of the locker, he pulled on his boots, swung his coat over his arm, grasped me by the wrist, and ran with me to the companion-ladder.

It was but a few paces, yet I was nearly swooning by the time I put my foot on the steps. Richard helped me up ; but though the night air—and, oh ! how can I describe the delicious sweetness of the first draught of it after the deadly vapor I had been drawing into my lungs ! —almost immediately recovered me, so far as my faintness was concerned, yet, so great had been the shock of waking from a dreadful nightmare into the reality of fire and the suffocation of the smoke, that I stood as one who has been dazed by a cruel blow on the head, sick and giddy, and trembling so violently that, had I not kept hold of my husband's arm, I should have fallen.

It was dark, but still a most beautiful, fine night. There was a draught of wind blowing, though but a very light air indeed. All was as still as death along the

19

decks. The black circumference of the wheel was visible against the stars over the horizon, but it was deserted. I could not make out the merest shadow of a human figure forward, and, glancing aloft, I perceived that the fore-yards were laid aback, and that the bark was hove to, though she was under all plain sail, from the main-royal to the gaff-topsail.

There was no appearance of fire; even the binnacle lamp had gone out or been extinguished; the only glimpse of light aboard the vessel came through the skylight from the dimly burning cabin lamp; but from all parts of the bark, round the coamings of the hatches, from the points where the masts penetrated the deck, from her sides and other places, which I should have believed impervious, there floated up thin rills and spiral drainings of vapor, breaking out with a kind of hovering motion, like steam from a bed of manure. The smoke was plainly to be seen in the starlight, and when it rose a foot or two above the bulwarks the light air settled it away to sea.

All this we saw, as I may say, in a breath, though it is not so quickly described. Richard stood at the compan-ion, looking round him, while I, letting go of his arm, began to clothe myself, with trembling hands, discover-ing, as I did so, that I had happily brought with me all that was essential, even to my shoes and hat.

"Is there anybody about?" shouted Richard, putting his hand to the side of his mouth.

His voice rang with a hollow note along the deck, and was faintly echoed in the canvas aloft. No answer came back.

"Mr. Short!" he shouted again.

The faint breeze sighed softly in the rigging, and there was a little tinkling sound of water rippling against the side of the vessel; but no reply was made, and no one appeared. I cannot express how shocking the silence made our situation.

Richard ran forward, but was gone barely a minute. "The crew have left us," he exclaimed. "They have gone away in the long boat. Look! do you see the tackles at the yardarms?" said he, pointing up. "How softly the villains did their work!"

"Oh, Richard!" I cried, his words bringing the mate to my mind, "Mr. Heron is below, locked up, and will be suffocated."

Before the sentence had fairly left my lips my husband rushed down the companion. The smoke oozed heavily up through this aperture, more fully charged than before with the foul, disgusting, poisonous, gaseous fumes I have mentioned; and I stood in agony, waiting for Richard to return with the mate. Indeed, I can never forget the torture of that short passage of waiting. Happily, it was but short. In a few moments my husband came running up the ladder, with his hands over his mouth, and the instant he reached the fresh air he threw himself down and was violently sick; and, what was much more terrifying to me, I perceived that his hands and the lower part of his face were covered with blood that had been forced from him by the poisonous gas.

I ran to one of the scuttle-butts, and, filling the dipper, brought it to him. The cold water, and the cleansing of his mouth, face, and hands, refreshed him, and he then got on his feet.

"Did you find the mate?" said I, afraid that he was going to tell me that the mate was dead, suffocated in the berth in which he had been locked up.

"He is gone with the others," he answered. "His door is wide open. The berth is full of smoke, and I had to grope about it, and feel in his bunk. He is gone," he repeated, but that was all he said on that subject then.

He now ran over to one of the quarter-boats, and looked at it, and when he returned he had recovered his composure, and spoke calmly.

"They have had humanity enough to leave us the choice of two boats," said he, "though I dare say they hoped the poisonous smoke would prevent us from wanting them. Thank God, there is no hurry. These fumes mean that the cargo is on fire, and that the mates and men are at the bottom of it. That it has been done in the belief that it may kill us outright, or at least prove a heavy professional disaster to me, I am as sure as that I stand here, if only from the manner in which the whole of the villains have sneaked away from us. Jess, we

must try and save our lives. Let us be cool—let us have
faith in God's mercy. Stay where you are ; nay, come
farther away from the companion, out of the road of the
smoke. I shall return in a moment."

He hurried forward and disappeared. He was absent
about three minutes, and then returned, bearing a bundle
in his hand, which he carried to the quarter-boat and
threw into her stern-sheets. At the same time he took a
small breaker out of the bows of the boat, and, bearing it
to the scuttle-butts, filled it with the dipper, afterwards
bringing the little cask and the dipper back to the boat.

I stood looking on, for I did not see how I could help
him. I will not say that even yet I realized all the horror of our situation. Had the least point of flame showed
itself, the full sense of our peril would have rushed upon
me. But, remaining to a certain extent dazed by the
rush and consternation which had followed the first
shock of discovery, and nothing appearing but the little
crawlings and creepings of smoke, while the vessel lay
still upon the black, star-tipped sea, with all her old beauty glimmering in spaces of spectral white in the darkness, it was impossible for me to master all the significance
of the shocking misfortune that had come upon us. It
seemed, indeed, no more than a dream—a mere change
in the nightmare that had paralyzed me in my sleep
below.

When Richard had stowed the breaker of fresh water
in the boat, he jumped inside, and again thoroughly tested
and felt over her, to make sure that the devilish malice
of the men had not converted her into a trap for us, and
then called me to him and told me to help him to lower
the boat into the water. I needed no instructions on this
head, for I understood all about the lowering-gear of
boats ; so that, when Richard was ready, I took a secure
turn round a belaying-pin with the hauling part of the
after-fall, and carefully lowered away with him. When
the boat was in the water my husband descended into
her by one of the falls, unhooked the blocks and brought
her to the main chains, where he made her fast by the
painter. He then came on deck. As he sprang from
the bulwarks he stumbled so as to fall lightly on his

hands. He instantly jumped up, exclaiming, "Jess, put your hand to the deck. The wood's as hot as an oven."

I did as he bade me, and found the deck hotter than if the meridian sun had been pouring upon it. This we had not noticed before : first, because we had our shoes on ; and, secondly, because the deck was hot only forward of where the cabin bulkhead was — that is, over the hold where the coal lay. But the discovery that the deck was hot frightened my husband out of his cool manner.

"Jessie, Jessie," he cried, "you must get into the boat at once ! at once ! The vessel is full of fire. The cargo must be in flames to make the deck so hot as this, and there may come an explosion at any moment."

And, so saying, he ran to the bulwarks and dragged me up, then helped me into the chains, and from the chains into the boat. He was hesitating a moment as he stood in the bows of the boat, with his hand on the hitch of the painter, as if considering whether he should stay where he was or go on deck again, when the forward canvas was thrown out on the darkness by a flash of greenish light. It came and went so quickly that I thought it was lightning, until a glance round at the cloudless sky assured me that it must have been caused by the leaping of a jet of flame from some aperture in the deck. The smoke that was rising from various points of the hull also grew denser and darker, and my husband, putting his hand against the vessel's side, exclaimed that it was hotter than the deck.

The sudden burst of flame and the increasing heat and smoke determined him. He cast the painter adrift, and picking up an oar shoved the boat's head off, and then came aft and sculled her for a distance of about fifty fathoms from the bark, where we lay watching the burning vessel.

Now that there was nothing more to do, and he could think and see the vessel lying out there like a dark picture, the full significance of our misfortune smote him, his manhood gave way, he leaned his elbows on his knees, and clasped his hands upon his forehead and gave several sobs as he drew his breath. His grief broke me down, and I threw my arms round his neck, unable to speak, though knowing he would understand what was in my heart by that caressing gesture. We sat thus in silence for several minutes, during which I felt his strong form shaking as he strove with his bitter grief and dismay; he then gently released himself from me, kissing my hand as he put it away.

"Oh, Jess, my darling wife," said he, "what have I brought you to?"

"I am in the only place in the world where I should wish to be, Richard," I answered. "I have no fear, dearest."

And, indeed, I spoke as I felt, for with him by my side I had no fear.

"For days and days I have been foreboding something of this kind," he continued. "But how has it happened? Did the men, as I believe, fire the vessel, or has the coal broken into fire? But think of them leaving us to perish, as they must have hoped, in the smoke! And how softly the scoundrels worked! I heard no stir. They liberated the mate, they swung the main-yards, they got the long boat over, and all so noiselessly that not a murmur reached us aft. How long have they been gone, I wonder?" And here he stood up in the boat and peered around the dark ocean circle. He seated himself again, and continued, "But I *cannot* believe they fired the ship. Yet they left us to our fate—they meant that we should perish. Oh, the villains! the villains!"

I seized his hand and clasped it, to restrain him and bring him to himself, for as he cried "Oh, the villains!" a perfect paroxysm of rage convulsed him, and he swayed like a man in a fit upon the thwart.

"We might have got the fire under, had they stopped," he continued, after a short interval of silence. "But they had other designs. They preferred to trust themselves in an open boat and take their chance, rather than enable me to save the vessel. It was their mode of revenging themselves. Great Heaven! what wrong did I ever do them to deserve this? Was it Heron's scheme? Did he fire the ship? And if so, how did he fire her? You saw no flames in the cabin?"

"No," I replied.

"The fire is in the coal, then. Did they smell the fire forward first, and then arrange with the carpenter to release Heron and leave us to our fate? That must have been it."

I listened, but had no heart to follow his speculations, beyond putting in a word here and there in the hope of bringing him back to his former coolness of manner and language. With him by my side, I say, I had no fear. I mean by that, that the feeling that he was with me, and that if we perished we should perish together, took so much of terror from death that there was but little left to affright me in the contemplation of it. But I could not look upon the vessel, from which the smoke was rising in a dark cloud that hung in a black shadow to leeward, and blotted out the stars that way, and upon the gleaming, inky vastness of the deep, whose nearness to us as we sat in that little boat converted it into an overwhelming presence, without a recoil of the very spirit, and a most cruelly torturing sense of our helplessness and insignificance and hopelessness.

Finding me scarcely able to converse, my husband fell into silence too, holding my hand, and gazing at his vessel without the least movement of his head.

Once, the idea rushing into my mind, I exclaimed, "Do you think any one has been left on board by the men, Richard?"

"He would have shown himself long before, if he is not dead," he answered; "and if he is dead we could not help him. No, no; only you and I were left, be sure of that."

It was about three o'clock in the morning, so that some time must pass before the day broke. The breeze was soft and cool, just enough of it to keep the water rippling, and the reflection of the larger stars running in it. The shadow of the night hung very heavily upon the whole circle of the horizon, so that if the boat in which the men had gone away was even not more than two miles distant we should not have been able to see her. From time to time my husband would throw an oar over the stern to scull the boat back to her place, since, being to windward, the breeze set us towards the bark, and would have brought

us much too near her for our lives were the vessel to ex-
plode.

No more fire appeared for a long time after the first
short lightning flash that had hove the canvas all green
out of the gloom; but the smoke went on growing in density until it was breaking away in heavy coils from apparently the whole range of the deck, as though the hull were
the mouth of a marine volcano, though I should have
thought the forecastle hatch and the companion the only
two places where it could have found egress, had I not
seen it with my own eyes, when on deck, rising up from
the sides and the water-ways and the foot of the masts
and through the pumps, like steam from the surface of
the solid earth. But at the expiration, as I may suppose,
of about half an hour, a shoot of clear red fire, leaping up
amidships from or near the main hatch, brightened the
heavy pall of smoke into a dark orange, and made a terrible picture of the bark, with her red sails and red masts
and red rigging standing like a painting wrought with a
brush dipped in liquid fire upon the canvas of the night.
The flame vanished and left all in darkness again, as if
the belch of dense black smoke that rolled up had extinguished the fire. But very shortly afterwards · a dull
report came booming along, with a tearing and rending
sound mixed up in its muffled note. An immense foun-
tain of sparks was hurled up out of the forecastle, and
filled the air with spangles which floated away upon the
smoke, and then came a dazzling gush of white fire that
ran up like a column of water under the lateral plunge of
a cannon-ball, and in a breath the whole of the fore canvas and gear were in flames.

Hardly had these been kindled when there was another
deafening explosion; this time aft. The deck was rent
by a force as furious as ignited gunpowder; and masses
of solid planking, portions of the deck, of the companion,
of the skylight, all of them burning, were hurled to an
incredible height in the air, shooting through the smoke
into the clear atmosphere above like rockets, rushing upwards on wings of flame, which roared like a heavy wind
over our heads, and falling in all directions, but all of
them close to the vessel.

The tearing up of the decks left a free vent for the immense body of fire in the hold; and the flames now shot up from every part, from the very eyes of the bark to the taffrail, for the most part of a uniform height, reaching to half-way up the mainmast, though there were tongues and lances of flame, dazzling bright red and white spiral columns, which darted their licking points to the very summit of the cross-trees, burning up the smoke until it was all clean fire from the line of the bulwarks to the topmost writhings of the conflagration. The sea lay like burning sulphur in the terrible glare for a mile around, completing the wildness and horror of the scene; and within the same compass there was an almost sunlike brightness in the sky.

Neither Richard nor I spoke a word. We sat crouched in the boat watching, I at least with spellbound eyes, saying to myself, "If the flames had prevented us from leaving the berth, what a coffin should we have found, what a funeral in that crimson, flashing, roaring vessel!" — the thought of which shrunk up the very soul within me.

Though we lay at a distance of four or five hundred feet from the vessel, the heat from the raging fire was so great as to oblige Richard to throw out an oar, and scull the boat another hundred feet or so farther off. The coal which formed the bark's freight was, indeed, of a very dangerous quality, full of iron pyrites, as we afterwards came to hear, and it burned with astonishing rapidity, all parts of the surface of it being exposed through the destruction of the deck, and fed by an incessant fall of flaming masses of sail or spar or rope from the fabric of masts and canvas on high.

By this time there was not the smallest fragment of the vessel that was not on fire ; flames as many-colored as the hues of a kaleidoscope wriggled like snakes along her stays, shrouds, and backstays, and crawled and hissed around her masts, yards, and jibbooms ; her side timbers being burned out of her, I could see the clear red, palpitating, incandescent mass in her hold, until her hull looked no more than a floating cage of red-hot wire, while every now and again the fall of a heavy fragment of spar or yard from aloft into this molten mass flashed up a great body of flame, and the glowing surface-coal poured in cascades of lava from the apertures in her sides. There is no language to express the roaring noise of the fire, nor the ear-piercing, seething, and hissing sounds of the burning coal and wood and gear, as they poured or dropped into the water. There was one moment when the flames in the hold slackened down, and left the vessel a most complete and terrific drawing in fire upon the gloom. Imagine the skeleton of a ship, completely rigged, and the fierce crimson of a tropical sunset shining through her. But this illustration is imperfect; for you want the dark night and the throbbing and surging molten redness heaving within the ribs of the ship, that is rigged with burning masts and spars and shrouds, while the metal about her is white-hot, so that there is not so much as a block banded with iron that is not expressed by the flaming pencil of the fire-fiend.

"Richard," I exclaimed, breaking a long, long silence, "is not that the dawn breaking yonder?"

He looked and said, "Yes, thank God. The rising sun may bring us help. Was there ever such a flashing beacon as our poor bark? What a fire she makes! Heaven have pity on us!"

The dawn brightened swiftly; the dark ocean grew a pallid gray, and a faint pink shone in the east. As quickly as the night falls in those latitudes, so rises the day. The glad morning soared out of the sea, sharpening its bland and beautiful rose-colored radiance until the cloudless heaven blushed to the zenith; while in the west the melting shadow of the night was leaving behind it an azure as tender as an English summer twilight sky. I saw the shoulder of the sun flash a long, sparkling silver stream of blinding radiance along the deep as he rose; but he was scarcely half above the horizon when the bark broke in halves, and, as though a magician had waved his wand over the scene, the whole dreadful picture vanished amid a furious hissing, as if a hundred locomotives were blowing off their steam at once, leaving behind but a few blackened fragments of the wreck, while a vast cloud of snow-white vapor soared up slowly out of the blue water, and went sailing away on the light breeze in the wake of the smoke that overhung the sea in the north, like a thunder-storm.

CHAPTER XXX.

IN AN OPEN BOAT AT SEA.

RICHARD sat like a stupefied man, staring at the water where the few charred remains of our sea-home floated. He then turned his head slowly and looked at me. Maybe the sight of my pale and worn face restored his mind to him; for, giving himself a kind of shake, he rubbed his eyes, stood up in the boat, and took a long, steady look round.

"I see nothing," said he ; " look yourself, Jessie; your sight may be better than mine."

I did so, but saw nothing. The daylight made the vast solitude of the sea more awful to my senses than I found it during the darkness. In the darkness its immensity was swallowed up; and though the burning bark had been a terrific object, yet while it was there, lighting up the sea, it called our thoughts to it, and took the edge off the horrible sense of loneliness. But the sun disclosed the ocean to its uttermost bends ; not the minutest object broke the continuity of the soft blue cincture that girdled the hemisphere of waters, and that was clasped in the east by the diamond-brightness of the reflected sunrise.

"There is nothing to be seen, Richard," said I, seating myself with a shudder, for whenever I looked over the gunwale of the boat the nearness of the sea gave me a shock as though my very heart recoiled in my bosom. Indeed, no imagination can realize the effect upon the mind of the change from the deck of a vessel, even so small as the *Aurora* was, to the interior of a little boat that brings the deep within a few inches of your hand from where it slopes away into the infinity of the arching heavens.

My husband, making no answer to what I had said, pulled a pencil from his pocket, and began to scribble with it on the stern-sheets, which were painted white. I watched him, and then asked what he was doing.

"I am endeavoring to get an idea of our longitude and latitude," said he, "so that I may know how to steer."

"Where do you make us to be?" said I, when he had done calculating.

"In round numbers," he answered, "Sierra Leone is about seven hundred miles distant; the African coast about three hundred, and the Cape Verde Islands about four hundred and fifty. We had better steer for the islands. By steering northwest we stand a good chance of falling in with a ship; whereas that chance will grow smaller the more we haul in to the African coast."

My heart sank in me to hear of all those miles lying between us and land. Noting this, he put on a brave manner, and looked at me with one of his old cordial smiles.

"Keep up your courage, Jess," said he; "with anything of a breeze in our favor, it will not take us many hours to fetch the islands."

"Hours!" I exclaimed; and then, making a calculation, I said, "Oh, Richard, if we should be able to sail regularly at even five miles an hour, it would take us four days to traverse four hundred and fifty miles."

"And what then?" cried he, heartily; "think of old mutiny Bounty Bligh making a voyage of some thousands of miles in a small boat full of men, and coming through it more safely than ever he did through the voyage in his ship. But must we believe that we shall sight no vessel between this and the Cape Verde Islands? Why, Jess, sailing to the westward will bring us right in the track of ships bound round the Cape. Before that sun sets, darling, we may find ourselves safe aboard some thousand-ton craft, telling our dismal story, and thanking God for our safety."

And so saying he jumped up, and, laying hold of the short mast that was stowed along the thwarts, rove the halliards of the little lug-sail, and stepped the mast. All the boats of the *Aurora* were fitted with masts and sails; indeed, father's hint had operated with Richard, who had had the boats well looked after, especially the long-boat; and one reason why the crew had been able to hoist that boat overboard promptly and quietly was because Richard had always had the gear necessary for that business kept handy, and the boat ready for use at a moment's notice. There would have been time, before the bark burst into flames, for him to have obtained the materials for a mast and sail for the boat we were in, had she not been already furnished with those things; but having them ready made us the better off, as the mast and sail fitted her properly, and were of the right size, with reefs in the sail, and an iron clamp in the thwart which firmly secured the mast.

Having set the sail, he came aft with the sheet, and then, fixing the yoke, got the boat round, bringing the sun on our starboard quarter. The light breeze blew along the sun's wake, and truly might we have supposed that it came out of the sun himself, for there was a fiery, parched, sandlike taste in it that dried up the skin, so that anybody who had been in Africa near the equatorial parallels might have known by the feel of the wind that that broiling, barbarous continent was not many leagues distant. The sea was very smooth, merely ruffled by the breeze, with here and there a little crisping of foam. Apparently we were to have another cloudless day. The moment the sail was full, the boat felt the impulse, and began to creep along, raising a tinkling sound round her as she broke the ocean ripples, and leaving astern of her a slender vein of a wake as hard and gleaming as glass, sprinkled over with bell-shaped bubbles.

As nearly as I can remember, she was about two or three and twenty feet long, painted green inside, with white thwarts and stern-sheets, plenty of beam for her size, and a spring forward that brought her bows well out of the water. She was a new boat, of course, belonging as she had to a new ship, and, like every other appointment of our unhappy vessel, was first-rate of her kind. Richard noticed me running my eyes over her.

"You have nothing to fear from her," said he; "she'd outweather a gale."

"What is in that bundle?" said I, pointing to a small white canvas bag lying in the bows of the boat.

"Biscuits," he answered. "I went to look in the galley for provisions, but the men had cleared it out. I then overhauled the bread-locker in the forecastle, and found

some handfuls of pieces. That bag lay on the deck, and
I filled it with all the biscuit I could find. There was no
use in looking for anything more to eat there, even had
the smoke allowed me to wait another minute. But there
are only two of us ; and the biscuit will last our turn—
though, Jess, you might bring it aft if you will, and stow
it away in this locker here, for fear of some salt water
coming aboard."

I did as he asked me.

"If I could have managed to breathe in the cabin," he
continued, " we should have had more to live upon than
dry ship's bread. But there was no use trying again.
When I came up, after looking for the mate, I was all but
suffocated.   I think my head would have burst if the
blood had not flowed.   What a horrible atmosphere !
What could there be mixed up in the coal to make the
fumes of it so disgusting and deadly ?"

I could not answer this, but I know, from my own experience of the smell, that no smoke was ever more nox-
ious and vile than that which came from the *Aurora's*
hold.

As the sun climbed the sky, its heat grew terribly fierce,
though, during the forenoon, at least, the sail threw shadow
upon the fore-part of the boat, and we both of us sat
there, Richard managing to steer very well by bending
on some pieces of stuff (which I had found in the locker
when I put the bag of bread there) to the lines, so that
he was able to steer and yet sit well forward too.   Our
talk was mainly about the bark and the crew, and the
disastrous incidents of the voyage. I asked him if he did
not think the coal had been burning in the bottom of the
hold for some time before the smoke leaked into the
cabin ; as it seemed incredible, if the fire had broken out
but a short time before I smelled the fumes, that the vessel should have been burned up and utterly destroyed in
the space of half a night.

" No," he answered ; " if the coal had been burning, as
you say, we should have smelled the smoke.   It would be
bound to show itself.   It was the explosions that helped
the fire, and made the whole dreadful business speedy.
When the decks were blown up and the sides burned out,

the draught of breeze kindled every fragment of coal in the hull, just as you'd draw up a fire by putting on what the servants call a blower. It did not take long to char the keelson, after which the weight of the burning freight forward and aft cracked her in halves, and down she went."

"Do you think she could have been saved had the men stood by you, Richard?" I asked.

"I believe," he replied, "that we might have made shift to keep the fire under, by drowning the freight and making the hold air-tight, until we fetched Sherborough or Sierra Leone."

"Surely," cried I, "villains as the men were, they would not hazard their own lives by setting fire to the bark."

"Well," he answered, gloomily, "I will not say they fired the bark. But they deserted us—they never called us—they meant that we should perish, and they nearly had their way—they nearly had their way!" he exclaimed passionately, bringing his hands together.

"But this loss cannot affect you professionally, Richard, if God preserves our lives, and suffers us to reach home," said I.

"I can't say, Jess. I shall tell the story ; but it is a strange one to relate. Your evidence will be thought biassed, and I have no other witness to prove that the mates and the crew were against me to a man, though, to my knowledge, I had never given them the least cause to complain of me. But don't let us trouble about that," said he, with a brave effort to brighten up again. "Our first business is to save our lives. Pray God this fine weather may last. Here is a nice little breeze, that should measure us a baker's dozen of leagues before the sun goes down, if it holds."

And he looked with a smile at me, and caressed my hand. But no masquerade of that kind could hide the truth from me : the loss of his ship, and the danger and hardships to which I was exposed, were too much for his manhood. No smile could conceal the heart-breaking trouble in his eyes ; grief had robbed his face of its old healthy color, and it had a grayness of complexion that made him appear ten years older than he had looked on the preceding day. I was pale and worn too; I knew that must be so, by the deep feeling of weariness and grief in me. Nor in any other respect could I have looked my old self; for though, thanks to Richard's sharp presence of mind, which had bid me collect my clothes, I was fully attired, even to my hat, yet I had hastily dressed myself on deck, and in the dark, and in the hurry and disorder of my mind had put on my clothes in a wild fashion indeed. This is but a trifling circumstance to relate, yet it is a little piece of color that will help out that picture of us as we sat in the boat, which I wish you to have in your mind.

There were moments when my bewilderment, as I gazed round upon the vast surface of blue water along which we were creeping, grew so violent that my feelings were numbed with it, and I felt like one in a trance. Calamity had followed us so fast, that I cannot say I had even yet fully mastered the meaning of all that had come. Every glance at the sea, at my poor husband, at the little boat, every reference to the events of the past night, was like a fresh disclosure. Only a few hours ago I was standing on the deck of the bark, everything safe and quiet, a heaven full of stars over me, the sea leaning, like a dark mirror, against the sky, with not the merest shadow of a foreboding in me of the perils and horrors in store for us. And now, here we were, two lonely figures in a boat, a mere speck, visible to no eye but God's; not, indeed, immediately threatened with the anguish of thirst and starvation, yet with no more of hope in us than what comes from the natural clinging to life; not a fragment left of the vessel that we had both loved and were proud of as our ocean-home, unless it were a few black bits of wreckage floating some miles astern upon the little ripples, whose frostlike heads the sunshine transformed into jewels. I thought of father; pictured him at Shields, talking and laughing among his old sea-friends there, thinking of us, perhaps, and guessing how far we should be by this time from our first port. Then I went back to the old house in Newcastle, to my childish dreams in it, my wish to be a sailor's wife, that I might be on the sea; and, as I turned up my eyes to the inexpressibly rich and glorious azure of the heavens, there recurred those old fancies of tropical skies and silver seas and green and feathery islands, aromatic with sweet perfumes.

Those dreams came back to me like curses now. But, even as I felt this, I looked at my husband, who sat near me, with his pale and sorrowful face drooping upon his breast; I thought of his love; our little dead child; a rush of tenderness overwhelmed my heart; I flung my arms round his neck, sobbing and crying, "Oh, Richard, I am with you! Thank God, I am with you!" as if he had known what was in my thoughts. And I believed he did, for, without speaking, he put his arm round me and held me to him, till I had done crying, and then, tenderly kissing me, he let me go, saying—

"Jess, you are a sailor's wife, and have a sailor's spirit. This old ocean, that you have loved from your childhood, will not betray such a trusting sweetheart as you. Come, darling, we shall meet father again; we shall sit by his fireside, and tell him of our adventures. Remember, while we have life, and while we believe, as we do believe, my little wife, that the eye of God watches over us, all is well."

"Yes," said I, "God watches over us; we are spared to one another; all is well. My tears have done me good. You'll not again find me wanting heart, Richard."

A little before noon, my husband asked me to steer the boat, and, going to the locker, pulled out the bag of bread and examined the contents of it.

"Why, Jess," cried he, "here is enough to last you and me a fortnight, with economy. I suppose that scoundrel Orange found the men something more to their taste, or, depend upon it, they would have left the bread-locker empty."

He gave me a biscuit, and also filled the dipper with water. This was our dinner! But I made no account of that. A sea-biscuit appeased my appetite as fully as a good dinner would, and though the water was warm, through standing in the sun, it was fairly sweet, and yielded me the most refreshing draught I ever remember swallowing; for by this time I was very thirsty, though, owing to the engrossing character of my reflections, I gave no heed to my thirst, until the sound of the water gurgling, as Richard filled the dipper, caused me to feel it very sharply.

But that which made this time truly dreadful was the sun. He was now almost over our heads. There was no escaping him. Let Richard have steered as he might, the sun would still have looked straight down. The sail made no more shadow than a thin line arching transversely across the boat. The paint blistered, and gave forth a faint oily smell; the woodwork was so hot that I could not keep my hand on it above a few seconds; the back of my neck seemed roasting, as though close behind it was a great fire. There was air enough to have kept us cool under shelter; but in the sun its fanning seemed only so many overpowering heat-waves. Of all this part of our experiences, I remember that giddy, blinding, beating sun chiefest. The heat streamed through my hat, and I felt it on my head, as though molten metal were straining through the covering of it. It was like having your eyelashes, nay, your very eyelids, cut off, to look abroad upon the blinding white glory which filled the sea, and in the very midst of which we were sailing. There was the most merciless cruelty symbolized to me, who sat crouched, with my hand over my tortured and dazzled eyes, by that stark, staring, flaming and maddening luminary poised over our heads, and pouring his scorching effulgence straight down upon us, as though the tiny speck we made upon the mighty ocean was singled out to receive, in concentrated form, the full rays of the burning light that hung in the pure, deep sapphire of the firmament.

But there was no help for it. A fair breeze was blowing; every hour of this progress was bringing us nearer to the islands we were making for, and to the track of ships bound to the southern hemisphere. And though Richard spoke once of lowering the sail, so as to make an awning of it, yet the moment after he said "No;" that, hard as the heat was to bear, it would be harder yet to lie idly on the sea, and lose the chance the pleasant breeze was giving us. And so fully was I of this mind, that I would have been content to go on enduring the heat for another twelve hours rather than have stopped the prog-ress of the boat.

However, the sun could not stand always in one place; and when he drew into the south and west the sail cast a shadow in the bows, and thither did Richard and I crawl, he hitching more of the small stuff we had providentially come across to the yoke-lines, and steering the boat, and steering her well too, in the very foremost end of her.

All the time, whether we talked or were silent, our eyes were incessantly employed in searching the horizon. Several times I imagined I perceived a sail; but it was always a cheat of the sight, due to the dazzling tremble upon the sea. But, oh, what mortal gaze had ever beheld a more beautiful, wonderful heaven than that under which we were sailing! As the gentle but furnace-hot breeze moaned past us, it seemed to deepen the thrilling violet in the quarter whither it blew. But all around the gleaming and flashing circle of the sea, save in the southwest, where the glory of the sun hung like an effulgent veil upon the face of the sky, the blue stood softly and purely dark behind the horizon, the line of which was as clear as the rim of a crystal cup inverted upon a piece of velvet.

CHAPTER XXXI.

NIGHT IN AN OPEN BOAT.

The afternoon was fast waning, as we might know by the sun. The breeze had freshened somewhat; each little surge, as it coiled over, ran with a sparkling feather-ing of spray, and the foam broke bravely from the stem of the boat as she swept along fast under the steady pull-ing of the lug-sail. We had no compass, and my husband could only steer by the sun; yet he spoke of the direction he was taking with confidence, and said that, when the sun was gone, there would be the stars to steer by.

All day long he had held the yoke-lines, suffering me to take them only when he went to the bread-bag or the little water-cask. He declared he was not tired; nor do

I believe he was, thanks to the length he had contrived to give. to the yoke-lines, which enabled him to get up and move about, and even go right forward, and yet control the boat too.

I was looking over the sea at our weather-bow, when I suddenly caught sight of a dark object not above a mile distant. I stood up to get a better view, and then asked Richard if he could see it. He peered about, and, after a little, said, "Yes."

"What is it, do you think?" said I, for, though it was but a mere waif, as I might tell, yet its breaking the eternal monotony of the blue surface caused me to view it with a degree of interest that made my question eager.

"Why," said he, after taking another good look, "it seems to be a bit of spar, or else a dead grampus. We'll luff the boat a bit and see."

He moved the helm, and brought the stem of the boat on a line with the object. A few minutes went by, when suddenly he exclaimed,

"Has the wind shifted? or are we in a current? or is that object out there alive? This minute the wind was abeam, but now, do you notice, it's drawing ahead, and yet we are going direct for that dark thing."

"I'm sure it can't be alive," said I; "it's a piece of spar, Richard."

"Let it be what it will," he exclaimed, growing excited, "it's moving. Look at the sun! it's right abeam, and here's the wind almost ahead!"

I was now as much amazed as he, for certainly the varying posture of the sun was conclusive proof that we were shifting our course, and yet we always kept the object right ahead.

"Why, what can it be?" said I. "There must be a current there!"

"It must be a very fast current," he replied, "and a mighty narrow one, too. We are not in it, or we should be setting to the eastward, too."

By this time he had brought the boat close to the wind, and the sail lay almost fore and aft. In a few minutes we had a full sight of the object.

It was indeed a piece of stout spar, blackened with paint

or tar; it looked like a piece of the pile of a small wooden pier, of about twelve to fourteen feet in length. To it was securely hitched a length of stout line that formed a loop, or bight; to this bight, that was in the water at what I may call the foremost end of the spar, was another line; and attached to this line, but in some manner it was impossible for us to make out, was a long, immensely powerful shark. It was a sight scarcely credible to our reason, though there it was, plain enough in our eyes.

Richard was dumfounded. Had some monstrous apparition risen out of the water, it could not have put an expression fuller of sheer, downright amazement into his face. The shark, scared perhaps by our boat, suddenly shifted his helm, and headed about northeast, which enabled us to stick to the skirts of the piece of timber he was towing. He was just beneath the surface of the water, the hempen trace of his unwieldy chariot not suffering him to sink out of sight; but as the bit of wreckage wobbled upon the brisk ripple, it would heave the afterpart of him up, from the spine, just in the rear of the dorsal-fin, to the hindmost spike of his hideous, piratical, barbed tail. I tried hard to see how the line was affixed to his body; but his head and shoulders were always under water, and the swift bewildering run of the ruffled surface rendered nothing distinguishable but his dark, massive, and savage outline. However, there could be no doubt that he had been harnessed by means of a rope collar secured on either side his immense flappers, so that he could neither forge ahead out of it, nor back himself clear of it. He showed no signs of exhaustion, though if he had been launched overboard from a ship the clear horizon was proof sufficient that he must have been in the water some hours, if not some days. Heavy as the spar was, he would tow it along for a space as fast as we sailed, then slacken down, and oblige Richard to let go the sheet of the lug-sail, that we might not run away from him.

Probably such a sight was never seen before, and for the time being it actually sent all thoughts of our perilous and miserable situation out of my head. Yet I should have defied the most tender-hearted person to have compassion for the monster. There is something in the very look of a shark that chills the blood, and awakes a kind of passion to destroy it. This beast, like the one that had lurked under the counter of the bark, was of immense size and length, but apparently not of the same species, the run of the jaws being round—so far, at least, as I could make out—instead of shovel-shape, and the color of the back a very sickly, evil-looking blue, though this hue might have been the effect of the refraction of the light in the water. Whether, harnessed as he was, he could have rolled on to his back to gorge his prey, I do not know; but, even were this privilege denied him, I should have been very sorry to have trusted myself near his malignant, oval, bluish head, in spite of the burden that he towed behind him. Every time his tail descended, after the jump of the timber had hove it up, he would make a savage and furious sweep that sent the water foaming along the sides of the wood, as though a screw-propeller were revolving there. He allowed us to keep him company for about five minutes, then, with a sudden revolving dash of his long and frightful body, that brought the piece of timber after him like a keel in tow of a tug, he struck off to the southwards; and on Richard bringing the boat back to her former position, as nearly as he could reckon by the sun, we lost sight of him.

"Did any man ever see the like of that before?" exclaimed my husband, looking at me with much of the downright consternation that the spectacle had at first excited in him lingering in his face.

"Where could he have come from?" I asked.

"Who can tell? As likely from the shore as from a ship. I can't imagine that any vessel would carry such a piece of timber as he was towing. But it is a sailor's job. If he comes from a ship, the crew settled upon this way of showing their love for him and his species. After hooking and hauling him aboard, instead of cutting him up they made him fast to that piece of timber, and sent them adrift together—though it would need some clever manœuvring to get the beast overboard again."

"But it's a wonder that he lived after being out of water," said I.

"Live!" he exclaimed. "Why, a shark's alive and

kicking after he's cut up. He'll go on towing that piece of wood until the rope's chafed through, ay, though it would take six months to disconnect him, and then he'll be as hearty as when the sailors hooked him, though hungrier. But what an object to come across in the middle of an ocean! What an entry it would make in a log-book!"

"If he came from a ship," said I, "she ought not to be very far off."

"I thought of that," he replied, throwing an eager glance round the sea. "But who can say how long he has been in the water?" and he stood up and again most carefully and intently searched the sea; but the clear, dark-blue line was as speckless as the vaulted azure overhead.

The excitement raised by the singular object we had encountered soon passed, and our minds turned again with fresh bitterness and sadness to our dreary, helpless, and perilous situation. At noontide, when the meridian sun was pouring his fierce fires upon our unsheltered bodies, I would have given five years of my life for him to set, and for the cool and shadow of the evening to descend upon the water. But, now that the night was at hand, I dreaded its approach.

The breeze had fallen light again, always blowing steadily from the east—with the sun setting on our port bow we could not mistake the quarter of the compass—yet it preserved weight enough to keep our sail full, and the boat went very softly along over a surface as meltingly blue as the sky that it reflected. When the sun was near the sea he went quickly. For a few minutes there lingered a most glorious western sky of crimson, and we both took advantage of this pause of daylight to search the sea-line.

"A little more patience, Jess," said Richard, as our eyes met. "At all events, in such weather as this we are as safe here as though we were ashore. The night may bring us something, and if not, then it will be marvellous indeed if we sight no vessel to-morrow."

The darkness came out of the east like a cloud, and as the folds of it vanquished the hectic tinge in the west, the stars shone out thickly; indeed, the coming on of that night was as though a black velvet carpet crested with silver points had been unrolled over the azure, wrapping the sea in a deep shadow. This sudden envelopment of gloom—for sudden it was, after the bright glory of the sunset—made me shiver and draw closer to Richard, and to comfort me he held me in one arm against him, and in that position we sat.

I had thought the ocean more lonesome-looking and affrighting by daylight than in the night, when the dawn broke in the morning, and showed us the boundlessness of the deep, and nothing remaining of our vanished bark but a few blackened fragments of wood. But now that the darkness was come, I longed for the daylight again, and was amazed to think that the heat of the sun should have made me eager to exchange his radiance for the mystery and the fear and the soul-subduing shadow of the night. The sea was as black as ink, though the white fires of the larger stars touched it in places. The horizon drew up around us, and made a wonder of the sky, for you could see the stars shining far beyond the motionless thickness which stood for the water-line. Oh, if there be one kind of solitude more terrible than all others, it is that which is felt by the shipwrecked occupants of a little boat, many leagues away out upon the surface of the great sea, and shrouded in the darkness of a quiet night, through which the wind floats moaning as though there went with it a long, invisible procession of complaining spirits. It was impossible to look at the liquid, pitch-like surface alongside without a recoil, for there was something in the blackness, here and there bearing upon it the gleam of a star-flake which widened on the brow of the light swell, that forced rather than courted the imagination into its depths ; and, as they say that the fancy is sometimes never more alive than in the brains of a dying man, so I, who, though not dying, yet may truly be said to have been hanging on the very brink of an ocean grave, found my fancies cruelly active too ; my imagination pierced to the very bottom of the ebony profound, and I well remember figuring the aspect of my husband and myself lying upon the rocks of a valley, the black shadows of mountains rising on either hand, and over all, like the blue atmosphere itself, the green ocean, silent as the tomb. I know little of the arguments which have been employed to prove to men what all but those who have not their minds must feel to be the truth—namely, that they have immortal souls; but of all testimonies to that immortality, I can conceive nothing stronger than the power that the imperishable soul has of standing apart when it wills, and figuring the body that holds it as dead, and surveying it, and musing over it, as though it were dead indeed. This I did that night until my overmastering fancies so wrought upon me that, had I not had my husband to turn to and accost, I am as sure as that it is I who am telling this story that the rising sun would have found me mad.

Well, how that night passed I can no more relate than I could the passage of a dream full of wild, inconsequential adventures. What I best recollect of it is, my husband begging me to lie down in the bottom of the boat, and my refusing, partly because I dreaded to quit his side, and partly because I could not surrender myself to sleep, and leave him alone and wearied almost to very death to steer and watch. I remember that we talked of the *Aurora's* crew, and wondered in which direction they had steered the long-boat; and then, at about eleven o'clock—for my husband had his watch—I fell asleep, with my head on his shoulder, dropping off like a little baby.

My dearest one let me sleep as long as I would, and for three hours I rested in that way—he never so much as moving for fear he would disturb me; and when I awoke there was he supporting me, motionless as a figure of wood, the wind still softly blowing over our starboard quarter, and the boat sailing true by the stars. That sleep refreshed me, and I begged him to take some rest too, and to use my shoulder as a pillow as I had used his; he refused, but I kept on pleading, telling him that I could steer a boat as well as he, and promising to awaken him should there come the least change of weather, or should there befall any circumstance to render my calling him necessary.

Well, after a while he yielded; and, pointing to a bright star, he told me to keep it over the mast, rather to the right than to the left of it, as we were steering northwest as nearly as we could guess, and the star would bring us west if we followed it too obediently; he then put his cheek upon my shoulder, and was presently in a deep sleep, breathing heavily, but very regularly. I found no difficulty in keeping the boat steady; the gentle, long-drawn swell sometimes threw her off her course, but she needed very little steering, for the breeze blew regularly, and leaving out a fall-off or a come-to of the boat at long intervals, I managed to hold the bright star to the mast, almost as much so as if it had been a lantern slung between the masthead and the end of the little yard.

I know not if any woman had ever kept such a vigil as this before. It comes back to me like a nightmare, and though, God knows, nothing was ever more real, there are times when I cannot persuade myself that it truly happened. And yet I have but to close my eyes and there comes before me the black sea, and upon it the awful silence of the night, and the dull shine of phosphorus in the run of the swell, and the crisping of expiring foam gleaming past the boat's sides, and the mournful plaining of the night breeze in the hollow lugsail.

For two hours my husband slept. When he awoke he refused to take any more rest.

"No, no," said he, putting his watch to his face to read the dial by the starlight, "two hours of sleep will do. It has made a new man of me. It is half-past four; we shall be having the dawn soon." And rubbing his eyes, for I still held the yoke-lines, he stood up to stretch himself, and putting his hand against his forehead to shelter his sight from the small silver beams that fell from the sky, he gazed intently into the darkness over the weather-quarter, followed the sea to the weather-bow, then began on the lee-quarter.

But when he got as far as about a point and a half before the lee-beam, his head remained stock-still. I was first attracted by his motionless posture, and exclaimed,

"What do you see in the darkness there, Richard?"

"Look as I point," said he, in a breathless way, levelling his arm, which showed very plainly against the stars over the horizon; "is that a shadow there?"

I stared with all my might, and sometimes I thought I

could catch sight of a sort of blotch upon the gloom, though it went when I looked full at it.

"I cannot say," I answered; "at moments I imagine I see something."

"But *I* see it!" he cried. "I cannot be mistaken. Put the helm to starboard, Jess—there, that'll do! Yes, I can see it plainly now. It must be a vessel."

His telling me to starboard the helm had brought the object he believed he saw right ahead, and the wind dead astern of us. He eased away the sheet of the sail, and with an oar "boomed" out the canvas, so that every inch of it might hold wind; and, leaving me with the yoke-lines in my hand, he went into the bows and crouched down, gazing fixedly in advance of him. His head and shoulders were right in a line with the object, and therefore blotted it out to me; but though I could see nothing, and was not even sure that what he beheld was real, yet the mere idea of there being a ship in sight so agitated me that I heard my heart beat furiously in my ears, and my hands and feet became as cold as the water over the side.

A whole quarter of an hour must have gone by, yet my husband made no sign, never addressed me, not so much as once shifted his posture; but now on a sudden he called out in a loud, ringing, excited voice,

"That's a ship, Jessie! and we are gaining on her!" and then, coming aft, he cried, "And see! yonder's the dawn breaking. We shall be plain in their sight against the sunrise! Oh, my love, thanks be to Almighty God for this, for your sake, my precious one!" and he broke down on a sudden, not weeping, but breathing with a heavy sobbing sound, as a man does to whom tears are denied.

I drew his hand to me and kissed it, and while I held it, and he struggled with his emotion, the dawn brightened astern, and, looking up at the sky over the masthead, I saw the greenish daylight spreading like a mist borne onwards by the wind into the west. The water remained black even when the western sky was glimmering with the light that brightened in the east; and bending my head so as to clear the foot of the sail, I perceived under the pallid heaven, against which the coal-black sea-line stood with startling sharpness, the outline of a little vessel about three or four miles distant, still wrapped in the shadow that blackened the deep, but showing out with exquisite distinctness against the dim gray of the sky, like a carving in jet, mounted upon a faint green ground.

"Do you see her now, Jess?" cried my husband.

I answered in a whisper, "Yes," being scarcely able to articulate in the wild hurry of passions and feelings which the vision of that vessel bore in upon me.

Now rose the sun—right behind us—following, with a speed that would have seemed magical to any one used to the gradual birth of the day, the light that heralded his approach, and flashed his magnificent beam across the still cloudless heaven, devouring the last of the languishing stars in the depths of the rich azure which his radiance evoked, and brightening the sea into a world of creeping waters, and giving color and brilliance to the little vessel ahead, whereby we perceived that she was a small brig, tolerably deep in the water, with a broad white streak along her sides, broken by painted ports.

"Surely, she sees us, Richard! Is she not hove-to waiting for us?" I exclaimed, my quickly beating heart causing me to speak as though I was out of breath.

He did not answer, but kept his head over the side, and watched her with scarcely a wink of the eyes.

"Something is wrong with her," said he, in the manner of a man thinking aloud. "Look at her yards! forward they are square, while her main-topsail is aback. If she's moving at all, she's drifting astern. Note the flying-jib hanging from the boom into the water. What can ail her people? Her trim looks older than daybreak. She's in some plight, and has been so for hours."

She grew rapidly as we went along, heading dead for her before the gentle breeze, which, almost ever since we had been adrift in the boat, had blown steadily from the east; and the brilliant light of the cloudless day being all abroad, we by this time could master almost every detail of her. There was nothing wrong with her aloft; every spar was standing, all her yards crossed; but the strange, uncouth manner in which those same yards were braced gave her something of a truly woe-begone and even wrecked aspect. Her royals and fore-topgallant-sail were loose, but the halliards had been let go, and the canvas hung before the sails under them. Most of the braces were slack and lay in bights; the peak halliards were gone, and the gaff drooped upon the folds of the spanker; and the flying-jib trailed from the end of the boom. You might have thought that she was manned by a number of landsmen, who, having attempted all sorts of experiments, had, in sheer despair of making proper use of the gear, given up working the vessel.

Fixedly and narrowly as we watched her, we could not discern the least sign of any living thing on board.

"Can she be abandoned?" exclaimed Richard, "and, if so, why? Her hull appears sound; it's nothing but the trim of her yards that makes her look in trouble, and there's no distress signal flying."

As we drew near it became still more evident that, so far as the vessel herself was concerned, there was little amiss; she floated with good buoyancy, and there was nothing whatever in her appearance to suggest any cause for her abandonment. Presently my husband took in the oar with which he had boomed out the sail, and when we had almost closed the brig he lowered the sail and stood in the bows, calling to me to steer the boat so as to run her broadside on to the main channels of the vessel. This I did, and, having made fast the painter to one of the plates, he got into the chains, helped me out of the boat, and we both got on board.

CHAPTER XXXII.

A FEVER-STRICKEN BRIG.

THE decks were flush and fairly white, but covered with the ends of the running-gear, the first sight of which impressed us both with the idea that there had been a struggle. There was a fair-sized deck-house abaft the foremast, and a similar but longer deck-house or cabin

aft, which where we stood prevented us from seeing the
wheel. A gangway went on either side this house, but
each one, like other parts of the deck, was strewn with
coils of running-rigging jerked off the pins, and left to
lie. All her boats were in their places ; the long-boat
was amidships, securely lashed, and there were good-looking boats, sharp at both ends, like a whaler's, at the davits.
The galley stood this side of the foremost deck-house,
but no smoke came from the little chimney. We stood
listening, but no sound of footsteps nor of human voices
was to be heard, nothing but the soft sweeping sound of
the breeze aloft, the stir of the canvas as the vessel leaned
with the delicate swell, the pattering of reef-points, or the
chafing of a block.

"Strange !" muttered my husband, almost in a whisper,
for the silence of the apparently abandoned vessel subdued and hushed his voice. "*Why* is she deserted?"
And as he said this he stepped over to the front of the
after deck-house, and peered in through the little windows.

I followed him, walking, as he did, with extreme difficulty, for our long confinement in the boat, and the sitting posture we had been forced to maintain in it for the
greater part of the time, had left our limbs numbed to
that degree that they were in a manner paralyzed. The
front of this deck-house, which I will call the cabin, contained four small windows, two on either side the door.
My husband, I say, went to one of these windows, and I
to another, and we peered in. The interior lay very
plain : we saw a small table with lockers on one side, and
a few wooden chairs on the other, standing on our left,
while on the right ran a bulkhead, partitioning off three
or four little sleeping-berths, every berth having a door
of about the height of a man. There was nothing living
to be seen ; no signs visible of the place having occupants.

My husband put his hand upon the door as if to enter,
but changed his mind and came away, followed by me,
who was losing sight of the perils we had escaped, and of
our deliverance from the danger of a little boat, in the
wonder and kind of awe that filled my mind as I looked
around upon this lonely, silent scene.

"This is a great puzzle, a great mystery," said he, always speaking in a whisper. "Hush! do you hear nothing?"

I listened, and answered, "Nothing but the flapping of the sails."

"I'll try forward," said he; "stop where you are, Jess."

"No, no," I exclaimed, "let me go with you. I don't like to be left alone," and I looked at the cabin, more frightened than I can remember feeling at any time in the boat.

As much to give me courage as to help my numbed limbs over the ropes which encumbered the deck, he took my hand, and we walked forward as far as the foremost deck-house. There was but one door, facing aft, and it was closed; he let go my hand to open it, and put his head in, but instantly sprang back, spitting violently on the deck.

"Great God!" he exclaimed, at the top of his voice, "what an atmosphere! It is worse than the fumes aboard the *Aurora*."

He had scarcely said this, when I, too, recoiled, raising a cry as I did so; for from the foremost end of the deck-house there emerged, and then stood stock-still, the figure of a haggard youth or man—which, I could not distinguish—with his face dark with dirt, a quantity of long red hair, through which his wild and bloodshot eyes showed like those of a Skye terrier, dressed in a red shirt and canvas trousers rolled up above the knee, his arms and chest bare, and his arms, like his face, as grimy as a pitman's. By the manner in which he stared at us I believed he was mad, and shrank close to Richard. The sight of us had petrified him. His jaw was dropped, and this posture of his mouth, by exhibiting his lower teeth, heightened the frightfulness of his appearance. His arms hung by his side, but the fingers were wide asunder, as though in another moment he would raise his hands in an attitude to fend us off.

"Are you one of the crew?" exclaimed Richard, as bewildered as I was, though certainly not alarmed, by this extraordinary and truly dreadful-looking apparition, and stepping in front of me as he asked the question.

The creature stood staring at us with the same gaping

air of astonishment, never stirring—no, not so much as
moving his hands or bringing his fingers together. I
whispered, "He may not be English." But on my husband trying him again in our tongue, a kind of rumbling
sound issued from him, and he answered in a painfully
hollow, but quite distinct voice,

"Yes. But who are you? Where d'ee come from?"

"We're shipwrecked people," said Richard. "We
sighted this vessel at daybreak, and made for her.
Where's the rest of your crew?"

"Dead," he answered.

"Ha!" exclaimed Richard, with a sudden recoil, and
throwing a hasty glance at the deck-house. "Where are
you from?"

"Sherborough," replied the poor creature, speaking
like one in a dream.

"Sherborough, near Sierra Leone?"

"Ay."

"What's your cargo?"

"Palm-kernels."

"Is there nobody left but you?"

"Nobody," he said; and, breaking out of his trance,
he dashed his hands to his face, and then held them
clasped above his head, crying, "Everybody's dead but
me, dead with the fever, sir! Oh, my good God! what
a time I've passed alone here! Have ye come to deliver
me, sir? Have ye come to deliver me?" and he ran towards us, but stopped short when within reach of Richard's
arm, and gazed at us with the most imploring, agonized
expression of face that can be imagined on a human
being.

"Ay," said Richard, "we'll save you, my man, with
God's help, and we'll save ourselves, too. Is there anything to eat aboard?"

"Plenty to eat, sir," said the poor fellow, who was crying like a child.

"Why, then, if that's the case," said Richard, "I suppose you've taken care to feed yourself, and that you're
middling strong."

"Ay, I can work," said the other. "I'll do anything
ye may set me to; and God bless 'ee for finding of me."

"I'll not ask for your story now," said Richard, "for we must turn to while the weather's fine, and get the brig ship-shape. First," said he, pointing with a kind of awe in his face to the deck-house, "how many of the poor fellows lie there?"

The other considered, counting upon his fingers, and answered, "Three."

"Are they all dead?"

"Ay, dead two days."

"Jessie," said my husband, "go aft, clear out of the way, while we get the bodies overboard. We must do that at once, for our own lives' sake, for there are a thousand fevers in the atmosphere of that deck-house."

I obeyed him, but trembling, and, I may say, in a perfect agony of mind to think that he should enter and stay even for a minute in an atmosphere that his manner of springing from it and spitting made me guess to be as bad as that of a pest-house. But our lives, as he had said, must certainly answer for it if the vessel was not rid of the dead bodies, and afterwards sweetened. So I went aft, finding that my legs were losing much of the cramped and numb sensation; and, making my way along the narrow passage or gangway on the starboard side of the cabin, I arrived right aft, where the wheel was, so as to put the cabin between me and the bodies which were to be taken from the deck-house.

But the moment I had the wheel in view, I stopped, as if struck to the heart, and felt the hair stir on my head; for, sitting up, with his back propped against the wheel, was a dead man, his chin on his breast, his hands lying on the deck, the knuckles downwards and the fingers curled up, and his legs straight out in front of him. Such a corpse as that—for I dare not describe the appearance of the face—would have shocked any one to view, even though thoroughly prepared beforehand for it; but coming upon it suddenly, finding it there, I say, where I had expected to see nothing but the clear deck and the wheel, chilled me to the marrow, and struck me motionless.

Thus I stood. Then, after a while, finding my tongue, I called loudly to Richard. He immediately quitted his loathsome and repulsive business.

21

"What is it?" he cried ; and then, coming upon the dead man, he shouted to the fellow on the main-deck. He arrived quickly.

"Who is he?" exclaimed my husband, pointing to the corpse.

"The cap'n, sir," answered the other. "I forgot to tell 'ee he was here. He was the last man the fever laid hold of, but he took no notice, and went on holding the wheel, till, coming aft, I found him fallen down. I picked him up and put him agin the wheel, and, there being nobody left but me, I went forrard and sat down, waiting for the fever to come and do my business too."

"Help me to carry him forward," said Richard ; and between them they raised the body and took it forward, and in a minute or two afterwards I heard the splash of it as they dropped it overboard.

I sat down on the little grating abaft the wheel, quite overcome by the sudden and dreadful encounter, but was soon driven away by the heat of the sun, and stood in the shadow thrown by the folds of the spanker upon the deck. But I suppose, being fresh from a peril the significance of which was fearfully apparent to me, as I gazed upon the vast sheet of blue water that waved very softly down to the remote horizon, my sensibilities were too hardened to allow such a circumstance as I have just related to impress me with the depth and sharpness they would have taken from it at any other time. As my husband and the man dropped the bodies one by one overboard, the splash in the water would send a shiver through me ; but I could not look at the stout little vessel which the hand of God had mercifully conducted us to, and think of our wonderful preservation from the hideous loneliness and the unspeakable perils of the little open boat that lay straining alongside at its painter, and filling my ear with the rippling sound of the breeze-swept surface against its bows, without a triumphant gladness, a swelling of the heart, a lifting up of my whole soul, which no horror, not even the horrors we had been called upon to view in this brig, could subdue, or in any degree qualify.

Some time passing, and hearing no more splashes, I walked a short distance forward, and perceived a quantity of smoke issuing from the deck-house. I called Richard, who came out of the house and told me that they were lighting the stove—for it seems that this deck-house was the crew's forecastle—in order to boil a kettle of pitch, that the fumes might purify the interior. He was covered with perspiration, and the mingled awe and disgust which such work as he was fresh from would put into any man's heart were strong in his face. But, like myself, the sense of our deliverance, and gratitude to God for his mercy were too powerful to be hindered. He spoke with a hearty, triumphant note in his voice, and made as if he would embrace me, but checked himself, saying, "No, I must not touch you until I have thoroughly purified myself." He added, that not only were the bodies overboard, but all the hammocks and bedclothes too, and that the deaths of the crew were undoubtedly owing to African and yellow fever, of which he knew nothing of the treatment, though he supposed that the fumes of boiling pitch would go far to kill the germs in the atmosphere. When he had done with the deck-house, he would fumigate the cabin the same way.

He then re-entered the deck-house, where he and the other stayed until they had adjusted a small pot or kettle of pitch upon the stove, which done, they both came out, closing the door after them, that none of the fumes from the pitch, when it boiled, should escape.

All this while the weather remained most beautifully clear and fine; overhead was the same cloudless, rich, darkly blue sky that had looked down upon us on the preceding day, and the light breeze that had blown us to this brig still lingered, coming as true from the east as when it first uprose. The sun, to be sure, was terribly fierce, though it was not yet eight o'clock; but the bulwarks, sails, and masts threw plenty of shadow on the deck, while the wafting of the lower canvas sent little circling draughts of air along, so that, after the exposure we had endured, this brig's deck was as if we had sailed twenty degrees farther north.

By this time I had managed to make out the appearance of the wretched survivor of the vessel's crew, and discovered that he was no more than a very coarse, rough youth, of about eighteen years of age; though, as I have said, when I saw him first I was not in the least able to guess whether he was man or boy. As we went towards the cabin Richard asked him the name of the brig, and he answered that she was the *Bolama*, belonging to Sunderland, and making for that port when her crew sickened and died.

"And what's your name?" asked Richard.

"Joe Spence," he replied.

"What was your rating?"

"Boy, sir."

"And how came your decks to be in this state?" said Richard, pointing to the ropes that lay as confused as raffle all about.

"Why," answered Spence, "before the cap'n was took ill, he was steering, all the hands but me being dead or down with the fever; there comes a shift of wind, and the cap'n he sings out to me to let go this and slacken away that, and see what I could do by a drag here and a pull there, and the likes of such work; so whatever I had to touch I chucks down on deck, where there was mess enough already, and never troubled to coil down again."

"Well," said Richard, "we shall have to coil down presently. The brig looks as if she'd been in an engagement."

He then threw open the cabin-door, and, putting his head in, took a long, suspicious sniff.

"I smell nothing wrong here," said he, drawing back. "How many mates did you carry?"

"One, sir," replied Spence.

"Where did he die?"

"In his berth," said Spence, pointing into the cabin. "He was the first to go."

"If we're to use this cabin, Jess," said Richard, "we must first fumigate it. You stop on deck and keep a lookout. I see a bit of a stove aft there, Spence. Jump forward, my lad, and collect what stuff you can for a fire, and get a bit of canvas to choke the flue with. Coal smoke's dirty, but it's good for fever. If there's not another pitch-kettle handy we'll use a saucepan."

The lad was back in a trice with all the necessary materials, for it seems there was a little pile of coal in the galley, and in about a quarter of an hour they had not only got the fire lighted, but were busy laying out on deck the blankets and bedding they had taken from the captain's and another berth, having bundled those found in the mate's berth overboard.

There is nothing better for infected clothes than hot sunshine and fresh air. Richard was right not to throw all the bedding overboard, for, though we were in warm latitudes now, yet we might find ourselves in cold ones before we met with help, and with nothing but the clothes we stood up in to cover us, and not a blanket on board, we should think ourselves poorly off indeed.

After Richard had closed the cabin-door and spread the bedclothes upon the deck, he stood looking around him very earnestly, closely examining the appointments and rig of the brig, and considering within himself what was to be done. Presently, his eye lighting upon the harness cask, that was lashed to ringbolts in the deck close against the cabin, he went to it, found it open, and, peering in, called out, "Here's plenty of beef, Jessie. Spence, are there any cooked provisions knocking about, d'ye know?"

"There should be store enough in the cabin, sir," answered Spence.

On this Richard went into the cabin, reappeared, holding a china dish containing the remains of a piece of salt pork.

"That is all I could see to find," said he, sneezing and puffing, and his eyes full of water. "There are no pitch fumes about yet, but the coal-smoke is abominably irritating. Spence, look into the galley for a plate and a knife or two."

The young fellow ran forward, his movements full of life and eagerness, and returned with a couple of tin plates, some black-handled knives, a pot of mustard and a bottle half-full of vinegar. These he set down on deck, looking as pleased as Punch that he should have found them for us, and Richard then told him to jump into the boat alongside and bring up the bag of bread out of the locker in the stern-sheets.

We had now the materials for a meal, and getting to-

gether in the port gangway, where the shadow of the
mainsail lay, we heaped up some of the gear into seats,
and fell to our repast. The pork was pretty sweet, and
by eating it with plenty of vinegar and mustard we found
it relishable enough. Both Richard and I were exhausted
rather than hungry; the biscuit we had with us in the
boat had appeased our appetite without yielding us the
nourishment we needed; but the pork made out a meal
for us, and this breakfast, and the rest we took while eating it, did us both a great deal of good. Spence ate heartily. Indeed, the poor fellow seemed half-starved.

"Why, my lad," said Richard, "I thought you told us
you had plenty to eat aboard the brig?"

"So I had, sir," he answered, "while all hands was up
and well. But when I found the cap'n dead, and myself
the only man left, I took no thought of eating. I went
forrard 'twixt the house yonder and the foremast, and sat
down, and gave myself up to die."

"That wasn't British sailor fashion, Spence," said Richard. "You should have hoisted a distress signal, and kept
a lookout. How many hands went to your complement?"

"There was the cap'n and the mate, two; four able seamen, six; two boys, eight; and the cook, nine," he answered.

"You say the mate sickened first and died?"

"Ay," answered the poor fellow, giving his wild reddish hair a jerk that exposed his eyes, which showed in
pink circles in the grime upon his flesh, "the mate went
first. That was a week arter we had left Sherborough.
He was ill two days, and in that time two others were
down, both able seamen. In five days these were all dead.
Then the other boy fell ill, and in two days he died, and
we dropped him overboard arter the others. That left
five of us, counting the cap'n. Then two more kept their
hammocks, and next day the third man lay ill. The cap'n
was wore out; we'd no medicine aboard, and couldn't attend to 'em. We could hear 'em shouting sometimes when
they was delirious, but the cap'n and me had to mind the
brig, and all we could do was to put pannikins of water
near 'em, so that they could help themselves when they
felt thirsty. Lord, what a time it was!" cried the poor

creature, lifting the back of his hand, that was shaking like an old man's, to pass it over his forehead, upon which large drops of sweat had gathered while he talked.

Richard looked at me, and said, under his breath, "This is the sailor's life. These horrors are standing portions of the perils of the deep; but how few landsmen know anything about them!"

He might well say that. Often had I flattered myself, when living at home with father, that my knowledge of the sea and the sailor's profession was a hundredfold greater than that of most people who belong to the shore; but what was it then as compared with what it was now, confronted as I was by the experience of three short days, in which I had stood upon the deck of a burning ship, had been exposed to the scorching light of the sun in a little open boat, with all the agony of the mighty solitude of the ocean in my soul, finally to come upon a vessel that had been the theatre of such lonely, helpless suffering, that to relate it bit by bit as it happened would be to tell a story which a heart of stone would recoil from, shocked, sick, and trembling?

Most surely, to know the sailor's life, and to be able to follow him into that universe of wild, thrilling, and indescribable realities in which he sinks as his ship draws down behind the distant water-line, you must have been to sea with him, suffered with him, felt with him the anguish of shipwreck, and those nameless tortures of flesh and spirit —for tortures come to him that have no names—which are among the gifts of the ocean oftenest inflicted on those who love the mighty mother best.

I said to Richard it seemed almost miraculous that Spence should have escaped a malady so deadly as this fever had been.

"Ay," said he, looking at him. "It's wonderful that he should not have been attacked; but it is more wonderful that all the men who sickened should have died. This sort of thing comes of sending vessels of this pattern to sea without medical stores—not so much as an ounce of quinine aboard. Only last year I heard of such another case as this. A steamer fell in with a little bark, five of whose crew had died of African fever, while four of them lay living, but prostrate with it, and there were only the master and one man left to work the vessel. There was not a drop of physic aboard. The steamer manned the bark with some of her own men, and brought away the sick seamen, all of whom were able to resume their duty within eight days, thanks to the steamer's medicine-chest. And now," said he, jumping up, " breakfast being over, and the three of us the better for it, let's turn to smartly and shove this brig into latitudes where there'll be other folks than ourselves. Spence, give us a hand here to clear these decks, that we may see where we are." And we all three of us fell to work to coil the ropes over the pins.

This did not take us very long, and when we had done Richard jumped on the top of the cabin, and took a long, long look around.

"There's nothing in sight," he called out ; "nothing but beautiful weather. Spence, run out on to the jib-boom, and pick up that flying-jib. If it's too heavy for you, sing out and I'll lend you a hand."

He then came off the top of the deck-house, taking a look at the compass as he did so, for the little deck-house ladder led close to the binnacle, and called to me to help him to get the yards round. Luckily, no manœuvring was wanted, for the vessel's head lay within a few points of the course he proposed to steer. I could now be of real help to him, for my knowledge of the rigging of a ship enabled me to obey his orders without any hesitation. When he told me to let go such and such braces I did so at once, and then crossed over and hauled with him. He seemed to have recovered all his old strength, and worked with wonderful energy and spirit.

"Jess," said he, pausing to speak to me, "this brig is a true Godsend to us, not only because it puts a solid fabric under our feet instead of a little, fragile, open boat, but because the money we shall get for saving her, if God wills that we should save her, will twentyfold repay us for the loss of our personal property in the *Aurora*."

"Yes," I answered, feeling the light of his smile upon my face, "and let Mr. Heron and the crew tell what false-hoods they will of you—if they escape being drowned, which will be more than they deserve, Richard—I am sure, when our story comes to be heard it will leave you high in the owner's esteem, and with a fine character for your brave, single-handed struggle with a gang of unprincipled wretches!"

"Maybe, maybe, Jess; any way, I shall have your father on my side," said he. "Now, my darling, let's get those foreyards swung. This weather looks too beautiful to last, and there is much to be done."

When I say that the size of this brig did not exceed two hundred tons, you will suppose that the yards were not very heavy nor hard to drag round in so light an air as was then blowing. And, light as the air was, it helped us when it got inside the sails by gently carrying the yards with it, and in a few moments we heard the lip, lipping of water over the side as the brig gathered way.

"Jessie, you can steer," said Richard; "run to the wheel, my pet. Keep her northwest by north for the present. That course will do until I can come across a chart and a sextant."

I ran aft, took hold of the wheel, and put it over until I had the course named by Richard against the lubber's point; this brought the wind on the starboard quarter; but, now that we were moving, it seemed to have died away, and I felt the sun striking down on my back as fiercely as ever it did in the boat; nay, the spokes of the wheel were so hot that I had to keep constantly shifting hands, holding first one spoke, then another. But, cruel as the biting sun was, it made but a light trial now. As I looked along the deck and then up at the sails, so deep a feeling of gratitude swelled my heart that the tears gushed from my eyes, and if I could have then let go of the wheel I should have knelt and given thanks to God for his merciful preservation of us from the torments and the loneliness of the open boat.

When I took the wheel Richard went to the side and peered over.

"Jessie," he called, "here is the *Aurora's* boat. We have no use for her now. Shall I send her adrift?"

"She is an old friend," I answered, not liking the thought that she should be sent adrift.

He hung over the side, musing, and then said, "Yes, she is an old friend, but we have three good boats, and there is no room for her." And, so saying, he reached over into the chains, cast the painter adrift, and let the end fall into the water. The boat veered slowly astern, and as she came clear of the counter and plain in my view, I turned my head to look at her. I never should have believed that the sight of any inanimate object could have moved me as that boat did. It was the letting-go of the last link of a chain of associations, bitter and happy, the bitter ones making the memory of those which were happy the more plaintive and tender for the mingling. She took me back, ay, to that very hour when father and Richard and I had first boarded the *Aurora* in the Tyne; and she unrolled the whole panorama of the voyage, the fading Tynemouth coasts, the sparkling Downs, the mutiny, the bark on fire, lighting up the heavens with a blood-red glow, the leagues of lonely sea on which the sun poured his scorching fires, the mystery and awe of the dark, silent, starlit night, and then this brig, a floating charnel-house, with death riding lazily upon the sluggish, sickly atmosphere of fever. As she receded and grew smaller, I thought of Richard and me seated in her, and I then gauged, in a manner that would have been impossible to me by other means, the immensity of that ocean on which we had floated; and how mere a speck we made I could judge by this—that though the boat was under the counter but just now, already she was swallowed up in the violet shadow of the blue swell, and was only visible when the heave of the gleaming surface of the gentle undulation threw her up into the white glory of the sunshine that flashed a beam of silver from her wet sides.

CHAPTER XXXIII.

OUR NEW SEA-HOME.

THE wheel, as I have said, was situated abaft the deck-house, which, as I might reckon, would be fully six feet high, and therefore the view of the decks was entirely blotted out from me. I cannot say it was an old-fashioned way of fixing the wheel, for our forefathers used to steer by tiller-ropes that led to the wheel on the main-deck, before the round-house, as it was called, as if they understood that the proper place for a helmsman is where he can command a clear view ahead. But, whether old-fashioned or not, I thought this fixing of the wheel behind the cabin a senseless arrangement, and the properest receipt in the world for producing collisions.

I felt troubled at not being able to see what Richard and the other were doing. I could perceive nothing below the reef-band of the mainsail. However, the being shut out, so to speak, forced me upon my own thoughts, and holding the wheel came so easily to me, particularly on this quiet day, when nothing was wanted but an occasional movement of the spokes to keep the vessel's course on a line with the jibboom, that I found little in the simple business to stop me from meditating on whatever came into my head.

One consideration that troubled me much was this: here was a brig that had been originally manned by nine men; she now had but two. It is true, I could steer, but that was all. I had but little strength to offer as help in hauling upon a rope, and could be of no use in furling or reefing. This being the case, would my husband and Spence be able to work the brig? Suppose bad weather came, what should we do? Suppose the days passed and no vessel came near to assist us, what would our plight be? I was sailor enough to feel these anxieties, but not sailor enough to answer or appease them. My heart, as I have said, was full of gratitude to God for bringing us to this brig; but, grateful as I was, I could not but feel that heavy peril yet lay before us unless help came while the weather remained fine.

From time to time I could hear my husband calling to Spence, and after a little they clewed up the fore and main royals and went aloft to stow them, my husband taking the main. Clearly all the numbness had gone out of his legs, for he ran aloft as nimbly as a monkey, and rolled up the sail with wonderful quickness. He stood in the cross-trees to take a long look round, and then called to me to know if I found it too hot where I stood.

"I can bear it," I answered, "but I can't say I am comfortable here, Richard."

On this he came down, and after a little arrived with a boat-sail, which he very expeditiously rigged up over my head to serve as an awning, tying the foremost end to the rail that went round the top of the deck-house, though contriving it in such a way as to leave a clear view of the mast from the wheel. This shelter was as grateful to me as a drink of cold water to a thirsty man. I could now stand without my hat and let the light air cool my head.

"You're a brave little woman, Jess," said Richard, kissing my forehead lovingly, forgetful of the fear of contagion he had expressed a while before. "It would do your old father's heart good to see how nobly his lass buckles to sailor's work when the call is made. Never, my darling, could you have thought that what you knew of your father's profession would some day come in to help you to save your husband's and your own life. How now should we manage if you couldn't steer?"

"Yes," said I; "but though I *can* steer, how are we to manage? Shall the three of us—one a boy and the other a woman—ever be able to navigate this brig?"

"We mustn't ask ourselves such questions," he exclaimed heartily. "All that we have to do is to go on shoving forward as best we may. I have a programme in my mind, and one item of it is to shorten sail while the weather remains fine, and keep her under easy canvas. Better to lose time than risk foundering in a sudden gale."

And then, seeing Spence coming down the fore-rigging, he left me.

There was the right kind of foresight in his determination to reduce sail while the two of them could do it. For the next hour and a half they were occupied in this work: furling the fore-topgallant-sail, reeving fresh peak-halliards, and snugging the spanker against the mast and furling the mainsail—though how they managed that job I am sure I cannot say, for the sail was a large and heavy one; yet manage it they did, taking one yardarm at a time and using a little watch-tackle in the bunt; and when they left the yard the sail could not have been better stowed had half a dozen men gone aloft to roll it up. It seemed a strange thing in such shining, glorious, placid weather as was then around us, to shorten sail down to a point that made the brig fit to meet half a gale of wind. And yet I wanted no better assurance of the wisdom of this procedure than the feeling of relief that came to me, when I looked up and beheld the provision that had been made against any sudden, violent uprising of wind. We were in the right kind of seas for tempestuous changes. And beautiful as the sky appeared at this hour, folds of the richest blue ether that seemed to waver and deepen in hue as the eye sought the mighty, radiant, soothing depths; and fair and lustrous as was the deep, whose tender breathings shot its vast surface with running, burnished violet shadows, which broke into long lines of flashing splendor as they passed under the wake of the sun—yet, in another hour the whole scene might be changed, the blue hidden by masses of dark cloud, and a storm of wind turning the ocean into rolling volumes of snow.

I supposed now, by seeing a quantity of bluish smoke blow lazily away over the bow, that Richard had opened the cabin-door. This proved to be the case, and, by opening the little scuttles that ran on either side the cabin, the deck-house was soon emptied of the fumes. However, I was kept at the wheel, seeing nothing, and yet comfortable enough under the awning that had been improvised, until I believed that Richard, by not having me in view, had forgotten all about me. At last Spence arrived, and I

own it startled me to see him, for Richard had made him
wash himself and shift his clothes, and there now presented himself a youth, with an abundance of red hair
stowed away under a cap, a yellow face, a pair of immense
brown hands, and an ungainly though muscular shape,
dressed in a blue jersey and a pair of drill trousers. I
imagined at first he was one of the crew supposed to be
dead but come to life again, and stared at him with astonishment as he sheepishly offered to take the wheel.

"Why," said I, "are you Spence?"

"Yes, 'm," he answered.

"I didn't know you," said I. "Where's my husband?"

"In the cabin," said he; "and he told me to tell you
he wants you there."

I gave him the course, and then went to the cabin.
There was no smoke left in it, but the smell of boiling
pitch was prodigiously strong, and I dare say I should
have found it very unpleasant if I had not thought of it
as a purifying agent. The cabin was a substantial little
box of a place, bulkheaded, as I have described, very
strongly built, and as plain as a ship's forecastle. A thin
slip of old carpet went along the deck on the right side of
the table. The ceiling was stained and varnished to resemble mahogany. The table travelled on stanchions, so that
when not in use it could be run up out of the road. The
chairs and lockers were the only other furniture that I can
remember, if I except a lamp that swung from an eye
screwed into the ceiling.

I found Richard in the berth that had belonged to the
captain, inspecting the contents of a bag of charts.

"I am anxious to get an observation at noon," said he,
"and yonder is a good sextant"—nodding towards a tri-
angular-shaped box on a little table up in the corner;
"though whether I can depend upon that chronometer"
—giving a second nod towards the timepiece that stood
near the sextant-case—"is another matter. Have you
looked into the other berths, Jess?"

"No," I answered.

"Then do so," said he, "and take your choice. They
are all the same size—too small for two."

There were four of them in all, mere boxes, all side by

side, and each one containing a sleeping-shelf under the little circular window, or scuttle, with which every berth was lighted. The foremost one had been made into a pantry, fitted with shelves and drawers similar to a kitchen dresser, and here I found a good array of plates and dishes, and knives and forks, and the like—indeed, all that was requisite to furnish a table with at meal-time, along with some dozens of red tins piled under the drawers, which, when I came to examine them, turned out to be tins of preserved meat, milk, and such things. The other berths were fitted with fixed washstands, lockers, pegs for hanging clothes, and other small conveniences; but, apparently, two of the three only had been used, and seeing this, and desirous that Richard should keep the captain's berth, as there he would find all the materials he needed for navigating the brig, I fixed upon the berth that had not been occupied.

"And where will Spence sleep?" said I.

"Oh, poor devil," exclaimed Richard, "let him have the mate's berth. I doubt if he'd have the courage to turn-in in the deck-house forward after what happened there. The poor creature is welcome to the cabin. The deck-house is best kept shut up, for, had you seen the bodies—tut! tut! where am I drifting to? All that sort of thing is behind us, Jess, and we're bound home now, my darling. Aren't you tired out by your long spell at the wheel? You've not had your clothes off for near upon forty hours; so take my advice, go to your berth, and, while I am shooting the sun, have what Jack calls a good wash-down. Here's a lump of marine soap; here are towels, somewhat rough, but you'll know how to use them; and if you'll wait a minute, I'll fetch you a bucket of sparkling green sea-water."

He could not have advised me better, and seeing a good-sized tin bath-tub under the bunk in the captain's cabin, I carried it into my berth, and enjoyed such a bath as you must have been shipwrecked in a tropical climate, and been obliged to keep your clothes on night and day, to appreciate the delight of. I poured the green, sweet sea-water right over me, and when I had dressed myself, and made shift to adjust my hair with a comb which was in the captain's cabin, but which I took good care to wash well before using, I felt as if youth and health had come back to me at a bound; my spirits rose, and I actually found myself humming, "Weel may the keel row," as I put on my hat and made ready to go on deck and see of what help I could be there.

It was fortunate that I was not troubled in those days with self-conceit, otherwise the reflection of my face in the little glass before which I combed my hair must have qualified the buoyant inspirations of the salt-water bath. The right side of my face was literally scarlet with sunburn; the rest of my skin, being too fair to brown, had developed a quantity of freckles; and the back of my neck, on which the sun had poured fiercely while I was in the boat, was of the complexion of a boiled lobster. But, so far from being astonished by my own appearance, I was surprised to find that it was not worse; indeed, I had fully made up my mind to discover that the previous day's roasting had changed me into a negress.

Before I left the cabin Richard entered it, with the sextant in his hand. He said he had taken the sights he wanted, and must now work them out, and when he had done he would follow my example, and duck himself with salt-water.

"Meanwhile, what can I do, Richard?" said I.

"You can attend to the dinner," said he; "you'll find everything ready. We lighted the galley fire before Spence relieved you at the wheel, filled the copper, and put a piece of beef in to boil."

Before going to the galley, I went aft to see how Spence was getting on at the wheel. I found him steering with great gravity, and looking very cool in the shadow of the sail my husband had spread for me.

"This has been a wonderful meeting, Spence," said I; "not more good for you than for us."

"Ay, 'm," he answered. "I should just think it is wonderful. Ye've saved my life. I was near going mad afore you came aboard."

"Well," said I, "what you've got to do is what *we've* got to do: give up thinking over what's passed, and go to work with might and main to save the brig and get home."

"You'll find me all there," he exclaimed. "There's naught I'll stick at. What's the gentleman's name, 'm, that I may know how to call him?"

"Captain Fowler, and I'm his wife. He's a sailor-man as well as you."

"It's easy enough to see that, missis," he answered, with a slow grin. "I never knew a man to pick up a royal faster than he did. An' in tricing up that bunt," said he, looking at the mainyard, "I'm blessed if there wasn't the strength of a whole ship's company in his arms."

I left him and went to the galley. The decks had been entirely cleared of the litter of sprawling ropes, and the little brig had a truly habitable look as she swung softly over the long-drawn, gentle, dark-blue ocean swell, her canvas barely held quiet by the languid breeze, the heavenly azure of the horizon showing over the bulwarks, and a faint tinkling of slowly passing water all around her. She was in no sense a good-looking vessel, having what sailors call a flaring bow, which made her appear as round as an apple forward when you viewed her that way, and a very square stern. Indeed, her beam was like an old East Indiaman's. But we found out afterwards that she fined down handsomely under the bends, while, as for strength, she was like one of those oak-built frigates which neither a succession of actions nor being laid up for three quarters of a century has been able to destroy, being as strongly put together as a stone pier, with bulwarks as stout as a castle parapet, and sturdy lower masts, painted white, spars which in these economical days would be thought strong enough for a vessel of six hundred tons.

The little caboose, or galley, stood by itself, like a sentry-box, a few paces before the main hatch. I entered it, and found a very good oven and coppers, and a couple of shelves, furnished with such odds and ends as a ship's cook would require. The fire was roaring merrily, the water in the coppers boiling, but, oh! the temperature! I took up a two-pronged fork, and, plunging it into the copper, brought out the piece of beef that had been dropped into the water; but, on inspecting it, perceived that it would need twenty minutes more boiling; so I

22

lingered in or about the galley until I considered the
meat sufficiently cooked, and then set it upon a tin dish
and carried it into the cabin, almost overcome by the
combined heat of the galley and the sun. Next, going
into the berth that had been used as a pantry and store-
room, I procured a table-cloth and the other necessaries
for dressing a table, and so got dinner ready.

There were more things to eat than the beef; for, while
hunting after a table-cloth, I came across some pots of
jam, a quantity of white biscuits, and several tins of sardines. I placed what I thought we should require of
these things on the table, and was going to seek Richard,
when he came out of his berth.

"I heard you bustling about," said he. "I have finished
my calculations, and enjoyed a grand bath." He looked
at the table, and said, "Why, here is a capital display,
Jess. What have you in that glass pot there?"

"Raspberry jam," I answered.

"One would think you had been shopping," he exclaimed, bursting into a laugh. "But stop till I overhaul the little hooker. The presence of that raspberry
jam points to a theory of life on the part of her late unhappy captain that should warrant us in forming large
expectations of the contents of the lazarette. I'll just tell
Spence we're going to dinner," and out he ran, more brisk
and cheerful, with more of his old cordial heartiness in
his manner than I had seen in him since that miserable
day of the mutiny on board the *Aurora*.

He soon returned, saying, as he sat down, that the deep
blue of the weather had a wonderfully steady appearance.

"I have told Spence to keep a bright lookout for ships,
not only ahead, but astern. We must both bear that in
mind, Jess. It's as important as steering."

"Where do your calculations make us to be, Richard?"

"Why," he replied, "farther to the west'ard and the
south'ard than I believed."

"You will have to alter your course, then," said I.

"Ay, by a trifle, and it is done. Upon my word, Jess,
this is an excellent piece of beef; or is its flavor owing
to shipwreck and my salt-water bath?"

"Why do you head the brig for the Cape Verde Islands," I asked, sticking to my subject as being more important than the beef, "instead of steering her for Sierra Leone or Sherborough, where she comes from?"

"For several reasons," he answered. "First of all, the islands are two hundred miles nearer to us than the ports you name. Secondly, I have no fancy for trying for any nearer point on the African coast, with only three of us to work the vessel should we find ourselves near a lee shore, crowded with the most inhuman and ferocious tribes of savages that are to be found in any part of the world. Thirdly, the farther we get to the north and west, the greater grows our chance of encountering assistance, either in the shape of a sailing-ship, that may be willing to lend us two or three hands, or else a steamer, that might favor us with the end of her hawser. Do these reasons satisfy you, my darling?"

"Oh, Richard, you know I am very ignorant of such matters. You are sure to be right."

"No, no," said he, smiling, "not sure; but I do my best. It is a mere matter of judgment. Many skippers would, I dare say, try and fetch the mainland, but I would rather keep driving or drifting north and west, with a clear sea all around me, and taking my chance — seeing that we have plenty of water and provisions aboard — of being sighted and assisted by some passing ship, than running for the African coast, and waking up one morning to find a stiff inshore breeze blowing, the land aboard, and only Spence as ship's company. But, let me decide as I will," said he, looking very grave, and regarding me with eyes full of pathos and love, "God's hand will be in it. We owe him thanks, my little wife, for our wondrous preservation, so far, from fire and the perils of an open boat. Such signal mercies make me feel sure we are watched over; and we can have but little faith if we do not go to work hopefully and heartily, and without the least misgiving."

In this he did but express my own thoughts, as he must have known by seeing the tears which filled my eyes as I took his hand and pressed it.

CHAPTER XXXIV.

A CRUEL BLOW.

WE sat a little while talking over our adventures, and
I was heartily glad to notice that he did not make the
great grief of his losing the *Aurora* that I expected to
find in him when he should come to have leisure for
thought, and his mind was freed from such pressing peril
as an open boat brings.   No doubt he was supported by
reflecting that what had happened was altogether outside
his duties, his courage, and his resolution as a seaman ;
that he was as innocent of the fire and the ultimate destruction of the bark as he was of the cruel and barbarous
mutiny.

This deck-house in which we sat was much cooler than
the cabin of the *Aurora*, owing to the door and the windows, which ventilated it freely.   The smell of the pitch
was still strong, and set us speaking of the fever.   Richard said that, though African fever was contagious, he
had no fear now that all the bodies were overboard, their
clothes thrown away, and the deck-houses well fumigated.
In all cases of the kind which he could recollect, he never
remembered that any of the fresh crew sent on board by
passing ships took the fever.   Infection was caused by a
sick man sleeping with the rest of the men in a small,
badly ventilated forecastle or cabin, and in such a vessel
as this, if the fever chose to spread, there was no medicine to check it.   Then, pulling out his watch, he asked
me to go and relieve Spence at the wheel, that the lad
might have his dinner.

"If we don't come to you quickly," said he, "it will be
because I want to overhaul the lazarette, and see what
provisions and water there are aboard.   Nothing can happen in the shape of weather," he added, "while the sky
keeps that most wonderful color ; though I wish I could
see a barometer about ; for these latitudes are as capri-

cious as a cat — all velvet one hour, and the next all claws."

I went on deck, feeling greatly refreshed, strengthened, and cheered by the meal and our quiet chat, and, taking the wheel from Spence, told him to go and get his dinner in the cabin. The same languid breeze was still blowing over the quarter. It was as hot as the sunshine itself, and it was amazing that the heat did not dry it up, and that it should prove so constant, for there seemed to be no place for it to come from; there was not the merest tip or vaguest feather of cloud upon the dome of blue. Fresh from an open boat myself, and knowing, though but for a day, the torture of the heat, and the dazing and maddening influence of the iteration of the surface of the sea upon the mind, I could well understand the language of sailors who, in describing their sufferings when ship-wrecked, have spoken of seeing their dying shipmates turn up their faces to the blue and cloudless heaven, and curse it with their glazed eyes. Majestic, wonderful, beautiful as that azure was, yet even I, standing safe and in good health upon the deck of a sound vessel, found, when I came to the wheel and looked up and saw the eternal blue void shining still, something malignant and cruel in the hot, breathless, measureless expanse; the weariness of finding it there yet, shadowless save in the deepening of its own hue in places, as though a swell ran through the great ocean of azure ether, became a pain; and a kind of passionate longing grew in me for a sweeping wind that would checker that staring, glaring face with clouds, and give life to the brass-like ocean, now scarcely wrinkled by the draught of air, and veil for intervals the burning, dazzling disk that was pouring its almost vertical fires over our mastheads.

I took notice, however, that while we sat at dinner the course of the swell, that had heretofore run in the wake of a faint breeze, had veered into the northeast, so as to bring it a little before the starboard beam. The heave of it was heavier than before, but not more noticeable, owing to the spaces between the folds being exceedingly wide, so that the rolling of the brig to it was very gentle and gradual. Nor was the horizon as clear as it had been.

There was no mist, and yet the natural boundary of the deep was so vague that here and there it was difficult to distinguish it from the sky.

I had been standing at the wheel about half an hour, and was lost in thought, having much, as you may conceive, to engross my mind. The brig was steering herself, and scarcely needed watching. Every now and again, as the swell heeled her tenderly, the topsails would come to the mast with a pleasant sound ; and a backdraught of air, disdaining the blowing of the wind, ran along like the waft of a fan, and hollowed the little sail that sheltered me from the sun. The complete silence, illustrated rather than broken by the swinging of the canvas, the occasional subdued wash of water under the counter, and the soft chafing of the gear, was altogether too soothing for me, who had had but little sleep, and that of the most uneasy kind, during the last forty-eight hours; and twice I started up and broke away from the weight of slumber that loaded my eyelids, with a feeling of fright, as though I had committed some dreadful crime.

I was rubbing my eyes with one hand, and with the other holding on to the wheel, for my unconquerable sleepiness was incessantly causing my legs to "give" under me, when Spence came along the narrow passage or gangway on the port side of the cabin. He approached so leisurely that I had no doubt whatever that Richard had sent him to relieve me at the wheel, and was feeling very thankful for the release, intending at all hazards to lie down in the cabin and take a nap, when he said—and there was something in the expression of his face, now fully perceived by me, that put sleep to flight before ever he had opened his mouth—

"The cap'n wants you, 'm. You're not to be alarmed. He's had a fall; but he hopes he's not much hurt."

When I heard him say that, my blood ran cold, a darkness came into my eyes, I let go the wheel, and my hands fell to my side as though I had been shot through the heart. But the dreadful feeling of faintness passed like a flash.

"Where is he?" I cried.

"In the cabin," he answered.

I ran there, and on entering the door perceived my husband lying on the deck with his head and shoulders supported against the locker. Beyond him, at the extremity of the cabin, was a small hatchway, not much bigger than a man-hole, the cover of which was raised. I had not noticed that hatch before.

"What has happened to you, Richard?" I cried, throwing myself down on my knees at his side, and taking his hand in both mine.

He was very pale, and the pain that he had suffered, or was suffering, was not only most visibly expressed in his features, but it had forced the perspiration on to his forehead, whence it trickled as though his face were being bathed with water.

"I am afraid," he answered, giving me a smile, nevertheless, "I have injured my left leg in some way. We had opened that after-hatch there, and I had thrown my legs over to drop below, when I slipped and fell. I felt no pain until I endeavored to rise, and then "—here a sudden pang twisted his face, and he broke off, saying, with a groan, "I have broken my leg, Jess."

I hid my face in my hands to master the dreadful swooning feeling that again rushed upon me. I knew, by the way he said, "I have broken my leg, Jess," that he was as conscious of the injury he had received as though a surgeon had been by his side to tell him, and next to his death no worse calamity could have befallen us. Yet, even as I so stood, though but for a moment or two only, with my face in my hands, there rushed upon me the feeling that everything now must depend upon my courage and fortitude and determination. It was a life-giving fancy, and in a breath, I may say, I found the strength I needed.

"Don't let this fret you, Jess," said my husband; "we shall manage yet, depend upon it."

"Oh, yes," said I, "my poor darling, we shall manage. And first to ease your pain, if possible, and make you comfortable," and so saying, I ran into his berth, and brought out the mattress and pillow, which I placed upon the deck close to where he sat, and then, getting him to lean upon me, I let him gently drop towards the mattress until he was upon it. He clinched his teeth until the veins stood out like cords upon his brow, as I raised his legs to bring them in a line with his body; but not a sound escaped him.

"Where is the injury, Richard?" I asked.

"Below the knee," he replied.

There was but one way of getting at it, and that was by cutting through his trousers and drawers. I took a penknife from his pocket, and cut with a light hand—for the Almighty had given me courage, and I do not remember that there was the least tremor in my hand—round the leg of his trousers, and by this means I exposed the portion of his leg where the injury was.

He asked me to put my arm under his head to support it while he looked at his leg, and then said—

"It is a simple fracture, evidently. You can do nothing but put splints on, and bandage it, Jess."

To obtain bandages and splints I fetched a sheet from his berth, and tore it into slips, and then cut some pieces of wood from a biscuit-box that was in the pantry, and, working with the most delicate touch I could employ, I swathed the fracture with lengths of the stout muslin, and then brought the leg of his trousers up to its place again. I had noticed some wicker-protected jars in the berth where the cabin provisions were kept, and, supposing that they contained lime-juice, went to mix him a drink of that refreshing cordial; but, on pouring out a small quantity from one of them into a tin pannikin, I discovered that the stuff was brandy. I gave him a draught, which greatly relieved him from the faintness produced by the heat and the pain, and then bathed his forehead and hands in a weak dilution of the same.

"Do you feel easier, my darling?" I asked him.

"Yes, in body, Jess; but not in mind—for how are we to manage now?"

"Oh, we shall manage, as you said awhile ago. The weather is fine; there is not much sail on the brig, should it come on to blow; and we must pray to God that a vessel may sight us soon and relieve us."

"What a misfortune! what a misfortune!" he cried, clasping his hands. "Think of me prostrate here—helpless as any of the corpses I threw overboard this morning —with only you and Spence to handle the vessel! What is to be the end of it? What have we done to merit these cruel blows, one following the other?"

"Oh, my darling!" I cried, "don't let your thoughts run in that strain; though you are helpless in one sense, you are still with me to advise and direct me how to act." And then, seeing him put his hand to his breast, I asked him if he was in pain there.

"No," he answered; "I am sound enough in all but my leg. It struck the corner of a case; but the rest of me fell upon a quantity of sacking, or some soft stuff just behind it."

"But how," said I, "did you manage to get out?"

"Why, Spence dragged me up, I helping him with my arms and right leg. The other one trailed behind me like a warp over a ship's stern. Do you know, the splints soothe and support it, Jess. The pain doesn't shoot so often as it did."

I was greatly comforted to hear this, for, dreadful as was this fresh misfortune, it would have been tenfold heightened to all my senses had the pain been great and constant. I knelt down and kissed him, and again bathed his forehead; but he now begged me to go on deck and have a look round, and see if Spence kept the vessel to her course; so I left him.

I felt as in a dream when I quitted the shadow of the cabin and found myself in the glaring sunshine. I had had no time as yet to think; the demands upon my attention had come so fast that there had been no room for reflection. But the fierce, white light of the sun, the sight of the spacious field of water running into the remote haze of the horizon, furnished on a sudden such a tremendous significance to the calamity that had befallen my husband, and to the probable consequences of it, that the extreme sharpness and vehemence of the realization defeated itself and filled me with the sensation of being in an evil and harrowing dream. I very well remember standing on the main-deck, and looking up at the tall masts and the sails, and then gazing mechanically round the ocean, and thinking to myself, What is to become of

us? How can this brig be managed by two people, one
of them a girl, whose strength may at any moment fail
her, and leave her as helpless and prostrate as her husband? The poet says that sudden joy, like grief, con-
founds at first. I can answer for grief doing that.

But as in the cabin, so here, this distracting, ay, and
truly deadly confusion of mind—for madness, more often
than not, is born of the mental condition I was then in—
passed away; the mere thought that it was my husband
now who had to look up to me, and whose life was in my
hand, as mine had been in his down to this time, restored
my old spirit to me, and, breaking away from my idle,
dreamy, staring posture, I walked aft to the wheel.

"Is the cap'n very badly hurt, 'm?" inquired Spence,
the moment I approached him.

"Yes; he has broken his leg," I replied.

"Oh, my good God!" cried the poor fellow. "I didn't
think it was as bad as that. He never once groaned. I
reckoned it was no more than a bit of a sprain. The
curse of the Lord seems on this brig. What's to be done
now?" and he rolled his pale eyes about, with a look of
wild consternation on his face.

"Why, we must do the best we can," I replied; "there
are two of us, and we shall have to keep watch and watch,
and relieve each other at the wheel. The captain will tell
us what course to steer."

"Ay, but how'll he know?" cried Spence, out of whose
face the fresh misfortunes had shocked every particle of
blood, so that with his red hair and the pink circles round
his eyes he was every whit as ghastly, dismal, and alarming as when covered with grime and stalking out from
behind the deck-house like a ghost. "If his leg's broke,
he'll not be able to come on deck and take sights."

I had not thought of this; but I was resolved to let no
fresh discovery in our trouble daunt me.

"We must pin our hopes upon sighting a ship," I replied. "Every hour, heading as we are, brings us nearer
to the track of vessels bound south. And now," I added,
"while I think of it, we may as well hoist a distress-
signal, for there is no telling how soon we may be within
reach of a telescope. Where are the flags kept?"

"In that locker, there," said he, pointing to a long box, painted black, and lashed to cleats close against the cabin bulkhead fronting the wheel.   I put all the animation I could muster into my manner, terrified lest despair should so settle upon this poor creature, whose sensibilities had been already unendurably wrung by the horrors he had passed through, as to deprive him of all power and will to work; being well aware that this state of mind and body is often induced among shipwrecked sailors, who, getting it into their minds that God is against them, and that all their struggles must prove useless, resign themselves to their fate, and refuse to lend a hand even when threatened with death by their comrades in misfortune for so doing. Turning over the flags, I lighted upon a pretty large ensign, which I bent on to the peak signal-halliards—the gaff, as I have said, having been hoisted into its place— and ran the flag half-way up, with the union down.   The red made a bright spot of color against the blue sky, and looked an object that could not fail to be seen by any vessel coming within the horizon.   The sight of it carried my mind back to our marriage-feast, when father had jumped from his chair on hearing of the distress-signal behind him; and there arose such a gush of memory as tightened my throat, and I had much ado to keep back my tears.

But I had made up my mind not to yield to any further weakness, and, pointing to the ensign, told Spence, with as strong a note of cheerfulness as I could throw into my voice, that that was but the first step, and that the next would be a ship bearing down to learn the meaning of it. My manner, I rejoiced to note, appeared to make him ashamed of his consternation; he said—

"I never had to work with a lady before, 'm; but there's no duty you're unequal to that ye need mind putting on to me.   I'll make a four hours' trick to your two, 'm, if ye like; and as to sleep, I reckon I can do with less than you; and so you may arrange the watches in the way that'll please you best."

"No, no," said I; "we'll share and share alike.   I'm a woman, it is true, but I am not afraid of doing sailor's work, and if it weren't for my clothes," said I, looking up at the spars, " I'd go aloft with you as cheerfully as I'd take the wheel. But, thanks to my husband's foresight, there'll not be much for you to do up there," and as I said this, I turned to look at the sea in the quarter whence the breeze was blowing, not yet having given any attention to the appearance of the weather.

The wind had slightly freshened, and had veered a little into the north, being about east-northeast. The yards, however, were braced sufficiently forward to keep the canvas full, and that was one reason why I did not sooner notice the shift. There was just enough weight in the wind to crisp the surface of the water, and fill it with flashing points and bright dazzling gleams of sharp, clear green and white, as though it were covered with floating diamonds which were set sparkling by the run of the little foam-flecked ripples.

Under such small canvas as was exposed, it was not to be expected that the brig should make much headway; accordingly, she surged along over the swell very slowly, with her foresail blowing out, and then dropping in as she rolled; yet there was a sound of the seething of froth forward under the bows that was pleasant to hear, and the short, oil-smooth surface of wake, fringed with the snow of the foam from the cutwater, was evidence, at least, that we were not stationary.

There was an old leather-covered telescope on brackets under the after-hatch or break of the cabin, immediately over the flag-locker; I adjusted the focus, and, finding the glass in good condition, took it on to the top of the cabin and swept the blue circle with it, not missing an inch of the circumference. The haziness yielded to the lenses, and I penetrated to where the water-line met the sky; but there was nothing to be seen; no, not the merest speck or shadow of any kind upon the whole of the mighty girdle.

CHAPTER XXXV.

I HELP TO WORK THE BRIG.

HAVING now had the look round that Richard desired me to take, I quitted the top of the cabin, and returned to him. It struck me to the heart to see him lying on his back, helpless as any little infant; but, compelling my manner into a kind of cheerfulness, I sat down on the deck at his side, and asked him how he felt?

"Oh," said he, "I must not trouble myself to think how I feel. There is a dull aching that may mend by-and-by, if nothing worse than the broken bone is to come of my fall. But we'll not anticipate trouble on that head. How looks the weather, Jess?"

"Still very fine; the wind has drawn out into the east-northeast."

"Don't the sails want trimming, or have you let her go off her course?"

"No," said I, "she is still heading as you wish. The yards are forward enough to hold the wind. You will remember we didn't brace them square."

"I hope I am doing right," he exclaimed in a restless way, "in making for the islands. While lying here, I've been thinking it would have been best, after all, to have tried back for Sierra Leone. I know nothing about the Cape Verdes, except that the navigation about those islands is mighty perilous. I was led to choose them first by their being nearer than any part of the African coast that's civilized, and by reckoning that, by heading their way we stood every chance of falling in with ships."

"The last is our only chance now, Richard," said I; "but it's a chance as good as a certainty. We had far better keep to the open sea and trust to God to bring us help, than try for the coast, and risk being wrecked upon it for the want of men to work the brig."

"Ay," he exclaimed, "and if that risk was great enough

this morning to determine me to keep clear of the pestilential, savage-haunted shore, what has it become now that I have been struck down and rendered as useless as that table? But the veering of this breeze promises more difficulty. In these waters the prevailing tendency of the wind is from the north and west. Should it come on steadily from that quarter, we shall have to decide whether to up helm and take our chance of fetching Sierra Leone, or somewhere betwixt the River Gambia and Cape Palmas, or of managing to get on a wind and let ourselves be blown to the southward and westward. But what am I saying? We are powerless! I am unable to take sights —it will be impossible for me to ascertain our whereabouts; and leaving you at the wheel, how could Spence, single-handed, be able to get the yards round."

The expression of his face, of bitter grief, worry, and pain, frightened me.

"If you allow your mind to harass you in this manner," said I, "it will bring a fever upon you. No fretting and worry can help us. Life itself, from beginning to end, is a mere chain of accidents, and surely our chances now are better than they were yesterday."

But it was no good reasoning with him at that time. His fortitude had temporarily given way under the cruel accident that had befallen him. He was naturally of an impatient and even of an impetuous disposition, and to be chained to the deck, as it were, by a broken leg, to be unable to be of the least use in our critical position, helpless and a burden in a brig which had but a boy and me to work her, and dependent upon my being within hail to satisfy the least want that arose in him, was a most unparalleled and soul-subduing condition for a man of his temperament to find himself in.

I did my best to cheer him, but gave up when I found it was no good, and went on deck again, thinking his mind would settle if I let him alone for a bit, and then he would be able to take a calmer and more hopeful view of our situation. Though the shock of the accident that had befallen him had driven all feeling of sleep out of my eyes, I was pretty sure that, if I did not manage to get some rest, I should break down. I therefore went to Spence, and

told him that I was willing to take the wheel for an hour
in order that he might be better able to stand at it for two
or three hours afterwards, that I might have that time for
rest, as I had slept but little for two nights and days.

"Go and turn in at once, missis," said he; "I'm good
to stand here for another four hours if ye like."

"No," said I, "your health is as precious to us as mine;
go and lie down in the cabin. Tell my husband of our
arrangement, and let him wake you in an hour's time.
And just look into the galley, will you, Spence? and make
the fire up if it's low, as we shall be wanting a cup of tea
by-and-by."

I took his place, and he went forward. The breeze had
gradually freshened until there was now strength enough
in it to give the brig a little heel. A few white clouds,
too, had floated out of the sea, but they were very high
and small, and far between. If all had been well with us,
had we had men to work the vessel, this would have been
a noble wind to help us into the northeast Trades. There
were studding-sails in the tops, and booms ready to rig
out, and three or four men would have helped us to cover
the spars of the little craft with canvas. Still, though
with but a topgallant-sail and two topsails on her, the brig
was pushing with something of briskness through the sea,
throwing the water in white sheets from her weather-bow,
and giving earnest, by the yeasty swirl to leeward, of her
capacity of raising what Jack calls a "smother" whenever
she should be pressed, whether she sailed fast or not. A
line of smoke went blowing into the hollow of the foresail,
by which I knew that Spence had thrown some coal on to
the galley fire. I thought, how strange and wonderful it
will seem to Richard, lying helpless upon the cabin floor,
to reflect upon my being alone on deck, steering the brig,
his life in my hand. Happy for him and me was it, I felt,
that I was a sailor's daughter, that I had learned how to
steer when I went to sea with father, and that my love of
the marine life had always kept me so close, in imagination, to the ocean, that when I was on it, and in peril, I
could play a sailor's part, ay, I may truly say, almost with
as much ease as if my training for this time of danger had
been in the forecastle and among seamen.

But there was one trouble on my mind, as I stood thinking at the wheel of that little brig, so heavy and black
that my very heart drew off affrighted from the mere contemplation of it. It was the fear of other and worse mischief than the fracture of the bone following the breaking
of my husband's leg. I was quite ignorant of surgery,
and could merely idly ask myself, did mortification ever
come of such an injury? Was my husband's health likely
to break down by leaving the broken limb as it was? I
say, the mere thought of these things was too much for
me ; they were a thousandfold worse than our helpless
situation. But my resolution to look courageously before
me, and my faith in God's mercy and love—so strong at
that time that sometimes, in recalling it, I am almost willing to believe that an angel had been sent into that lonely
deep to watch by my side and put a trust in me by whispering to the ear of my soul—I say, my resolution and
faith came to my aid. I drove away the black thought,
and fixed my imagination on other things, attentively
scanning the sea always, and more than once with a sudden
start, for as the little white clouds broke up, like puffs of
smoke from a musket upon the horizon, one of them now and
again took the very form and complexion of a ship's sails,
until by watching it rise I would see it was only a cloud.

After I had been at the wheel about half an hour the
wind drew yet more into the north, so that the brig would
not lie her course as the yards then were. I did not dare
quit the wheel to call Spence, and therefore had no alter-
native but to shift the helm so as to keep the sails full,
and this brought the brig's course a very little to the
north of west. It seemed to me, however, that it could
not much matter in what direction we steered, provided
we made plenty of westering ; for, as I had told Richard,
we had but one chance, and that was being seen and relieved by a ship, and it would be strange indeed if, by
steering to the westward, that chance did not befall us ;
whereas, if we went on heading for the Cape Verde Islands, what should we do if one day we found them a lee
shore, the brig among the shoals, and only Spence and
myself to handle the vessel whose safe navigation de-
manded eight or ten men?

It seemed a very long hour before Spence came to relieve me ; and yet it was only an hour. He arrived with a very sleepy look in his face, but said that his nap had done him a deal of good, and that he was willing to stand a four hours' trick if I pleased. I thanked him heartily, and told him I would see. If I could start with a good rest, so as to have a foundation to work on, I'd take care, I said, that we divided our watches afterwards equally. I also explained that the wind had drawn ahead, but that he must keep the brig as she was, unless my husband wished otherwise, in which case we should have to make the wheel fast while we endeavored to brace the yards up.

I then hurried to the cabin, where my poor husband lay upon the mattress as still as a sleeping man. His eyes were open, and a look of animation and happiness came into his face as I approached.

"Spence told me of your arrangement," said he, "and it is a wise one. Bring the mattress and bolster from your berth, and place them alongside mine and lie down at once. You need sleep, and must take it."

I fetched the mattress, and laid it close against his, so that he could arouse me by putting his hand upon me, and while I did this I asked him if his leg gave him pain.

"Nothing that I can't bear," he replied. "The splints keep the broken bone in its place. My pulse is quiet, too, which is a good sign. Of course there is nothing in sight, Jess ?"

"Nothing," I replied ; "but I must tell you that the wind has drawn farther ahead, and that I had to let the brig fall off to keep her sails full. She now heads about west-northwest. Does it matter ?"

He reflected, and said, "No, it does not matter. You were right when you said we had but one chance now, and that was a passing ship. Spence tells me you have the ensign half-masted."

"Yes."

"You can do no more," said he. "As it is, you have done wonders. Lie down now and get some sleep."

However, before doing so, I ran forward to see to the galley fire and fill the little copper with water from the

23

scuttle-butt, as there was tea in the pantry, and I knew Richard would enjoy a cup by-and-by. I then returned, removed my hat, and lay down on the mattress, and, with my husband's hand in mine, fell asleep almost at once.

I was aroused by Richard gently pulling my arm. I sat up and found the cabin dark.

"Why," I cried, "it is night. How long have you let me sleep?"

"No, no," he answered, "it is not night. The sun has not been gone above five-and-twenty minutes. You have slept three hours and a half, and a wonderful sleep it has been; you never once moved. Has it done you good?"

"Yes," said I, getting up, "it has indeed."

"You had better go and take the wheel," said he, "that Spence may light the cabin and binnacle lamps. He'll know where to find the oil. Then you'll return and get some supper. I feel a little hungry."

This was joyous news, and raised my spirits as nothing else could have done. There could be no better sign than for him to tell me he felt hungry. So, putting on my hat, I went on deck, and found the poor lad very faithfully standing at the wheel, but full of anxiety, for the moment I drew near he exclaimed, "She's broke off two points since you was on deck, 'm."

I looked at the binnacle-card and found the vessel was heading west by north.

"No matter," said I.

"I could swing them yards a bit myself, I believe," said he. "With the weather-braces all gone, there's plenty of wind to help 'em, if ye'd bring her to quietly. Shall I try?"

"Not at present," I replied. "If she continues to break off, then we must brace up if we can, for we don't wish for any southing. My husband wants you to trim and light the binnacle and cabin lamps, and at the same time you can give an eye to the galley fire."

Although, as Richard had told me, the sun was not long set, the night could not have been darker had it been midnight. The stars shone with extraordinary brilliance, as though the northing in the wind had clarified the atmosphere and sharpened the greenish and white fires of those matchless tropical luminaries. The new moon stood over our mastheads. I had not noticed it before, though it should have been visible during the latter portion of the afternoon ; but there it was now, like the paring of a new silver dollar fixed among the stars in the velvet-black heights, with just enough of power to give a delicate gossamer hue to the puffs of vapor which came sailing down the spangled canopy upon the brisk wind that blew steadily from the north and east. The sea was as black as the sky, but fuller of phosphoric light than I had yet seen it. Every little surge as it curled over flashed into radiance, and the wake of the brig looked as though burning spirits of wine were being poured over the stern, so wavering, wild, and sparkling at times was the shining, lambent trail that streamed into the darkness.

I searched the gloom with eager, penetrating eyes, always now when on deck looking round and round the eternal liquid circle, as anybody would whose only hope lay in sighting a vessel. But the horizon loomed up dark and desolate against the low, shining stars, not the least shadow of a darker hue than the night that hung over it to win and detain the eye for an instant.

Spence did not keep me long waiting at the wheel ; yet during the short while I stayed there the strange and menacing character of the peril we were in came more sharply home to me than it had yet done. The darkness and the mystery that night-time flings upon the deep gave, no doubt, an edge to my perception of our situation such as it would lack when the brilliant sunshine was abroad. The wind streamed with melancholy sounds through the rigging and under the foot of the sails ; the water made a sobbing noise against the sides of the moving vessel, and my imagination found something sad beyond expression in the thin slice of moon, the darkened portion of whose disk was clearly defined upon the sky. Hope might have found a symbol of herself in that planet, the dawn of whose full light was just begun ; but, though I was not without hope, yet the mood then upon me left but little of it ; so that when I looked up at the moon I could not but think she typified our own condition, being all but extinguished by the shadow upon her, as we were by the heavy misfortunes which had fallen like the very hand of death upon us.

However, Spence's arrival with the binnacle lamp drew me away from these miserable reflections. He fitted the lamp under the brass hood, and then took the wheel.

"I've got my supper in the bosom of my shirt," said he. "The cap'n told me to take it aft. He also told me to take a drink of spirits and water, which I've done; so ye needn't hurry. I don't want no hot tea. I'm not fond of tea. In these here climates there's naught like cool drinks."

"When I've waited upon the captain, and had something to eat," said I, "I'll come and settle the matter of watches with you. Meanwhile, keep a sharp lookout for ships, Spence."

"Trust me to do that," said the poor fellow.

On entering the cabin I found the lamp burning brightly, and Richard reading some papers from a box by his side.

"I got Spence to bring me these from the captain's berth," said he. "They are papers concerning the brig's cargo, crew, and the like. I find she's a trifle bigger than I thought her—three tons under two hundred. She's chock-full of palm-kernels, and I should say her cargo alone is worth not less than four thousand pounds."

"What concerns me more than her cargo," said I, "is your health. Does your leg give you any uneasiness?"

"Not much more than the uneasiness of not being able to move it," he replied. "My darling, you know my temperament. It's a frightful hardship for me to be nailed to this deck as if I were some strange kind of moth or butterfly pinned on a cork. I must occupy my mind, or take the chance of falling imbecile. The next thing I meant to do after overhauling that cursed lazarette was to examine the brig's papers."

"Well," I said, "you can go on reading while I get supper ready. But let me do that at once, for I suppose waiting has not decreased your appetite?"

He answered, "No; I should be glad of a bite." So I went into the pantry, whither Spence had removed the things after he had eaten his dinner, and brought out the cold beef and the other provisions, and, putting some tea into an earthenware teapot, I went to the galley, where I found a good fire, and the small copper full of boiling water. It was very dark on deck, but the fire gave light enough in the galley to enable me to see. I will own I did not linger. The nervous condition I was in made the proximity of the deck-house, which might have been more fitly called a dead-house, seeing the sufferings it had witnessed, and the shocking objects it had held, violently distressing to me. I looked at it fearfully, and came away from it quickly, and I remember thanking God, as I entered the cabin, that it was in the forward part of the ship, instead of being near the wheel, where I should have to stand alone during a portion of the night.

In respect of plates and cutlery, and the odds and ends of the pantry, the *Bolama's* cabin could not have been better furnished had she carried passengers—which she might have done in her day, too, for her papers showed her to be over ten years old, taking her back into 1850, at which time the voyage to Sierra Leone and the ports on the west side of the African continent was chiefly made in small vessels. I mention this brig's equipment to show that we were not utterly unfortunate, and that, dismal as that time was, there was here and there a bright point in it.

I know not what a stranger would have thought who, unknown to us, should have boarded our apparently abandoned vessel, and peered into the cabin, and found that little interior looking extraordinarily hospitable in the illumination of the lamp, that gave a very brilliant, cheerful light, and the table covered with as good a repast as any one could hope to find in a vessel of the tonnage of the *Bolama*—cold salt beef, sardines, jam, white biscuit, a tin of preserved mutton, and the like. But the truly amazing part of this strange ocean picture, to a stranger, would have been the seeing me, a young woman, with my hair rough, the sleeves of my dress turned above my elbows, my dress "triced up," as sailors say, in order that my legs might have plenty of liberty, and a piece of canvas, which I had found on a shelf in the pantry, fastened round my waist, to preserve my dress from being blackened and destroyed by the galley grime—for, you will remember, it was the only dress I had, and if it should be torn or rendered unwearable, there was positively nothing else, if I except the dead captain's clothes, I could attire myself in—I say, the strangest part would have been the seeing me waiting upon my husband, bolstering up his head and shoulders so that he might get at his plate without twisting his body, while on deck there stood but a single figure at the wheel, not a living thing to be found elsewhere, and the silence of death and the black shadow of the night upon the forward part of the brig, from the mainmast to where the bowsprit launched itself towards the gleaming stars over the sea. The wild, impressive legend of the Phantom Ship was, indeed, being imitated to the very life by this brig, as she went dimly sailing through the gloom of the tropical night, her white sails vaguely glistening under the crescent moon, and the black ocean breaking into pale flashes of fire around her, as though the deep preserved the reflection of a storm that had passed over it, and was full of the lightning that had whizzed in sparks and lances into its mighty heart.

"Landsmen may think sea-life prosaic and monotonous," said Richard, turning his eyes slowly round the cabin; "but my experience is that there is no theatre in the world fuller of wonders and thrilling changes. A magician is perched on the main-truck of every vessel afloat, and day after day he waves his wand, and transforms the picture."

"That is the true fascination of the sea," I replied; "but why should its very beauties be so deadly? I felt that in the open boat last night, when I looked up at the sky filled with stars, like chips from a glorious rainbow."

"Well," said he, "if God preserves our lives, you will have had enough of the ocean by the time you get home."

"We'll see," I replied, feeling that he was pretty near the truth. "Anyway, I sha'n't be sorry to quit this brig. The thoughts of her dead crew haunt me. Sometimes I seem to taste a thickness in the air, as if the fever still lingered."

"No, no," he cried, "that *must* be fancy, Jess. Fever's not to be tasted in that way. Keep your mind clear of thoughts of that kind. If I had the least misgiving I would own it. Many others besides ourselves have boarded fever-stricken ships, but I cannot remember that any harm ever befell them, as I told you. The bodies are overboard, their clothes and hammocks destroyed, the fore deck-house well smoked and kept shut, and this cabin thoroughly fumigated. What is there to be afraid of?"

I plucked up my spirits, and answered that I was not afraid; that if it had not been for the unfortunate and most cruel accident that had befallen him, I was sure I should have learned to feel by this time happier and easier in mind in this brig than I had been in the *Aurora*, from the hour when misgivings of Mr. Heron's character first troubled me; and that, even as it was, the load upon my spirits would be lightened to a degree that would enable me to confront our present peril with a comparatively gay heart if I could be quite sure that the injury to his leg would stop at the broken bone.

"What do you fear, Jess?" he asked.

"Well," said I, "I am wicked to fear anything at all; yet if I could but get a surgeon to come and set your leg, and tell me that it will be well and sound again by-and-by, I should be content, for such happy news, to go on sailing about in this brig, and doing the work of a cook, steward, and ordinary seaman all in one, for the next six months."

"Indeed, then, my darling," said he, "you may .be as sure of that news as if a surgeon had given it to you. I know what is the matter; it is what the doctors call a simple fracture of the bone. I don't apprehend any further mischief than that, Jess, unless—and now I'll be perfectly frank with you—the reuniting of the bone should leave me one leg a trifle shorter than the other—enough to give me an aristocratic halt in my gait."

Alongside my fears that his leg might mortify, or that something of that kind might happen, this notion of the broken leg being shorter than the other when it came to be healed did not sound in the least alarming. I left the table, saying that before I went on deck I must make him comfortable, which I did by bathing his face, adjusting his pillow and the like, and fetching from the captain's

berth a few books which stood upon a shelf—odd volumes
of magazines, novels, and such things, which I put by his
side on the deck.

"What are your arrangements with Spence?" said he,
as I put on my hat.

"We have arranged nothing as yet," I replied. "But
the poor fellow must not be allowed to do more than his
share. His life is as precious as mine—"

"No, no," interrupted Richard.

"Why, yes," continued I, "in one sense certainly. What
should we do without him? God's goodness is surely visible in the circumstance of the lonely lad being left to
receive us here and help us. I think we had better make
four hours each at the wheel."

"Four hours will exhaust you," he exclaimed with a
shake of the head, and looking at me with the passionate,
restless, yearning expression of a prisoner.

"No, it will not, and certainly not if the weather remains
fine," said I. "There is refreshment to be got out of four
hours at a stretch, as you sailors call it; whereas you wake
from two hours still weary and unsatisfied."

"Take my watch, then," said he, pulling it out of his
waistcoat pocket, and giving it to me, "that you may know
the time. But how are you to make yourself heard should
you want Spence?"

"I have been thinking of that," I replied. "One way
will be to tie the end of a line to him, bringing it through
one of the cabin scuttles to the wheel."

"A good idea!" he exclaimed, his face brightening.
"But, instead of making the end fast to Spence, make it
fast to me. I am a lighter sleeper—should I sleep at all—
than Spence, who snores like a pig with a cold in his
head."

"No," said I, laughing, "I want you to sleep. I'll engage to wake Spence, when I want him, if he isn't clever
enough to slip the line off him before he lies down."

"I'll see to that," he exclaimed. "Shall you take the
first watch?"

I answered, "Yes."

"What time is it now?"

I looked, and said it was ten minutes past eight.

"Then you'll come below at twelve? It can't be helped. But, oh, Jessie!" he cried, with a sudden burst of sorrow, "what would I give to have saved my darling from this!"

"Not a word more, Richard," I said, kissing him. "My courage is dependent on yours. Keep up your heart, for by doing so you will be keeping up my heart. Pray God before this time to-morrow comes we may be relieved of all this bitter anxiety."

And not trusting myself to speak another word I hurried out of the cabin, in time to save him from seeing the hot tears that rolled down my cheeks, in defiance of my desperate struggle to force them back.

CHAPTER XXXVI.

WE SIGHT A SAIL.

I FOUND Spence at his post, and, peering into the binnacle compass, perceived that the vessel's course was still due west. The breeze was very steady, and the little puffs of cloud which were driving along the stars made me suppose it was the Trade-wind, which, near the African coast, blows, as I have been informed, more northerly than in mid-ocean. I told Spence that I had arranged to divide the watches into four hours each, and asked him to get a lead-line, or some piece of long, thin stuff, and attach one end of it to his arm and pass the other end through one of the after-cabin scuttles. This he did, but first I thought I would try whether the line would work freely; so I told him to go into the cabin and lie down with the line fast to him, and when he had done this I pulled the line, on which he came out immediately, saying it was all right, and that the line gave me a purchase that would enable me to heave him out of his grave, if he were buried a hundred fathoms deep.

It comforted me, as you may believe, to have this line, which, when dragged, would bring me help, or, at least, companionship, at once when I desired it. And yet, in spite of that and of my reflection that Richard and the lad were lying not above twenty feet from where I stood, I felt all the horror of complete loneliness to a degree it would be hopeless for me to attempt to express. The thin, wisp-like curl of moon was sailing down the black heavens on a line with our bowsprit, and stood just over the fore-royal-yard. The stars shone brightly, upon the very edge of her, and gemmed the rim of the blackened disk so as to make the picture of her strangely beautiful. Sometimes a meteor would flash out from the soft mass of starry points, and, after floating gently for a little space, break into a kind of silvery smoke. The wind filled the air with many sounds.

At any time there is something peculiarly melancholy in the moaning and wailing of the night-breeze among the rigging of a vessel; but to me, who stood alone upon those dark decks, the noises up aloft were unspeakably depressing, and colored my thoughts to a complexion very fit to render solitude insupportable. They were like spirit-voices calling to one another in lamenting tones. They brought up the dead crew of the brig to my mind, and memory so painted the body of the captain, as I had beheld it propped up against this very wheel which I was holding, that I viewed it there—just in front of me—as if indeed it were at my feet; and I actually drew away at arm's-length from the spokes, with a long, tremulous sigh, momentarily affrighted beyond all self-government by the vision conjured up by my fancy.

I cannot suppose that I should have suffered from this timidity had it not been for the strain to which my nerves were subjected by the trials and misfortunes which had come upon us previous to our boarding the brig. My imagination, it is true, was always an active one—too active sometimes for my peace of mind; yet in health I was not a woman to be alarmed by superstitious thoughts. But this night they mastered me; nor can I wonder that it should have been so, when I look back and recall the ponderous shadow of the night (which made the thin streak of moon and the stars visible without taking any light from them), in the midst of which the brig was sailing, her black decks silent as the grave, voices of the wind in her rigging uttering sounds which seemed articulate to my keen and feverish hearing; while imagination gave such substance to memory that every flutter in the folds of darkness on either hand of the cabin took the form of a spectre, whose presence had an almost supernatural setting in the ghostly fires which swarmed in the water, and which broke out with a greenish shining in the curl and fall of the little surges, and in the hollow, washing sound of the sea, as the stem of the brig divided the ink-like billows, and sent a line of seething foam along the sides of the moving vessel.

I thought the time would never pass. After glancing at the watch I would put it away, resolving not to look at it for a long while, so that when I produced it again I should find that a good spell of time was gone; but so deceptive was my impatience that, when I drew the watch out once more and put it to the binnacle lamp, I would discover that, instead of an hour having passed, as I supposed, only twenty minutes had elapsed.

Happily, I did not feel weary. The spindle of the wheel was protected by a box-like cover, with a ledge on either side, which enabled me to sit and yet hold the spokes too, and this saved my legs. Likewise, my nervous condition kept me very wide awake, without the least desire in me, that I can remember, to sleep. Shortly after ten o'clock the binnacle lamp grew dim and wanted trimming; but, beyond the loss of the companionship of the bright light, the waning of it signified nothing, since the moon would be over the bows until Spence's watch came round, and all that I had to do was to keep her there.

All this while the half-masted ensign was blowing over my head. Its rippling made a noise that soothed me to hear. I know not why this should have been, unless it was that its noise was a familiar one, and broke into and qualified the dreary crying and moaning of the wind in the rigging, or because, in their way, its dark folds were a kind of beacon that promised to court help to us when the daylight was abroad and a ship came in sight. So often as the flapping and rattling of the flag drew my attention to it, so often would I send my eyes round the dark sea. The mere anxiety to get my mind away from the gloomy,

chilling, superstitious fancies which trooped upon it made
me doubly vigilant in watching the black ocean circle,
and in humoring all the thoughts which were put into my
head by reference to our perilous situation.

Whether my description of our plight at this time en-
ables you to grasp it, I cannot guess ; but, for myself, I
can truly say that I doubt if ever I compassed it in its
entirety. Its possibilities of peril were too numerous to
be mastered by me. That my husband was lying, with a
broken limb, as helpless and useless to our chances of preserving our lives as the mattress that supported him I very
fully knew and quite understood the significance of ; likewise that, if a storm arose, we should have no other hope
than God's mercy. These two things stood out blackly
on my mind, and I never lost sight of them. But the other
conditions and chances of our situation occurred to me fit-
fully, and one pushed the other out of my memory, so that,
as I have said, my mind never thoroughly embraced our
plight, as Richard's did or any salt-water sailor's would ;
which was all the worse for me, because, by not seeing all,
or rather by not being able to guess all, my imagination
stepped in to complete the picture, and made our prospects
appear truly frightful.

For instance, I would suppose that we did not sight a
vessel for days and days. Again and again this dreadful
curse had fallen upon famine-stricken sailors, as the maritime annals show. Was it to be hoped that I could reckon
for any length of time upon my strength ? and, if nature
gave way with me, what could Spence do ? He could not
always be at the wheel ; he would need rest ; and might
not his strength fail him, too ? And then figure our condition, floating about in a vessel we could not control, and
without the least knowledge of our whereabouts ; all three
of us prostrate, I too sick and feeble to attend to my husband's wants !

I say, this was only one of the horrible but probable
fancies that came into my head as I stood alone at the
wheel that night, starting at the imagined stirring of some
delusive shadow in the black air on either side the cabin,
listening to the hollow, mournful notes in the rigging, and
to the plaintive, sobbing cadence of washing water, while

the horned moon took a faint, pinkish tinge as it sank to
a level with the fore-topsail-yard, and the sea was flushed
up around by the radiance of its own emerald-green fires,
and filled my ear with the multitudinous creaming and
seething of its innumerable surges.

I had looked at the watch, and made out, with great
difficulty, by the faint flame of the binnacle lamp, that it
was twenty minutes before midnight; and I had put the
watch in my pocket, with my face turned in the direction
of the sea over the weather beam, when I thought I could
see a kind of gray shadow that way. I rubbed my eyes,
to efface the impression of the white face of the watch
from my sight, and looked again; and then, seeing the
shadow very plainly against the stars, which shone purely
down to the very sea-line, my heart began to beat fast.
To make sure I let go the wheel and seized the glass; but
the darkness was very deceptive. I thought the lens out
of my focus, and, the tubes being stiff, I had some trouble
to get the telescope to give me a clear picture. This
bother cost me some minutes, but at last I had the right
focus, and on bringing the glass to bear upon the shadow
I distinctly made it out to be a large ship, heading as we
were, under a great crowd of canvas.

No sooner was my mind satisfied that the shadow was
a ship, than I seized the line attached to Spence, and pulled
it vigorously with both hands. Three times I had to tug
the line before I could awaken the lad, proving that I
should have done better to let Richard have the end tied
to him. My impatience became an agony, for the ship
was moving swiftly and drawing ahead like a roll of
smoke, and I was running towards the cabin when Spence
came hurriedly along.

"What is it, mistress?" he called out; "is it eight bells
yet?"

"See! there's a ship out there!" I exclaimed, pointing,
and articulating in my wild excitement with the greatest
difficulty. "How are we to make her know we are in distress?"

"Why, we must burn a flare!" he roared out, rendered
half-mad on a sudden by the news. "Mind the helm, 'm
—we're aback!" he bawled, and rushed forward.

It was true enough. I had let go the wheel, to use the glass, and, in the delay occasioned by my clumsy bothering over the stiff tubes, the brig had swept round in a semicircle, bringing the wind on the bow and the shadow of the ship on the lee beam. The sails were rattling smartly, but in a few moments they were right aback, and lay silently pressing against the masts.

I ran to the wheel and put it hard over. But the brig's way was stopped; indeed, by this time she may have gathered stern-way, in which case I ought to have put the helm hard a-port. But I never thought of that. I considered the stoppage of the vessel a death-blow to our chance of being seen and helped by the ship that was fading away out in the darkness ; for, though she outsailed us fast, still we might have managed to keep within the compass of her horizon long enough to enable us to make a flare that should be visible to her, had it not been for my unhappy letting-go of the wheel, and the rounding of the brig into the wind.

Finding that the vessel lay motionless, slightly leaning under the breeze, with her canvas bellying out abaft the masts, I quitted the helm, and ran on to the main-deck, where I found Spence in the act of firing a small pile of wood he had removed from the galley, on the top of which was a tar-barrel and divers odds and ends which he had collected I know not where, oakum, and canvas, and the like. He may have found them in the deck-house, but he had closed the door of that place again, and I never thought of asking where he obtained his materials. But, such as they were, they were of the right kind to make a blaze, especially the tar-barrel. He fired them with a piece of oakum lighted at the cabin-lamp, and in a few moments there soared up a strong, brilliant flame, that threw out the sails and spars of the brig as though the yellow moonlight lay upon them ; a thick smoke went up from the tar, and, as the flames rose and sank, the coming and going of the red lustre was like the play of lightning upon the decks and sails.

"Just take the glass, and see if they mind us, will'ee, missis!" shouted Spence, who looked terribly unearthly in the wild glare of the fire, as he ran round it, poking and stirring it, and reminding me of the picture of the cannibals in "Robinson Crusoe."

"Take care that you don't set the brig on fire!" I cried.

"I'll see to that," he answered.

I ran aft, took the glass, and pointed it in the direction where I had last seen the ship. I saw her at once, but she was the merest phantom of a shadow now. That she had not altered her course I knew by the squareness of her outline. If she saw the light and meant to come to us, she would take in her studding-sails; and her keeping that canvas aloft, as I could judge by the shape of the darkness she made, proved that she was heading away from us. Nevertheless, I stood watching her through the glass until her shadow completely faded out—and then, turning round, chilled to the heart by the bitter disappointment of the eager hopes that had filled me while she remained in sight, I found the brig in darkness.

I went on to the main-deck, and saw Spence trampling out a mass of glowing embers.

"It's no use," said I; "she did not see us, and is out of sight."

"She may be out of sight, but I dunno about her not seeing us," he exclaimed, stamping and making the sparks fly as he crushed the embers with his big feet.

I entered the cabin, to tell Richard what had happened, and to ask him to advise me how to get the brig before the wind. The lamp burned brightly. My husband lay motionless on his back, with his arms by his side, but his face worked with the excitement kindled by our proceedings on deck, which he knew very well the meaning of, and with the torment raised in his mind by his helplessness and inability to move at such a time.

"I know what has happened, Jess," said he at once, as I knelt by his side to take his hand and kiss his forehead. "You have sighted a ship and burned a flare, but she is gone."

"Yes," I replied; "but we have no right to expect help from the first vessel we sight—on a dark night, too, and with nothing better at hand than a few pieces of wood and a tar-barrel to make a light."

"How was she heading?"

"As we were," I answered ; "due west, as nearly as I could make out."

And then I told him that, having let go the wheel when I first sighted the ship, in order to view her through the glass, the brig had come up in the wind, and now lay aback.

"Has the breeze freshened ?" he asked.

"Nothing to speak of," I replied.

He was silent for a while, and then said, very despondently, "I don't know whether it would not be best to haul up the foresail—which Spence can manage by taking the clew-garnets through a snatch-block to the forecastle capstan or aft to the winch, if the sail should prove too heavy for him and you—and swing the foreyards, and let the brig remain as she is. If our only chance lies in being picked up by some passing vessel, we may as well keep quiet, take things easily, and wait for something to turn up. It is too much that you should be at the wheel—day and night—getting but little rest, exposing yourself on deck to the sun by day, and to the damp and chill by night, and perhaps planting the seeds of a lifelong ill-health, and all for no purpose. Better heave the brig to, Jess," said he, speaking with the manner of one who has no hope left.

"No, no !" I exclaimed, earnestly. "It would end in my falling mad outright, Richard, to go on deck hour after hour, and day after day, and find ourselves motionless, and nothing in sight but the empty, desolate sea. The mere sense of moving keeps up the heart ; and surely we must multiply our chances tenfold by pushing towards the ocean highways."

"Very well," said he, softly, and without the least spirit. "Be it so, since you wish it. You are captain, and can do as you like," he added, with a wan, faint smile. "I'm but a sheer hulk, indeed, only fit to be tossed overboard."

"Come, Richard," said I, smartly, guessing that, if I let the feelings his words excited master me, I should only deepen his despondency; "this is not language for a sailor to hold. We have to preserve our lives ; and if God will but continue my health, it shall not be my fault if we don't both of us see the canny town again, and relate our

adventures to Thomas Snowdon, master-mariner. Is there
no magic in the memory of father's hearty old presence to
quicken the true seaman's heart that beats in you ?"

"It's my broken leg," said he, catching hold of my hand,
"and my being floored, with will enough in me to raise
the dead, and not physical power enough to crawl an inch,
that breaks me down. Here have I been lying for near
upon twelve hours—and for how much longer must I go
on lying ?—and at a time, too, when, but for that damned
lazarette, I should be able to do the work of three men, so
as to bring you to that canny town which you tell me we
shall yet see. But this is only a passing mood, Jess.
Take no notice of it. I was half maddened by knowing
there was a ship in sight, and hearing you at work with
Spence, and not being able to stir so as to advise and lend
a hand. If it will make you feel happier to have the brig
sailing, by all means get her started afresh on her voyage
to nowhere."

"How am I to do that ?"

"Why," said he, "first of all, I suppose, she has stern-
way. If that's so, put the helm hard a-port, and take a
turn with a rope's end over one of the spokes to keep the
wheel steady. Then flatten in your jib and staysail sheets.
Let me see ; the jib is set, I think ?"

"Yes," said I.

"Get those head-sheets flattened in—you and Spence
can manage that. Then make shift to swing the main-
yards, so as to point them to the wind, that there may
be no pressure on the canvas. Keep the foreyards as
they are. When the brig pays off, reverse the wheel ;
and, as she comes to her course, trim the yards as best
you can."

"Since we shall have to drag the yards about," said
I, "had we not better brace them up, so as to be able
to steer more north than we have been going ?"

"Oh, it doesn't matter," he answered. "If we are to
shove forward at all, we had best go westward. The
sooner we're out of these seas the better."

I went on the main-deck, where Spence was kicking
the ashes of the fire into the scuppers, and told him to
help me to get the brig on her course again. I clearly

remembered Richard's instructions, and the first thing I did was to look over the side, and watch the little gleams of froth upon the surface of the water, which speedily satisfied me that the vessel was moving sternwise. I then went aft to the wheel, put it hard a-port, and secured it by the bight of a rope over one of the spokes. This done, I called to Spence to give me a hand to flatten in the jib and staysail sheets. Of course, I could not see his face; but I had not the least doubt that he was thunderstruck to hear me giving these orders, and correct orders, too; nor was I without surprise myself, for I certainly never could have believed that my knowledge of the sailor's vocation was sufficiently minute to qualify me to carry out all the instructions Richard had given me without blundering.

The youth bundled about in a very handsome manner, hauling heartily, and singing out at the top of his voice. He was as uncouth as a ploughman, but strong as a horse, and was of the utmost assistance besides in knowing the right ropes, and in being able to put his hand upon them at once. The yards ran round much more easily than I had imagined, Spence dragging with all his weight upon the braces, while I kept the hauling part under a belaying-pin, taking in the slack as it came; and in ten minutes' time I was at the wheel, waiting for Spence to trim and light the binnacle lamp, the brig once more following the wake of the moon, that stood like an angry wound or blood-red scar in the black sky over the jibboom end, and the yards braced as they had been before the brig had come up into the wind.

Relating this sort of work is not hard; but let me assure you that the actual thing was very desperately fatiguing to me, who had never had to haul and pull before, and who was already worn out by the four hours' watch I had kept. My hands glowed like hot iron with the toil, the perspiration streamed from my face, and there was such a tormenting tingling of weariness in my legs that, but for being able to rest myself upon the ledge of the spindle-cover I have before described, I must have sank down upon the deck. Still, it soothed my fear and comforted my heart to hear the wash of the passing water,

and to feel that we were once more moving. I am sure
the stagnation of being hove-to hour after hour, and perhaps day after day, would have affected my mind, as I
had told Richard. A sense of life was communicated
by the mere circumstance of moving, and hope could not
sink while every hour that came round held a chance in
it of our progress bringing a sail into view. But to
heave-to would be like giving up, and sitting down to
die. That such a suggestion should have come from my
husband, who in health would have been the first to indignantly and angrily denounce it, was the saddest proof
that could have been offered me of his shattered spirits,
and of the mental sufferings induced in him by the cruel
accident that had befallen him at a time in his life when
his health and strength could never be more precious to
him and to me.

Presently Spence returned with the lamp, which he put
into the binnacle.

"There's the end of the line," said I, pointing to it
on the deck. "I will attach it to my arm; but a very
slight pull will be enough," I added, thinking that, if he
should see some object to excite him, he might haul as
though he had got hold of the topsail-halliards, and hurt
me.

"All right, missis," said he; "I'll take care not to do
more nor twitch it."

I lingered to take a last look around. The moderate
breeze blew pleasantly, and kept the sea trembling with
phosphorescent flashes; the stars seemed to have gathered brilliance with the deepening night, and those of
the first magnitude shone with extraordinary richness and
beauty, some of them touching the dark ocean with points
of silver light, as though they were little moons. The
small, steam-colored clouds drifted swiftly and steadily
under them. The air was warm, yet the dew lay so thick
that the starlight glittered on the decks, and I could have
thrown the water in showers off the companion or skylight or bulwark rails with my hand. I went on top of
the cabin with the telescope; and, resting it on the iron
rail, swept the sea-line slowly and carefully on both sides
the brig as far forward as the foresail would let me level

the glass ; and now, feeling quite exhausted, I replaced
the telescope, told Spence to keep a sharp lookout, and
gave him my husband's watch to put in his pocket ; then
made my way, with trembling legs, to the cabin.

CHAPTER XXXVII.

A STRANGE MEETING.

SPENCE had occupied the mattress I had placed for myself next to Richard ; but fastidiousness would have been
very much out of place at such a time as that ; and I
had to content myself by turning the mattress over and
reversing the bolster.

"You look tired out, Jessie," exclaimed my husband.
"And what a bed for you to come to !"

"Yes," said I ; "but it's a more comfortable bed than
other shipwrecked people have found to lie upon. Is
there anything I can do for you, Richard ?"

"Nothing."

"Does your leg pain you?"

"Why, yes," said he, "there is always a pain in it.
I must expect that ; but shall not mind it, if it stops
there. In other respects, I am none the worse for my
fall and breakage."

"In body, you mean," said I, "and I thank God to
hear you say it ; but I wish your spirits were what they
were."

"They would be if I could get up and go to work,"
he exclaimed ; "but there is nothing here for me to do,
except to think ; and though we were on board a fine
steamer, Jess, fast making for home, instead of on a little brig, with but one man to work her, and though, instead of having a broken leg, I was as sound as I was
aboard the *Aurora*, yet surely there would be enough
in the incidents of our short voyage in that unhappy
bark to keep me miserable and dejected."

"Yes, I have to admit that," said I, removing my hat,
and preparing to lie down.

"But," continued he, speaking with excitement, "take everything that has happened together—the mutiny, all the trouble I had with that miscreant of a mate, the fire, the dastardly desertion of us by the crew, the loss of the noble little bark, our sufferings since, and the perils which still confront us—how would you have me hold up my spirits, forced as I am to lie like a baby upon this deck, with nothing to think of but the dark past and the yet darker present?"

"Have you not slept to-night?" I asked.

"For an hour about—not longer," he replied.

"Try now to get some sleep, then. Two or three hours' rest will stop you from thinking. I am more afraid of your mind than of the injury you have received. This kind of fretting may end in throwing you into a fever, and what shall I do if that happens?"

He fondled my hand, saying he hoped it would not come to that.

"Then," said I, "for my sake, Richard, shut your eyes, and endeavor to obtain some rest."

He did so, and lay quiet, and I closed my eyes too; but, in spite of my weariness, I could not sleep; my fatigue was an aching all through the body, too excessive for repose. I lay listening to the light, creaking noises in the vessel, as she swayed with the swell, and to the muffled, rushing sound of the wind, that came very audibly from the main-deck though the open cabin-door. I often recall the picture we must have presented as we rested side by side upon the plain, hard mattresses, completely dressed, with no other covering on us than our clothes. This time last night I was in an open boat, asleep on my husband's shoulder; and now, though twenty-four hours had passed, they found us still together and alive; but could I say better off, when I thought of the terrible misfortune that had rendered Richard as helpless as a child, and left me alone with a young seaman to navigate a brig of hard upon two hundred tons? How far did these present experiences correspond with my early seductive fancies of the sea? What had become of those dreams of glorious freedom, the speeding fabrics leaning in towering and gleaming heights of white upon

the flashing waters, those visions of green islands stretching their golden sands into the glass-like blue of the
perfumed ocean, which had colored my young imagination, until the very name of the sea thrilled through me
like the whisper of a sweetheart in a girl's ear? I was
answered by the solemn motion of the brig rhythmically
rolling as she went slowly along, by the blackness out
upon the main-deck, where the gloom stood like a wall
of ebony against the cabin-windows and the open door,
by thoughts of the loneliness there, and of the men who
had died one by one in the deck-house forward. The
spirit of the deep had changed its shape indeed; it was
no longer a radiant form, wooing me into realms of tender azure and prismatic waters; but a skeleton, crouching motionlessly, and looking steadfastly upon me with
its frightful grin, keeping watch over a mighty liquid
grave, full of the dark outlines of drowned men and
women.

There was something febrile in such thoughts as these,
as you may suppose, and they kept me awake for full
three quarters of an hour after I had put my head upon
the bolster. But Richard had fallen asleep, and his regular respiration fell at last soothingly upon my ear, for
it gladdened me to feel that, for a time, at all events,
his mind had ceased to fret and chafe him. But truly
nothing happens to one in this world that somehow does
not turn out to be for the best; for, while lying awake
I got thinking of Spence alone on deck, and the thought
of him instantly put it into my head that I had forgotten to attach the line to my arm. This I promptly rec-
tified; though but for my not being able to fall asleep
speedily, it is certain that Spence might have gone on
standing at the wheel for hours, unless by quitting the
helm to arouse me he had let the brig take her chance
of rounding into the wind, and falling aback again.

My sleep was deep and refreshing; and never mortal
rose more reluctantly from his bed than I from my mattress when I was awakened by my arm being gently
jerked by the line. I pulled in response, to let Spence
know I was awake, and would be with him in a moment.
The cabin lamp, which was shining pretty brightly when

I fell asleep, had burned out the oil, and the cabin was pitch-dark. I spoke Richard's name softly, and listened; but he made no answer. His deep and regular respirations told me that he still slept, and in order not to arouse him I crept away from the cabin on tiptoe, guided by the door, through which I spied a little fragment of starlit sky glimmering beyond the bulwarks.

The night air struck cold, and made me shiver; but then, to be sure, I had been sleeping in a dress that hung heavy upon me with the damp of the dew when I lay down.

"Well, Spence," said I, going up to the wheel, "here I am, you see; easier to arouse than you."

"I'm a man," he answered, "to manage without much sleep; but when once I'm down, missis, and snorin', I'm a rare 'un to 'waken."

"What time is it?" I asked.

"About twelve minutes arter four," he replied, pulling out the watch and giving it to me.

"Has the wind kept steady?" I inquired, looking for the moon, and finding that she was gone.

"Ay," he answered; "steady as a house."

"The binnacle lamp burns low," said I, taking his place at the wheel; "but don't bother to trim it. I dare say it will last till the break of the dawn, which cannot be far off. Do you think you can manage to enter the cabin and lie down without disturbing the captain? He's sound asleep, and I want him to sleep. But there's no light."

"Oh, I'll manage, missis," said he. "Where shall I find the end of the line?"

"On the mattress. You'll feel it after groping a little."

"Well, good-night again, 'm," said he, and vanished in the darkness.

I found the wind a trifle lighter than when I had left the deck. The sky had the deep pitchy gloom it will take before the dawn, and some of the stars shone with almost startling brilliance. The sea, too, was not so phosphoric as it had been, possibly because there was less wind to agitate it, and it made a shadow under the stars that would have been dreadful for a much stouter heart than mine to behold, in the situation we were then in. I looked round and round the darkness in the hope of seeing the lights of

a ship, and very soon after I had taken the wheel I perceived what I was so sure was the red lantern or port
light of a ship, that my heart began to beat fast, just as
it did when I sighted the shadow before midnight; but I
did not dare let go the wheel again to get the telescope,
neither had I the heart to bring Spence on deck; I therefore stood staring with all my might, and with every pulse
in my body hammering sharply, until, by observing that
the light never shifted its position by so much as a hair's-
breadth away from a star that hung just over it, and that
it would sometimes twinkle, and even lose its reddish color
and become yellow, I discovered that it was no more than
a star.

Alas! how often have such appearances deceived and
helped to craze the brain of the poor shipwrecked mariner!
Unless you have gone through the experience yourself,
you cannot know the anguish caused by these illusions.
The sailor, half-mad with thirst, upon some water-logged
vessel or in some little open boat, turns his glazed eye
upon the sea, and searches the desolate and lonely horizon yet once more for a ship.   Then a sudden transport
of joy forces a dreadful laughing shout from him.   "A
sail!" he cries, huskily, and madly points.   His broken-
hearted, dying comrades struggle to their feet, and behold, with the light of life rekindled in their glazed eyes,
a little, gleaming, white object, that looks to be the canvas of a vessel indeed, bearing right down.   But it grows
fast, and as it rises it loses its shape, and the miserable
seamen fling themselves down with dying moans into the
bottom of the boat, as they see that what they took to be
a ship is but a cloud.   I have gone through it.   I know
what that disappointment is, and solemnly declare that I
cannot conceive of any kind of mental anguish comparable to the agony that is wrought in the mind of shipwrecked persons by these deceptions of clouds and stars.

To my inexpressible comfort, the dawn broke after I
had been standing at the wheel a little while.   The sky
in the east changed from a faint green into a light pink,
and from that into radiant rose, as though the hues of a
prism were being flashed upon the heavens in that quarter; and, gazing intently round the ocean circle that still

stood dark against the illuminated sky, I spied, dead to
leeward, a little forward of the beam, a dim, white object,
which the searching beams of the sun, that rose at that
moment, showed to be a sail.

The several disappointments I had gone through, however, under this head, kept me quiet, and thinking and
looking cautiously. It might prove anything else than
what I thought it; or, if it were a ship, then she was a
great deal too far off to signal, and might cheat our hopes
by passing away, as the other had done. But after waiting a little, and observing that the object remained stationary, I let go the wheel a second to take down the
glass, and then grasping the spokes again before the wheel
had time to move—for it certainly would not do to let the
brig come aback every time we sighted a sail—I pointed
the glass with one hand, contriving to keep it sufficiently
steady to enable me to perceive that what I had taken to
be the topmost canvas of a ship, whose hull was below the
horizon, was the lug-sail of a boat about four or five miles
distant from us.

I could scarcely credit my senses at first, for the circumstance of a little boat sailing in these seas, with some
hundreds of miles of water between us and the nearest
land, seemed truly extraordinary; but then it came into
my mind that the people in her had perhaps been shipwrecked; and this brought the further notion that, let
them be what they might, they would certainly be able to
help us to navigate the brig to some port. I was determined, however, not to let any excitement govern me. I
put down the glass, and softly pulled the line attached to
Spence. This time he answered at once, by jerking the
line at his end, just as I had done to let him know that I
was awake and coming; and in a few moments he arrived.

"Do you see that?" I exclaimed, pointing over the lee
beam.

"Ay!" cried he, breathlessly, rounding his eyes and
clasping his hands; "it's a sail!"

"Hold this wheel, Spence, while I examine her," said I.

He came to the wheel, and I took the glass on to the
top of the cabin, and, resting it and kneeling down, had a
long look at the boat. She had altered her course, evi-

dently, the moment she saw us, luffing and heading up so as to strike us at an angle. The swell that ran towards her hid her at intervals, nor was it possible at that distance to distinguish more than the sail and hull of her.

I told Spence what she was, and then inquired if my husband was awake. On hearing that he was, I came down from the top of the deck-house and ran into the cabin.

Richard raised his head as I entered, and, seeing in my face that I had news, called out eagerly, "Is there a ship in sight, Jessie?"

"Not a ship, but an open boat, Richard."

"An open boat!" he cried. "How does she bear?"

I told him.

"Are there any people in her?"

"I cannot tell yet. She is too far off," I answered.

"Have you put the helm up—are you running down to her?"

"No," I replied.

"Then do so, my darling, at once!" he cried, raising himself on to his elbows in his excitement. "We must pick her up, for, though there be but one man in her, he is bound to be a Godsend to us."

I hastened on deck and told Spence to shift the helm so as to run down to the boat. This he did, bringing her about two points on the bow; and now, as the foresail hid her from the top of the cabin, I took the glass and got upon the bulwarks, and watched her by steadying the glass against a backstay. She was sailing almost as fast as we were, lying over, and swinging on to the top of the swell, and then vanishing behind the blue folds, and shining like a piece of burnished silver when her streaming sides soared into the sunshine, while her white lugsail glittered like a square of mother of pearl. It seemed like being in the Downs once more to see this boat—as though she were some little galley-punt—sailing along, and I might easily have persuaded myself that, by dropping the glass and looking around, I should find vessels under way and vessels at anchor all about us.

But by this time I could very clearly discern that she was full of men—at least, she seemed so. I could not

count them, but there was a little crowd of black heads
forward as well as aft. I called out to Spence, "She appears to have a whole ship's crew in her."

"I can't see her," he answered. "Ye must mind an'
not let me run over her, missis. We'd best bring the brig
to the wind when we get anigh 'em, and stop our way;
or, if ye'll come and take the wheel, I'll go forrard with a
rope's end ready to heave to 'em, and 'll tell ye when to
put the helm down."

This was a sensible proposal, for I should have made
but a sorry job of flinging a coil of line into a boat; I
therefore replaced Spence, who went forward to watch
the boat and tell me what to do.

The sight of the crowd of men had filled me with a
feverish exultation. I strove hard to master the wild
play of emotions, and partially succeeded. But my heart
throbbed painfully; the excitement raised by a prospect
of deliverance from our dreadful situation made me feel
sick, and there was so strong an hysteria upon me that my
struggle to restrain the passionate desire to cry and give
vent to myself was a real agony. I could not see the boat,
nor even Spence, for, as I have said, the cabin blotted out
the whole brig, from the reef-band in her mainsail down,
and I could, therefore, do nothing but wait until he should
tell me to shift the helm. Amid all the confusion and
tumultuous hurry of my mind at that moment, I was
wondering who that crowd of men were, and what plight
we should find them in. When you sight an open boat
far out at sea, you never know what scene of horror you
are to be called on to witness. Father used to tell a story
of coming across a boat with three dead bodies in her—
corpses, which in life had been full-grown, robust seamen,
but which famine had so horribly reduced that any one of
them could have been raised by one hand by the smallest
boy in his vessel.

I was speculating upon the boat, and wondering how
long she had been adrift and how far distant she was
from us, when I heard Spence calling for me to put the
helm down. I did so instantly, and then, as the brig
came round, shifted the helm afresh to prevent her from
being taken aback, until I had her with her sails shaking,

and her way stopped. Presently Spence bawled out, "Look out for the line!" and, after another interval, there arose a murmur of voices alongside, and then a silence, in the midst of which Spence came running aft, half out of breath, and shouting, in a choking voice, "There are eleven of 'em, missis—all sailor-men! They're coming over the side! Will 'ee go and receive 'em?"

I at once surrendered the wheel, and walked down the port gangway, or passage between the bulwarks and the cabin, until I came in view of the main-deck; but no sooner did my eyes fall upon the men, than a low cry escaped me, and I stopped, transfixed with astonishment, mingled with fear and aversion.

The very first man my sight encountered was Mr. Short.

The last of the men was at that moment coming out of the boat alongside and tumbling inboard over the bulwarks; and, looking from one face to another, I beheld the whole of the crew of the *Aurora* before me—the carpenter, Orange, Snow, Quill, the mulatto, Craig, Cutter, Gray, the cook, Moore, and Green—all but Heron!

I stood petrified by this most unexpected encounter, and ran my eyes over them, too astounded to speak. Their consternation, on the other hand, far exceeded my amazement. Some of them literally recoiled when they saw me, and then stood stock-still, their mouths open, and most of them with an expression of terror in their faces. Then, one by one, they broke away from the kind of trance my apparition had flung them into, and began staring around as if to see where the rest of the brig's crew were, bringing their eyes back again to my face, but never speaking a word, and not the least sound escaping them. The alarm expressed in their faces was greatly heightened, and in the case of Dan Cock and Anthony Moore, the apprentice, raised into something positively grotesque, by their haggard, worn looks. I could not imagine a completer picture of a shipwrecked crew than those men made as they stood together in the sunshine, whose brilliant, searching light microscopically expressed their attenuated, downcast, and forlorn countenances. Their parched and burned skins were good assurance of the sufferings the sun had caused them in the two long days during which they had been exposed to its fires. They stood in the posture of men whose limbs were paralyzed; and all this, as I have said, inexpressibly heightened the looks of terror with which they regarded me, who but a few minutes ago they would have sworn, to a man, was as dead as any one at the bottom of the ocean can be.

"Surely, you be Mrs. Fowler, wife of the master of the *Aurora?*" said Mr. Short at last, looking at me with bent eyebrows, and such an interrogative expression of face as gave an extraordinary twist to his ugly features.

"Yes," I replied, scarcely able to control the deep aversion the man raised in me; "and you and the others there are the crew of the *Aurora*, who left us to perish on board a burning vessel."

"Some of us were against that," exclaimed James Snow, who, I thought, looked at me with a certain shame and contrition. "Here's Mick Craig and Timothy Gray as 'll tell ye all hands wasn't in that job."

"Are you alone here, mum?" inquired the carpenter, rolling his eyes curiously around the decks, and then bringing them to bear upon me again.

"No," I replied; "my husband is in the cabin; but he lies with a broken leg, and cannot move. You can follow me, if you wish to speak to him;" and I stepped to the door of the cabin, noticing, however, that when I said my husband lay with a broken leg, two or three of the men glanced at one another with an appearance of dismay.

I found Richard supporting himself on his elbows, leaning his head forward in an intensely eager, listening posture.

"Who do you think the men who have come aboard are?" I exclaimed hurriedly.

"Not the *Aurora's* crew?" he cried.

"Ay," said I, "as true as that the sun is overhead."

"Heron—"

"No," I interrupted, "I do not see Heron among them;" and, hearing their footsteps, I turned and found them entering the cabin.

Short, who came in first, made a stand close to the door. Quill and Orange stood near him; but the others

approached Richard more closely, Snow being the first to
pull off his cap, which the others did, one after the other,
until they all stood bareheaded. My husband fell back
upon his bolster when he saw them. Grief and horror
and rage, induced by the memories they called up, so
worked in him that for some moments he could not utter
a word. His bosom heaved fast, as though he had been
running, and nothing could have more plainly expressed
the sharpness and violence of his emotions than the death-
like pallor that made his face as white as my neck. The
passage of silence lent a peculiar emphasis and pathos to
this picture of the helpless sea-captain lying prone on his
back, and watched by the rugged group of seamen, whose
vile conduct had greatly contributed to bring us to this
pass. And yet, maddening as it was to recall the heart-
less brutality of their desertion of us, and to think that
this very brig that had delivered us from the perils of an
open boat should also prove an asylum for the wretches
who had coldly left us to perish aboard a burning vessel
—I say, maddening as this thought was, yet when I looked
at the men and reflected that, if they chose, they could
enable Richard to save the brig, and carry us back to our
old North Country home, my aversion and fear of them
gave way. I considered that it must surely be the hand
of God that had directed them to us; and that, detestable as their conduct had been, yet it was fit that our
gratitude to the Almighty, and the sense of our plight
without them, should make us receive them as men sent
by Heaven to assist us.

My husband soon recovered himself, and, having asked
me to prop up his back by a second bolster, said, looking
at Short, "You thought we were dead, no doubt. You
did well to leave us in a ship on fire. It was a proper ter-
mination of the conduct you pursued, from the day you
brought a curse upon the bark by joining her. You come
now and find me with a broken leg, aboard a little vessel,
with no one to work her but my wife and a boy. Now
that you have come—eleven of you; ay, twelve, for I
suppose Heron is not far off—what do you mean to do?
You see I am very much at your mercy. Look!" he
cried, baring his bandaged leg by pulling down the por-

tion of the trousers I had severed, "here it is, you see, men. I am quite defenceless, and my wife can do nothing. What is it to be?" He folded his arms, and ran his eyes slowly along the group of faces which confronted him.

There was a short silence, and then Snow said, "If nobody else 'll answer, I will. So far as I am concerned, an' I'll speak for Craig, Cutter, and Gray, as well as myself, we're not here to do you harm ; but to help you and your lady, if you'll let us turn to. If I'd ha' known you and her was alive, it 'ud ha' saved me some grievin'. So help me God, Captain Fowler, as I stand here, I've cursed myself o'er and o'er again for having made one to leave you and your lady aboard the *Aurora*. It was Mr. Heron's doing, and the devil was in it as well as that man ; but the men knew, if I'd ha' had my way, I'd ha' put back before ever we had fetched a hundred fathom arter leaving the bark !"

"It's the Lord's truth, Captain Fowler," said Craig. "There was more besides Jim Snow as felt the shame of it afterwards. Whatever our notions might be consarning the bark's complement of men, we never meant 'em to carry us so far as to leave you and your lady to perish aboard a burning vessel."

"But you *did*," said Richard.

"Mr. Short," cried Snow, turning sharply upon the carpenter, "you know it was me as came and reported the smoke to you first. You went smelling about, and said the cargo was on fire. I says, 'Call the cap'n,' and says you, 'I'll go and see if there's any smoke in the cabin.' You went below, and five minutes arterwards you comes up with Mr. Heron. All hands was now on deck, sir," said he, addressing Richard ; "and seeing the smoke drawing up middling thick from the hatches and elsewheres, we took fright, and turned to, and got ready to sway the long-boat overboard ; and in the midst of this comes Mr. Heron and Mr. Short, telling us to bear a hand, as, if an explosion took place, the vessel would founder under our feet. One of us sings out, 'Where's the captain and his wife?'"

"Me ! I sung that out," interrupted Craig.

"And Mr. Heron," continued Snow, "says, 'Bear a hand, my lads, with your work; I'll see to the captain and his wife.' Some got the boat over, and put water and provisions in her, thinking Mr. Heron was looking arter you and the lady; and when all was ready, Mr. Heron comes running out of the companion, calling, 'There's fire in the cabin, and the smoke's so thick that there's no getting aft without suffocation. Over with ye, boys, before she blows up!' and all hands, believing what he said, and being in a regular fright at the notion of her blowin' up, tumbled into the boat, I for one thinking we'd hold off a bit to give you and the lady a chance of joining us; instead of which, the carpenter hoists the sail, Mr. Heron takes the tiller, and we leave the vessel for good. Aren't I speaking God's truth to the captain, Mr. Short?"

The carpenter made no reply.

"Me and Craig and Gray was for putting back," continued Snow, speaking fast, and with much excitement. "I said, 'Mates, sooner than leave 'em to perish, I'll take my chance, and seek 'em in the cabin; and, if they be alive, I'll bring 'em out of it;' but Mr. Heron says, 'No. There's no use going back,' he says; 'there was fire in the cabin, and the smoke was so thick that it was impossible the captain and his wife could be alive.' Gray was on my side, and so was Craig; but the rest said nothen, and so we had to let the matter be. But I've cursed myself o'er and o'er again," cried the man, with passionate vehemence, "for having made one to leave you and your lady to such a death as a burning vessel makes for human people."

"Well, Snow," said Richard, speaking very gently, "I'm glad from my heart to hear you talk like this; and glad too to know that you are not the only man who would not have deserted us. I believe every word you say."

"Ay, but don't let Jim Snow take all the credit to himself," suddenly exclaimed Isaac Quill, stepping forward from the side of the carpenter and Orange. "If I said nothing when he and Craig was asking the mate to put back, it was because I believed Mr. Heron spoke the truth when he told us that the cabin was on fire, and that

you and your lady was bound to have been suffocated
some time. Ye've had to put me in irons, captain, and so
maybe you won't believe me ; but, as I stand here alive,
and talking to ye man to man, my words is this : that I'd
ha' no more thought of leaving the bark without bringing you and the lady along, if it hadn't been for Mr.
Heron, who said you was both suffocated, and kept all
on hurrying and terrifying of us by swearing that the
bark was full of fire, and that if we didn't look sharp
she'd blow up, than Jim Snow there would, and that's
making as much allowance for his honesty as he can ask
for."

"Where is Mr. Heron ?" asked Richard.

"Overboard and drowned," replied two or three voices
at once.

"How did that happen?" said Richard quietly, though
he could not conceal the effect of this plain-spoken piece
of news upon him.

"Why, it came about in this way," replied Short, speaking for the first time since he had entered the cabin, and
in a sort of forced way, as though he felt it was time for
him to say something, though not liking to address Richard either. "It was yesterday afternoon. We'd sighted
a sail, and Mr. Heron he stood up in the stern-sheets of
the boat to see her. There was a bit of a swell on, and
not wind enough to keep the boat steady, though she was
going through the water too ; and we was all looking
towards the sail, when we hears a splash, and found that
it was Mr. Heron who had fallen overboard. I can't tell
ye how it happened, and I don't suppose none of us can,
all hands looking the contrairy way at the time; anyways,
there he was. He came up once, while we were getting
the boat round, and Quill chucked him an oar ; but he
couldn't swim a stroke, and went down agin with the oar
within a fathom of him, and we saw him no more."

I scrutinized the faces of the others while the carpenter told this story ; for when I had heard that Heron was
drowned, there rushed upon me the suspicion that he
might have been murdered in a quarrel in the long-boat ;
and any one who had seen those men standing in that little cabin, haggard, rough, and wild-looking from their ex-

posure and crowding in the boat, would not have thought it very wonderful that such a thought should have come to me.

But there was something in their looks that persuaded me that Heron had met his death as the carpenter had described. There was no restlessness, no hang-dog manner; they kept their eyes fixed fairly and straight upon Richard while the carpenter spoke; and when he had ended, Quill said, "There was no time to jump overboard arter him. He rose but once."

"Well, men," said Richard, drawing a deep breath, as though the news of Heron's death had both shocked and relieved his mind, "you see what you've come to. If you are willing to work the brig home, here she is—not big enough to make you short-handed; and though I was stopped by breaking my leg from overhauling the lazarette, I believe you'll find provisions and water aboard to last all hands until we make an English port. As for me, my share must lie in getting some of you to carry me on deck every day before noon to take sights. That I'll do; and as to the past, since our present danger is as much yours as mine, and since no good can come of this meeting unless we all pull together, and work with a will and with friendly feelings, then I am willing that the past shall be the past—understanding by this that on our arrival I shall of course make a deposition as to the loss of the *Aurora*, wherein I'll tell the whole story, or as much of it as I know, and any action that may be taken upon it, more especially in dealing with *you*, Mr. Short, will be the concern of others, and nothing to do with me."

"There's nothing I'm afraid of that you can put into your deposition," answered the man, in his gruff, raw voice, but with very little of his old impudent manner left. "I always did your bidding—"

"I have told you to let the past rest," interrupted Richard. "Men, are you willing to turn to and work this brig home?"

"Yes, sir, heartily willing," said Snow, quickly; and in a moment they were all saying they were willing.

"Very well," said Richard; "you'll want a captain, which I can't make, for I can't oversee you, and can do no more than navigate the brig. Whom among you would you wish to give the charge of the brig to?"

"We'd rather you'd keep that berth," replied Snow, who, having put himself forward as spokesman, had plainly won the consent of the others to his answering for them. "Though you remain below all the time, we'll recognize no one else as skipper."

"Very well," said Richard; "but you'll want a couple of mates to head the watches."

Snow looked at Mr. Short, and then at Richard, and said, "Suppose Mr. Short is chief mate?"

"I am quite willing," replied Richard, promptly, which somewhat surprised me, for I believed he would have opposed that suggestion at once. "Now choose a second mate, so as to waste no more time."

The men glanced at one another, but evidently would not make a choice, until Richard said, "I choose James Snow. If that choice is agreeable to you, say so."

They all said, "Ay, Snow would do."

On this Richard briefly informed them that when we had boarded the brig we had found but one man living, and three men dead of African fever in the deck-house; that the deck-house had been fumigated, and all the hammocks and clothes belonging to the crew flung overboard; and that therefore the first thing they had to do was to throw open the deck-house and ventilate it thoroughly, and then turn to and get up some spare sails, and place them on the deck in the house to lie on. "As for your breakfast," said he, "all you've got to set about, cook, is to get the galley fire lighted, and the lad Spence, who, I suppose, is at the wheel, will tell you where to find provisions to go on with."

Some of them thanked him, and all of them kept their heads uncovered until they were out of the cabin.

The moment I was alone with my husband, I knelt down by his side, and threw my arms round his neck. "Oh, Richard, thanks be to God for sending us these men!" I cried, breaking into sobs, for the thought that one bitter anxiety at least was over, and that I should be able to be with my husband and nurse him, instead of wearing out my strength in steering and pulling at the ropes with Spence, flooded my eyes, in spite of all I could do to keep my tears back.

"Yes, indeed, thanks be to God!" he replied. "There'll be no further trouble with the men—I'm sure of that. We shall see old Newcastle again, Jess. And what shall I have to tell your father about you? How shall I ever be able to make him understand your courage and your skill as a sailor? Jess, you are a true Sea Queen, and that is my name for you henceforth."

We talked in this strain for a few minutes, he pressing me to his heart, and I feeling that our love had taken an immeasurable depth from our companionship amid the disasters and perils which had happened to us; and then we got speaking of the crew. I asked him if he thought Mr. Heron had met his death in the manner described by the carpenter.

"Yes," said he, "I do. Villanously as they treated us, they are not such villains as to commit a murder."

"I only asked the question to hear your opinion," said I. "I have not the least doubt that Heron fell overboard, and that the men would have rescued him had they been able. And though, God knows, Richard, much as I hated him, I cannot help feeling sorry that he is drowned, yet I am wicked enough to own that I would rather he should have been drowned than come on board this brig with the others."

"Drowning has merely saved his neck," said Richard, coldly. "The man would have left us to perish in the *Aurora*. He was a murderer at heart; and, had he lived, would have done something to bring him to the gallows."

"Do you believe Snow's story?"

"I do. I believe it because nothing could be more probable. The men had run up in a fright on smelling and seeing the smoke. The carpenter, quite as willing as the mate that you and I should be left to stifle, sneaks down, releases the mate by quietly prizing open the door, and tells Heron what the matter is; and when Heron comes on deck, hating me as you and I hate the devil, and witnessing in the smouldering vessel a fine opportunity for revenge, he frightens the men into getting the long-boat over, and then, pretending that the cabin is full of

smoke and fire, and that we must be already dead of suffocation, he terrifies the crew into jumping into the boat by
swearing that the bark will blow up in a minute. Snow
could never have invented all this. Such a story would
have required preparation. He never dreamed of seeing
us again; and yet, no sooner does he see us, than out it
comes, as only the truth can."

"But Heron and Short must have been content to sacrifice their belongings for the sake of getting away in a
hurry, so as to leave us to be burned," said I, puzzled by
this view, for I knew that the mate had a chestful of
clothes, besides mathematical instruments and the like.

"And what of that, Jess?" exclaimed Richard. "He
knew that, whether he left the bark in a hurry or not, he'd
have to leave his clothes and belongings behind. I don't
say that he may not have foreseen from the smoke that
was rising from all parts of the deck that the vessel was
doomed, whether the crew stayed to try to extinguish the
fire or not; but his hatred of me determined him to leave
us to our fate, let what would happen. Everything is explained by keeping that in mind, and remembering the
fright that the sight of the smoke would raise in the crew,
and the command over them their fears would give him."

"Strange," said I, "that we should not have heard them
getting the long-boat over, and calling out."

"Not so strange either," he replied, "if you will recall
how heavily I lay sleeping when you aroused me. The
fumes acted like an opiate on me, and deadened you, too,
though, I dare say, had you heard any noise you would not
have found anything unusual in it. Heron took care not
to come aft to the quarter-boats over our heads. The
men worked on the main-deck, where the cargo, coming
nearly flush with the hatch, killed the sound of their feet
as solid earth does."

"Do you think the fire was accidental?"

"Oh, unquestionably. I never doubted that after I had
got over the first shock and alarm. But, Jessie," said
he, under his breath, "understand me, Short is as bad as
Heron. They were both at one in their wish that we
should sink or blow up with the *Aurora*. A man is not
the less your murderer because the pistol he levelled at

you missed fire. Whether the law, when we get home, will give me any hold upon him I don't know. He can swear he never refused to execute my orders, nor did he. He can also put the whole barbarous cruelty of deserting us upon the mate."

"Yes," said I, feeling the hot blood in my cheeks as I thought of the villain; "but what would be thought when you proved that he released the mate without coming on to our berth to call us?"

"He'll say that he couldn't see for the smoke, and that had he stopped another minute he would have dropped dead," answered Richard, "and who's to contradict him? Why, he'll make a virtue of releasing the mate! He'll say, 'See what a hero I am! I saved one man, anyway; and would have saved the others had the smoke given me a chance of breathing another minute.'"

I felt the truth of all this, and could only impotently hope, nevertheless, that the wretch would be punished as he deserved.

CHAPTER XXXVIII.

A FRESH START.

AT this moment John Orange came into the cabin, and, pulling off his cap, asked with a very submissive face if it was my husband's will that he should turn to and act as his steward again, or go forward and do sailor's work along with the others.

"We shall want some one to look after us," answered Richard, "especially now that I'm little better than useless lumber. But how's your temper, man? D'ye think you can learn to carry a cheerful face if I give you back your old berth?"

"It's news to me to larn that I've got a bad temper," answered Orange, looking at us with his sour face, into which he could no more have infused an expression of good-nature than he could have sweetened a citron by moistening the roots of the tree it grew on with syrup. "But as the past is to be the past, captain, I'm willing to do my best. I know my dooty as steward, and 'ud run easier in cabin harness than in forecastle work."

"All right, then," said Richard; "you're at liberty to fill your old post. There's the pantry; but you'll have to sleep forward."

"I sha'n't mind that, sir," answered the fellow, evidently well pleased to be reinstated. "Shall I get breakfast at once?"

Richard answered "Yes," and the man went into the little pantry; and in a few moments we heard him clattering among the dishes.

My husband now asked me to go on deck and see what the men were at, and tell Mr. Short that he wished to speak to him. The carpenter was standing on the main-deck, staring about him as a man might who has purchased a vessel and wants to see what he has bought. I gave him Richard's message, on which he touched his hat—a civility I don't remember that he had ever shown me aboard the *Aurora*—and very promptly went into the cabin. I found that the brig was still lying close to the wind, the weather leeches of the canvas lifting, and the vessel without way, just as I had left her when I quitted the helm to receive the men. The crew were forward, most of them stripped to their waists, sluicing one another with buckets of salt water, which was no doubt a refreshment they much needed, after their long confinement in the boat, and as good a medicine as they could have hit upon to set them up and qualify them to go to work briskly. Smoke was pouring out of the galley chimney; and that, and the men's voices, and the sense of there being a plentiful crew aboard, so transformed the brig in my imagination, that, after giving Richard's message to Short, I stood like a woman in a trance, amazed almost to stupefaction by our sudden change from a condition of most perilous and distracting loneliness to the companionship of eleven men, not counting Spence, who would complete a crew of twelve active seamen!

But the truth is, I had already undergone so many surprises and narrow escapes, that my mind, so to speak, had grown used to wonders and unexpected things. In fact, I was falling into that state of thought which I have found

to be habitual among seamen who have seen much and
suffered much: that habit, I mean, of taking things as
they come, and allowing nothing to amaze them. It was,
indeed, remarkable rather than wonderful that we should
have fallen in with the *Aurora's* long-boat, after having
been separated three days from her; but then she had had
the same breezes as we; she must also have headed as we
had, and our reduced canvas would enable her to keep
pace with us; so, taking it altogether, there was nothing
miraculous in the encounter, unless the providence visible
in it must be called so. But it was altogether another
thing when I looked at the brig and reflected upon the
change the presence of the crew wrought in her and in our
prospects.

I walked aft and found Spence still at the helm, just
holding the wheel to prevent it from shifting.

"Why, they seem to have forgotten you," said I.

"No, 'm," he answered; "they know I'm here. A man
came aft just now and would have sent a hand to relieve
me. But I told him there was no hurry: I could wait till
the men had rested themselves and got summat t' eat, and
the wessel started afresh and the watch called."

"Well, Spence," I exclaimed, with a deep feeling of
kindness for the poor fellow who had worked faithfully
and honestly, and with such a consideration for me as no
born and polished gentleman could have surpassed, and
who also took a further interest in my sight from the horrors he had witnessed and the passage of dreadful loneliness that he had endured before we sighted the brig, "we
shall yet, please God, see the old home again. You have
acted the part of a true sailor, and I heartily thank you,
now that our anxiety is over, for having done all you
could to lighten my share of the work." And so saying I
gave him my hand.

He was a good deal moved by this, and embarrassed
too, mumbling that it wasn't for the likes of him to be
thanked by the likes of me; he had done naught but
what was right, and what any other sailor-man would do;
he owed his life to the captain and me, and it would be a
poor job if he hadn't turned to with all his might and
main to do what he could for us all.

Hearing a wobbling noise over the side, I went to the bulwarks and perceived the *Aurora's* long-boat riding to a line just under the quarter. Often as I had noticed her when she stood on chocks amidships of the bark, I had never supposed her so big and fine a boat as she looked on the water; she would have accommodated a large number of men, and I no longer wondered that the crew should have thought her big enough for the whole of them to quit the bark in. They had taken care to provision her well. There were three good-sized casks of water in her bows, and a bag of bread and a quantity of tins of preserved meat aft, together with other eatables, the nature of which I forget, though I remember there was plenty; so that the men certainly had not boarded us in a famishing condition. A bitter feeling of indignation arose in me when I contrasted the care the fellows had taken of themselves with their abandonment of their captain and me in a burning vessel; and, though I fully believed all that Snow had said as to that barbarous act having been wholly contrived by Heron, who was abetted by the carpenter, I was still sure that there was no other crew who, to a man, would have exhibited so much cowardly haste as they had in abandoning the bark without some of them turning a deaf ear to the mate's assurance that we were suffocated, and making one attempt at least to rescue us.

However, I could not but remember that these were the same men who had refused to let Richard stand by the water-logged Danish bark. They might be contrite now; sick of insubordination; well punished by exposure in an open boat; anxious to get home, and for that reason willing to obey orders; but nevertheless they were villains at heart, some worse than the others, but not an honest man among them, not even James Snow, penitent as he seemed, and no doubt was; and, though their coming was a most precious Godsend to us, I knew that with them on board I should not feel perfectly easy until the English coast had hove in sight, and the time arrived when I should be able to turn my back, never to set eyes on them again.

While I hung over the rail, looking at the boat and musing over her, I heard Short call out, "Now then, my lads, bear a hand and get yourselves dressed. One of you jump aft and relieve the wheel. The lad's been at it on and off all night;" and he gave some further instructions, but what they were I did not hear. In a few moments who should come along to relieve the wheel but Dan Cock, the mulatto, who had been the sauciest and one of the worst-disposed of all the men in the mutiny; but so much had the open boat, and the fire, and the influence of such repentant shipmates as Snow and Craig sobered him, that the villain had the civility to touch his cap as he passed me, and to keep his eyes down and to appear ashamed that I should see him.

However, I was determined that neither he nor the others should imagine that Richard and I had any resentment against them, now that the bark was gone and we had been brought together again to make a general effort for the sake of the lives of all concerned; for, thought I, if they should suppose that Richard meant to revenge himself when we got home, they might send us adrift, and run away with the brig, so as to effectually stop any intention he might have to set the lawyers at them. Therefore, when Spence had left the wheel, I went up to Dan Cock and asked him if he and the others had had anything to eat since they came aboard.

"No, mum," he answered, evading my eye; "but we're none of us berry hungry. We war eatin' our breakfast when we sighted dis hooker, and dar was food enough in de long-boat to gib us pretty good 'lowance each man."

"I hope we shall be more comfortable than we were in the *Aurora*," said I, speaking as kindly as I could. "You'll not be short-handed here, at all events. This brig is nearly two hundred tons smaller than the bark, and you'll suppose that the yards are not very heavy when I tell you that I and the boy belonging to the vessel managed to swing and trim them without much trouble."

"Oh, dere'll be no more trouble about bein' short-handed," said he, rolling his dusky African eyes upon me, for, though he was a mulatto, he was very nearly as dark as some black men I have seen, and talked with the thick, throaty utterance of the negro; "all hands is plaguey glad to be out ob de long-boat, and dere's ne'er a man but what's willin' to 'pologize for what's gone afore, by doing his dead best now. It war de mate's work; he hated de cap'n like pison. He'd come to me when I war stannin' at de wheel—you and de skipper out ob sight—and curse and talk agin the cap'n for an hour at a time. S'elp me, lady, as my name's Dan Cock, dat's de libing troof. It war him as started us agin going to Sierra Leone. 'Cock,' him say to me once, 'was you ebber at Sierra Leone?' 'No, sar,' I answer. 'Hab you any relation?' him say. 'Yes,' I say, 'I hab a moder and two sister.' 'Can you write?' him say. I say, 'No; was nebber taught writin'.' 'Bekase,' him say, 'if you knew how to write, de berry fust ting you should do when you git to Sierra Leone is to sit down and write to your moder and sister, tellin' dem dat afore dey receive your letter you'll be dead. Oh, Cock!' him say, 'it's an awful place;' an' he'd go on talkin', lady, till de pusperation trickling upon my head make my hair feel as if it war a bed o' worms."

"And I suppose," said I, willing to learn all I could, since I found him disposed to be very much more communicative than I had expected, "that he talked in the same manner to the other men?"

"Ay," he answered, nodding with great vehemence, "him and de carpenter—but him sheefest. Lady, I'll tell yah de whole story in de wink ob an eye," said he, letting go the wheel with his dusky hands in order to gesticulate, meanwhile steadying the helm by laying his knee upon a lower spoke; "de mate him puts it into Quill and me, and some ob de oders, to hate de notion ob going to Sierra Leone. So we make up our mind to oblige de cap'n to go back home again. We turns to, and talks it ober in de fo'ksle, and all hands agrees to make out dat de wessel's weak-handed, and dat tree ob de hands—Dan Cock, dat's me, bein' one, Micky Craig de oder, and Jim Snow de tird —was no good at all as able seamen. De mate finds out our meanin' from Ikey Quill, and he talk to de carpenter, and de carpenter him talk to us. Berry well; de cap'n puts down de mutiny, and locks up de mate, and den we agrees not to refuse to work de bark, but to gib all de trouble we can, and to desert her at Sierra Leone. De fire was a pure haccident. I dunno, I'se sure, who war de

fust to smell de smoke ; Jim Snow him say he war. You
heard Jim's story to de cap'n, lady? S'elp me de Lord it
war de troof itself. De mate and de carpenter war run-
nin' about all de time swearin' dat de bark 'ud bust open
if we wasn't quick, and dat you and de cap'n war smodered. It made us all hurry; and if I, Dan Cock, said nuf-
fen when Jim Snow him say in de boat, 'Let's put back,
boys, and gib de cap'n and his wife a chance for dere
lives,' it war because de mate took his solemn haffidavy,
swearing great oaths, lady, dat you and your husban' war
smodered, dat de fire war ragin' in de cabin, and de smoke
so tick and full ob pison dat any man who took but one
sniff would fall down dead."

In any other humor I should have lost my gravity over
the fellow's gestures and play of features ; he slapped his
knee, shook his fist, and rolled his eyes about as though
he were striving with all his might to work them out of
their sockets. All these contortions he no doubt considered necessary to convince me of the truth of his story.
I was about to ask him another question when I was interrupted by the arrival of several men to drag the boat
alongside, and get it on board; at the same moment the
steward came along to tell me that breakfast was ready.

As I entered the cabin James Snow came out of it,
saluting me respectfully as he passed me. The steward
had made an excellent display of the table, but best of all
was my husband's appearance ; the careworn, almost haggard, look had disappeared as if by magic ; there was a
little color in his cheeks, enough to make his eyes bright,
and in spite of the many marks in his face of his heavy
trials and the expression of bitter impatience of his helplessness which shot into his countenance every time he
shifted the posture of his head and shoulders, I had not
seen him looking so much like his old self since the first
week of our voyage in the *Aurora*.

"Jessie, you can take your ease now, my darling," he
exclaimed. "Remove your hat and sit down and make a
good breakfast, and, when you have done, go and lie down
and sleep away the rest of the day, for if ever a hard-
worked girl wanted rest you do."

"Your appearance is better than rest to me, Richard,"

I answered. "It is twenty-four hours since you met with your accident, and you are looking better now than I have seen you for a long while past. Surely that should mean that we have nothing further to dread from the fractured bone?"

"Not if I may judge by my feelings," he answered. "I never felt better. But it is this manning of the brig that has done me good. It cheers me, I can tell you, to hear the voices of the men about, and to feel that my darling may rest herself after her noble exploit."

"Hush!" I cried. "I have done nothing noble—"

"Do you think not?" he interrupted. "Wait till I tell the story ashore—describe you at the wheel, keeping a lonely watch on deck, your husband prostrate in the cabin, dependent for his life upon your love and courage! Wait till I tell the story; you'll then know by what others think whether you have acted a noble part or not! But take off your hat, darling, and let us get some breakfast. I'm as hungry as a wolf."

That was enough for me, and I instantly bustled about to set his breakfast by his side, the steward—probably guessing this was a duty I should not allow him or anybody else to discharge—remaining on the main-deck within call. The voices of the men rang with a hearty note, as they got tackles on the yardarms and made ready to get the boat out of the water and stow her. However, my mind was too full of what Dan Cock had told me to give much attention to what was passing on deck; and while I put Richard's breakfast by his side I repeated to him the account the mulatto had given me of the reason of the growth of the mutiny. He listened very attentively, and then said, "Cock's a liar. There's a little truth mixed up in what he says; but he leaves out the most important part. Snow was with me just now; I saw him passing and called him in, and said I was heartily glad to see that he was ashamed of the part he and others had taken aboard the bark, and I asked him to tell me honestly the reason of their revolting against a man who had done them no wrong, and who would have been a good master to them had they used him fairly. He answered that after leaving the Downs the crew took a dislike to the voyage.

They cast about for an excuse for refusing to work the vessel, and it was agreed among them that he and Cock and Craig should sham inefficiency. Heron had no hand in this. But when he found what was going forward he countenanced it out of hate of me, from a wish to embarrass me in all ways possible, and ultimately to drive me home, so that I might lose credit with my employers. The carpenter chimed in, and, of course, when the men found out that both mates were with them, they did not take long to break out into open mutiny. That is Snow's account, and I believe it."

"It seems more probable than the mulatto's," said I. "I suppose they may be trusted to work the brig home?"

"Oh, yes. They want to get home as much as we do. Besides, they pretty well know they have not much to fear from me. They mutinied, but then they can swear that I forgave them, which is true; and though afterwards they refused to let me stand by the Danish bark, yet they went on doing the ship's work until the vessel took fire, so that I doubt if any good would come of my prosecuting them."

"The mulatto said that the fire was a pure accident."

"Snow says so, too," he replied, "and there can be no doubt of it."

"Is Mr. Short to take his meals with us here?" I asked.

He looked at me and laughed. "Why, Jess, that beauty seems to serve you as the Old Man of the Sea served Sindbad. But he is mate now, remember, and has a right to live in the cabin. I'll leave him to choose. If he wishes to live aft, we must let him do so."

"He'll not do so if he has an atom of conscience in him," said I. "He'd need to have the courage of his first cousin, Old Nick, to sit and eat his meals with people whom he would have left to die in fire and smoke."

By this time, as I could see by looking through the cabin-door, the men had got the long-boat aboard and were busy in making and trimming sail. The sunshine poured with blinding brilliance upon the decks, but there were small clouds rolling along the blue to checker the streaming effulgence, and the swift coming and going of the shadows was pleasant assurance of a merry breeze being abroad. The carpenter had mounted to the top of the cabin, and we could hear his voice overhead bawling orders to the men. Sailors have a knack of putting a deal of meaning into their songs, and it was impossible to miss, in the way the men sung out as they boarded the main-tack and ran the staysails aloft and mastheaded the top-gallant and royal yards, their anxiety to let us in the cabin understand that they worked with a will, and that there was to be no more "sogering" among them. As the sails gave their folds to the wind the brig slightly heeled, and it was like being aboard the *Aurora* once more to hear the humming of the breeze in the rigging and the sharp washing of water as the stem of the little vessel broke through the bright blue sea, and flung it away from her bows in sheets of foam.

I asked Richard what course he was heading.

"Westerly, for the Trades," he replied.

"Shall you steer straight for England, Richard?"

"Ay, Jess, straight as the wind'll let me. Sunderland is our destination. The old hooker was bound to that port when we found her, and the consignees shall have their palm-kernels yet, and without delay, I hope, either."

You may suppose such talk as this set my heart beating gayly. Only a few hours ago we were in an open boat, in such peril that we durst scarcely call our lives our own; and now here we were in a stout old brig, manned by twelve seamen, and heading for old Sunderland, which is but a half-hour's ride by railway from Newcastle!

"And now, Richard," said I, when we had finished our breakfast, "how shall we manage that you may be perfectly comfortable? you cannot remain lying on the deck upon that mattress."

"I'll ask Short to rig me up some contrivance, a kind of stretcher on supporters, on which I can lie during the day, and at night a couple of men can lay me, mattress and all, in my bunk," he answered. "Perhaps it had better be done at once. Just call the steward, Jess. He's out there on the main-deck."

The man came, and Richard directed him to ask the carpenter to come to the cabin when he had done making sail. In a few minutes Mr. Short arrived. He stood awk-

wardly in the cabin door, twisting his cap in his hands. I
was pleased to find the rogue capable of sustained embarrassment. It proved, at least, that there went a thread of
conscience through his evil qualities.

"Well, Mr. Short," said Richard, speaking as though
they had always been the best friends in the world, "have
you got all the canvas the brig requires on her?"

"All plain sail's made," answered Short. "She'll bear
all the stun'sails she has, but I thought the men had better knock off and get their breakfast afore rigging the
booms out."

"Quite right; and you'll see that they make themselves
as comfortable as circumstances will permit in their deck-
house. I noticed a bit of a table there, and any plates
and such things which they may be short of they can have
from the cabin. See that they keep the place ventilated.
And now, Mr. Short, as regards yourself; will you join
us here?"

He hesitated, and looked around him, and answered,
"I'm agreeable to use this cabin for meals, sir, when you
and the lady are done; but I'd rather sleep forward—take
my chance with the men."

"Very well," said Richard, giving me a sly look;
"there's breakfast on the table—you'll find some hot tea
in that pot. Is Snow on deck?"

"Yes, sir."

"Then sit down, man, sit down and get your breakfast;" and down he sat, and at once fell to eating with
great appetite and relish.

"Mr. Short," continued Richard, "you see the sort of
fix I'm in here. Had I been shot through the head I
couldn't be more completely floored."

"I'm sorry for that job, captain," replied Short, answering with his mouth full, and the arteries in his neck and
forehead standing out like whipcord. "I hope the waitin'
before it can be set'll do the limb no harm."

"I don't know; I'm not surgeon enough to say," said
Richard, always preserving his friendly tone, which I
thought exceedingly wise in him; "but I'm going to ask
if you think you could manage to rig up some contrivance that will enable the men to carry me handily on

deck when I want to take sights, or have a look around and breathe the air, and that can be set up in this cabin, so that when I'm below I need not be confined in my berth all day?"

"Are there any carpenter's tools aboard, d'ye know, sir?" asked Short.

"Ay," replied Richard, "you'll find a whole chestful in the fore deck-house."

"Then," said Short, "leave it to me, and give me a couple of hours, and I'll undertake to knock up the werry contrivance that's needful, sir."

Richard thanked him, and said that the work, when done, was sure to be the thing he wanted. It was strange to my ears, as you may suppose, to hear my husband conversing genially with the man who had left us, meaning that we should perish by the most dismal and horrible of all deaths, as cold-bloodedly as if we had been rats instead of fellow-creatures. Yet, strange as it was, I recognized, as I have said, the policy of it. Had God suffered my husband to have had the use of his limbs at that time, he would, I may be sure, have put himself into a very different posture in his reception of and dealing with the miscreant who, with the mate, had done him the most injury that it lay in his power to inflict; but he was helpless and defenceless; in a sense, the carpenter had command of the brig. Penitent as the crew seemed to be, we were assuredly not yet disposed to trust them; and consequently both Richard's and my policy was, since the strange, capricious fortunes of the deep had brought the crew and us together again, to behave in such a manner as to make them believe that any hatred and aversion and resentment we might have felt was sunk, and, so to speak, extinguished, by our joy in having them with us to work the brig and carry us home.

Mr. Short was all eagerness to set about his job for Richard. It gave him a chance of showing that he was well-disposed; and he made such despatch with his breakfast that in a few minutes he jumped up, and, without addressing us, hurried out of the cabin.

"He's glad of the opportunity to oblige me," said Richard, in a low voice. "It's a good sign, for it means that,

26

though he may hate me more now than ever he did aboard the *Aurora*, he knows that the fire and long-boat have given the men's minds a twist that leaves him pretty nigh single-handed in his sentiments, and that his game is to act an honest part."

"Let us hope so," said I; "and could the men be got to believe that they lost all their clothes simply because the carpenter and Heron wouldn't give them time to collect them, for fear that we should come on deck, they'd not view Mr. Short with kindlier feelings."

"That's it, Jess," he exclaimed, laughing; "you understand sailors."

Here the steward came in to remove the breakfast things, and the next quarter of an hour I dedicated to making Richard comfortable, putting on fresh bandages, sponging his face, bringing him papers, charts, books, and other things he asked for out of the captain's berth, and so forth. This done, I said I would step on deck, to have a look round, and then come below and lie down and get an hour's sleep.

The crowd of sail under which the brig was now swarming along had completely transformed her. She looked, indeed, a fine, handsome boat, and as big again as when under topsails and topgallant-sails only. On my way to the steps that led to the top of the cabin I found Craig at the wheel, and stopped to give him a smile and a word.

"It is pleasant to see a familiar face once more," said I. "So much has happened since the *Aurora* foundered, that that event seems weeks old."

"Ay, much has happened, mum, as you say—more than ought need to have happened," he replied, shifting uneasily on his feet, and yet meeting my gaze very fairly. "I hope as you believe what Jim Snow said in the cabin about some of us being willing to put back to the bark arter we had shoved off."

"Fully," I replied; "but we'll say no more about that."

And giving him another smile, I mounted the little steps and stood on top of the cabin. The breeze was a merry one, but the sea was smooth, with a light swell rolling up on the weather bow. The water was as blue as the sky, over which the clouds, white as steam, were sailing, and touching the glittering, streaming deep with little shadows of violet. The air was full of those strange, mingled wailing and joyous notes which are yielded by the vibration of taut wires ; and, as the breeze poured out of the cotton-colored concavity of the mainsail and swept away under the foot of the cloths, you could see it skurrying in darts and rushings upon the rush of froth over the lee side. Every now and again might be heard a smart, fountain-like fall, as the round weather-bow of the brig struck the swell and tossed up and away a glass-clear green slope of water. The vessel was, however, evidently as stiff as a church, to quote from Jack once more. Her angle was very small, though the same weight upon a like surface of canvas would have heeled the *Aurora* so as to have brought the lee channels flush with the sea. And she was slow, too, as I might tell by looking at the passing foam ; though, like all round-bowed vessels, she made a great clatter as she went, and flaked up a wake astern of her that would have done very well for paddle-wheels. I could scarcely realize, as I stood looking around me, that a few short hours ago there were only myself and Spence to work the brig. The men had done breakfast, and some hands were aloft on the main, and also on the fore-yard, rigging out the topmast-studdingsail-booms, while others made ready to run the sails up ; and James Snow stood just under me, with his hands behind him, and his face upturned, singing out directions, and acting his part as second mate with all the gravity and show of consequence and importance that can be imagined. Forward I could catch a glimpse of the carpenter and Dan Cock sawing and hammering, and full of business over the manufacture of some contrivance that was to render Richard portable. Smoke broke briskly away from the little galley-chimney, and every now and again the cook would put his head out and cock his eye up at the men on the yards and then disappear, exhibiting by his movements and face perfect contentment with this new order of things. The scene was full of life and flashing sunshine and sea-beauty. It was a marvellous change to come about in a few hours ; a very reprieve, indeed, from death. I thought of my lonely watch, the dark decks, the superstitious fears

which every stir of the shadows had excited, my agony of
mind, when I found Richard with his leg broken, and
when I reflected upon the helpless condition which that
disaster reduced us to ; and as I cast my eyes up at
the white sails, bravely doing their work, and round upon
the brilliant, windy sea, over whose dark-blue and foamy
breast this old brig was sailing, and thought of the home
to which we were bound, and of the reception father
would give us when he heard our story, I turned my face
up to God, my heart swelled with gratitude, and I had to
walk to the side and lean my head over the rail that the
men might not see me crying.

CHAPTER XXXIX.

THE CARPENTER ENABLES RICHARD TO TAKE SIGHTS.

I WAS now resolved to take some rest, and entered
the cabin, feeling that two or three hours' sound sleep,
coming on top of this happy change in our prospects,
would make a new woman of me. The steward had
picked up my mattress from the deck and placed it in the
bunk in the berth I had chosen ; and having prepared the
bed with a couple of blankets, which had been well aired
and purified by having been left in the sun and wind
throughout the preceding day, I lay down and was soon
fast asleep.

When I awoke it was half-past eleven. The sleep had
done me the good I had expected from it ; the aching in
my limbs was abated, my head was clearer, and all that I
felt to need was the refreshment of a complete change of
clothes. But this, of course, was not to be obtained ;
though the prospect of wanting clothes for a voyage that,
in so slow a vessel as the *Bolama*, might, even under
favorable circumstances, last a couple of months, began
now for the first time to bother me exceedingly. The
dress I stood up in, the only dress I may truly say I had
in the world at that time, was a merino ; but then it was
new, and, though the sun and dew had not improved its

color, I had no fear that it would not last me until I was able to replace it. My hat, too, kept its shape, and the feather was to be made comely by a little coaxing. Also my boots were new and strong, and I had, moreover, come away from the *Aurora* in a jacket, which was sure to prove useful when our northing made the weather cooler. For outer garments, therefore, I was in a condition to manage ; but how was I to do for underclothing? If you who are reading this are a woman, you have but to figure yourself, who have been used to a plentiful wardrobe all your life, on board a ship, with a long voyage before you, not one of your own sex at hand to help you with loans from her own stock, with no better outfit than the bare clothes upon you, to comprehend my feelings when I stood looking down upon my dress and wondering what I was to do for clothes.

I do not remember that the least regret had been caused me before by the loss of all our little personal property in the *Aurora*. I was too thankful to God for having preserved our lives, to murmur because we had not saved our boxes too. I was better able to bear the loss since neither Richard nor I had brought to sea any object whose destruction would have been irreparable. All my treasures—such precious memorials as a lock of my dead baby's hair, little gifts from my mother, presents from my husband, and the like—I had left in my father's keeping. Richard's heaviest loss lay in his nautical instruments, books, and papers ; yet these were all to be replaced, and at no great outlay either ; and so, as I say, I was content to think that we had saved our lives, and thought nothing of the rest. But now that we were no longer in peril, and I could afford to think of my attire and comfort, I could not but regretfully recall the plentiful stock of underlinen and wearing apparel that had gone to the bottom of the ocean. With a roll of muslin and needles and thread I might have made shift ; but it was not to be hoped that a brig that had been manned wholly by rough seamen would yield me such things ; and, full of this little trouble, for little it was after what we had suffered—though, our other troubles being over, it did not seem so little to me then—I left the berth intending to confer with Richard, and see what was to be done.

Much to my surprise I found him lying on a rough but strongly constructed stretcher, the arms or carrying parts of which were sustained on crutches that raised him above the deck about three feet. The carpenter had done his work cleverly and quickly. The bottom of the stretcher was composed of canvas tightly nailed across, and the whole rude machine swung like a cot upon the crutches to the rolling of the brig. Richard laughed as I stood looking, and exclaimed,

"What do you think of this notion, Jess? Could I be more comfortable in a hospital bed?"

"It's capital," I answered. "Why, with a couple of men to wait upon you, you'll be able to go about almost as well as if you had the use of your legs."

"And only think of my convenience being studied by Thomas Short, of all men in this world?" he exclaimed, laughing again. "How the wheel goes round, to be sure! and how certain the unexpected is to come up! I hope the men didn't disturb you, Jess, while they rigged up this apparatus!"

"I never heard them," I answered. "I have only just woke up, and feel all the better for my sleep."

"Yes, you look all the better. They'll be carrying me on deck in about ten minutes' time to let me grope about for the sun. If this wind holds we should be feeling the Trades soon, though I hear the brig's not a clipper."

"Clipper or not, she's better than an open boat, Richard."

"Ay, my darling, for she'll let you have all the rest you want, and be a lady once more, instead of a poor Jack-tar hauling and singing out at the ropes; and she'll carry us home, too, and put money in our pockets, Jess," said he, taking my hand and kissing it and looking at me lovingly.

After a pause, I said, "Richard, I want to talk to you about myself. What am I to do for clothes—I mean for underlinen? I have nothing but what I am wearing. How am I to make them last until we get home?"

"Why, you can't make them last," he replied, looking puzzled. "What's to be done? Couldn't you turn to and convert some of the sheets knocking about in the berths into underlinen?"

"Upon my word," said I, "I never thought of the sheets. They are muslin, and if I had needles and thread I could make them do, I believe."

"Needles and thread!" he exclaimed. "If you'll overhaul the locker in the captain's berth there, you'll find a regular sailor's housewife full of cotton and thread and needles, little and big. Few sailors go to sea without such things. Open the locker, and I think you'll find it in the left corner, near a leather bag of money. I meant to have handed it to you when I saw it, but something took my thoughts off it."

I entered the berth and lifted the lid of the locker, in which I perceived a quantity of clothes, neatly folded, some papers and other things, and up in the left-hand corner, as my husband said, a large bag of money, and next it a roll of sealskin, which on opening I found to be a pouch with pockets, full of thread and cotton in skeins, together with several papers of needles, a pair of scissors, a bodkin, and indeed most of the fittings of a work-basket.

"Have you found it?" called Richard.

"Yes," I answered, coming out of the berth; "and it contains all the things I require. If I can only muster muslin enough from the sheets, I shall manage."

"If the sheets run short, use the table-cloths," said Richard. "But you'll find enough sheets. How many changes do you want? A couple will do, surely?"

"I'll see what material I have," I replied, delighted by Richard's suggestion and by the discovery of the needles and thread, for, though the sheets were not quite the sort of stuff I should have chosen in a shop to make underlinen out of, yet they would provide me with a refreshing change, besides supplying me with work enough to keep me occupied and amused for some days.

"So, you see," said Richard, glancing at me with a half-smile, as if he found something very innocent and childish and humorous in the pleasure the prospect of a change of underlinen yielded me, "that there is no difficulty in life that may not be overcome by looking at it steadily and patiently, and grappling it courageously. Think of a shipwrecked woman manufacturing a suit of underlinen out of the heart of a masculine old brig! It beats Robinson Crusoe. *He* found his tailor's shop on the back of goats; but you have converted an old Geordie into an underclothing establishment. However, Jess, if you find the sheeting won't do, we must keep a bright lookout for a sail, and see if there's a captain's wife aboard, and if she has anything in your line to sell or exchange. There's plenty of money in that bag. I did not count it, but I looked at it, and saw more gold than silver among the pieces."

And then, perceiving the steward approaching the cabin-door, he called to him to tell Mr. Short to send some hands to carry him on deck.

In a few moments there arrived Gray, Moore, Quill, and the carpenter himself, whom I took care to thank very earnestly for the capital contrivance he had furnished my husband with.

"Nothen to thank me for, mum," he answered. "It's a rough job, but I wouldn't keep the captain waiting. Yet, though it's rough, I'll warrant it strong enough to bear a house. Now, boys, all together and gently."

The four men seized the spokes or arms of the stretcher, hoisted it out of the crutches, and bore it without a shake on to the deck, I following with the sextant-case under my arm. I was afraid it would not pass through the little door; but Short had foreseen this, and provided for it by making the stretcher of the exact size to go through it. The men conveyed Richard round the cabin to the steps leading to the top of it; and after a little manœuvring they got him up on top, and, one of them fetching the crutches, he was presently sitting erect, supported by a couple of bolsters, his sextant at his eye, and as comfortable as any man could hope to be under the circumstances.

Mr. Short hung about us, obviously anxious to be of use. How easy this demeanor of his made me feel I cannot express. I do not say that we were at his mercy, because I had already discovered by several signs that the men—most of them, at least, for I could never feel

sure of Quill and Dan Cock—seemed anxious to atone for
the past by behaving well now ; but, having regard to
the helplessness of Richard's condition, any surliness and
insolence on the part of the carpenter would always have
kept us restless and anxious. As it was, though I did
not in the least believe that the fellow had a nature capable of regret for misconduct, I could not doubt that he
was finding a conscience in his interests. I dare say he
supposed that Richard could procure a very serious punishment for him for his conduct in the *Aurora*, and that
his policy now was to behave well and help Richard to
his uttermost to carry the brig home, so that he might
be sure of an excellent character for the voyage in the
Bolama, at least.

Well, as you may imagine, it made me very light-
hearted to see Richard on deck, breathing the pure air,
and capable of taking sights and navigating the brig as
well as if he walked about.

"This does me a world of good, Jess," he exclaimed,
glancing about him with cheerful eyes during the intervals of watching the sun. "I feel a new man already."

I kept my eyes on him as he held the sextant before his
face. I had married him for love, and believed when I
married him that I never could love him better than I did
then. But, in reality, how had my love deepened and
strengthened since! Handsome he always was, but never
so handsome as he seemed now, with lines of care and
pain in his face, and as helpless as the little babe I had
borne him, before death came to pluck that lonely bud
whose root was in my heart.

The wind was blowing due north, and had gathered
more weight while I had been asleep. But there were
topmast and topgallant studding-sails on the brig, and to
judge from her steadiness she could have carried half as
much sail again. The water flashed up around her, and
fell back in white clouds full of rainbows from her weather-
bow. The wind had deepened the color of the sea into a
dark violet, which furnished a beautiful contrast to the
glorious snow of the foaming surges. You could hear the
stem of the brig hissing like red-hot iron as she drove
through the billows, taking them with a certain rhythmi-

cal grace that made her motion singularly easy and regular. The clouds had enlarged their forms, and swarmed
in heavy-bosomed squadrons along the sky, with a shadow-
ing upon their skirts that made them appear like distended
sails, and here and there a prismatic light on their brows
as they rolled up towards the sun, whose heat was so
greatly qualified by their ceaseless passage, and by the
clear and rushing wind, as to render shelter from it unnecessary.

Although the crew had been divided into watches, the
watch below were on deck hanging about the galley,
where the cook was preparing their dinner, and among
them I saw Spence, talking with great energy, and evidently repeating, perhaps for the twentieth time, the story
of the fever-stricken crew, and his own anguish when he
found the captain dead and himself the only living man
left. And, indeed, such a yarn as this, coming on top of
their own experiences, would have gone far to account for
the improved behavior of the *Aurora's* men, even had
penitence had no place among them. Sailors are prover-
bially reckless, but only up to a certain point. They value
their lives as much as any other class; and, backed by
their own knowledge of the sea, are to be impressed by
narratives of marine horrors to a degree beyond the capacity of landsmen to arrive at. I could easily figure
Spence in the deck-house, surrounded by listeners, describing, in words they could better understand than I, how
first Bill died, and then Jim, and then Dick, and how they
raved, and how it was upon those very hooks that Bill's
hammock swung, and the dreadful sight the poor fellows
made when they were dead. Our men were fresh from
hardships, had escaped destruction in a burning ship, and
all the dangers of an open boat leagues and leagues away
out upon the high seas; and they would, therefore, bring
with them the right kind of mood to be impressed by
Spence's stories, and to make up their minds so to behave
that if any more disasters befell us they would be able to
say that they had had no hand in them.

In a few minutes Richard made eight bells, but, as there
was no bell to strike the hour upon, Mr. Short announced
the news to the men by shouting it out in a hoarse voice

from the top of the cabin; and at the same time he ordered the three fellows who had helped him to carry Richard on deck to lay aft and carry him below again. I asked my husband why he did not stay on deck and work out his sights there, and offered to fetch him all he needed; but he said no, it would not do to be dragging the chronometer about; besides, he wanted to inspect the chart and do other work which was better to be performed in the shelter and quietude of the cabin than on deck. And so, the men coming aft, he was lifted and carried into the cabin, and this time into his berth, where I stayed with him a while, handing him the books and charts, etc., which he required.

I then said, when I found he no longer needed my services, that it might be good policy in me, as representing him, to go forward among the men, look into their deck-house, ask if they were comfortable, and if their provisions and water were good.

"Yes, Jess," said he, "you might do that. And it also reminds me to tell the carpenter to overhaul the stores, that we may know how much provisions and water we have to depend upon. But he can attend to that after dinner."

I went forward, leaving him full of figures and calculations. The crew were in the deck-house, the carpenter keeping the lookout while Snow dined, and one hand being at the wheel. The time was when I would have gone among a ship's crew without misgiving, promising myself plenty of amusement and interest from a chat with them. Indeed, my old fancies of the sea had always included a ship's forecastle, myself sitting on a chest, a group of sailors around me telling strange yarns of distant countries and wild adventures; and, though the forecastle was the one part of a ship I knew the least about, my imagination was quite strong enough to figure a darksome interior, dimly lighted by an oil-lamp, whose oscillations vigorously indicated the plunging and rolling of the vessel, and whose dim illumination barely disclosed the bronzed and toughened faces of the men, and the massive, rugged details of the great bowsprit vanishing betwixt the knight-heads, the huge windlass barrel, the bights of great chain cable and the wavering outlines of thick deck-beams, the whole made impressive by the hollow voice of the blast sweeping out of the staysail and fore-course, and by the thunderous wash of the bow-wave as the vessel plunged into the roaring hollows.

But, though I will not say that my old love for sailors and their calling had been extinguished by the experiences I had gone through in the *Aurora*, it had been rudely shocked. It is sometimes one's first impressions which last longest, and I was pretty sure that henceforth, whenever I thought of sailors, the memory of the seamen who had revolted against my husband, and left us to take our chance aboard a burning vessel, would rise up and sadly tarnish my old brilliant and romantic pictures of the sea.

I hesitated a little when I came to the door of the deck-house and heard the men's voices, and should have returned ; but the carpenter was watching me from the top of the cabin, and I feared he might suppose I was hanging about as a kind of spy if I did not go through with my errand. So I stepped up to the door and looked in. The house was a fair-sized compartment for so small a vessel : a middling long table, that swung on hinges, went down one side of it, and athwart the top was a bench like a carpenter's. The men had got up some sails out of the sail-locker, and coiled them in rolls along the deck, so as to serve them for seats as well as beds : and there they sat, nine of them, counting Spence and the cook, some of them eating their dinners and the others smoking from a couple of pipes, which it seems was all they could muster among them, and which they would pass one to another, one man cutting from a small stick of tobacco—all they had—ready to replenish the pipes as they came round.

It was a curious scene, and I shall always remember it as one of the many picturesque details of those hard times. There was a lump of smoking salt beef in a small wooden tub in the middle of the deck, and from it the men helped themselves, cutting off pieces with their knives, which most of them had brought away with them from the bark, and eating the meat with biscuit and pickled onions, of which there stood a large square bottle full near the tub. They had to a certain extent lost the look of fatigue I had noticed in them when they first came aboard—the salt water they had sluiced themselves with had done that for them; yet they had a ragged, soiled look, too, with their uncombed hair tossing upon their heads, some of them in bare feet, their trousers rolled up to the knees, and their throats and hairy breasts left naked by their loose shirts of flannel or coarse linen. They stared at me when I put my head in, but went on eating and smoking and sitting still, though I noticed they infused a certain kind of respectful bearing into their postures.

"I have come from Captain Fowler to learn how you are getting on, men," said I. "You know, of course, that he is incapable of seeing that you make yourselves as comfortable as our circumstances will allow."

"We're doing first-rate," answered Snow. "A deal better than we did in the long-boat, eh, mates?"

"Ay, you may swear to that, Jim," said Craig.

"Do you find the provisions pretty good?" I asked.

"Yes, mum, they're all right," replied Craig. "It's a treat to get a bit of real junk to gnaw upon after two days o' tinned meats."

"It's a pity you're short of clothes," said I; "but for that I think you'd find yourselves comfortable enough, though with only a sail for a mattress."

"There's a slop-chest in the lazarette, missis," exclaimed Spence.

"So much the better," said I. "I'll tell my husband, who will no doubt give orders for the clothes to be distributed. Is there any message you wish me to take to him? Is there anything I can do to add to your comfort?"

One or two of them hung their heads, and I noticed that Quill turned his face aside. In truth, my kind manner and words produced the very effect I wished them to achieve; and it was a good sign, I thought, that the forecastle ringleader of our trouble in the *Aurora*—I mean Isaac Quill—should be capable of confusion and shame enough to render him incapable of meeting my eyes.

"No, mum, there's nothen ye can do, thanking you all the same," replied Snow, after a little pause.

"Onless, lady," exclaimed Craig, "you'll make us under-

stand that you don't believe there's ne'er a man in this
house who'd have consented to leave you and the cap'n
aboard the bark if the mate hadn't swore that ye was both
dead, and not to be come at for the fire and smoke."

"Ay, it's God's truth," cried Quill, turning suddenly,
and speaking with great energy ; "it was the mate's drivin'
and crying out that brought that sogering job about."

"My husband told you he believed you," I replied.
"But it's best not to talk of what is past and over. Mr.
Heron's dead, he can do my husband no more harm, and I
am pretty sure that you have thrown all your old notions
about Captain Fowler overboard, and are willing to help
him, who is now but a broken and prostrate man, to carry
this vessel home to England."

"Trust us !" cried Snow, bringing his hand heavily
down upon his knee ; "we'd do that for your sake, for
you never had any of our ill-will. Young Joe Spence
here has told us how you took charge and did sailor's
work with him when the cap'n broke his leg ; and the
woman who'll behave as you did, under sarcumstances as
'ud send most ladies fainting away to their beds, is a
woman to sail round the world with—that I take my oath
of ; and here's my hand upon it !" and so saying he struck
his knee again. A murmur of acquiescence followed this
speech, and, there being nothing more to say, I gave them
a nod and a smile and came away.

By the time I returned to the cabin, dinner was on the
table. Richard had finished his calculations, marked our
whereabouts down upon the chart, and, believing the wind
then blowing to be the Trades, had told the carpenter to
turn the hands up when they had done dinner, and brace
the yards up so as to bring the brig into a more northerly
course.

"Whether it be the Trades or not," said he to me,
"we'll use it as if we could reckon upon it. We want to
get north, not west, and one degree of latitude is worth
more to us than all the longitude put together."

While I prepared his dinner and put it before him in
the berth, where he chose to remain until after the meal,
meaning then to be carried on deck, I told him how I had
looked in upon the men, and repeated our short conversa-

tion. He was mightily pleased with Snow's remarks about me, and the crew's approval of them; and said that he wanted no better assurance of their good intentions than their recognition of the part I had played in the brig.

"Vilely as they behaved," said he, "they're still sailors; and if they've taken a fancy to you, they'll be loyal."

"Will you punish them when we get home, if we ever get home?" I asked.

"Not unless I am forced by the *Aurora's* owners," said he. "And even were I disposed to prosecute them, I don't see what case I have. There's no law that I know of to prevent a crew from making their escape from a burning ship, and leaving the master and his wife behind. Besides, I have no official log-book to produce. Also, I should be bound to declare that I promised to forgive them if they turned to, and that they *did* turn to, though sulkily and badly enough."

"Then, if I were you, Richard," said I, "I would make a merit of necessity, and give the men clearly to understand that you will not prosecute them when you get ashore."

"They know it. I have told the carpenter," he replied. "He asked my forgiveness for the past while he was fixing these supporters in the cabin; swore that it was all Heron's doing, and that he was now cursing himself day and night for ever having chummed, as he called it, with that wretched creature, and hoped if he and the others did their work honestly I'd let them go their ways when we arrived in port, as a term of imprisonment—the rascal has read the Merchant Shipping Act—would ruin him."

"If you have promised," said I, "I am sure we need fear no more trouble."

"No, make your mind easy, Jess; I only wish my damage," said he, looking at his leg, "was a smaller one. The pain is atrocious when I move that unhappy limb, which I am apt to do when I am not thinking about it."

"Does the movement of the stretcher, when the men lift it, pain you?"

"Not in the least," he answered; "I suffer only when I forget that my leg is broken, and twitch it. The freedom from pain when I am perfectly at rest makes me hope that your splintering of the fracture has brought the broken ends into their place. If so, the bone may reunite fairly, and I sha'n't have to go about with one lower spar shorter than the other."

"How long will it take us now to get home?" I asked him.

"Why," said he, "this brig must be an old crab with a vengeance if, with anything like favorable weather, we have not the waters of the English Channel under us in six weeks from to-day."

Six weeks! it was a kind of eternity to look forward to, when I reflected that he would be suffering all that time, and that no medical aid could come to him before. But fretting was idle work, nor would it do to let him see me downcast, for if ever cheerfulness was an obligation upon a wife nursing her husband, it was so to me in the presence of my poor, stricken, imprisoned darling, who had but me to talk to and cheer him, and whose mind was heavy, not alone with his grievous accident and the perils and hardships my going to sea had brought me into, but with the memory of the loss of his bark, that was bound to fill him with gloom when he thought of his professional future.

My reflections, however, were presently diverted by hearing the hoarse notes of Mr. Short shouting orders on deck, and by the songs of the sailors, and the flapping of canvas. Richard cocked his ears like a dog to a whistle.

"They're taking in the topgallant and main-topmast stu'nsails," said he. "When they've braced up we'll go on deck."

In a few minutes coils of rope were flung down, more songs raised, and the brig's heel grew sharper. We could hear the breeze humming like a distant roll upon a drum as the little vessel, by being brought close to it, made it seem to come the harder through the rigging, and the motion grew lively as the round-bowed brig courtesied to the surges. I waited until all was quiet on deck, and then, at Richard's request, told the steward to tell some men to come aft and carry my husband on to the top of the cabin. The pitching of the brig made me feel very nervous while this was doing, but the men took great care, moved very slowly, and swayed to the motion of the brig as easily and lightly as a pendulum.

They soon had him safe and in the full eye of the warm, sweet, rushing wind; and as it would be impossible for me to do any cutting-out on deck, in the face of a breeze that would blow my work overboard if I let go of it with my hands for a second, I deferred the setting about making myself some underclothing for a little, to sit by Richard's side and enjoy the glorious afternoon through which the brig was heavily crushing along, her yards braced up to a point that just allowed the fore-topmast-studdingsail to keep full, the water tossing in beautifully tinted crystals upon her weather-bow, a white band of froth seething and creaming past to leeward, and dancing like a path of snow over a hilly ground far away astern on the blue, foam-crested billows, while the little royals high above our heads strained at the black yards like imprisoned clouds seeking to break their bonds and join the graceful fleet of swan-white bodies of vapor which sailed in swift processions over our mastheads ; and the hollow cloths of the lower canvas were lined with the ebony rulings of the standing-rigging, whose shadows were as black as those of objects seen in clear moonlight, in the tropical splendor of the stooping sun, whose flying beams flashed up the ocean in the south into blinding spaces of brilliant silver, athwart which the spray from the breaking heads of the rolling surges blew in a kind of mist that might have passed for fragments of a great silken veil, rent by the wind and borne on its wings headlong down the slope of the bright, rushing, azure expanse of the mighty deep.

CHAPTER XL.

I SEND A LETTER TO FATHER.

I HAVE now arrived at a point in my narrative when I find that the sea leaves me little to say. The ocean never could be monotonous to me, but it does not follow that I should not tire and tease you by lingering over those marine pictures of calm and storm which could never miss of a deep fascination to me; no, not even when my mind was most harassed and terrified by peril. I am aware that many landsmen's idea of the sea is that it is nothing but a dull circle of water, sometimes blue, when the sun shines, and sometimes dark, when the heavens are overcast; at one hour smoothly sleeping, at another hour filled with the commotion of roaring waves, and with little else to break the tediousness of a voyage than the occasional sighting of a ship, the forming of a water-spout, or the hooking of a shark.

Well, it would be like admitting that a good deal I have already written in this story flatly fails as an expression of my own notions were I to argue against such opinions here. When some marine Wordsworth rises to interpret the ocean-mysteries, as the Lake poet did the glories and miracles of the earth, the field, the river, and the wood—giving a voice to that wondrous liquid universe whose green transparency is filled with many strange and many nameless and many unseen and unknown shadows; bright-eyed, silver-armored shapes floating like sunbeams over their golden territory; huge, rhinoceros-colored forms hanging like thunder-clouds in the heights of their own death-silent crystal realms—when the spirit of such another poet as Wordsworth, mingling with the colors and suggestions of the deep, translates the magic of them into rich words, so that the very soul as well as the eye of the beholder comes to the spectacle of the storm and the calm; the sunset that flashes a body of fire into the water; the windy moonlight touching with pearl the glimmering crests of the rolling, pallid surges; the gleaming sail that passes like a morning mist along the shining line against which the firmament leans its weight of blue folds—then to the student of such a poet at least there shall be found but little monotony at sea; not a fragment of dark green weed, not a foam-bell tinkling in the wake of the ship, not the faintest chord of plaintive music moaned by the breeze through the rigging of the vessel, but shall make the bosom of the ocean a field of surpassing interests, every one more pregnant than the flower-teeming earth herself, with suggestions to bring the soul close to that

God whose glory, whose majesty, whose terror, and whose peace that passeth all understanding every mood of the deep mirrors.

Sailors know that it is a good thing when a voyage leaves a person little to relate ; for a barren log-book is a sure sign of fine. weather and prosperous sailing. Fate had apparently exhausted her malice in burning our bark and breaking my husband's leg ; and from the hour when the *Aurora's* long-boat came alongside the *Bolama* to the hour when, under God's providence, we moored the brig safely in the Sunderland Docks, hardly an incident befell us that you would think worthy of particular relation.

On that same afternoon on which we braced up and headed for the north, accepting the fine wind then blowing as the Trades, which it really proved to be, the carpenter went to work to overhaul the provisions, and, having submitted the list to my husband, we discovered, to our great satisfaction, that the supplies were ample to last the number of people we carried for as long again as the time we calculated on occupying in making the voyage home. We made out some hundredweights of bread, many tierces of beef, a good supply of salt pork, with a quantity of sundries, such as flour, pease, rice, sugar, tea, coffee, lime-juice, and such matters, besides the dainties, such as jam, white biscuit, brandy, and the like, for the use of the cabin. The fresh water was equally abundant. One discovery that greatly pleased the men was a case of plug tobacco, and I believe no one was more rejoiced at it than Richard, who was an inveterate smoker, and who, when the news was brought him, whispered to me that he had been yearning for a smoke ever since he had found himself adrift in the open boat, though there were too many troubles upon him all at once, at that time and afterwards, to allow him to make a grievance of such a want as tobacco. The men had but two pipes ; but when the carpenter came and said there was a case of tobacco among the other stores, Richard made me go and thoroughly rummage the lockers in the berth he used, hoping I should find a pipe there. I searched, unsuccessfully at first, but, bethinking me of feeling in the pockets of the coats, I found two well-smoked wooden pipes, which I brought in triumph to Richard, who, giving one to the carpenter for the crew, handed me the other to fill for him ; and presently there he was, lying on his back, with a soothed and contented face, blowing out clouds of smoke with a relish I could not view without laughing.

There was also found a slop-chest full of clothes—sailors' shirts and drawers and coats—which Richard ordered the carpenter to bring up on the main-deck, and distribute such of the contents among the men as they wanted. These clothes and the tobacco completed the good temper of the crew. It was impossible to mistake their bearing. They seemed like a new ship's company. Every order set them running about like men-of-war's-men, and when I came on deck the same evening in the second dogwatch, a fine sunset in the sky, the strong, steady wind blowing, and the brig bursting through the surges, plunging as friskily as a young cart-horse, and yet sailing with nearly erect spars, though the whole pressure of her canvas, including the fore-topmast-studdingsail, was to leeward, I found all hands, saving the fellow at the wheel, squatting near the galley, handing their pipes about like Indians, singing songs. Such are sailors ! even when they are rascals—as I shall always consider the crew of the *Aurora* to have been—they are still children ; and, like children, who are to be made happy and set romping by an old rag-doll or broken go-cart, so a pipe of tobacco and an hour's spell of rest will fill Jack with good spirits and his mouth with yarns and songs. Indeed, there is no man comparable to him for delightful artlessness and simplicity of heart ; no man one can more respect and even have a hearty affection for when he is honest and a true sailor. Pity he should not always be so, for the sake of his noble and manly calling !

As for myself, I found employment for a week in making underlinen from the sheets. The material was somewhat stout for such apparel, as you will suppose, if you are a woman ; still, when the things were finished, they supplied me with a change that was a true luxury. And I may honestly say that I do not know what I should have done without those sheets, which Richard told me he had been very nearly flinging overboard. They yielded me

enough material to furnish me with three changes, counting what I had on; and only women who have been shipwrecked can appreciate the inexpressible comfort I found
in those rude garments, and how tolerable and even pleasant, in some respects, their possession made our voyage
home to me. Richard was better off than I, there being
a good wardrobe for him in the lockers in the captain's
berth. There were a few good linen shirts, socks, handkerchiefs, and the like, not to mention a whole bundle of
coats, trousers, and waistcoats, the cut and pattern of
some of which made us fancy that poor Captain Grange
—for that, it seems, was the name of the late master of the
Bolama—must have been somewhat of a dandy. All that
we found in that way, however, we took the utmost care
of, as, from a pile of letters we came across in the locker,
we discovered that Captain Grange had a wife and three
children living in Sunderland, for whose poor sakes it was
our duty, and a sacred duty too, to take the utmost care
of the dead man's little property and money.

What with sewing—for when I had completed my
underlinen I found other work for my needle—I say,
what with sewing and waiting upon Richard, who required to be dressed and washed by me as though he
were a baby, his leg paining him sometimes exquisitely if
he moved it, or even sat upright, unless I pushed him
into an erect posture with my hands, and then propped
him with bolsters, the time passed quickly. Regularly
every morning my husband was carried on deck to take
sights, and as regularly carried below again to work them
out ; and this business marked the passage of time like
the hand of a clock, for I would over and over again say,
"Another morning gone, Richard; how fast the days
roll along ! it seems but just now that the men carried
you first on deck."

I gave up worrying myself with fears about the consequences of his accident when the first week went by, and
his health and spirits kept sound. I clearly understood
that had we had a surgeon on board, he could have done
no more than put splints on the leg, and order Richard
to lie, as he now did, until the broken bones were reunited.
One great satisfaction the presence of a surgeon would,

of course, have afforded us; I mean, he would have set
the leg properly, that is, if he understood his business;
whereas the broken limb had to take its chance in my
hands, and there was the dismal prospect before my poor
husband of having to suffer his leg to be broken again in
order that it might heal in such a manner as to enable
him to use it. However, we should have to wait until we
could see a doctor before we could be sure that more torment and imprisonment were in store for Richard; and
meanwhile, as I have said, after the first week had passed
we could make our minds easy on the score of worse than
the fracture following the accident.

The Trades blew us along finely day and night, and
twelve days after we had braced up and headed the *Bolama* for home, we were on the parallel of the island of
Madeira. It was slow work, to be sure, showing but little
more than one hundred and fifty miles a day, or a speed
of between six and seven nautical miles an hour; yet to
hear that we were in the latitude of Madeira was to feel
that we were drawing near home indeed, and I remember
that when Richard said to me, after he had worked out
his observations, "If we carry this weather for another
twenty days, Jess, we shall be ashore, and in Sunderland,
ay, and perhaps in South Shields, yarning with your father,
at the end of that time," my heart beat foolishly, and I
wanted but a very little to start me off crying like a
child.

I enjoyed the sea more now than ever I did aboard the
Aurora, in spite of my husband's helpless condition, that
was always a depressing weight upon my heart. In the
Aurora, from the very hour of our bringing up in the
Downs, I was always uneasy and troubled; every day
something unpleasant was happening to take the edge off
my enjoyment of the ocean: either the men were grumbling or rebelling, or the mate was at hand to chill and
vex me with his cold, insolent indifference of manner; or,
if it was not Heron, then it was Short, and if not Short,
then it was the steward. But I was now free from all
those trials. Orange, it is true, could never alter his sour
face; but he took his tone from the others, showed that
he valued his own interests, gave us even more attention

than he had bestowed upon Heron, and though, after Mr. Short, I disliked him the most of all the crew, yet his presence was no longer a discomfort to me.

Mr. Short, of course, I was obliged often to see ; for he would come to my husband for instructions, besides eating in the cabin when we had done ; but he was no longer the rough, uncouth, surly sea-bear of the *Aurora.* He would touch his cap to me whenever we met ; he pitched his tone into the pleasantest key his growling voice could take when he addressed me ; and in his gross, coarse way did his utmost—I will not say to atone for the past, for he was no more capable of the kind of contrition James Snow, for instance, exhibited, than he was of lengthening his legs or shortening his body, but to confirm in my husband the promise he had made him, that the past should be the past, so far as he, I mean Richard, was concerned.

The rest of the crew were equally well-behaved. It was not only the being homeward bound, and the hope that they had heard the last of their mutiny and disobedient conduct, that kept them straight ; the fire and exposure in the long-boat were such physic to them that they wanted no more doses of that kind. Besides, what had they gained ? They had lost all their clothes but those they stood up in, and though I do not know what expectations they had as regards their pay, or of sharing in the salvage-money that would follow the carrying of the brig into port, I might easily guess they would tell one another that if any prosecution followed the deposition my husband would be forced to make, they stood a chance not only to lose their pay, but to go to jail. This would be quite enough to render them disgusted with the business into which they had been urged, willingly enough, by Mr. Heron, and to determine them, without any regard to remorse, which I never will believe that more than two or three of them felt, to do their work quietly, and take their chance of my husband's kindness by acting as best they could to please him.

So I say that, being relieved of all the troubles that depressed and kept me restless and uncomfortably expectant on board the bark, I enjoyed this voyage home in the brig with much the same kind of spirit I had got from

the sea when I was many years younger and went to the
West Indies with my father. The *Bolama* was a wonderfully dry vessel, both as regards her bottom and the
weather she made. She never required pumping more
than once a day ; and, though we met with some strong
winds off Cape Finisterre, and a high, confused sea, her
decks from forward of the deck-house to right aft were
as dry as a carpet, and all the water that came aboard
was an occasional bucketful that was hove or blown over
the weather forecastle rail.

I remember one afternoon sitting on the top of the
cabin at the side of Richard. The temperature was fresh
but not cold, and a strong breeze of wind a little to the
southward of west was sweeping the brig along under a
main-topgallant-sail only. The ocean as far as the eye
could pierce was of a uniform dark green, every ridge as
it arched over before breaking into snow being as trans-
parent as bottle-glass, and showers of frosty spray blew
along it like bursts of steam. At long intervals a handful of flying fish would spark out from the side of a surge
and quiver like a discharge of little silver arrows as they
vanished in the green fold of a farther billow ; and in
our wake were a few of Mother Carey's chickens, adapting their flight to the motion of the waves whose surface
they skimmed, charming my eyes by the exquisite grace
of their airy accentuation of the running seas. The sky
was full of large white clouds, many of them rain-laden,
as you might know by the fragments of rainbow which
hung about them like jewels in their brows or trains, and
here and there the horizon was gray with showers from
them. It was, indeed, the very perfection of an ocean
day ; the wind sweet, fresh, and strong, the sunshine
leaping among the green troughs and flinging sheets of
silver over the coiling seas, which looked to be struggling like imprisoned monsters under the shining tangle
until the passage of a cloud-shadow dissolved the white
splendor and left the dark-green billows rolling steadily.

Suddenly, looking over our weather quarter, I spied the
gleam of a ship's canvas hanging fixedly upon the running waters. I fetched the old leather-cased telescope,
and, after inspecting her attentively, made her out to be

a ship heading our course and apparently overhauling us hand over fist, as sailors say, under an immense press of sail. Richard could not turn on his stretcher so as to see her, but his curiosity was tickled by my report of the rate at which she was gaining on us, and he asked me to keep watching her and to let him know when she hove such and such canvas up; which I did until I was able to report to him that her topsails were above water.

"Why," cried he, "she must be the Phantom Ship! She's not sailing, she's flying." A quarter of an hour went by, and then he said, "Give Snow the glass, Jess, and see what he makes of her."

The man, who was standing near, took the telescope, and, after scrutinizing her a while, said that she was a large, full-rigged ship.

"She's got all three royals on her, and fore-topmast and main-topgallant stu'nsails. Dashed if ever I seed the like of it, sir!" he exclaimed. "She looks to be all foam forrards as high as the fo'ksle rails, and she's layin' over so that I'm jiggered if I don't believe she'll be showing her keel clean out of water to wind'ard."

"Jess," exclaimed Richard, "if that ship is bound to England she'd carry a letter to your father to say you are coming home, if we could only manage to chuck it aboard. Shall we try?"

"I'll gladly write the letter," said I, "if the rest can be done."

"Then go and write it," he exclaimed, "while we signal her."

I ran below into the berth that my husband occupied, where there were plenty of writing materials, and, seating myself at the little corner table, wrote as follows:

"Brig *Bolama*, at sea, May 8, 1860.
"Lat. 38° N., Long. 19° W.

"DEAREST FATHER:—The *Aurora* was destroyed by fire at sea on [such and such a date]. Richard and I and the rest of the *Aurora's* crew, with the exception of the mate, boarded this brig, that was fever-stricken and all her crew dead but one man, and we are bringing her home. We are quite well and in good spirits. A ship is overhauling us fast, and I am writing this in a hurry, in the hope that we shall be able to throw it on board as she passes us, as she seems to be a fast ship, and will let you hear of us some days before we arrive. Please look out for us at Sunderland, to which port we are bound. Cannot imagine when we shall arrive, but my superscription will tell you where we are at this time of writing. Our speed is about six. We send you our fondest love.

"Ever your affectionate child,

"JESSIE FOWLER."

This being written, I hunted for and found an envelope, which I addressed to "Captain Thomas Snowdon, care of Messrs. ———, Shipowners, South Shields," and then returned to Richard.

The brig's yards had been braced sharp up and the little vessel jammed into the wind so as, if time permitted, to cross the hawse of the approaching ship and get to windward of her, or to give her a chance of passing us to leeward without obliging her to deviate very greatly from her course. I quite understood that her passing close to leeward would give us a better chance of flinging the letter fairly aboard her than we should get by throwing it against the wind. Owing to the head sea and the manner in which the brig lay squeezed in the wind, her pace was now little more than four knots, whereas Richard and Snow had calculated, from the growth of her canvas upon the horizon, that the speed of the coming ship was a full twelve knots, and perhaps more. She was about eight or nine miles distant, and broad upon our weather-beam, the shifting of our helm having brought her so as to appear as if she wished to cross our weather-bow. We had some colors flying at the peak, and the fore-topgallant-sail and main-royal had been set while I was writing in the cabin, Richard explaining to me, when he saw me looking aloft, that the faster we could make the old *Bolama* spin when the stranger came alongside the better our opportunity would be to sling the letter into her. He asked me what I had written, and I gave him the letter. He read it and said, "You don't speak of my accident?"

"No," I answered. "The news I give is alarming enough as it is. If I told father your leg was broken he would be miserably anxious about you until we met, and was able to judge how bad things were for himself."

"You're right," said he. "But it's a very short letter, Jess."

"Ay," said I; "but it will be too long if it falls into the water when we try to fling it aboard the ship."

"Mr. Snow," said he, addressing the man, for now that Snow was second mate, we all called him *mister*, "is there any man among our crew capable of smartly heaving this letter aboard yonder vessel, should we succeed in bringing her close enough?"

"I'll undertake to put it aboard, if she'll come near enough to leeward," answered Snow.

"Very well," said Richard; "take charge of it, and rig it up as best you please. It's not of first-rate consequence; still, we should be glad to get it aboard."

"It's for my father, Mr. Snow, telling him we are coming, and asking him to meet us at Sunderland," said I, thinking that without this explanation he would suppose it had something to do with the crew, relating their conduct, or asking the ship to report the facts of the mutiny, or something of that kind, which might tempt him to aim at the sea, instead of the ship, when he came to fling the letter.

He took it and went forward, and in about five minutes returned with it, securely fastened to a piece of holy-stone to which was attached about three quarters of a fathom of small line.

"There, sir," said he to Richard, swinging the stone, "let yon ship draw close enough, and it'll go hard, with the wind to help me, if I don't post this here letter safely aboard her."

An hour went by, but it was a very short one to me, for I forgot the passage of time in watching the beautiful sight of the approaching vessel. I cannot now remember, if, indeed, I ever thought of inquiring, what message our signal was intended to convey. Three times were different strings of various colors hoisted, by order of Richard, who read from the signal-book, and told Snow what numbers to fly; and that we were understood was abundantly proved by the behavior of the ship, that altered her helm to pass under our stern. She was an English vessel, of about twelve hundred tons, built of iron, painted green, with a bow like a racing schooner. She was so deep in the water as to look a mere black line upon the foam that she heaped up all round her. It seemed incredible that so slender a basis could support the enormous structure of canvas that rose from it. She was willing to oblige us by nearing us as close as she durst, but she would do no more; not a rope was touched aboard of her. Onward she rushed, under the thunderous square white stretches of her mountain-high canvas, her studding-sails curving to the boom-ends, every cloth standing with the gleam and stirlessness of carven marble; a whole flight of jibs ballooning out from her long spear-like jibbooms; her green hull flashing with the wet, as it was hove up hissing with foam on the send and coil of the surges; while the westering sun sparkled in the red paint of her lower plates, and in the gilt tracery about her figure-head, and in the glass of her windward scuttles, and in the brass-work upon her white decks, which lay at so steep an angle that it looked as if a lead, dropped from her foretop, would have plumbed the water five fathoms distant from her lee side.

As she swept up to us the sight so thrilled and transported me that for the life of me I could not have spoken. Oh, what words, what painter's brush, what most eloquent and incomparable figuring of the reality could express, with any approach to the truth, the majesty and beauty of that ship in full career; her sails echoing in thunder; her iron-stiff weather-shrouds and backstays ringing out a hundred clear notes, as though bells were hung all over her; her sharp iron stem hissing as though it were red-hot, as it crashed through the green transparency of the surge-crests, hurling them into foam for many feet ahead of her, and turning them over into two steel-bright combers, which leaned like standing columns of glass under each cathead, while from them there broke a roaring torrent of brilliant foam, such as you may see rushing away from under the sponsons of a paddle-steamer, which fled aft in a broadening band that looked to turn the billows white for a whole league astern of her!

In two hours from the time I had first sighted her she was close to us; but then, of course, our own way had been greatly checked by the choking luff we had held. The carpenter had come on deck, and, hearing what Richard wanted, had chalked in big white letters on a hatch or board, or something of that kind, "*If we can send the letter, please post on your arrival*," and this was held up in clear view upon our taffrail by one of the seamen. There was a crowd of men looking at us over the forecastle rail of the ship, and a number of people, some ladies among them, on her long poop, most of them examining us through binocular glasses and telescopes, while somebody—one of the mates, if it were not the captain—stood on the weather-rail, holding on by the mizzen-royal-backstay, conning the ship, and perhaps ready posted for speaking us.

On she came, roaring and hissing, and her canvas booming as though she were in a heavy thunder-squall. Never before did I so thoroughly realize the horrors of a collision at sea as when I watched that deep and massive iron fabric tearing through the surges, and thought of her running full tilt into another vessel aiming at her at the same rate of speed. I literally trembled with excitement, and even had I possessed the strength of a steam-engine I could no more have flung my letter on board of her than I could have jumped on to her poop. I cannot say how close she passed to us, for water distances are extraordinarily deceptive; but she was so close that I could distinctly make out the faces and complexions of the women, and see the feather in the hat of a very pretty blonde girl trembling in the wind, and note a sort of alarm in her posture as the ship swept broadside past us. What they could have thought of me in my weather-soiled apparel, and of Richard swinging in his rude stretcher, I am sure I cannot imagine. But those were not my speculations then. Indeed, I paid little attention to the people on the ship's decks. My whole being was absorbed in contemplation of that long, heeling iron shape; the flashing swirl that leaped in snow upon her red plates; the magnificent stretch and shining heights of gleaming sail, and the wild ringing and roaring noises she filled the wind with.

I was startled by a loud and echoing shout from Snow: "Ship ahoy! look out for the letter!" I shrank away to give him room; he fell back a step, whirling the piece of stone with great velocity; and taking the measure of the distance of the object he aimed at with his eye, the stone and line fled from his hand and whizzed through the air like a projectile from a cross-bow; I could not follow it, but in an instant he roared out in a voice of triumph, "Done it, by jingo!" and at the same moment two or three people ran to the foot of the mizzen-mast and picked up the stone and line, which had struck the weather hollow of the topsail and fallen plump on deck out of it.

"Did ye aim at the tops'l, Jim?" bawled the carpenter.

"Ay, as true as you stand there!" cried Snow.

"Splendidly done!" exclaimed my husband.

"We'll post it for you all right," shouted the man who stood on the weather-rail, and waved his hand, a gesture we all returned, the people on the ship responding.

The noble vessel swept by us too fast for any further speaking. The brig was luffed to let the ship get well away, and in a breath almost, so it seemed to me, she was ahead, dipping her elliptical stern, on which was written the single word "Lilian," into the foaming billows, and leaving behind her a wake on which our old brig wallowed heavily, like a ship's boat sent adrift. In less than an hour she was a small leaning column as pink as the clouds which floated overhead in the streaming rays of the windy sunset.

"I wish she had offered to take our tow-rope aboard, Jess," said Richard, after the men had carried him below; "but no matter. She has your letter, and in a few days your father will know that the *Aurora* is at the bottom of the sea, and that his canny daughter is homeward bound, after having seen more of sea-life in ten weeks—mutiny, fire, open boats, the African fever, and a broken leg—than most men experience in four times that number of years."

CHAPTER XLI.

IN SOUNDINGS.

WELL, as I have said, with the exception of some rough tumbling off Cape Finisterre, we had all the fine weather our hearts could desire, and at last came a day when my husband said, after working out the position of the brig, that if the northwest wind then blowing held out throughout the afternoon we should be well into soundings by eight o'clock that evening. By this he meant that sudden jump from two thousand into seventy and eighty fathoms, which expresses the boundary between the waters of the Atlantic and those of the English Channel; and you can imagine my feelings when I understood by this that in all probability next day we should be sailing in sight of the English coast.

But this was a memorable day for me, from a circumstance I never could have foreseen, though it would have saved me many fits of despondency and a very great deal of worry had I been able to do so. For hard upon a fortnight now my husband had made no complaints of his leg. I had noticed that he would sit up or move without that flinching and grimacing which formerly accompanied the least motion that gave activity to the muscles of the injured limb; but I had only allowed myself to hope from this that the pain was much less frequent and severe. Well, on this day, when we had done dinner, and I was getting him some cold water to sponge his face as he lay swinging upon the stretcher in his berth, he said to me, "Jessie, do you know, my darling, I am not at all sure that my leg has not grown sound again."

"What makes you think that?" said I.

"Why," said he, "to begin with, I can move it without pain. For the last three or four days I have been experimenting with it, and at first the pain was pretty sharp, so in order not to raise your hopes and then disappoint them, I held my tongue. But now I can move it without pain. See here," and so saying he lifted the leg, and swayed it to and fro just as easily as he would have moved it before it was broken.

"Do you feel no pain at all?" said I.

"Not in the least," he answered.

"Why, Richard," I exclaimed, "this is very wonderful. Do you think, after all, your leg really was broken.

"Oh, Lord, yes," he replied, making a face. "Broken! ay, as you might break a pipe-stem. But I'll tell you what I think, Jess: there's good luck in your bonnie fingers, and by great and rare fortune either the bone put itself into proper trim to set correctly when you clapped the chafing-gear on to my shank, or else your loving hands unconsciously set the limb as though a surgeon had fallen to work. That's my notion. The broken bone has come together again and made a right union in the process. If that were not so, I could no more do this without squealing than I could shove a pig into a bag without disturbing the neighbors," and he waved his leg to and fro once more.

I threw my arms round his neck and gave him a hearty kiss, beside myself with joy at the news; and then asked him what he meant to do now.

"Why," he replied, "get up, to be sure."

This frightened me; for not only was there something alarmingly novel in the idea of seeing him erect and using his legs, after he had been lying prostrate all these weeks, but I was terrified by the prospect of his putting his weight upon his leg, and finding that, so far from its being well, he ought not to have tried it for another month or two, and then having to go back to his stretcher again much worse than when he quitted it. I expressed my alarm, and begged him not to dream of walking.

"Why, do you think I shall hurt, with crutches?" he asked.

"No," I replied, "for then you can keep your leg off the ground. But where are you going to get a pair of crutches?"

"The carpenter will make me a pair in an hour," said he. "A couple of scrubbing-brush handles and sockets for the arms are all I shall want."

Well, that I may complete this little episode, he sent for the carpenter, who went to work as willingly upon a pair of crutches as he had upon the stretcher; and before supper-time he brought them to the cabin, and they were as neat a job, considering that he had but very rough materials to use, as any instrument-maker could have turned out. The stretcher was put upon the deck; Richard, leaning on me, got up on one leg, the crutches were put under his arms, and he began to hobble about with such a face of happiness on him at the recovery of his liberty that my eyes swam to see him. No child was ever more pleased with a handsome toy than he was with those crutches. When he had them under his arms he stood gazing down at them and admiring them to the carpenter, and telling the rough, pock-marked fellow, who tried to look modest, that in all his life he had never seen a neater piece of work.

"Well, sir," said Mr. Short, politely, "the *Aurora's* crew made ye uncomfortable enough when that wessel was afloat; and its gratifying to me to feel that it should ha' fallen to my share to set you on your legs again."

"Come, Jess," said Richard, "we'll go the rounds of the brig and let the crew have a look at their skipper on his pins once more."

There was not much sea on, yet the brig rolled somewhat, and the unsteadiness of the decks made me keep close to Richard, with my hand upon his arm ready to uphold him should his crutches slip. The crew were at supper in their house; but Spence, seeing us coming, called to the others, and they all came out of the house and gave my husband a ringing cheer. How they could have uttered such a cheer, with the memory in them of their conduct to the man they were now shouting for, was not to be conceived. However, we were too near to English waters now to render any further speculations into their motives profitable. If they were sorry for their vile behavior in the *Aurora*, they had need to be so. I had learned to think well of them during this voyage in the brig, for they had done their best and shown as much smartness as can be expected from merchant seamen of their kind; but I could not repress the old feeling of

28

aversion when I turned my eyes from Richard's crippled figure to them, and reflected that though, indeed, they were innocent of the destruction of the *Aurora*, the fire was a fitting sequel to their infamous, unsailorly behavior; and that, by leaving the vessel without calling their captain and giving him a chance to extinguish or keep the fire under, they were as morally responsible for our heavy misfortunes and for the death that came close to us as they would be for the drowning of the helpless Danes, if they had not been rescued after we left them to their fate.

What Richard's thoughts were I cannot say; but he spoke in his usual cordial tone when he limped up to the house and looked in, and asked if the sails gave them warmth enough as beds, now that we were out of the hot latitudes.

"Plenty ob warmf, sar," said Dan Cock. "When de deck-house door's closed de place am snug as an oven. Isn't dat de troof, mates?"

"Ay, we all lie soft and warm enough, sir," replied Tom Cutter. "It don't give a man the convenience of a hammock, but I reckon a thickness of good sail-cloth's a better mattress than ye'll find in most fo'ksles."

Just then the brig gave a bit of a jump, and made Richard lurch. There was no fear of his falling, but when the men saw him lurch half a dozen of them sprang forward to catch him. He thanked them, and then saying that he trusted that before another day had passed we should be well into the English Channel, he bade me lay hold of his arm, and we left them to go on with their supper.

"If those fellows," said he, as we made our way aft, "had condescended to be as civil aboard the *Aurora* as they now are, the poor old girl might still have been afloat."

"That was my exact thought when they cheered," said I.

"We might, at any rate, have made shift to carry her to Sierra Leone, even though we should have had to scuttle and sink her there to put the fire out. In that case we should have preserved our clothes, and the gold-fish, and the old harmonium," said he, with a laugh that was half a sigh. "But I am a young man, Jess; my leg, I dare say, will be quite well in a week or two; and, with youth on

one side and the world on the other, it needs more than
the loss of a ship to sew a man up."

"If you should never go to sea again, Richard,
I'll not cry."

"Not go to sea! How am I to clothe this pretty little
figure?" said he, laying his hand on my shoulder.

"Father shall answer that question," I replied.

"What do you mean, my darling?"

"Don't you remember him once telling you that what
was his is mine, and what's mine is yours?" said I. "If
there's enough for him there's enough for me; and what
will keep you will keep me; be sure of that."

"Why, what strange logic!" said he, laughing.

"Now, Richard," said I, speaking out what had been in
my thoughts for some days, "this voyage out and home
has been enough for me. I shall always continue to love
the sea and sailors; but henceforth I mean to love them
only from the top of a cliff or from the end of a pier. I
have had enough of the ocean, and want no more. But
you'll have to stop at home too. You shall remain a
sailor to the end of your days, but you shall do no more
business in deep waters."

He puffed a little, shook his head, laughed, and looked
grave in a breath, and then catching himself up in something he meant to say, he exclaimed, "Well, well, let us
leave that matter until we get home."

It was a real disappointment to me, when I went on
deck at half-past nine that same night, to find that the
bright, strong wind that had run us into the chops of the
Channel had gone. The calm was unbroken when I
gained the deck, and the shadow of the night, pierced by
the host of rayless stars, intensified it. And yet, chafe as
I would, there was so much dark and reposeful beauty in
the scene, that insensibly my impatience melted away before it, and I stood near Richard's chair, on the top of the
cabin, absorbed in contemplation of the silent, shadow-
enfolded picture. It was the last scene of the kind I
have viewed, and that, maybe, is why I am able to recall
it so clearly, and why I find a kind of pathos in the recollection of it. Never is the beauty of a vessel—I care not
what her rig is, though the larger she be and the nearer

she comes to being a full-rigged ship the better—more
solemn than when, with all sail set, she lies motionless
upon the deep, and the darkness of night makes a mystery of her towering fabric of canvas, and the stars
wave among her slender rigging as she leans with the
silent breathing of the sea. On this night the stars were
almost as bright as in the tropics, and their light fell
straight into the water, filling the depths with silver lines,
which there was not the least breath of air to make tremulous. The influence upon the mind of that immense
gloom, those shining stars, and the huge and visionary
space of water, heaving in its sleep, was like that of
solemn music. The pale stretch of spanker overhead,
extending from beyond the taffrail to the glimmering
mainmast, hung in the gloom like a surface of phosphorus. The shrouds and backstays soared into the
darkness and were lost. Forward all was dark, but there
was a light in the deck-house that made a little haze, and
in that faint illumination were just to be seen the loom of
the foremast, a short length of cable, a few coils of running
rigging on the belaying-pins, and such matters. There
was one man on the forecastle on the lookout; where the
rest of the watch were I could not say, but I might suppose that a single cry from my husband or James Snow,
who had the watch, would fill the decks with them at
once. Sometimes the man on the lookout would stand
motionless, when his figure would be clearly marked
against the sky, that was a vast galaxy, amid which now
and again a meteoric light flashed and vanished in dust.
The movement of the sea was so steady, the swell so
broad, and the intervals between the rolls of the brig so
long that the rudder was almost stirless, and the wheel-
chains clanked feebly only when her bows lifted and she
dipped her counter in the black water.

At times Richard would rise on his crutches, and we
would move here and there, stopping at intervals to look
around, and beholding always the same huge, oily, gray-
black surface stretching down to the stars, and reflecting
their lustre with the flashful brilliancy of mirrored moonlight. Those spaces of silent canvas overhead, delicately
stretched, their pale apexes like summer clouds, made the

picture like a dream. The masts and yards of the brig, the network of rigging, took in the gloom an appearance of the most exquisite fragility. The shadows magnified their heights into a star-searching altitude of marble-like sail, and the whole fabric took a mystery of color that seemed to lift it out of the sphere of human creation. As I cast my eyes upon those still and pallid heights, and then on the silent length of dark deck, to where the arching foot of the foresail left exposed the glittering stars shining over the bows, and looking like small white fires kindled upon the forecastle rail, and then round upon the black and breathless leagues of ocean, I could not help saying to Richard that few things more deeply illustrate man's kinship with the Creator than the familiar but always impressive wonder of strength and beauty, a ship.

"Quite true, Jess," said he; "though, unhappily, a ship is not always a wonder of strength, and seldomer yet a wonder of beauty."

"Oh, you are too literal," said I. "You may be a good sailor, but you are no poet, Richard."

"You're right, my darling. I was born a poet; but weevils and salt pork have undone me."

The swell, if indeed this long and solemn respiration could be so called, was now right aft, and the swinging brig would presently have it on her port beam. The clank and grind of the wheel-chains was a little more frequent now, the sob and moan of water under the counter more defined; at times the light sails rattled hopefully, as though they felt a stir of wind up there, but the mainsail, that was hauled up, hung its folds with little perceptible motion, and the brig seemed to be as sound asleep as the sea. From water-line to water-line the great arch of blue-black sky was cloudless—a May-night heaven, full of balm, and fit for the green lands of the old home we were nearing to slumber under.

A man came out of the deck-house with a lighted pipe in his mouth. I could see the glow of the hard-sucked tobacco in the tip of red light that centred the black outline of his head, like the blazing eye of the goat in Crusoe's cavern. He stood a moment gazing our way, then joined the man on the lookout. They paced their short

walk lightly, but as steadily as the ticking of a clock, and
I could catch the growl of their voices whenever a stoop
of the bow gave a sweep to the fore-course and sent a
little rush of dewy air to where Richard and I stood.
The solemnity of this calm was deeper than any I remember having experienced. The soft moaning wash of water
alongside, the vague whispers of circling draughts of air
up aloft, the flapping of the lighter canvas, were sounds
which did not in the least degree break the spell of peace;
on the contrary, they appeared to me to increase the intensity of it by furnishing to the ear those delicate contrasts by which an ocean silence is best to be measured.

As I stood with my hand on Richard's arm, and my eye
fixed upon one of the richest of the stars, my thoughts
went to Newcastle, to Elswick, to the cemetery in which
our darling lay. Oh, there would be peace there on such
a night as this. The Durham hills would stand dark
under the stars, and the voice of the river flowing in the
valley inaudible. But could even the peace amid which
my beloved little one was sleeping—could even the peace
of a night whose shadow took a sanctity from the holy
dead upon whose graves it rested, and a beauty from the
distant looming hills and the gleaming coil of river and
the virginal sweetness of the young year sleeping in trees
and shrubs and flowers, compare with *this* peace, and *this*
beauty? I looked up at the tall masts, and round upon
the deep ocean, whose ebony bosom the night had made
another sky of by the glories it had kindled in it. Well,
I did feel the peace of such a scene as I am here most im-
perfectly describing, as such a peace on shore never could
be felt by me. To be alone on the deep, in a night of
starlit tranquillity, with never a cloud to sully the vernal
beauty of the sky, with never a break to intercept your
gaze into the farthest reaches of the visionary distance,
is to realize something of the magnitude of eternity,
something of the unspeakable being and presence of God,
and that whole and perfect repose of the spirit which can
only be felt by one from whom shore life, with all its sorrows and temptations and strifes, is sundered by distance
as large and impressive to the mind as time.

Suddenly the light sails flapped. The royals were aback,

and right ahead the reflected starlight was broken within a dark space of water, clear-lined, and quickly broadening, like smoke flowing our way.

"Man the port main-braces!" shouted Snow.

The men came tumbling along, making a hollow patter on the deck with their feet. They looked like a gang of shadows. Coils of running rigging were thrown down with a noise that vexed the ear, accustomed for some time to no harsher sound than the melodious gurgle of water or the soft waving of the cloud-like sails. All being gone to windward, the men tailed on to the lee-braces. Half-a-dozen hoarse songs were raised, and the blocks squealed as the ropes set the sheaves revolving, and the chain topsail-sheets rattled, and the trusses creaked as the lower yards swept round.

"So! well; the main-topsail-yard! too much the royal yard! slacken a bit to leeward! get the main-sheet aft!"

Every sail was now silent and drawing. The brig stood on a level keel to it, but she was already breaking the water at her bows, and astern ran a thin wake glancing in eddies and bubbles into the darkness of the farther sea, while the silence was broken by the hoarse chorus of the men, singing as they boarded the main-tack,

> "For we are homeward bou-hou-hound,
> For we are homeward bound."

CHAPTER XLII.

HOME.

On the night of the 22d of May we were abreast of the Yorkshire coast, somewhere betwixt Flamboro' Head and Whitby, and Richard said that he hoped to be in sight of Sunderland early next morning.

I shall never forget the feelings with which I withdrew to my berth to sleep for the last time in the bunk that had furnished me with a bed ever since I had been aboard the *Bolama*. All the incidents of the voyage out in the *Aurora* and home in the brig arose before me; and few hearts ever felt more grateful for great mercies shown than mine did when I knelt down in the little berth that night to say my prayers. From the hour we had entered the English Channel Richard had kept the deck, more or less, which he managed to do very well with his crutches, not choosing to trust the navigation of the brig through those perilous waters to Mr. Short. This night he told me he was not likely to close his eyes, a resolution I did not attempt to combat, first, because I knew I should not be able to dissuade him from it ; and secondly, because, drawing into the land as we were, I quite saw it would never do to leave the brig all through the darkness in the hands of two uncertificated men, as Snow and the carpenter were. I kept him company until nearly eleven o'clock, and then, making him promise to call me the moment the Sunderland coast should heave in sight, I went to bed, as I have written, first thanking God with streaming eyes for his long, merciful care of me and my dear husband.

Well, I lay tossing and thinking a long, long while, hearing the patting of Richard's crutches, as he crossed and moved about the cabin-top over my head ; but it did not seem to me that I had slept longer than an hour when I was awakened by a hand on my shoulder ; and who should it be but Richard come to tell me that it was half-past seven o'clock, and that Sunderland was not above five miles distant.

No sailor responding to a shout of "Tumble up for your lives, men !" ever sprang out of bed with more breathless haste than I did. My excitement and impatience were so great that I could hardly stay to dress myself. In five minutes I was dressed and on deck, and then I saw stretching all along our port beam the low, dark cliffs of Durham, with the Yorkshire coast fading on our weather quarter.

I stood looking with clasped hands and rapt eyes. What emotion is comparable to the sudden, yearning joy that is kindled in the mind by the first sight of the shores of one's own home after a long voyage ? But think how the transport is heightened in one who has been in dire peril, who has been in a situation where he has thought of home as a dying person would, recalling it with sighs and tears, as a beloved object, never more to be seen by him!

"Oh, Richard!" I cried, "do you think father will be waiting for us?"

"If he is not," he answered tenderly, taking and fondling my hand, "it will not be long before we have him with us."

The wind was light and off-shore, forcing us to lie with our yards braced hard against the lee rigging, and barely enabling us to head up for the port, whose position on the coast was marked by a haze of brownish smoke discoloring the sky in the north and west. It was a beautiful May morning, warm as a June day, the sky clear, save in the east, where there hovered a bank of pearl-colored clouds, and the sea smooth and blue that way, though changing into a sparkling green as it approached the land.

"You had better go below and pack up, Jessie," said Richard, laughing.

"Yes," said I; "and when I have done, however shall we manage to get all our luggage ashore!"

"Never mind," said he, still laughing; "we return, it is true, with a beggarly account of empty boxes, but there's money enough in this old bottom to enable us to walk in silk attire, and silver hae, or haw, or hoo—what's the true twist of the confounded spelling?—to spare."

Well, we went on creeping and crawling in this way until the steward told us breakfast was ready; but you may suppose that neither of us lingered over the last meal we should ever take aboard the *Bolama*, and when we went on deck again there were the Roker houses clearly to be seen with the naked eye, and a tugboat making for us as hard as ever her wheels could urge her, with a trail of smoke following in her wake like a mighty corkscrew. In twenty minutes she was alongside, asking us where we were bound to, and if she should tow us. My heart went out to the bluff seaman on the bridge. No music ever fell more sweetly on my ear than his rough north-country accent. Well do I remember that tug. The sight of her sent me back to that day when I watched the steamer that had towed us out of the Tyne returning to the river I had then believed I should not set eyes on

again for months. I was too much excited, however, to
take close notice of what passed ; and that was one reason,
I suppose, why I was greatly astonished by the apparition
of a pilot suddenly coming over the side from a cobble-
built boat, that had crept up to us quite unseen by me.
He knew my husband, and stood staring when he saw
him on crutches.

"Why, Captain Fowler !" he exclaimed, glancing with
an amazed face round the brig, "what brings *you* here?
Bill so-and-so (naming the man) told me ye had command
of the *Aurora*, and that ye were gone for six or eight
months—or was it a year ?"

"Ay," replied Richard, "Bill spoke the truth in that ;
which means, you see, that there's a bit of a yarn to spin."

"But what have ye done with the bark, captain?"
cried the pilot.

"Why, man, I've left her to the nor'west of the Gulf of
Guinea, out of soundings, and therefore I can't tell you
how many fathoms deep."

"Well, well !" said the pilot, "ye shall give it me all
presently." And forthwith he addressed himself to the
duties he had come aboard to discharge.

In a moment the order was given to let go and clew
up ; and while the tug manœuvred with the tow-rope,
the crew sprang about, hauling with all their might, and
singing out at the top of their voices. Sail after sail was
clewed up, and as the hands went aloft to stow the canvas
the steamer lifted the bight of the hawser out of the
water, and the brig followed, spurning the foam from the
paddle-wheels with her broad bows, and making the stem
of the pilot-boat, that was attached to us by a line astern,
hiss as it swept through the smooth wake formed by the
bottom of the brig upon the surface of froth that was
flung in seething cataracts from the wheels of the tug.

Richard stood near me, talking to the pilot, and telling
him all about the voyage and the particulars of the loss
of the *Aurora*. He often referred to me, and I would
catch the pilot staring hard ; but I took very little notice
of what was said, for my thoughts were with the land we
were rapidly approaching, and I had no attention to give
to anything else. By this time the harbor, the docks, the

town of Sunderland lay all clearly to be seen, with a foreground of ships' masts and spars — a dense, exquisitely
complicated cluster — behind which here and there the
windows of a house caught the light of the flashing sun,
that now stood high above the horizon of the North Sea.
Away past the north pier I could see the yellow Roker
Sands, with the roofs of the houses on the summit projecting their tops above the soft chocolate of the long,
low, stubborn-looking range of cliffs ; farther yet was the
cavernous and wave-washed Holey Rock, while in the far
north, blue in the distance, and hanging with a film of
white under it upon the delicate green of the ocean that
way, was Souter Point, beyond which trended a line of
coast, that, after a few miles, gaped to let flow the waters
of my well-loved Tyne. As we neared the harbor, a fine
bark, fresh from port and well freighted, as I might suppose, with coal, swept past us, under topsails, her topgallant-sails flying, and hands aloft on the royal yards.
Some people on the quarter-deck waved their hats to us
—a mere sailor's adieu—for we were too far separated to
distinguish faces.

"That's the *Albion*, bound to Pernambuco," said the
pilot.

She was not unlike the *Aurora*, and I watched her a
minute or two for that reason. Bound to Pernambuco!
Would she ever get there, I wondered. The *Aurora*, too,
had started bravely, lifting her beautiful wings high,
heeling to the iron-cold February wind, and dominating
the sea like the queen that she was. My breath came and
went quickly as I thought of her now—all her regal stateliness dissolved, ay, not less completely than had she been
a radiant soap-bubble blowing along over the ocean-
billows; and of all the brave and noble show she made
no fragment remaining, save the few bits of charred timber we saw floating on the calm sea when the smoke of
the explosion settled away, and we found ourselves alone
in a little open boat.

But here was home right before my eyes, almost within a stone's-throw; it was not a moment for miserable
reflections. There were a number of people on the north
pier, and as we entered the mouth of the river I ran

my eye along the faces with a beating heart until, seeing a figure standing on the upper end of the pier, wildly
waving his hat, and in such a demonstrative fashion that
the people near him had opened so as to leave him a
clear space for his vehement gestures, I shrieked out,
"Richard! Richard! there's father!"

"Ay, there he is!" shouted Richard; and putting his
hand to the side of his mouth, "How are you, captain?
how are you, captain? here we are—sound enough! here's
Jessie, full of spirits, and in grand health!"

Whether the crowd on the pier had any notion of our
story—which was likely enough, because my father had
got my letter, and had, no doubt, gone about talking of
it—I cannot say; but when Richard had shouted out,
they gave us a cheer which quite drowned my father's
answer, if indeed his emotion suffered him to make any,
and in a minute we were gliding past the Polka Hole,
and the hailing house, and on to abreast of the Custom-house quay. What with the tug letting go of us,
and the Custom-house officers boarding us, and fasts being got over for mooring, together with a host of con-
flicting shouts from the shore as well as from our decks,
my mind was so excited and confused that I can remember little more than seeing my father and Captain
Robinson (who was at my wedding) waving their hands
and calling to us from the quay, and then a plank being thrown over, and my father, followed by his friend,
rolling on board.

I was in father's arms before he was fairly over the
side. What kissing! what hand-shaking! what ceaseless
inquiries! what exclamations!

"Four months gone!" cried father, holding both my
hands and falling away from me; "and in that time
ye've seen fire and shipwreck and what other wonders!
was there ever such a lass, Robinson! but, Lord! how
well she looks! brown as a berry, and a true tropical
sparkle in her eyes to let us know where she's been.
And Dick! on crutches, too! God guide us!" and here
followed more hand-shaking, more kissing, tears and
laughter on my side, laughter and a strong look of tears,
too, on father's.

Well, such a meeting as this must be left to your imagination, for in real truth I find myself utterly unable to give you the least idea of the spirit or character of it. There were certain formalities to be gone through by Richard before the Receiver of Wrecks, which would prevent him from accompanying us in the town; so Captain Robinson stayed with him while father and I walked into High Street to the Saddle Inn, kept in those days by Mrs. Davison and her daughter Lizzie, there to order dinner and wait for Richard and Captain Robinson to join us.

"Have ye no luggage, Jessie?" said father.

"Not a scrap, father; not so much as would fill a pocket-handkerchief," said I, "except what is in this little parcel, which I shall preserve as a memorial of what we have suffered."

He asked me what that was; and I told him it was some rough underlinen I had been forced to make for myself, having no clothes whatever to wear except those I stood up in when we left the *Aurora*.

"Oh, my poor Jessie!" he cried; "didn't I tell ye what the sea was? but ye'll have no more of it, my birdie. One shipwreck's enough for a lifetime, and since Dick's had his way for one bout, it'll be my turn now."

Fortunately it was not far from the quay to the Saddle Inn; but, short as the distance was, I was heartily ashamed to walk it in the dress I was attired in. My hat, as you may suppose, had a most terribly draggled appearance; the salt water had rusted my boots until they looked to be made of bronze; my jacket was discolored in a dozen places by exposure to wet, either of dew or rain or sea; and my dress hung upon me more like a sack than a gown make by a dressmaker. The people stared, especially the women, who would stand and look after me; but we walked fast, and heartily glad was I when we found shelter at last in the Saddle Inn, with its bay-window, and bright, sturdy, hospitable, old-world aspect.

We were expected, for my father had sent a message to Mrs. Davison to apprise her of our coming when the brig was made out (for, belonging to Sunderland, the *Boluma* was well known to the people connected with the piers and docks), and I was received by the kind landlady with such hearty, respectful cordiality as made me feel that I was at home and among friends at last, indeed.

"Now, Lizzie," said father, turning to Miss Davison, "I want ye to do me a favor, my lass. Mrs. Fowler here has been shipwrecked, and has come home with no other luggage than what ye see on her back and under her arm. Run out, like a good girl, first to some milliner and bid her send round a show of pretty hats to choose from; then go to a bootmaker's, and order some ladies' boots along; then whip round to where they keep women's underclothing, and tell 'em to send in such articles as I'll give ye leave to name to 'em. You'll know what to order. It's for a shipwrecked lady, my lass— a female Jonah, Lizzie, who is fresh from the belly of a big whale, called the ocean, which ye'll not need to read the Bible to know has a trick of stripping its victims naked before disgorging them, which last it only condescends to do now and again."

The errand delighted Lizzie, who ran off to put on her hat. My father then gave orders for dinner to be ready for four of us by half-past one, and we went into a snug room where, when Mrs. Davison had closed the door upon us, he once more hugged me to his heart, thanking God for giving him back his lassie, his Jessie, while I lay crying upon his shoulder as people will cry when they are safe, and look back and recall much suffering.

I had a great deal to tell him, as you may suppose; and yet it did not take me very long to relate the whole story. He listened with a great deal of indignation when I told him of the mutiny, and on my saying that Richard had forgiven the men, and, I was quite sure, had no intention of taking any steps against them, he jumped up and was for running out of the room, when I stopped him by asking where he was going.

"Why," cried he, "to give the police a chance of nabbing them before they up keeleg and away."

"No, no," said I, "do nothing of the sort, father. Richard has passed his word, and you'll not make him break it."

"Ay," said he, "it's not a question that concerns Dick; it's a question that concerns the whole mercantile marine. If mutineers are to be forgiven, what's to become of shipmasters? If these villains are not punished, the owners of the *Aurora* 'll have them upon 'em for wages, and the owners of the *Bolama* for salvage money."

"It can't be helped," said I. "Do sit down, father, and listen to the rest of my story."

Well, he sat down, chafing a great deal; but when I came to that part of the voyage where the crew left us aboard the burning bark, he hopped off his chair once more, and actually struggled with me while I held his arm, so mad was he to set the police at the fellows.

However, I managed to cool him down when I explained that it was all due to the chief mate's villainy, and that he was drowned, and that from the hour of boarding the *Bolama* the men had shown great remorse for the past, and had endeavored to atone for their behavior by working cheerfully and helping Richard to their uttermost to carry the brig home.

"They had us in their power," said I, "and had they been the rascals my story makes them seem, they might have sent us adrift in the boat they had saved themselves by, or have thrown us overboard. For who was to prove that we did not perish in the bark?" and then, seeing his temper rising again, I spoke of Richard's broken leg.

His manner instantly changed. "Is it well, Jess?"

"I don't know," said I. "The bone has set, but whether properly or not we cannot guess. We hope for the best, because there is no pain. I'll send for a doctor this afternoon and learn the truth, however it goes."

"Yes," said he, "and we'll have the best doctor in Sunderland. Mrs. Davison will tell us whom to send for. But there'll be no nursing here, Jess. Ye'll both come along home with me after dinner."

"Where have you taken a house, father?"

"Why," he replied, "at South Shields, on the Lawe. It looks right on to the sea. It was a rare chance my finding it, for the pilots are hot on that terrace. Mind ye, Jess, it's but a box of a place—nothing like the old

Newcastle house; but there'll be plenty of room for you two, ay, and for your bairns, too, when they come."

Here we were interrupted by a knock on the door, and Lizzie Davison came in to say that there was a girl with some hats down-stairs; and by the time the girl was in the room, a fellow with a bag of boots over his shoulders was shown in, and close behind him came another girl with a large, stout boy breathing heavily under a load of underlinen. I began with the hats, and chose a shape that suited me very well; and to get rid of the bootmaker, I fitted on his boots till I got a pair to please me; after which I made a selection of such articles from the stock of underlinen as I stood in need of.

"Now, Lizzie," said father, "take Mrs. Fowler to a bed-room and let her make herself comfortable."

This pleasant and pretty girl—for pretty she was, and I am happy to know she is still alive and hearty, and doing well, I trust—had given a complete catalogue of my wants to the shop people; so that, though I kept my old dress on, yet the articles I had selected enabled me to make a quite new figure, and in nice clean cuffs and collar, a bow for my hair, and new boots, I felt that I was a lady again, and fit for company. I was a long time in the bedroom, talking with Lizzie Davison, and showing her the clothes I had made on board the brig, and giving her a history of my adventures. When I went back to the sitting-room I heard voices, and on entering found Richard and Captain Robinson talking with father, and the cloth laid ready for dinner. Captain Robinson started up and came hastily forward to meet me, catching me by both hands.

"Good news, Mrs. Fowler!" he cried, in his cheery voice. "What do you think I am able to report?"

"What?" said I, looking eagerly at Richard, who was smiling at me.

"Why," said he, "we have been to Dr. ———, our best man in Sunderland. He examined the leg, said it was quite sound and handsomely set, and would not believe that it was not the work of a surgeon."

I ran up to my husband, and flung my arms round his neck. "Oh, my darling!" I cried, "this is a crowning happiness."

"It is, Jessie," he replied, fondling me; "all that re-mains to be done is not to use the leg for some time, to lie about as much as my temper will let me, and to stick to my crutches. Captain Snowdon," said he, turn-ing to my father, "this is one more obligation I owe your daughter. I have told you of her courage as a sailor; but let me add that, cruel as the shock of this accident, happening at such a time, was to her, she fell to work with a lion heart to patch me up, soothing me, encouraging me—great God!" he cried, breaking off and passionately grasping my hand, "what should I have done without her?"

"You called her a Sea Queen just now, Dick," said my father, whose dear, beaming old face was made all the dearer to me by the shadow of proud and happy tears in his eyes, "and a sea queen she is. Robinson, that's a nautical title that shall stick. She's Dick's wife, and she's my sea queen. It's a good term, and I'm obliged to ye, Dick, for the fancy. Robinson, henceforth, when ye have occasion to ask after Jessie's health, ye'll be good enough to say, 'How's the Sea Queen?' Her figure-head answers to the name, and there are facts enough in her wake to make the sound the properest that ever I shall hear in this life."

I was too happy and delighted with the news that Cap-tain Robinson had just given me to mind this talk about myself. I took it as it came. A heavy load had been lifted from my mind, and I knew how heavy it had been by the sense of delicious ease its removal gave me.

I found that Richard had satisfied my father on the subject of the *Aurora's* crew, by representing to him that, if even he had not resolved to keep his word with them, the grounds for legal proceedings were so small that it was exceedingly doubtful whether any magistrate would be found to punish them. Whether this was really Richard's opinion I cannot say; but he had certainly represented their behavior in such a light that father was obliged to agree with him that on the whole it was best to let the rascals be.

I need not linger, for my story is nearly done, as much of it, I mean, as is likely to interest strangers; and I should merely be retelling my experiences to repeat our conversation at table and afterwards. It was all about our voyage, and such dry matters as salvage, insurance, and such things; dry, that is, to write about, though mightily interesting to us, who looked for a substantial reward for the salving of the brig. But one incident let me not forget.

The dinner-cloth had been removed, and a bottle of wine and some glasses set upon the table. Father, Richard, and Captain Robinson had lighted their pipes, and were arguing with great animation on the character of seamen ; my father and Captain Robinson asserting that the British merchant sailor was no longer the man he used to be, being a mutinous, saucy, skulking fellow, who knew more about marine law than the sea, and whose main business in signing articles was not to help the shipmaster to navigate his vessel, but to plague and ruin him by bringing him into trouble ; while Richard, on the other hand, said no, the British sailor was as good a man as his father, and perhaps better ; and that it was as unreasonable to condemn all seamen because of the sprinkling of scowbanks and sogers among them, as it would be to condemn the whole race of parsons, because now and again a clergyman fell into mischief and forgot some of the commandments.

The window of the room we occupied overlooked High Street ; it was open, for the day was warm and sunny, and the bustle of the thoroughfare, the sound of voices, the rattling of wheels, the whistling of boys, the barking of dogs, came into the room, not so noisily as to vex the arguers, though, had it been twice as noisy, it would have been delightful to me, who for four months had heard no more than the hoarse songs of sailors, the roaring of the wind, the washing of water, or the faint moan of a fold of air stirring like a spirit-pinion amid the deathlike calm of a tropical ocean night.

Suddenly Mrs. Davison came into the room, and, looking from one to the other of us, said, in a subdued manner, "The wife of the dead captain of the *Bolama* has called to know if Captain Fowler will see her and tell her what he can of her husband."

"Ask her to walk up, Mrs. Davison," said Richard.

My father put down his pipe and clasped his hands upon his waistcoat.

"What have ye got to tell the poor body?" said he to Richard.

"Little enough," answered my husband, with a sigh.

"Robinson," exclaimed father, turning to his friend, "it's not for me to speak against the sea. It used m᷈ well, and left me a whole man, with enough to give m᷈ a change of linen twice a week, and a leg of mutton ever᷈ day, had I mind for a monotonous course of eating, afte᷈ seven-and-forty years of its waves and its winds. But I'm bound to say it's a merciless tyrant to some folk ; and in reflecting upon it I often think there's truth in what old Bob Perkins, who was master of the *Commodore Anson*, once said to me after a gale of wind : 'Thomas,' says he, 'the saying is that the devil's a person as can't manage for even a short spell without fire ; but ye may boil and then eat me, skipper, if I'm out of my reckonings in giving it as my solemn opinion that Satan is again and again shifting his quarters from where there's nowt but flames to where there's nowt but water, finding hell too hot for him, and so out of pure malice and wickedness making the ocean too hot for sailors.'"

As he said this the door was opened, and Mrs. Davison ushered in a young woman of about eight-and-twenty. I half rose, meaning to receive her and say a few kind words, but when I saw her I kept my seat. She was very good-looking, but had the sauciest, most mocking expression of face I ever saw. Her eyes were large, and black as coal, her cheeks red, and she was gayly dressed in a silk skirt, plentifully trimmed, and a black hat with a bright scarlet feather. She gave us a bow, and Captain Robinson handed her a chair. My father eyed her askant, and then took up his pipe. He had put it down out of deference to the widow's grief ; but finding no grief, he went on smoking.

"Which is Captain Fowler?" said she, looking briskly around her, and speaking without the least affectation of sorrow.

"I'm Captain Fowler," said Richard.

"I hear that you've brought my husband's brig home,"

she exclaimed; "was he alive when you found him, or what?"

"He was dead," answered Richard, shocked, as I was, by her levity. And, as if intending a rebuke, he related the story with great solemnity to her, and was excusing himself for having cast the body overboard in the unceremonious manner that the fear of infection had obliged him to adopt, when she cut him short by asking him where the property belonging to her husband was.

"Why," says Captain Robinson, scowling at her, "in the hands of the Receiver of Wrecks."

"Thank you," she answered, getting up, "I wanted to know for certain that the poor fellow was dead. Can any of you gentlemen tell me if I am entitled to his pay up to the time of the arrival of the brig home, or can I draw it only up to the day of his death?"

"Ye'd better go and ask the shipping-master," said father, sternly. "We'd have been willing to console ye had we thought you required consoling; but we're not here to give ye opinions on marine law, mistress."

"Oh, really," cried she, with a mocking and highly impudent shake of the head at father. "I didn't come here for your consolation, nor for your law either, but to be treated as a lady. You're seafaring people, as I can see, and, consequently, no rudeness from you can surprise me. Sailors, indeed!" cried she, with an hysterical toss of the head, "d'ye think women are fools enough ever to want consoling for the loss of the likes of *you*?"

And shaking her body like a negress in a new dress, she walked out of the room, slamming the door behind her.

I was very much shocked, and no doubt looked so; and Richard tried to appear equally disgusted. But it would not do; his sense of the ridiculous would have its way, and he burst into a laugh, which he immediately apologized for, by saying he was glad the interview had proved so easy, for had she come crying and talking of her children and her poverty it would have upset him for a week.

"But, Lord, what a woman!" cried father; "what a moral Jack may get from such wenches by studying 'em."

"Moral!" exclaimed Captain Robinson, "there are no morals to be got from her, Thomas, let Jack study her as he will. Don't you know who she was?"

"Not the least notion," answered father.

Here Captain Robinson whispered, and father tossed his hands.

"Well, well," cried he, "you Sunderland folk are a nice lot!" An observation which, to judge from Captain Robinson's smile, seemed on the whole to please him.

We left Sunderland at three o'clock, driving to Monk-wearmouth, where the railway station then was. On our arrival at South Shields we drove down the Ocean Road and up to the Lawe, and stopped before a cheerful little bright-windowed house, with a brass plate on the door bearing the name "Thos. Snowdon." Father entered first to receive us, and as we followed him he took me in his arms, and then wrung Richard's hands, exhibiting as much extravagant delight at having us as if this were his first welcome. We entered the little parlor, and father watched me with a happy face as I stood looking round upon the old familiar Newcastle furniture, the curiosities, the shields and arrows and spears, the old dark chairs, and mother's arm-chair, that stood on one side of the fireplace, as though she were still alive to occupy it. I went to the window. The North Sea stretched its grayish surface into the distant blue of the horizon. On the left were the dark Tyne-mouth cliffs, the white lighthouse and the old ruins near it standing as clear as a pen-and-ink drawing against the blue heavens. There was a flash and tremble of foam upon the Black Middens, and the river's mouth was lively with cobbles and larger vessels, inward and outward bound.

"Have you truly had enough of it, my darling?" said Richard, limping up to me on his crutches and pointing at the sea.

"Yes," I answered, "and so have you."

"Right!" cried father. "Dick, your wife has spoken; make up your mind, my lad. This has been your last voyage."

The lady who concludes her story in the above words resided up to a recent period in South Shields. Her husband, as you have read, was the first to call her a Sea Queen ; her father caught at the name, and always spoke of her as his sea queen ; until at last she came to be known to all her friends by that title. Whether she deserved it the reader can judge. As to her narrative, I had it from her lately, and in small bits at a time, and my memory, therefore, may have failed to give it all the color and exactness I found in her relation of it. Imperfect, however, as my rendering of it is, I feel no reluctance in offering it as a small contribution to English marine literature. We have been praising sailors so long, that some may think it is about time we gave their wives a turn. At all events, I believe this Newcastle lady is the first sailor's wife whose nautical experiences have been put into a book and made public in that way ; and if this really be so, then, if her example does but influence others of her sex who have shared the perils and trials of their sailor-husbands to relate their stories, she will have placed all lovers of marine literature under an obligation to her, whether this first attempt in a new field pleases them or not.

It may interest those who have followed her story to know that she had her way as regards the keeping of her husband at home. She told me there were many long disputes. Richard did not at all like the notion of hanging on, as it were, to his father-in-law ; but the father and daughter ultimately prevailed. The salvage money awarded to Captain Fowler went to purchase an interest in a vessel belonging to the firm that had owned the *Aurora*. This interest, coupled with what Captain Snowdon had, procured Fowler a well-paid post in the office of the firm, which he filled not only with great satisfaction to his employers, but to his own commercial advancement, so that, as he would say, in five years he made more money by stopping ashore than he could have earned by following the sea for tenfold that length of time.

The old novelists had a homely and satisfactory fashion of winding up their narratives with accounts of the various personages who had figured in their books. This is easily done when the stories are fictitious ; but truth is restrictive. I never hoped to learn what became of the

Aurora's crew after the *Bolama* was moored in the river Wear. The town was full of crimps in those days, and when a man left a vessel newly arrived he often vanished as utterly as if he had fallen overboard. I asked some questions of Mrs. Fowler about Short the carpenter, however; but all that she could tell me was that the owners of the *Aurora* resisted his application for wages, on the grounds of his insubordination while in that vessel, that he got some pettifogging attorney to threaten them with proceedings, and then either died or went to sea, for nothing more was heard of him.

THE END.

SOME POPULAR NOVELS

Published by HARPER & BROTHERS, New York.

The Novels in this list which are not otherwise designated are in Octavo, pamphlet form, and may be obtained in half-binding [leather backs and pasteboard sides], suitable for Public and Circulating Libraries, at 25 cents, net, per volume, in addition to the price of the respective works as stated below. The Duodecimo Novels are bound in Cloth, unless otherwise specified.

For a FULL LIST OF NOVELS published by HARPER & BROTHERS, see HARPER'S NEW AND REVISED CATALOGUE, which will be sent by mail, postage prepaid, to any address in the United States, on receipt of nine cents.

PRICE

BLACKMORE'S Clara Vaughan.........................4to, Paper $	15
Cradock Nowell...	60
Cripps, the Carrier...	50
Erema	50
Lorna Doone	60
Mary Anerley ....16mo, Cloth 1	00
4to, Paper	15
The Maid of Sker..	50
BENEDICT'S John Worthington's Name...............................	75
Miss Dorothy's Charge..	75
Miss Van Kortland..	60
Mr. Vaughan's Heir...	75
My Daughter Elinor...	80
St. Simon's Niece..	60
BULWER'S Alice...	35
A Strange Story. Illustrated	50
12mo 1	25
Devereux...	40
Ernest Maltravers..	35
Eugene Aram..	35
Godolphin..	35
12mo 1	50
Harold, the Last of the Saxon Kings..............................	60
Kenelm Chillingly..	50
12mo 1	25
Leila...	25
12mo 1	00
Lucretia	40
My Novel...	75
2 vols. 12mo 2	50
Night and Morning..	50
Paul Clifford..	40
Pausanias the Spartan..	25
12mo	75
Pelham..	40
Rienzi...	40
The Caxtons...	50
12mo 1	25
The Coming Race....................................12mo, Paper	50
Cloth 1	00
The Disowned	50
The Last Days of Pompeii..	25
4to, Paper	15
The Last of the Barons...	50
The Parisians. Illustrated..	60
12mo 1	50
The Pilgrims of the Rhine...	20
What will He do with it ?...	75

PRICE

CRAIK'S (Miss G. M.) Sylvia's Choice	$	30
Two Women	4to, Paper	15
COLLINS'S Antonina		40
Armadale. Illustrated		60
Man and Wife. Illustrated		60
	4to, Paper	15
My Lady's Money	32mo, Paper	25
No Name. Illustrated		60
Percy and the Prophet	32mo, Paper	20
Poor Miss Finch. Illustrated		60
The Law and the Lady. Illustrated		50
The Moonstone. Illustrated		60
The New Magdalen		30
The Two Destinies. Illustrated		35
The Woman in White. Illustrated		60
COLLINS'S Illustrated Library Edition	12mo, per vol.	1 25

After Dark, and Other Stories.—Antonina.—Armadale.—
Basil.—Hide-and-Seek.—Man and Wife.—My Miscel-
lanies.—No Name.—Poor Miss Finch.—The Dead Secret.
—The Law and the Lady.—The Moonstone.—The New
Magdalen.—The Queen of Hearts.—The Two Destinies.
—The Woman in White.

DICKENS'S NOVELS. Illustrated.

A Tale of Two Cities...		50	Nicholas Nickleby		1 00
	Cloth	1 00		Cloth	1 50
Barnaby Rudge		1 00	Oliver Twist		50
	Cloth	1 50		Cloth	1 00
Bleak House		1 00	Our Mutual Friend		1 00
	Cloth	1 50		Cloth	1 50
Christmas Stories		1 00	Pickwick Papers		1 00
	Cloth	1 50		Cloth	1 50
David Copperfield		1 00		4to, Paper	20
	Cloth	1 50	Pictures from Italy, Sketch-		
Dombey and Son		1 00	es by Boz, and American		
	Cloth	1 50	Notes		1 00
Great Expectations		1 00		Cloth	1 50
	Cloth	1 50	The Old Curiosity Shop		75
Little Dorrit		1 00		Cloth	1 25
	Cloth	1 50	The Uncommercial Traveller,		
Martin Chuzzlewit		1 00	Hard Times, and Edwin		
	Cloth	1 50	Drood		1 00
				Cloth	1 50

Harper's Household Dickens, 16 vols., Cloth, in box, $22 00.
The same in 8 vols., Cloth, $20 00; Imitation Half Mo-
rocco, $22 00; Half Calf, $40 00.

DE MILLE'S Cord and Crease. Illustrated		60
The American Baron. Illustrated		50
The Cryptogram. Illustrated		75

PRICE

HAY'S (M. C.) Into the Shade, and Other Stories...4to, Paper $ 15
    Lady Carmichael's Will............................32mo, Paper   15
    Missing..32mo, Paper   20
    My First Offer, and Other Stories......................4to, Paper   15
    Nora's Love Test   25
    Old Myddelton's Money....................................   25
    Reaping the Whirlwind............................32mo, Paper   20
    The Arundel Motto...   25
    The Sorrow of a Secret ....32mo, Paper   15
    The Squire's Legacy   25
    Under Life's Key, and Other Stories.................4to, Paper   15
    Victor and Vanquished....................................   25
HELEN Troy...16mo, Cloth 1 00
HUGO'S Ninety-Three. Illustrated......................   25
                         12mo 1 75
    The Toilers of the Sea....................................   50
                   Illustrated. Cloth 1 50
JAMES'S (Henry, Jun.) Daisy Miller..................32mo, Paper   20
    An International Episode...........................32mo, Paper   20
    Diary of a Man of Fifty, and A Bundle of Letters............
                         32mo, Paper   25
    The four above-mentioned works in one volume. 4to, Paper   25
    Washington Square. Illustrated..................16mo, Cloth 1 25
LAWRENCE'S Anteros......................................   40
    Brakespeare...   40
    Breaking a Butterfly......................................   35
    Guy Livingstone...................................12mo 1 50
                         4to, Paper   10
    Hagarene   35
    Maurice Dering   25
    Sans Merci..   35
    Sword and Gown   20
LEVER'S A Day's Ride.....................................   40
    Barrington..   40
    Gerald Fitzgerald...   40
    Lord Kilgobbin. Illustrated..............................   50
    Luttrell of Arran..   60
    Maurice Tiernay   50
    One of Them..   50
    Roland Cashel. Illustrated...............................   75
    Sir Brook Fosbrooke......................................   50
    Sir Jasper Carew..   50
    That Boy of Norcott's. Illustrated.......................   25
    The Bramleighs of Bishop's Folly.........................   50
    The Daltons...   75
    The Dodd Family Abroad..................................   60
    The Fortunes of Glencore.................................   50
    The Martins of Cro' Martin...............................   60

PRICE

MULOCK'S (Miss) Young Mrs. Jardine.................4to, Paper $ 10
NORRIS'S Heaps of Money... 15
OLIPHANT'S (Mrs.) Agnes.. 50
    A Son of the Soil.. 50
    Athelings... 50
    Brownlows... 50
    Caritá... 50
    Chronicles of Carlingford.. 60
    Days of My Life.............................12mo 1 50
    For Love and Life.. 50
    Harry Joscelyn................................4to, Paper 20
    He That Will Not when He May......................4to, Paper 15
    Innocent. Illustrated... 50
    It was a Lover and His Lass.......................4to, Paper 20
    John : a Love Story.. 25
    Katie Stewart.. 20
    Lady Jane ....4to, Paper 10
    Lucy Crofton...............................12mo 1 50
    Madonna Mary... 50
    Miss Marjoribanks.. 50
    Mrs. Arthur.. 40
    Ombra.. 50
    Phœbe, Junior.. 35
    Squire Arden... 50
    The Curate in Charge... 20
    The Fugitives...................................4to, Paper 10
    The Greatest Heiress in England...................4to, Paper 15
    The House on the Moor.......................12mo 1 50
    The Laird of Norlaw.........................12mo 1 50
    The Last of the Mortimers...................12mo 1 50
    The Minister's Wife.. 50
    The Perpetual Curate... 50
    The Primrose Path.. 50
    The Quiet Heart.. 20
    The Story of Valentine and his Brother........................... 50
    Within the Precincts.............................4to, Paper 15
    Young Musgrave... 40
PATRICK'S (Mary) Christine Brownlee's Ordeal......4to, Paper 15
    Marjorie Bruce's Lovers.. 25
    Mr. Leslie of Underwood.........................4to, Paper 15
PAYN'S (James) A Beggar on Horseback............................ 35
    A Confidential Agent............................4to, Paper 15
    A Grape from a Thorn............................4to, Paper 20
    A Woman's Vengeance... 35
    At Her Mercy... 30
    Bred in the Bone... 40
    By Proxy... 35
    Carlyon's Year... 25

PRICE

PAYN'S (James) Cecil's Tryst...$ 30
    For Cash Only...4to, Paper   20
    Found Dead..   25
    From Exile ....4to, Paper   15
    Gwendoline's Harvest..   25
    Halves   30
    High Spirits..4to, Paper   15
    Kit. Illustrated..4to, Paper   20
    Less Black than We're Painted.......................................   35
    Murphy's Master   20
    One of the Family..   25
    The Best of Husbands...   25
    Under One Roof...4to, Paper   15
    Walter's Word..   50
    What He Cost Her..   40
    Won—Not Wooed..   35

READE'S Novels: Household Edition. Ill'd......12mo, per vol. 1 00

A Simpleton and the Wandering Heir.	It is Never Too Late to Mend.
A Terrible Temptation.	Love me Little, Love me Long.
A Woman-Hater.	Peg Woffington, Christie Johnstone, &c.
Foul Play.	Put Yourself in His Place.
Griffith Gaunt.	The Cloister and the Hearth.
Hard Cash.	White Lies.

READE'S (Charles) A Hero and a Martyr...........................   15
    A Simpleton..   35
    A Terrible Temptation. Illustrated.................................   40
    A Woman-Hater. Illustrated.......................................   60
    Foul Play..   35
    Griffith Gaunt. Illustrated..   40
    Hard Cash. Illustrated...   50
    It is Never Too Late to Mend.......................................   50
    Love Me Little, Love Me Long.......................................   35
    Multum in Parvo ....4to, Paper   15
    Peg Woffington, &c..   50
    Put Yourself in His Place. Illustrated..........................   50
    The Cloister and the Hearth...   50
    The Jilt..32mo, Paper   20
    The Wandering Heir. Illustrated   25
    White Lies..   40

RICE & BESANT'S All Sorts and Conditions of Men...4to, Paper   20
    By Celia's Arbor. Illustrated.....................8vo, Paper   50
    Shepherds All and Maidens Fair...................32mo, Paper   25
    "So they were Married!" Illustrated ....4to, Paper   20
    Sweet Nelly, My Heart's Delight.....................4to, Paper   10
    The Captains' Room......................................4to, Paper   10
    The Chaplain of the Fleet..............................4to, Paper   20

PRICE

RICE & BESANT'S The Golden Butterfly.............................$ 40
    'Twas in Trafalgar's Bay............................32mo, Paper 20
    When the Ship Comes Home......................32mo, Paper 25
ROBINSON'S (F. W.) A Bridge of Glass............................. 30
    A Girl's Romance, and Other Stories............................ 30
    As Long as She Lived... 50
    Carry's Confession... 50
    Christie's Faith...12mo 1 75
    Coward Conscience............................4to, Paper 15
    For Her Sake. Illustrated... 60
    Her Face was Her Fortune...................................... 40
    Little Kate Kirby. Illustrated.................................... 50
    Mattie: a Stray.. 40
    No Man's Friend... 50
    Othello the Second..................................32mo, Paper 20
    Poor Humanity... 50
    Poor Zeph!..32mo, Paper 20
    Romance on Four Wheels.. 15
    Second-Cousin Sarah. Illustrated............................... 50
    Stern Necessity... 40
    The Barmaid at Battleton.........................32mo, Paper 15
    The Black Speck...................................4to, Paper 10
    The Hands of Justice ....4to, Paper 20
    The Romance of a Back Street...................32mo, Paper 15
    True to Herself... 50
RUSSELL'S (W. Clarke) Auld Lang Syne..............4to, Paper 10
    A Sailor's Sweetheart.............................4to, Paper 15
    A Sea Queen...........................16mo, Cloth. (*Now ready.*)
                                    4to, Paper .
    An Ocean Free Lance.............................4to, Paper 20
    My Watch Below...................................4to, Paper 20
    The "Lady Maud:" Schooner Yacht. Ill'd.......4to, Paper 20
    Wreck of the "Grosvenor"....................................... 30
                                    4to, Paper 15
SHERWOOD'S (Mrs. John) A Transplanted Rose....12mo, Cloth 1 00
TABOR'S (Eliza) Eglantine... 40
    Hope Meredith... 35
    Jeanie's Quiet Life.. 30
    Little Miss Primrose ....4to, Paper 15
    Meta's Faith... 35
    St. Olave's.. 40
    The Blue Ribbon.. 40
    The Last of Her Line.............................4to, Paper 15
THACKERAY'S (Miss) Bluebeard's Keys............................. 35
    Da Capo..32mo, Paper 20
    Miscellaneous Works.. 90
    Miss Angel. Illustrated.. 50
    Miss Williamson's Divagations....................4to, Paper 15

PRICE

THACKERAY'S (Miss) Old Kensington. Illustrated.............$ 60
    Village on the Cliff. Illustrated................................. 25
THACKERAY'S (W. M.) Denis Duval. Illustrated............... 25
    Henry Esmond, and Lovel the Widower. 12 Illustrations.. 60
    Henry Esmond.. 50
                                       4to, Paper 15
    Lovel the Widower.. 20
    Pendennis. 179 Illustrations 75
    The Adventures of Philip. 64 Illustrations.................... 60
    The Great Hoggarty Diamond...................................... 20
    The Newcomes. 162 Illustrations................................ 90
    The Virginians. 150 Illustrations............................... 90
    Vanity Fair. 32 Illustrations...................................... 80
THACKERAY'S Works: Household Edition ......12mo, per vol. 1 25
    Novels: Vanity Fair.—Pendennis.—The Newcomes.—The
    Virginians.—Philip.—Esmond, and Lovel the Widower.
    6 vols. Ill'd. *Miscellaneous:* Barry Lyndon, Hoggarty
    Diamond, &c.—Paris and Irish Sketch-Books, &c.—Book
    of Snobs, Sketches, &c.—Four Georges, English Humorists,
    Roundabout Papers, &c.—Catharine, &c. 5 vols. Ill'd.
TROLLOPE'S (Anthony) An Eye for an Eye...........4to, Paper 10
    Ayala's Angel...4to, Paper 20
    Brown, Jones, and Robinson... 35
    Can You Forgive Her? Illustrated............................... 80
    Castle Richmond...12mo 1 50
    Cousin Henry ....4to, Paper 10
    Doctor Thorne 12mo 1 50
    Doctor Wortle's School..................................4to, Paper 15
    Framley Parsonage.......................................4to, Paper 15
    Harry Heathcote of Gangoil. Illustrated....................... 20
    He Knew He was Right. Illustrated............................. 80
    Is He Popenjoy?...4to, Paper 15
    John Caldigate..4to, Paper 15
    Kept in the Dark...4to, Paper 15
    Lady Anna.. 30
    Marion Fay. Illustrated...............................4to, Paper 20
    Miss Mackenzie.. 35
    Orley Farm. Illustrated 80
    Phineas Finn. Illustrated.. 75
    Phineas Redux. Illustrated....................................... 75
    Rachel Ray.. 35
    Ralph the Heir. Illustrated....................................... 75
    Sir Harry Hotspur of Humblethwaite. Illustrated........... 35
    The American Senator 50
    The Belton Estate... 35
    The Bertrams..4to, Paper 15
    The Claverings. Illustrated....................................... 50
    The Duke's Children ....4to, Paper 20

PRICE

TROLLOPE'S (Anthony) The Eustace Diamonds. Illustrated.. $ 80
   The Fixed Period...4to, Paper   15
   The Golden Lion of Granpere. Illustrated......................   40
   The Lady of Launay..................................32mo, Paper   20
   The Last Chronicle of Barset. Illustrated......................   90
   The Prime Minister..   60
   The Small House at Allington. Illustrated....................   75
   The Three Clerks...12mo 1 50
   The Vicar of Bullhampton. Illustrated........................   80
   The Warden, and Barchester Towers. In one volume.......   60
   The Way We Live Now. Illustrated.............................   90
   Thompson Hall. Illustrated...................... 32mo, Paper   20
   Why Frau Frohman Raised her Prices, &c.........4to, Paper   10
TROLLOPE'S (T. A.) Lindisfarn Chase.................................   60
   A Siren...   40
   Durnton Abbey..   40
   Diamond Cut Diamond 12mo 1 25
WALLACE'S (Lew) Ben-Hur............ ....16mo, Cloth 1 50
WAVERLEY NOVELS:
      THISTLE EDITION: 48 Vols., Green Cloth, with 2000
      Illustrations, $1 00 per vol.; Half Morocco, Gilt Tops,
      $1 50 per vol.; Half Morocco, Extra, $2 25 per vol.
      HOLYROOD EDITION: 48 Vols., Brown Cloth, with 2000
      Illustrations, 75 cents per vol.; Half Morocco, Gilt Tops,
      $1 50 per vol.; Half Morocco, Extra, $2 25 per vol.
      POPULAR EDITION: 24 Vols. (two vols. in one), Green
      Cloth, with 2000 Illustrations, $1 25 per vol.; Half Moroc-
      co, $2 25 per vol.; Half Morocco, Extra, $3 00 per vol.
      Waverley; Guy Mannering; The Antiquary; Rob Roy;
      Old Mortality; The Heart of Mid-Lothian; A Legend of
      Montrose; The Bride of Lammermoor; The Black Dwarf;
      Ivanhoe; The Monastery; The Abbot; Kenilworth; The
      Pirate; The Fortunes of Nigel; Peveril of the Peak;
      Quentin Durward; St. Ronan's Well; Redgauntlet; The
      Betrothed; The Talisman; Woodstock; Chronicles of the
      Canongate, The Highland Widow, &c.; The Fair Maid of
      Perth; Anne of Geierstein; Count Robert of Paris; Cas-
      tle Dangerous; The Surgeon's Daughter; Glossary.
WOOLSON'S (C. F.) Anne. Illustrated................16mo, Cloth 1 25
YATES'S (Edmund) Black Sheep...   40
   Kissing the Rod   40
   Land at Last..   40
   Wrecked in Port...   35
   Dr. Wainwright's Patient..   30

☞ HARPER & BROTHERS *will send any of the above works by mail, postage*
prepaid, to any part of the United States, on receipt of the price.

1483338R0

Printed in Great Britain by
Amazon.co.uk, Ltd.,
Marston Gate.